NORA ROBERTS

writes for Silhouette's Special Edition and Intimate Moments lines and is one of Silhouette Books's most popular and prolific writers, as well as a multi-*New York Times* bestselling author in both hardcover and paperback. Nora was the first author inducted into the Romance Writers of America Hall of Fame and has received awards for her fiction, her creativity, her sales and her contribution to the genre. She has received lifetime achievement awards from the Romance Writers of America, Waldenbooks and *Romantic Times* magazine, and bestselling title and series awards from booksellers, readers and peers.

Nora Roberts is a consummate storyteller. She is known for her humor, creativity and willingness to take chances. Nora's commitment to her characters, to her writing and, most especially, to her readers, has earned her fans all over the world.

NORA ROBERTS

THE STANISLASKI SISTERS

Silhouette Books

Published by Silhouette Books

America's Publisher of Contemporary Romance

SILHOUETTE BOOKS

by Request

THE STANISLASKI SISTERS

Copyright © 1997 by Harlequin Books S.A.

ISBN 0-373-20134-6

The publisher acknowledges the copyright holders of the individual works as follows:

TAMING NATASHA
Copyright © 1990 by Nora Roberts

FALLING FOR RACHEL
Copyright © 1993 by Nora Roberts

Printed in U.S.A.

CONTENTS

TAMING NATASHA   9

FALLING FOR RACHEL   257

Those Wild Ukrainians

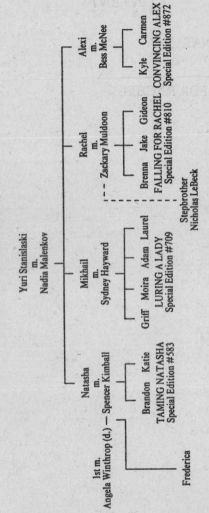

Yuri Stanislaski
m.
Nadia Malenkov

Natasha
m.
Spencer Kimball

1st m.
Angela Winthrop (d.) — Spencer Kimball

Frederica

Brandon   Katie
TAMING NATASHA
Special Edition #583

Mikhail
m.
Sydney Hayward

Griff Moira Adam Laurel
LURING A LADY
Special Edition #709

Stepbrother
Nicholas LeBeck

Rachel
m.
Zackary Muldoon

Brenna Jake Gideon
FALLING FOR RACHEL
Special Edition #810

Alexi
m.
Bess McNee

Kyle   Carmen
CONVINCING ALEX
Special Edition #872

THE STANISLASKI SISTERS brings you Natasha's and Rachel's stories.
Look for Frederica and Nicholas's story in
WAITING FOR NICK
Silhouette Special Edition #1088
Now on sale!

TAMING NATASHA

For Gail Link
Welcome to the fold

Lord, it's tweed. I didn't know a guy in tweed could make me salivate."

"A man in cardboard can make you salivate."

"Most of the guys I know *are* cardboard." A dimple winked at the corner of Annie's mouth. She peeked around the counter of wooden toys to see if he was still at the window. "He must have spent some time at the beach this summer. His hair's sun-streaked and he's got a fabulous tan. Oh, God, he smiled at the little girl. I think I'm in love."

Choreographing a scaled-down traffic jam, Natasha smiled. "You always think you're in love."

"I know." Annie sighed. "I wish I could see the color of his eyes. He's got one of those wonderfully lean and bony faces. I'm sure he's incredibly intelligent and has suffered horribly."

Natasha shot a quick, amused look over her shoulder. Annie, with her tall, skinny build had a heart as soft as marshmallow cream. "I'm sure his wife would be fascinated with your fantasy."

"It's a woman's privilege—no, her obligation—to weave fantasies over men like that."

Though she couldn't have disagreed more, Natasha let Annie have her way. "All right then. Go ahead and open up."

"One doll," Spence said, giving his daughter's ear a tug. "I might have thought twice about moving into that house, if I'd realized there was a toy store a half mile away."

"You'd buy her the bloody toy store if you had your way."

He spared one glance for the woman beside him. "Don't start, Nina."

The slender blonde shrugged her shoulders, rippling the trim, rose linen jacket of her suit, then looked at the little girl. "I just meant your daddy tends to spoil you because he loves you so much. Besides, you deserve a present for being so good about the move."

Little Frederica Kimball's bottom lip pouted. "I like my new house." She slipped her hand into her father's, automatically aligning herself with him and against the world. "I have a yard and a swing set all of my own."

Nina looked them over, the tall, rangy man and the fairy-sized young girl. They had identical stubborn chins. As far as she could remember, she'd never won an argument with either one.

"I suppose I'm the only one who doesn't see that as an advantage over living in New York." Nina's tone warmed slightly as she stroked the girl's hair. "I can't help worrying about you a little bit. I really only want you to be happy, darling. You and your daddy."

"We are." To break the tension, Spence swung Freddie into his arms. "Aren't we, funny face?"

"She's about to be that much happier." Relenting, Nina gave Spence's hand a squeeze. "They're opening."

"Good morning." They were gray, Annie noted, biting back a long, dreamy, "Ahh." A glorious gray. She tucked her little fantasy into the back of her mind and ushered in the first customers of the day. "May I help you?"

"My daughter's interested in a doll." Spence set Freddie on her feet again.

"Well, you've come to the right place." Annie dutifully switched her attention to the child. She really was a cute little thing, with her father's gray eyes and pale, flyaway blond hair. "What kind of doll would you like?"

"A pretty one," Freddie answered immediately. "A pretty one with red hair and blue eyes."

"I'm sure we have just what you want." She offered a hand. "Would you like to look around?"

After a glance at her father for approval, Freddie linked hands with Annie and wandered off.

"Damn it." Spence found himself wincing.

Nina squeezed his hand for the second time. "Spence—"

"I delude myself thinking that it doesn't matter, that she doesn't even remember."

"Just because she wanted a doll with red hair and blue eyes doesn't mean anything."

"Red hair and blue eyes," he repeated; the frustration welled up once more. "Just like Angela's. She remembers, Nina. And it does matter." Stuffing his hands into his pockets he walked away.

Three years, he thought. It had been nearly three years now. Freddie had still been in diapers. But she remembered Angela—beautiful, careless Angela. Not even the most liberal critic would have considered Angela a mother. She had never cuddled or crooned, never rocked or soothed.

He studied a small, porcelain-faced doll dressed in pale, angelic blue. Tiny, tapering fingers, huge, dreamy eyes. Angela had been like that, he remembered. Ethereally beautiful. And cold as glass.

He had loved her as a man might love a piece of art—distantly admiring the perfection of form, and constantly searching for the meaning beneath it. Between them they had somehow created a warm, gorgeous child who had managed to find her way through the first years of her life almost without help from her parents.

But he would make it up to her. Spence shut his eyes for a moment. He intended to do everything in his power to give his daughter the love, the structure and the security she deserved. The realness. The word seemed trite, but it was the only one he could find that described what he wanted for his daughter—the real, the solid bond of family.

She loved him. He felt some of the tension ease from his shoulders as he thought of the way Freddie's big eyes would shine when he tucked her in at night, at the way her arms would wrap tightly around him when he held her. Perhaps he would never fully forgive himself for being so involved with his own problems, his own life during her infancy, but things had changed. Even this move had been made with her welfare in mind.

He heard her laugh, and the rest of the tension dissolved on a wave of pure pleasure. There was no sweeter music than his little girl's laugh. An entire symphony could be written around it. He wouldn't disturb her yet, Spence thought. Let her indulge herself with the bright and beautiful dolls, before he had to remind her that only one could be hers.

Relaxed again, he began to pay attention to the

shop. Like the dolls he'd imagined for his daughter, it was bright and beautiful. Though small, it was packed from wall to wall with everything a child might covet. A big golden giraffe and a sad-eyed purple dog hung from the ceiling. Wooden trains, cars and planes, all painted in bold colors, jockeyed for position on a long display table with elegant miniature furniture. An old-fashioned jack-in-the-box sat beside an intricate scale model of a futuristic space station. There were dolls, some beautiful, some charmingly homely, erector sets and tea sets.

The lack of studied arrangement made the result all the more appealing. This was a place to pretend and to wish, a crowded Aladdin's cave designed to make children's eyes light in wonder. To make them laugh, as his daughter was laughing now. He could already foresee that he'd be hard-pressed to keep Freddie from making regular visits.

That was one of the reasons he'd made the move to a small town. He wanted his daughter to be able to reap the pleasures of local shops, where the merchants would know her name. She would be able to walk from one end of town to the other without those big-city worries about muggings, abductions and drugs. There would be no need for dead bolts and security systems, for "white noise" machines to block out the surge and grind of traffic. Even a girl as little as his Freddie wouldn't be swallowed up here.

And perhaps, without the pace and the pressure, he would make peace with himself.

Idly he picked up a music box. It was of delicately crafted porcelain, graced with a figure of a raven-haired Gypsy woman in a flounced red dress. In her ears were tiny gold loops, and in her hands a tambourine with colored streamers. He was certain he wouldn't have found anything more skillfully made on Fifth Avenue.

He wondered how the owner could leave it out where small, curious fingers might reach and break. Intrigued, he turned the key and watched the figure revolve around the tiny, china camp fire.

Tchaikovsky. He recognized the movement instantly, and his skilled ear approved the quality of tone. A moody, even passionate piece, he thought, finding it strange to come across such exquisite workmanship in a toy store. Then he glanced up and saw Natasha.

He stared. He couldn't help it. She was standing a few feet away, her head up, slightly tilted as she watched him. Her hair was as dark as the dancer's and corkscrewed around her face in a wild disarray that flowed beyond her shoulders. Her skin was a dark, rich gold that was set off by the simple red dress she wore.

But this woman was not fragile, he thought. Though she was small, he got the impression of power. Perhaps it was her face, with its full, unpainted mouth and high, slashing cheekbones. Her eyes were almost as dark as her hair, heavy-lidded and thickly lashed. Even from a distance of ten feet he sensed it. Strong, undiluted sex. It surrounded her as other women surrounded themselves with perfumes.

For the first time in years he felt the muscle-numbing heat of pure desire.

Natasha saw it, then recognized and resented it. What kind of man, she wondered, walked into a room with his wife and daughter, then looked at another woman with naked hunger in his eyes?

Not her kind.

Determined to ignore the look as she had ignored it from others in the past, she crossed to him. "Do you need some help?"

Help? Spence thought blankly. He needed oxygen. He hadn't known it was literally possible for a woman to take a man's breath away. "Who are you?"

"Natasha Stanislaski." She offered her coolest smile. "I own the store."

Her voice seemed to hang in the air, husky, vital, with a trace of her Slavic origins adding eroticism as truly as the music still playing behind him. She smelled of soap, nothing more, yet the fragrance completely seduced him.

When he didn't speak, she lifted a brow. It might have been amusing to knock a man off his feet, but she was busy at the moment, and the man was married. "Your daughter has her selection down to three dolls. Perhaps you'd like to help her with her final choice."

"In a minute. Your accent—is it Russian?"

"Yes." She wondered if she should tell him his wife was standing near the front door, bored and impatient.

"How long have you been in America?"

"Since I was six." She aimed a deliberately cold glance. "About the same age as your little girl. Excuse me—"

He had his hand on her arm before he could stop himself. Even though he knew the move was a bad one, the venom in her eyes surprised him. "Sorry. I was going to ask you about this music box."

Natasha shifted her gaze to it as the music began to wind down. "It's one of our best, handcrafted here in the States. Are you interested in buying it?"

"I haven't decided, but I thought you might not have realized it was sitting out on that shelf."

"Why?"

"It's not the kind of merchandise one expects to find in a toy store. It could easily be broken."

Natasha took it and placed it farther back on the shelf. "And it can be mended." She made a quick, clearly habitual movement with her shoulders. It spoke of arrogance rather than carelessness. "I believe children should be allowed the pleasures of music, don't you?"

"Yes." For the first time a smile flickered over his face. It was, as Annie had noted, a particularly effective one, Natasha had to admit. Through her annoyance she felt the trickle of attraction, and strangely, kinship. Then he said, "As a matter of fact, I believe that quite strongly. Perhaps we could discuss it over dinner."

Holding herself rigid, Natasha battled back fury. It was difficult for one with her hot, often turbulent nature, but she reminded herself that the man had not only his wife, but his young daughter in the store.

The angry insults that rose to her throat were swallowed, but not before Spence saw them reflected in her eyes.

"No," was all she said as she turned.

"Miss—" Spence began, then Freddie whirled down the aisle, carrying a big, floppy Raggedy Ann.

"Daddy, isn't she nice?" Eyes shining, she held out the doll for his approval.

It was redheaded, Spence thought. But it was anything but beautiful. Nor, to his relief, was it a symbol of Angela. Because he knew Freddie expected it, he took his time examining her choice. "This is," he said after a moment, "the very best doll I've seen today."

"Really?"

He crouched until he was eye to eye with his daughter. "Absolutely. You have excellent taste, funny face."

Freddie reached out, crushing the doll between them as she hugged her father. "I can have her?"

"I thought she was for me." As Freddie giggled, he picked up the pair of them.

"I'll be happy to wrap her for you." Natasha's tone was warmer, she knew. He might be a jerk, but he loved his daughter.

"I can carry her." Freddie squeezed her new friend close.

"All right. Then I'll just give you a ribbon for her hair. Would you like that?"

"A blue one."

"A blue one it is." Natasha led the way to the cash register.

Nina took one look at the doll and rolled her eyes. "Darling, is that the best you could do?"

"Daddy likes her," Freddie murmured, ducking her head.

"Yes, I do. Very much," he added with a telling look for Nina. Setting Freddie on her feet again, he fished out his wallet.

The mother was certainly no prize, Natasha decided. Though that didn't give the man a right to come on to a clerk in a toy store. She made change and handed over the receipt, then took out a length of blue ribbon.

"Thank you," she said to Freddie. "I think she's going to like her new home with you very much."

"I'll take good care of her," Freddie promised, while she struggled to tie the ribbon through the yarn mop of hair. "Can people come in to look at the toys, or do they have to buy one?"

Natasha smiled, then taking another ribbon, tied a quick, sassy bow in the child's hair. "You can come in and look anytime you like."

"Spence, we really must be going." Nina stood holding the door open.

"Right." He hesitated. It was a small town, he reminded himself. And if Freddie could come in and look, so could he. "It was nice meeting you, Miss Stanislaski."

"Goodbye." She waited until the door jingled and closed, then let out a muttered stream of curses.

Annie peeked around a tower of building blocks. "Excuse me?"

"That man."

"Yes." With a little sigh, Annie waltzed down the aisle. "That man."

"He brings his wife and child into a place like this, then looks at me as if he wants to nibble on my toes."

"Tash." Her expression pained, Annie pressed a hand to her heart. "Please don't excite me."

"I find it insulting." She skirted around the checkout counter and swung a fist at a punching bag. "He asked me to dinner."

"He *what*?" Delight showed in Annie's eyes, before a look from Natasha dampened it. "You're right. It is insulting, seeing as he's a married man—even though his wife seemed like a cold fish."

"His marital problems are no concern of mine."

"No...." Practicality warred with fantasy. "I guess you turned him down."

A choked sound caught in Natasha's throat as she turned. "Of course I turned him down."

"I mean, of course," Annie put in quickly.

"The man has a nerve," Natasha said; her fingers itched to hit something. "Coming into my place of business and propositioning me."

"He didn't!" Scandalized and thrilled, Annie grabbed Natasha's arm. "Tash, he didn't really proposition you? Right here?"

"With his eyes he did. The message was clear." It infuriated her how often men looked at her and only saw the physical. Only wanted to see the physical, she thought in disgust. She had tolerated suggestions, propositions and proposals since before she had fully understood what they meant. But she understood now and tolerated nothing.

"If he hadn't had that sweet little girl with him, I would have slapped his face." Because the image pleased her so much, she let loose on the hapless punching bag again.

Annie had seen her employer's temper fly often enough to know how to cool it. "She was sweet, wasn't she? Her name's Freddie. Isn't that cute?"

Natasha took a long, steadying breath even as she rubbed her fisted hand in her other palm. "Yes."

"She told me they had just moved to Shepherdstown from New York. The doll was going to be her first new friend."

"Poor little thing." Natasha knew too well the fears and anxieties of being a child in a strange place. Forget the father, she told herself with a toss of her head. "She looks to be about the same age as JoBeth Riley." Annoyance forgotten, Natasha went behind the counter again and picked up the phone. It wouldn't hurt to give Mrs. Riley a call.

Spence stood at the music-room window and stared out at a bed of summer flowers. Having flowers outside the window and a bumpy slope of lawn that would need tending was a new experience. He'd never cut grass in his life. Smiling to himself, he wondered how soon he could try his hand at it.

There was a big, spreading maple, its leaves a dark, dark green. In a few weeks, he imagined they would grow red and vibrant before they tumbled from the branches. He had enjoyed the view from his condo on Central Park West, watching the seasons come and go with the changing trees. But not like this, he realized.

Here the grass, the trees, the flowers he saw belonged to him. They were for him to enjoy and to care for. Here he could let Freddie take out her dolls for an afternoon tea party and not have to worry every second she was out of his sight. They would make a good life here, a solid life for both of them. He'd felt it when he'd flown down to discuss his position with the dean—and again when he'd walked through this big, rambling house with the anxious real-estate agent dogging his heels.

She hadn't had to sell it, Spence thought. He'd been sold the moment he'd walked in the front door.

As he watched, a hummingbird swooped to hover at the cup of a bright red petunia. In that instant he was more convinced than ever that his decision to leave the city had been the right one.

Having a brief fling with rural living. Nina's words rolled through his mind as he watched the sun flash on the bird's iridescent wings. It was difficult to blame her for saying it, for believing it when he had always chosen to live in the middle of things. He couldn't deny he had enjoyed those glittery parties that had lasted until dawn, or the elegant midnight suppers after a symphony or ballet.

He had been born into a world of glamour and wealth and prestige. He had lived all of his life in a place where only the best was acceptable. And he had relished it, Spence admitted. Summering in Monte Carlo, wintering in Nice or Cannes. Weekends in Aruba or Cancun.

He wouldn't wish those experiences away, but he could wish, and did, that he had accepted the responsibilities of his life sooner.

He accepted them now. Spence watched the hummingbird streak away like a sapphire bullet. And as much to his own surprise as to that of people who knew him, he was enjoying those responsibilities. Freddie made the difference. All the difference.

He thought of her and she came running across the back lawn, her new rag doll tucked under her arm.

She made a beeline, as he expected, to the swing set. It was so new that the blue and white paint gleamed in the sunlight, and the hard plastic seats were shiny as leather. With the doll in her lap, she pushed off, her face lifted skyward, her tiny mouth moving to some private song.

Love rammed into him with a velvet fist, solid and painful. In all of his life he had never known anything as consuming or as basic as the emotion she brought to him simply by being.

As she glided back and forth, she cuddled the doll, bringing her close to whisper secrets into her ear. It pleased him to see Freddie so taken with the cloth and cotton doll. She could have chosen china or velvet, but had picked something that looked as though it needed love.

She'd spoken of the toy store throughout the morning, and was wishing, Spence knew, for a return trip. Oh, she wouldn't ask for anything, he thought. Not directly. She would use her eyes. It both amused and baffled him that at five, his little girl had already mastered that peculiar and effective feminine trick.

He'd thought of the toy store himself, and its owner. No feminine tricks there, just pure womanly disdain. It made him wince again to remember how clumsy he'd been. Out of practice, he reminded himself with a self-deprecating smile and rubbed a hand over the back of his neck. What was more, he couldn't remember ever experiencing that strong a sexual punch. It was like being hit by lightning, he decided. A man was entitled to fumble a bit after being electrified.

But her reaction... Frowning, Spence replayed the

scene in his mind. She'd been furious. She'd damn near been quivering with fury before he'd opened his mouth—and put his foot in it.

She hadn't even attempted to be polite in her refusal. Just no—a single hard syllable crusted with frost at the edges. It wasn't as if he'd asked her to go to bed with him.

But he'd wanted to. From the first instant he had been able to imagine carrying her off to some dark, remote spot in the woods, where the ground was springy with moss and the trees blocked out the sky. There he could take the heat of those full, sulky lips. There he could indulge in the wild passion her face promised. Wild, mindless sex, heedless of time or place, of right or wrong.

Good God. Amazed, he pulled himself back. He was thinking like a teenager. No, Spence admitted, thrusting his hands into his pockets again. He was thinking like a man—one who had gone four years without a woman. He wasn't certain if he wanted to thank Natasha Stanislaski for unlocking all those needs again, or throttle her.

But he was certain he was going to see her again.

"I'm all packed." Nina paused in the doorway. She gave a little sigh; Spence was clearly absorbed in his own thoughts again. "Spencer," she said, raising her voice as she crossed the room. "I said I'm all packed."

"What? Oh." He managed a distracted smile and forced his shoulders to relax. "We'll miss you, Nina."

"You'll be glad to see the back of me," she corrected, then gave him a quick peck on the cheek.

"No." His smile came easier now, she saw, dutifully wiping the faint trace of lipstick from his skin. "I appreciate all you've done to help us settle in. I know how tight your schedule is."

"I could hardly let my brother tackle the wilds of West Virginia alone." She took his hand in a rare show of genuine agitation. "Oh, Spence, are you sure? Forget everything I've said before and think, really think it through. It's such a big change, for both of you. What will you possibly do here in your free time?"

"Cut the grass." Now he grinned at her expression. "Sit on the porch. Maybe I'll even write music again."

"You could write in New York."

"I haven't written two bars in almost four years," he reminded her.

"All right." She walked to the piano and waved a hand. "But if you wanted a change, you could have found a place on Long Island or even in Connecticut."

"I like it here, Nina. Believe me, this is the best thing I could do for Freddie, and myself."

"I hope you're right." Because she loved him, she smiled again. "I still say you'll be back in New York within six months. In the meantime, as that child's only aunt, I expect to be kept apprised of her progress." She glanced down, annoyed to see a chip in her nail polish. "The idea of her attending public school—"

"Nina."

"Never mind." She held up a hand. "There's no

use starting this argument when I have a plane to catch. And I'm quite aware she's your child."

"Yes, she is."

Nina tapped a finger on the glossy surface of the baby grand. "Spence, I know you're still carrying around guilt because of Angela. I don't like to see it."

His easy smile vanished. "Some mistakes take a long time to be erased."

"She made you miserable," Nina said flatly. "There were problems within the first year of your marriage. Oh, you weren't forthcoming with information," she added when he didn't respond. "But there were others all too eager to pass it along to me or anyone else who would listen. It was no secret that she didn't want the child."

"And how much better was I, wanting the baby only because I thought it would fill the gaps in my marriage? That's a large burden to hand a child."

"You made mistakes. You recognized them and you rectified them. Angela never suffered a pang of guilt in her life. If she hadn't died, you would have divorced her and taken custody of Freddie. The result's the same. I know that sounds cold. The truth often is. I don't like to think that you're making this move, changing your life this dramatically because you're trying to make up for something that's long over."

"Maybe that's part of it. But there's more." He held out a hand, waiting until Nina came to him. "Look at her." He pointed out the window to where Freddie continued to swing high, free as the hummingbird. "She's happy. And so am I."

Chapter Two

"**I**'m not scared."

"Of course you're not." Spence looked at his daughter's brave reflection in the mirror while he carefully braided her hair. He didn't need the quaver in her voice to tell him she was terrified. There was a rock in the pit of his own stomach the size of a fist.

"Some of the kids might cry." Her big eyes were already misted. "But I won't."

"You're going to have fun." He wasn't any more certain of that than his nervous daughter. The trouble with being a parent, he thought, was that you were supposed to sound sure of everything. "The first day of school's always a little scary, but once you get there and meet everyone, you'll have a great time."

She fixed him with a steady, owlish stare. "Really?"

"You liked kindergarten, didn't you?" It was evasive, he admitted to himself, but he couldn't make promises he might not be able to keep.

"Mostly." She lowered her eyes, poking at the yellow, sea horse-shaped comb on her dresser. "But Amy and Pam won't be there."

"You'll make new friends. You've already met JoBeth." He thought of the pixieish brunette who had strolled by the house with her mother a couple of days before.

"I guess, and JoBeth is nice, but..." How could she explain that JoBeth already knew all of the other girls? "Maybe I should wait till tomorrow."

Their eyes met in the mirror again; he rested his chin on her shoulder. She smelled of the pale green soap she loved because it was shaped like a dinosaur. Her face was so much like his own, yet softer, finer, and to him infinitely beautiful.

"You could, but then tomorrow would be your first day of school. You'd still have butterflies."

"Butterflies?"

"Right here." He patted her tummy. "Doesn't it feel like butterflies dancing in there?"

That made her giggle. "Kind of."

"I've got them, too."

"Really?" Her eyes opened wide.

"Really. I've got to go to school this morning, just like you."

She fiddled with the pink ribbons he'd tied on the ends of her pigtails. She knew it wasn't the same for him, but didn't say so because she was afraid he'd get that worried look. Freddie had heard him talking to Aunt Nina once, and remembered how impatient he had sounded when she'd complained that he was uprooting *her niece* during her formative years.

Freddie wasn't sure exactly what formative years were, but she knew her daddy had been upset, and that even when Aunt Nina had gone again, he'd still had that worried look. She didn't want to make him worried, or to make him think Aunt Nina was right. If they went back to New York, the only swing sets were in the park.

Besides, she liked the big house and her new room. Even better, her father's new job was so close, he would be home every night long before dinner. Remembering not to pout, Freddie decided that since she wanted to stay, she'd have to go to school.

"Will you be here when I get home?"

"I think so. But if I'm not, Vera will be," he said, thinking of their longtime housekeeper. "You can tell me everything that happened." After kissing the top of her head, he set her on her feet. She looked achingly small in her pink and white playsuit. Her gray eyes were solemn, her bottom lip trembling. He fought back the urge to gather her up and promise that she'd never have to go to school or anywhere else that frightened her. "Let's go see what Vera packed in your new lunch box."

Twenty minutes later he was standing on the curb, holding Freddie's hand in his own. With almost as much dread as his daughter he saw the big yellow school bus lumbering over the hill.

He should have driven her to school, he thought in sudden panic—at least for the first few days. He should take her himself, instead of putting her onto that bus with strangers. Yet it had seemed better to make the whole event normal, to let her ease into the group and become one of them from the outset.

How could he let her go? She was just a baby. *His baby*. What if he was wrong? This wasn't just a matter of picking out the wrong color dress for her. Simply because it was the designated day and time, he was going to tell his daughter to get onto that bus, then walk away.

What if the driver was careless and drove off a cliff? How could he be sure someone would make certain Freddie got back onto the right bus that afternoon?

The bus rumbled to a halt and his fingers tightened instinctively on hers. When the door clattered open, he was almost ready to make a run for it.

"Hi, there." The driver, a large woman with a wide smile, nodded at him. Behind her, children were yelling and bouncing on the seats. "You must be Professor Kimball."

"Yes." He had excuses for not putting Freddie on the bus on the tip of his tongue.

"I'm Dorothy Mansfield. The kids just call me Miss D. And you must be Frederica."

"Yes, ma'am." She bit her bottom lip to keep from turning away and hiding her face against her father's side. "It's Freddie."

"Whew." Miss D gave another big grin. "I'm glad to hear that. Frederica sure is a mouthful. Well, hop aboard, Freddie girl. This is the big day. John Harman, you give that book back to Mikey, less'n you want to sit behind me in the hot seat the rest of the week."

Eyes swimming, Freddie put one foot onto the first step. Swallowing, she climbed the second.

"Why don't you take a seat with JoBeth and Lisa there?" Miss D suggested kindly. She turned back to Spence with a wink and a wave. "Don't worry about a thing, Professor. We'll take good care of her."

The door closed on a puff of air, then the bus rumbled ahead. Spence could only stand on the curb and watch it take his little girl away.

He wasn't exactly idle. Spence's time was eaten up almost from the moment he walked into the college. He had his own schedule to study, associates to meet, instruments and sheet music to pore over. There was a faculty meeting, a hurried lunch in the lounge, and there were papers, dozens of papers to read and digest. It was a familiar routine, one that he had begun three years before when he'd taken a post at the Juilliard School. But like Freddie, he was the new kid in town, and it was up to him to make the adjustments.

He worried about her. At lunchtime he imagined her sitting in the school cafeteria, a room that smelled of peanut butter and waxy cartons of milk. She would be huddled at the end of a table scattered with crumbs, alone, miserable, while other children laughed and joked with their friends. He could see her at recess, standing apart and looking on longingly, while the others raced and shouted and climbed like spiders on jungle gyms. The trauma would leave her insecure and unhappy for the rest of her life.

All because he'd put her onto that damn yellow bus.

By the end of the day he was feeling as guilty as

a child abuser, certain his little girl would come home in tears, devastated by the rigors of the first day of school. More than once he asked himself if Nina had been right all along. Perhaps he should have left well enough alone and stayed in New York, where at least Freddie had had friends and the familiar.

With his briefcase in one hand and his jacket slung over his shoulder, he started for home. It was hardly more than a mile, and the weather remained unseasonably warm. Until winter hit, he would take advantage of it and walk to and from campus.

He had already fallen in love with the town. There were pretty shops and rambling old houses all along the tree-lined main street. It was a college town and proud of it, but it was equally proud of its age and dignity. The street climbed, and here and there the sidewalk showed cracks where tree roots had undermined it. Though there were cars passing, it was quiet enough to hear the bark of a dog or the music from a radio. A woman weeding marigolds along her walkway looked up and waved at him. Cheered, Spence waved back.

She didn't even know him, he thought. But she had waved. He looked forward to seeing her again, planting bulbs perhaps, or sweeping snow from her porch. He could smell chrysanthemums. For some reason that alone gave him a shot of pleasure.

No, he hadn't made a mistake. He and Freddie belonged here. In less than a week it had become home.

He stopped on the curb to wait for a laboring sedan to pass, and glancing across the street saw the sign for The Fun House. It was perfect, Spence thought. The perfect name. It conjured up laughter and surprises, just as the window display with its building blocks, chubby-cheeked dolls and shiny red cars promised a childhood treasure trove. At the moment he could think of nothing he wanted more than to find something that would bring a smile to his daughter's face.

You spoil her.

He could hear Nina's voice clearly in his ears.

So what? Glancing quickly up and down the street, he crossed to the opposite curb. His little girl had walked onto the school bus as bravely as any soldier marching into battle. There was no harm in buying her a small medal.

The door jingled as he entered. There was a scent, as cheerful as the sound of the bells. Peppermint, he thought and smiled. It delighted him to hear the tinny strains of "The Merry-Go-Round Broke Down," coming from the rear of the shop.

"I'll be right with you."

He had forgotten, Spence realized, how that voice could cruise along the air.

He wouldn't make a fool of himself again. This time he was prepared for what she looked like, sounded like, smelled like. He had come into to buy a present for his daughter, not to flirt with the proprietor. Then he grinned into the face of a forlorn panda. There didn't seem to be any law against doing both.

"I'm sure Bonnie will love it," Natasha said as she carried the miniature carousel for her customer. "It's a beautiful birthday present."

"She saw it in here a few weeks ago and hasn't been able to talk about anything else." Bonnie's grandmother tried not to grimace at the price. "I guess she's old enough to take care of it."

"Bonnie's a very responsible girl," Natasha went on, then spotted Spence at the counter. "I'll be right with you." The temperature of her voice dropped a cool twenty degrees.

"Take your time." It annoyed him that his reaction to her should be so strong, while hers played tug-of-war at the opposite end of the spectrum. It was obvious she'd decided to dislike him. It might be interesting, Spence thought, while he watched her slender, capable hands wrap the carousel, to find out her reasons.

And change her mind.

"That's $55.27, Mrs. Mortimer."

"Oh no, dear, the price tag said $67."

Natasha, who knew Mrs. Mortimer juggled expenses on a fixed income, only smiled. "I'm sorry. Didn't I tell you it was on sale?"

"No." Mrs. Mortimer let out a little breath of relief as she counted out bills. "Well, this must be my lucky day."

"And Bonnie's." Natasha topped the gift with a pretty, celebratory pink bow, remembering it was Bonnie's favorite color. "Be sure to tell her happy birthday."

"I will." The proud grandmother lifted her package. "I can't wait to see her face when she opens this. Bye, Natasha."

Natasha waited until the door closed. "May I help you with something?"

"That was a very nice thing to do."

She lifted a brow. "What do you mean?"

"You know what I mean." He had the absurd urge to take her hand and kiss it. It was incredible, he thought. He was almost thirty-five and tumbling into puppy love with a woman he barely knew. "I'd meant to come in before."

"Oh? Was your daughter dissatisfied with her doll?"

"No, she loves it. It was just that I..." Good God, he was nearly stuttering. Five minutes with her, and he felt as awkward as a teenager at his first dance. He steadied himself with an effort. "I felt we'd gotten off on the wrong foot before. Should I apologize?"

"If you like." Just because he looked appealing and a little awkward was no reason to go easy on him. "Did you come in only for that?"

"No." His eyes darkened, just slightly. Noting it, Natasha wondered if she'd erred in her initial impression. Perhaps he wasn't harmless, after all. There was something deeper in those eyes, stronger and more dangerous. What surprised her further was that she found it exciting.

Disgusted with herself, she gave him a polite smile. "Was there something else?"

"I wanted something for my daughter." The hell with the gorgeous Russian princess, he thought. He had more important things to tend to.

"What was it you wanted for her?"

"I don't know." That was true enough. Setting down his briefcase, he glanced around the shop.

Unbending a little, Natasha came around the counter. "Is it her birthday?"

"No." Feeling foolish, he shrugged. "It's the first

day of school, and she looked so...brave getting on the bus this morning."

This time Natasha's smile was spontaneous and full of warmth. It nearly stopped his heart. "You shouldn't worry. When she comes home, she'll be full of stories about everything and everyone. The first day is much harder, I think, on the parent than on the child."

"It's been the longest day of my life."

She laughed, a rich smoky sound that seemed impossibly erotic in a room full of clowns and stuffed bears. "It sounds like you both deserve a present. You were looking at a music box before. I have another you might like."

So saying, she led the way to the back of the shop. Spence did his best to ignore the subtle sway of her hips and the soft, fresh-scrubbed flavor of her scent. The box she chose was carved of wood, its pedestal topped with a cat and a fiddle, a cow and a quarter moon. As it turned to "Stardust," he saw the laughing dog and the dish with the spoon.

"It's charming."

"It's one of my favorites." She'd decided that any man who adored his daughter so blatantly couldn't be all bad. So she smiled again. "I think it would be a lovely memento, something she could play on her first day of college and remember her father was thinking of her."

"If he survives first grade." He shifted slightly to look at her. "Thank you. It's perfect."

It was the oddest thing—his body had hardly brushed hers, but she'd felt a jolt. For an instant she forgot he was a customer, a father, a husband, and thought of him only as a man. His eyes were the color of the river at dusk. His lips, as they formed the barest hint of a smile, were impossibly attractive, alluring. Involuntarily she wondered what it would be like to feel them against her own—to watch his face as mouth met mouth, and see herself reflected in his eyes.

Appalled, she stepped back and her voice grew colder. "I'll box it for you."

Intrigued by the sudden change in tone, he took his time following her back to the counter. Hadn't he seen something in those fabulous eyes of hers? Or was it wishful thinking? It had gone quickly enough, heat smothered in frost. For the life of him he could find no reason for either.

"Natasha." He laid a hand on hers as she began to pack the music box.

Slowly she lifted her eyes. She was already hating herself for noticing that his hands were beautiful, wide-palmed, long-fingered. There was also a note of patience in his voice that stretched her already frayed nerves.

"Yes?"

"Why do I keep getting the feeling you'd like to boil me in oil?"

"You're mistaken," she said evenly. "I don't think I'd like that."

"You don't sound convinced." He felt her hand flex under his, soft and strong. The image of steel-lined velvet seemed particularly apt. "I'm having some trouble figuring out exactly what I've done to annoy you."

"Then you'll have to think about it. Cash or charge?"

He'd had little practice with rejection. Like a wasp it stung the ego. No matter how beautiful she was, he had no desire to continue to ram his head against the same brick wall.

"Cash." The door jangled open behind them and he released her hand. Three children, fresh from school, came in giggling. A young boy with red hair and a face bursting with freckles stood on his toes in front of the counter.

"I have three dollars," he announced.

Natasha fought back a grin. "You're very rich today, Mr. Jensen."

He flashed her a smile that revealed his latest missing tooth. "I've been saving up. I want the race car."

Natasha only lifted a brow as she counted out Spence's change. "Does your mother know you're here spending your life savings?" Her new customer remained silent. "Scott?"

He shifted from one foot to the other. "She didn't say I couldn't."

"And she didn't say you could," Natasha surmised. She leaned over to tug at his cowlick. "Go and ask her, then you come back. The race car will still be here."

"But, Tash—"

"You wouldn't want your mother to be mad at me, would you?"

Scott looked thoughtful for a moment, and Natasha could tell it was a tough choice. "I guess not."

"Then go ask her, and I'll hold one for you."

Hope blossomed. "Promise?"

Natasha put a hand on her heart. "Solemnly." She looked back at Spence, and the amusement faded from her eyes. "I hope Freddie enjoys her present."

"I'm sure she will." He walked out, annoyed with himself for wishing he were a ten-year-old boy with a missing tooth.

Natasha locked the shop at six. The sun was still bright, the air still steamy. It made her think of picnics under a shady tree. A nicer fantasy than the microwave meal on her agenda, she mused, but at the moment impractical.

As she walked home, she watched a couple stroll hand in hand into the restaurant across the street. Someone hailed her from a passing car, and she waved in response. She could have stopped in the local pub and whiled away an hour over a glass of wine with any number of people she knew. Finding a dinner companion was as simple as sticking her head through one of a dozen doors and making the suggestion.

She wasn't in the mood for company. Not even her own.

It was the heat, she told herself as she turned the corner, the heat that had hung mercilessly in the air throughout the summer and showed no sign of yielding to autumn. It made her restless. It made her remember.

It had been summer when her life had changed so irrevocably.

Even now, years later, sometimes when she saw the roses in full bloom or heard the drunken buzz of bees she would ache. And wonder what might have happened. What would her life be like now, if...? She detested herself for playing those wishing games.

There were roses now, fragile pink ones that thrived despite the heat and lack of rain. She had planted them herself in the little patch of grass outside her apartment. Tending them brought her pleasure *and* pain. And what was life, she asked herself as she ran a fingertip over a petal, without them both? The warm scent of the roses followed her up the walkway.

Her rooms were quiet. She had thought about getting a kitten or a pup, so that there would be something there to greet her in the evening, something that loved and depended on her. But then she realized how unfair it would be to leave it alone while she was at the shop.

So she turned to music, flicking on the stereo as she stepped out of her shoes. Even that was a test. Tchaikovsky's *Romeo and Juliet.* She could see herself dancing to those haunting, romantic strains, the hot lights surrounding her, the music beating like her blood, her movements fluid, controlled without looking it. A triple pirouette, showing grace without effort.

That was past, Natasha reminded herself. Regrets were for the weak.

She moved out of habit, changing her work clothes for a loose, sleeveless jumpsuit, hanging up her skirt and blouse neatly as she had been taught. It was habit again rather than necessity that had her checking the cotton skirt for wear.

There was iced tea in the refrigerator and one of those packaged meals for the microwave that she both depended on and detested. She laughed at herself as she pushed the buttons to heat it.

She was getting like an old woman, Natasha decided, cranky and cross from the heat. Sighing, she rubbed the cold glass over her forehead.

That man had started her off, she thought. For a few moments in the shop today she had actually started to like him. He'd been so sweet, worrying about his little girl, wanting to reward her for being brave enough to face that momentous first day in school. She'd liked the way his voice had sounded, the way his eyes had smiled. For those few moments he had seemed like someone she could laugh with, talk with.

Then that had changed. A part of it was surely her fault, she admitted. But that didn't diminish his blame. She had felt something she hadn't felt, hadn't chosen to feel in a long, long time. That frisson of excitement. That tug of need. It made her angry and ashamed of herself. It made her furious with him.

The nerve, she thought, as she yanked her dish out of the microwave. Flirting with her as if she were some naive fool, before he went home to his wife and daughter.

Have dinner with him, indeed. She jammed her fork into the steaming seafood pasta. That kind of man expected payment in full for a meal. The candlelight and wine type, she thought with a sneer. Soft voice, patient eyes, clever hands. And no heart.

Just like Anthony. Impatient, she set the dish aside and picked up the glass that was already dripping with moisture. But she was wiser now than she had been at eighteen. Much wiser. Much stronger. She was no longer a woman who could be lured by charm and smooth words. Not that this man was smooth, she remembered with a quick smile. He—Lord, she didn't even know his name and she already detested him—he was a little clumsy, a little awkward. That was a charm of its own.

But he was, she thought, very much like Anthony. Tall and blond with those oh, so American good looks. Looks that concealed a lack of morals and a carelessly deceitful heart.

What Anthony had cost her could never be tallied. Since that time, Natasha had made very, very certain no man would ever cost her so dearly again.

But she had survived. She lifted her glass in a self-toast. Not only had she survived, but except for times when memories crowded in on her, she was happy. She loved the shop, and the chance it gave her to be around children and make them happy. In her three years there she had watched them grow. She had a wonderful, funny friend in Annie, books that stayed in the black and a home that suited her.

She heard a thump over her head and smiled. The Jorgensons were getting ready for the evening meal. She imagined Don was fussing around Marilyn, who was carrying their first child. Natasha liked knowing they were there, just above her, happy, in love and full of hope.

That was family to her, what she had had in her youth, what she had expected as an adult. She could still see Papa fretting over Mama when she neared her time. Every time, Natasha remembered, thinking of her three younger siblings. How he had wept with happiness when his wife and babies were safe and well. He adored his Nadia. Even now Natasha knew he still brought flowers home to the little house in

Brooklyn. When he came home after a day's work, he kissed his wife, not with an absent peck on the cheek, but robustly, joyfully. A man wildly in love after almost thirty years.

It was her father who had kept her from shoveling all men into the pit Anthony had dug for her. Seeing her father and mother together had kept that small, secret hope alight that someday she would find someone who would love her as much and as honestly.

Someday, she thought with a shrug. But for now she had her own business, her own home and her own life. No man, no matter how beautiful his hands or how clear his eyes, was going to rock her boat. Secretly she hoped her newest customer's wife gave him nothing but grief.

"One more story. Please, Daddy." Freddie, her eyes heavy, her face shiny from her bath, used her most persuasive smile. She was nestled against Spence in her big, white canopy bed.

"You're already asleep."

"No, I'm not." She peeked up at him, fighting to keep her eyes open. It had been the very best day of her life, and she didn't want it to end. "Did I tell you that JoBeth's cat had kittens? Six of them."

"Twice." Spence flicked a finger down her nose. He knew a hint when he heard one, and fell back on the parent's standard. "We'll see."

Sleepy, Freddie smiled. She knew from his tone that her father was already weakening. "Mrs. Patterson's real nice. She's going to let us have Show and Tell every Friday."

"So you said." And he'd been worried, Spence thought. "I get the feeling you like school."

"It's neat." She yawned hugely. "Did you fill out all the forms?"

"They'll be ready for you to take in tomorrow." All five hundred of them, he thought with a sigh. "Time to unplug the batteries, funny face."

"One more story. The made-up kind." She yawned again, comforted by the soft cotton of his shirt beneath her cheek and the familiar scent of his aftershave.

He gave in, knowing she would sleep long before he got to the happy ever after. He wove a story around a beautiful, dark-haired princess from a foreign land, and the knight who tried to rescue her from her ivory tower.

Foolishness, Spence thought even as he added a sorcerer and a two-headed dragon. He knew his thoughts were drifting toward Natasha again. She was certainly beautiful, but he didn't think he'd ever met a woman less in need of rescuing.

It was just his bad luck that he had to pass her shop every day to and from campus.

He'd ignore her. If anything, he should be grateful to her. She'd made him want, made him feel things he hadn't thought he could anymore. Maybe now that he and Freddie were settled, he'd start socializing again. There were plenty of attractive, single women at the college. But the idea of dating didn't fill him with delight.

Socializing, Spence corrected. Dating was for teenagers and conjured up visions of drive-in movies, pizza and sweaty palms. He was a grown man, and it was certainly time he started enjoying female companionship again. Over the age of five, he thought, looking at Freddie's small hand balled in his palm.

Just what would you think, he asked silently, if I brought a woman home to dinner? It made him remember how big and hurt her eyes had been when he and Angela had swept out of the condo for evenings at the theater or the opera.

It won't ever be like that again, he promised as he shifted her from his chest to the pillow. He settled the grinning Raggedy Ann beside her, then tucked the covers under her chin. Resting a hand on the bedpost, he glanced around the room.

It already had Freddie's stamp on it. The dolls lining the shelves with books jumbled beneath them, the fuzzy, pink elephant slippers beside her oldest and most favored sneakers. The room had that little-girl scent of shampoo and crayons. A night-light in the shape of a unicorn assured that she wouldn't wake up in the dark and be afraid.

He stayed a moment longer, finding himself as soothed by the light as she. Quietly he stepped out, leaving her door open a few inches.

Downstairs he found Vera carrying a tray of coffee. The Mexican housekeeper was wide from shoulders to hips, and gave the impression of a small, compact freight train when she moved from room to room. Since Freddie's birth, she had proven not only efficient but indispensable. Spence knew it was often possible to insure an employee's loyalty with a paycheck, but not her love. From the moment Freddie had come home in her silk-trimmed blanket, Vera had been in love.

She cast an eye up the stairs now, and her lined face folded into a smile. "She had one big day, huh?"

"Yes, and one she fought ending to the last gasp. Vera, you didn't have to bother."

She shrugged her shoulders while she carried the coffee into his office. "You said you have to work tonight."

"Yes, for a little while."

"So I make you coffee before I go in and put my feet up to watch TV." She arranged the tray on his desk, fussing a bit while she talked. "My baby, she's happy with school and her new friends." She didn't add that she had wept into her apron when Freddie had stepped onto the bus. "With the house empty all day, I have plenty of time to get my work done. You don't stay up too late, Dr. Kimball."

"No." It was a polite lie. He knew he was too restless for sleep. "Thank you, Vera."

"*¡De nada!*" She patted her iron-gray hair. "I wanted to tell you that I like this place very much. I was afraid to leave New York, but now I'm happy."

"We couldn't manage without you."

"*Sí.*" She took this as her due. For seven years she had worked for the *señor*, and basked in the prestige of being housekeeper for an important man—a respected musician, a doctor of music and a college professor. Since the birth of his daughter she had been so in love with *her baby* that she would have worked for Spence, whatever his station.

She had grumbled about moving from the beautiful high rise in New York, to the rambling house in the small town, but Vera was shrewd enough to know that the *señor* had been thinking of Freddie. Freddie had come home from school only hours before, laughing, excited, with the names of new best friends tumbling from her lips. So Vera was content.

"You are a good father, Dr. Kimball."

Spence glanced over before he sat down behind his desk. He was well aware that there had been a time Vera had considered him a very poor one.

"I'm learning."

"*Sí.*" Casually she adjusted a book on the shelf. "In this big house you won't have to worry about disturbing Freddie's sleep if you play your piano at night."

He looked over again, knowing she was encouraging him in her way to concentrate on his music. "No, it shouldn't disturb her. Good night, Vera."

After a quick glance around to be certain there was nothing more for her to tidy, she left him.

Alone, Spence poured the coffee, then studied the papers on his desk. Freddie's school forms were stacked next to his own work. He had a great deal of preparation ahead of him, before his classes began the following week.

He looked forward to it, even as he tried not to regret that the music that had once played so effortlessly inside his head was still silent.

Chapter Three

Natasha scooped the barrette through the hair above her ear and hoped it would stay fixed for more than five minutes. She studied her reflection in the narrow mirror over the sink in the back of the shop before she decided to add a touch of lipstick. It didn't matter that it had been a long and hectic day or that her feet were all but crying with fatigue. Tonight was her treat to herself, her reward for a job well done.

Every semester she signed up for one course at the college. She chose whatever seemed most fun, most intriguing or most unusual. Renaissance Poetry one year, Automotive Maintenance another. This term, two evenings a week, she would be taking Music History. Tonight she would begin an exploration of a new topic. Everything she learned she would store for her own pleasure, as other women stored diamonds and emeralds. It didn't have to be useful. In Natasha's opinion a glittery necklace wasn't particularly useful, either. It was simply exciting to own.

She had her notebook, her pens and pencils and a flood of enthusiasm. To prepare herself, she had raided the library and pored over related books for the last two weeks. Pride wouldn't allow her to go into class ignorant. Curiosity made her wonder if her instructor could take the dry, distant facts and add excitement.

There was little doubt that this particular instructor was adding dashes of excitement in other quarters. Annie had teased her just that morning about the new professor everyone was talking about. Dr. Spencer B. Kimball.

The name sounded very distinguished to Natasha, quite unlike the description of a hunk that Annie had passed along. Annie's information came from her cousin's daughter, who was majoring in Elementary Education with a minor in Music. A sun-god, Annie had relayed and made Natasha laugh.

A very gifted sun-god, Natasha mused while she turned off lights in the shop. She knew Kimball's work well, or the work he had composed before he had suddenly and inexplicably stopped writing music. Why, she had even danced to his Prelude in D Minor when she had been with the corps de ballet in New York.

A million years ago, she thought as she stepped onto the street. Now she would be able to meet the genius, listen to his views and perhaps find new meanings in many of the classics she already loved.

He was probably the temperamental artiste type,

she decided, pleased with the way the evening breeze lifted her hair and cooled her neck. Or a pale eccentric with one earring. It didn't matter. She intended to work hard. Each course she took was a matter of pride to her. It still stung to remember how little she had known when she'd been eighteen. How little she had cared to know, Natasha admitted, other than dance. She had of her own choice closed herself off from so many worlds in order to focus everything on one. When that had been taken away, she had been as lost as a child set adrift on the Atlantic.

She had found her way to shore, just as her family had once found its way across the wilds of the Ukraine to the jungles of Manhattan. She liked herself better—the independent, ambitious American woman she had become. As she was now, she could walk into the big, beautiful old building on campus with as much pride as any freshman student.

There were footsteps echoing in the corridors, distant, dislocated. There was a hushed reverence that Natasha always associated with churches and universities. In a way there was religion here—the belief in learning.

She felt somewhat reverent herself as she made her way to her class. As a child of five in her small farming village, she had never even imagined such a building, or the books and beauty it contained.

Several students were already waiting. A mixed bag, she noted, ranging from college to middle age. All of them seemed to buzz with that excitement of beginning. She saw by the clock that it was two minutes shy of eight. She'd expected Kimball to be there, busily shuffling his papers, peering at them behind glasses, his hair a little wild and streaming to his shoulders.

Absently she smiled at a young man in horn-rims, who was staring at her as if he'd just woken from a dream. Ready to begin, she sat down, then looked up when the same man clumsily maneuvered himself into the desk beside her.

"Hello."

He looked as though she'd struck him with a bat rather than offered a casual greeting. He pushed his glasses nervously up his nose. "Hello. I'm— I'm...Terry Maynard," he finished on a burst as his name apparently came to him at last.

"Natasha." She smiled again. He was on the sunny side of twenty-five and harmless as a puppy.

"I haven't, ah, seen you on campus before."

"No." Though at twenty-seven it amused her to be taken for a coed, she kept her voice sober. "I'm only taking this one class. For fun."

"For fun?" Terry appeared to take music very seriously. "Do you know who Dr. Kimball is?" His obvious awe made him almost whisper the name.

"I've heard of him. You're a Music major?"

"Yes. I hope to, well one day, I hope to play with the New York Symphony." His blunt fingers reached nervously to adjust his glasses. "I'm a violinist."

She smiled again and made his Adam's apple bob. "That's wonderful. I'm sure you're very good."

"What do you play?"

"Five card draw." Then she laughed and settled back in her chair. "I'm sorry. I don't play an instrument. But I love to listen to music and thought I'd enjoy the class." She glanced at the clock on the wall.

"If it ever starts, that is. Apparently our esteemed professor is late."

At that moment the esteemed professor was rushing down the corridors, cursing himself for ever agreeing to take on this night class. By the time he had helped Freddie with her homework—how many animals can you find in this picture?—convinced her that brussels sprouts were cute instead of yucky, and changed his shirt because her affectionate hug had transferred some mysterious, sticky substance to his sleeve, he had wanted nothing more than a good book and a warm brandy.

Instead he was going to have to face a roomful of eager faces, all waiting to learn what Beethoven had worn when he'd composed his Ninth Symphony.

In the foulest of moods, he walked into class. "Good evening. I'm Dr. Kimball." The murmurs and rattles quieted. "I must apologize for being late. If you'll all take a seat, we'll dive right in."

As he spoke he scanned the room. And found himself staring into Natasha's astonished face.

"No." She wasn't aware she'd spoken the word aloud, and wouldn't have cared. It was some sort of joke, she thought, and a particularly bad one. This— this *man* in the casually elegant jacket was Spencer Kimball, a musician whose songs she had admired and danced to. The man who, while barely into his twenties had been performing at Carnegie Hall being hailed as a genius. This man who had tried to pick her up in a toy store was the illustrious Dr. Kimball?

It was ludicrous, it was infuriating, it was—

Wonderful, Spence thought as he stared at her. Absolutely wonderful. In fact, it was perfect, as long as he could control the laugh that was bubbling in his throat. So the czarina was one of his students. It was better, much better than a warm brandy and an evening of quiet.

"I'm sure," he said after a long pause, "we'll all find the next few months fascinating."

She should have signed up for Astronomy, Natasha told herself. She could have learned all kinds of interesting things about the planets and stars. Asteroids. She'd have been much better off learning about— what was it?—gravitational pull and inertia. Whatever that was. Surely it was much more important for her to find out how many moons revolved around Jupiter than to study Burgundian composers of the fifteenth century.

She would transfer, Natasha decided. First thing in the morning she would make the arrangements. In fact, she would get up and walk out right now if she wasn't certain Dr. Spencer Kimball would smirk.

Running her pencil between her fingers, she crossed her legs and determined not to listen.

It was a pity his voice was so attractive.

Impatient, Natasha looked at the clock. Nearly an hour to go. She would do what she did when she waited at the dentist's office. Pretend she was someplace else. Struggling to block Spence's voice from her mind she began to swing her foot and doodle on her pad.

She didn't notice when her doodles became notes, or when she began to hang on every word. He made fifteenth-century musicians seem alive and vital—and their music as real as flesh and blood. Rondeaux, vieralais, ballades. She could almost hear the three-part chansons of the dawning Renaissance, the reverent, soaring Kyries and Glorias of the masses.

She was caught up, involved in that ancient rivalry between church and state and music's part in the politics. She could see huge banqueting halls filled with elegantly dressed aristocrats, feasting on music as well as food.

"Next time we'll be discussing the Franco-Flemish school and rhythmic developments." Spence gave his class an easy smile. "And I'll try to be on time."

Was it over? Natasha glanced at the clock again and was shocked to see it was indeed after nine.

"Incredible, isn't he?"

She looked at Terry. His eyes were gleaming behind his lenses. "Yes." It cost her to admit it, but truth was truth.

"You should hear him in theory class." He noticed with envy that several students were grouped around his idol. As yet, Terry hadn't worked up the nerve to approach him. "I'll—see you Thursday."

"What? Oh. Good night, Terry."

"I could, ah, give you a ride home if you want." The fact that he was nearly out of gas and his muffler was currently held on by a coat hanger didn't enter his mind.

She favored him with an absent smile that had his heart doing a cha-cha. "That's nice of you, but I don't live far."

She hoped to breeze out of the classroom while Spence was still occupied. She should have known better.

He simply put a hand on her arm and stopped her. "I'd like to speak with you a moment, Natasha."

"I'm in a hurry."

"It won't take long." He nodded to the last of his departing students, then eased back against his desk and grinned at her. "I should have paid more attention to my roster, but then again, it's nice to know there are still surprises in the world."

"That depends on your point of view, Dr. Kimball."

"Spence." He continued to grin. "Class is over."

"So it is." Her regal nod made him think again of Russian Royalty. "Excuse me."

"Natasha." He waited, almost seeing impatience shimmer around her as she turned. "I can't imagine that someone with your heritage doesn't believe in destiny."

"Destiny?"

"Of all the classrooms in all the universities in all the world, she walks into mine."

She wouldn't laugh. She'd be damned if she would. But her mouth quirked up at the corners before she controlled it. "And here I was thinking it was just bad luck."

"Why Music History?"

She balanced her notebook on her hip. "It was a toss-up between that and Astronomy."

"That sounds like a fascinating story. Why don't we go down the street for a cup of coffee? You can tell me about it." Now he saw it—molten fury that turned her eyes from rich velvet to sharp jet. "Now why does that infuriate you?" he inquired, almost to himself. "Is an offer of a cup of coffee in this town similiar to an illicit proposition?"

"You should know, Dr. Kimball." She turned, but

he reached the door before her, slamming it with enough force to make her step back. He was every bit as angry as herself, she noted. Not that it mattered. It was only that he had seemed a mild sort of man. Detestable, but mild. There was nothing mild about him now. Those fascinating bones and angles in his face might have been carved of stone.

"Clarify."

"Open the door."

"Gladly. After you answer my question." He *was* angry. Spence realized he hadn't felt this kind of hot, blood-pumping rage in years. It felt wonderful. "I realize that just because I'm attracted to you doesn't mean you have to return the favor."

She threw up her chin, hating herself for finding the storm-cloud-gray eyes so hypnotic. "I don't."

"Fine." He couldn't strangle her for that, however much he'd like to. "But, damn it, I want to know why you aim and fire every time I'm around you."

"Because men like you deserve to be shot."

"Men like me," he repeated, measuring out the words. "What exactly does that mean?"

He was standing close, all but looming over her. As in the shop when he had brushed up against her, she felt those bubble bursts of excitement, attraction, confusion. It was more than enough to push her over the edge.

"Do you think because you have a nice face and a pretty smile you can do whatever you like? *Yes,*" she answered before he could speak and slapped her notebook against his chest. "You think you have only to snap your fingers." She demonstrated dramatically.

"And a woman will fall into your arms. Not this woman."

Her accent thickened when she was on a roll, he noted, somewhat baffled by her claim. "I don't recall snapping my fingers."

She let loose one short, explicit Ukrainian oath and grabbed the knob. "You want to have a cup of coffee with me? Good. We'll have your coffee—and we'll call your wife and ask her to join us."

"My what?" He closed his hand over hers so that the door was jerked open, then slammed shut again. "I don't have a wife."

"Really?" The single word dripped with scorn; her eyes flashed at him. "And I suppose the woman who came with you to the shop is your sister."

It should have been funny. But he couldn't quite get the joke. "Nina? As a matter of fact, she is."

Natasha yanked open the door with a sound of disgust. "That is pathetic."

Filled with righteous indignation, she stormed down the corridor and out the main door. In a staccato rhythm that matched her mood, her heels beat on the concrete as she started down the steps. When she was abruptly whirled around, she nearly took the last two in a tumble.

"You've got a hell of a nerve."

"I?" she managed. "I have a nerve?"

"You think you've got it all figured out, don't you?" Having the advantage of height, Spence could stare down at her. Natasha saw shadows move over his face as temper colored his voice. He didn't appear awkward now, but every bit in control. "Or I should say you think you've got me figured."

"It takes very little." The fingers on her arm were very firm. She hated knowing that mixed with her own anger was basic sexual attraction. Fighting it off, she tossed back her hair. "You're really very typical."

"I wonder, can your opinion of me get any lower?" Now fury ground edge to edge with desire.

"Doubtful."

"In that case, I might as well satisfy myself."

The notebook flew out of her hand when he dragged her close. She managed a single, startled sound in her throat before his mouth covered hers. Covered, crushed, then conquered.

Natasha would have fought him. Over and over she told herself she *would* fight him. But it was shock— at least, she prayed it was shock—that had her arms falling limply to her sides.

It was wrong. It was unforgivable. And, oh God, it was wonderful. Instinctively he'd found the key to unlock the passion that had lain dormant in her for so long. Her blood swam hot with it. Her mind hazed. Dimly she heard someone laugh as they strolled down the sidewalk below. A beep of a car horn, a shout of greeting, then silence once more.

She murmured, a pitiful protest that shamed her and was easily ignored as his tongued glided over her own. His taste was a banquet after a long fast. Though she kept her hands balled at her sides, she leaned into the kiss.

Kissing her was like walking through a mine field. Any moment he expected the bomb to go off and blow him to pieces. He should have stopped after the first shock, but danger had a thrill of its own.

And she was dangerous. As his fingers dived into her hair, he could feel the ground quiver and quake. It was her—the promise, the threat of titanic passion. He could taste it on her lips, even as she fought to hold it back. He could feel it in her taut, terrified stance. If she released it, she could make him a slave.

Needs such as he'd never known battered his system with heavy fists. Images, all fire and smoke, danced in his brain. Something struggled to break free, like a bird beating at the bars of a cage. He could feel it straining. Then Natasha was pulling away from him, standing apart and staring at him with wide, eloquent eyes.

She couldn't breathe. For an instant she was genuinely afraid she would die on the spot with this unwanted, shameful desire on her conscience. In defiance she took a huge gulp of air.

"I could never hate anyone as much as I hate you."

He shook his head to clear it. She had left him dizzy, dazed and utterly defenseless. For his own sake he waited until he was sure he could speak. "That's a lofty position you put me in, Natasha." He stepped down until they were at eye level. There were tears on her lashes, but they were offset by the condemnation in her eyes. "Let's just be sure you've put me there for the right reasons. Is it because I kissed you, or because you liked it?"

She swung her hand out. He could have avoided the blow easily enough, but thought she deserved a hit. As the crack of the slap echoed, he decided they were even.

"Don't come near me again," she said, breathing hard. "I warn you, if you do, I won't care what I say

or who hears me. If it wasn't for your little girl—"
She broke off and bent to gather her things. Her pride
was shattered, along with her self-esteem. "You don't
deserve such a beautiful child."

He caught her arm again, but this time the expression on his face made her blood go cold. "You're
right. I never have and probably never will deserve
Freddie, but I'm all she has. Her mother—my wife—
died three years ago."

He strode off, was caught in the beam of a street
lamp, then disappeared into the dark beyond. Her
notebook pressed against her chest, Natasha sank
weakly onto the bottom step.

What in hell was she going to do now?

There was no choice. No matter how much she
hated it, there was really only one course to take.
Natasha rubbed the palms of her hands on the thighs
of her khakis, then started up the freshly painted
wooden steps.

It was a nice house, she thought, stalling. Of course
she'd seen it so often that she rarely noticed it anymore. It was one of those sturdy old brick places
tucked back from the street and shielded by trees and
box hedges.

The summer flowers had yet to fade, but the fall
blooms were already staking their claim. Showy del-
phiniums vied with spicy scented mums, vivid dahlias
with starry asters. Someone was caring for them. She
could see fresh mulch on the flower beds, damp with
watering.

Wanting a little more time, she studied the house.
There were curtains at the windows, thin ivory sheers

that would let in the light. Higher up she caught a glimpse of a fanciful pattern of unicorns that identified a little girl's room.

She gathered her courage and crossed the porch to the front door. It would be quick, she promised herself. Not painless, but quick. She rapped, released her breath and waited.

The woman who answered was short and wide with a face as brown and wrinkled as a raisin. Natasha found herself fixed by a pair of small, dark eyes while the housekeeper dried her hands on the skirt of a stained apron.

"May I help you?"

"I'd like to see Dr. Kimball if he's in." She smiled, pretending she didn't feel as though she were stepping into the pillory. "I'm Natasha Stanislaski." She saw the housekeeper's little eyes narrow, so that they nearly disappearing into the folds of her face.

Vera had at first taken Natasha for one of the *señor*'s students, and had been prepared to nudge her on her way. "You own the toy store in town."

"That's right."

"Ah." With a nod, she opened the door wider to let Natasha in. "Freddie says you are a very nice lady, who gave her a blue ribbon for her doll. I promised to take her back, but just to look." She gestured for Natasha to follow.

As they made their way down the hall, Natasha caught the hesitant notes of a piano. When she saw her reflection in an old oval mirror, it surprised her that she was smiling.

He was sitting at the piano with the child on his lap, looking over her head while she slowly tapped out "Mary Had a Little Lamb." The sun streamed in through the windows behind them. At that moment she wished she could paint. How else could it be captured?

It was perfect. The light, the shadows, the pale pastels of the room all combined to make the perfect backdrop. The alignment of their heads, their bodies, was too natural and eloquent ever to be posed. The girl was in pink and white, the laces of one sneaker untied. He had taken off his jacket and tie, then rolled up the sleeves of the pale dress shirt to the elbows like a workman.

There was the fragile shine of the child's hair, the deeper glow of his. The child leaned back against her father, her head resting just under his collarbone; the faintest smile of pleasure lighted her face. Over it all was the simple nursery rhyme music she was playing.

He had his hands on the knees of her jeans, his long, beautiful fingers tapping the time in tandem with the tick of the antique metronome. She could see it all, the love, the patience, the pride.

"No, please," Natasha whispered, holding out a hand to Vera. "Don't disturb them."

"You play now, Daddy." Freddie tilted her head toward his. Her hair wisped around her face where it had escaped from its clips. "Play something pretty."

"Für Elise." Natasha recognized it instantly, that soft, romantic, somehow lonely music. It went straight to her heart as she watched his fingers stroke, caress, seduce the keys.

What was he thinking? She could see that his thoughts had turned inward—to the music, to himself. There was an effortlessness in the way his fingers flowed over the keys, and yet she knew that kind of beauty was never achieved without the greatest effort.

The song swelled, note after note, unbearably sad, impossibly beautiful, like the vase of waxy calla lilies that rested on the glossy surface of the piano.

Too much emotion, Natasha thought. Too much pain, though the sun was still shining through the gauzy curtains and the child on his lap continued to smile. The urge to go to him, to put a comforting hand onto his shoulder, to hold them both against her heart, was so strong that she had to curl her fingers into her palms.

Then the music drifted away, the last note lingering like a sigh.

"I like that one," Freddie told him. "Did you make it up?"

"No." He looked at his fingers, spreading them, flexing them, then letting them rest on hers. "Beethoven did." Then he was smiling again, pressing his lips to the soft curve of his daughter's neck. "Had enough for today, funny face?"

"Can I play outside until dinner?"

"Well... What'll you give me?"

It was an old game and a favorite one. Giggling, she swiveled on his lap and gave him a hard, smacking kiss. Still squealing from the bear hug, she spotted Natasha. "Hi!"

"Miss Stanislaski would like to see you, Dr. Kimball." At his nod, Vera walked back to the kitchen.

"Hello." Natasha managed to smile, even when Spence lifted his daughter and turned. She wasn't over the music yet. It was still pouring through her like tears. "I hope I haven't come at a bad time."

"No." After a last squeeze, he set Freddie down, and she immediately bounded to Natasha.

"We're all finished with my lesson. Did you come to play?"

"No, not this time." Unable to resist, Natasha bent to stroke Freddie's cheek. "Actually I came to talk to your father." But she was a coward, Natasha thought in disgust. Rather than look at him, she continued to address Freddie. "How do you like school? You have Mrs. Patterson, don't you?"

"She's nice. She didn't even yell when Mikey Towers's icky bug collection got loose in the classroom. And I can read all of *Go, Dog, Go.*"

Natasha crouched so that they were eye to eye. "Do you like my hat?"

Freddie laughed, recognizing the line from the Dr. Seuss classic. "I like the dog party part the best."

"So do I." Automatically she tied Freddie's loose laces. "Will you come to the store and visit me soon?"

"Okay." Delighted with herself, Freddie raced for the door. "Bye Miss Stanof—Stanif—"

"Tash." She sent Freddie a wink. "All the kids call me Tash."

"Tash." Freddie grinned at the sound of the name, then streaked away.

She listened to Freddie's sneakers squeak down the hall, then took a long breath. "I'm sorry to disturb you at home, but I felt it would be more..." What was the word? Appropriate, comfortable? "It would be better."

"All right." His eyes were very cool, not like those

of the man who had played such sad and passionate music. "Would you like to sit down?"

"No." She said it too quickly, then reminded herself that it was better if they were both stiffly polite. "It won't take long. I only want to apologize."

"Oh? For something specific?"

Fire blazed in her eyes. He enjoyed seeing it, particularly since he'd spent most of the night cursing her. "When I make a mistake, I make a point of admitting it. But since you behaved so—" Oh, why did she always lose her English when she was angry?

"Unconscionably?" he suggested.

Her brow shot up into her fall of hair. "So you admit it."

"I thought you were the one who was here to admit something." Enjoying himself, he sat on the arm of a wing chair in pale blue damask. "Don't let me interrupt."

She was tempted, very tempted, to turn on her heel and stalk out. Pride was equally as strong as temper. She would do what she had come to do, then forget it.

"What I said about you—about you and your daughter was unfair and untrue. Even when I was...mistaken about other things, I knew it was untrue. And I'm very sorry I said it."

"I can see that." Out of the corner of his eye he caught a movement. He turned his head in time to see Freddie make her sprinter's rush for the swings. "We'll forget it."

Natasha followed his gaze and softened. "She really is a beautiful child. I hope you let her come into the shop from time to time."

The tone of her voice had him studying Natasha more carefully. Was it longing, sorrow? "I doubt I could keep her away. You're very fond of children."

Natasha brought her emotions under control with a quick jerk. "Yes, of course. In my business it's a requirement. I won't keep you, Dr. Kimball."

He rose to accept the hand she had formally held out. "Spence," he corrected, gently tightening his fingers on hers. "What else was it you were mistaken about?"

So it wasn't going to be easy. Then again, Natasha thought she deserved a dose of humiliation. "I thought you were married, and was very angry and insulted when you asked me out."

"You're taking my word now that I'm not married."

"No. I looked it up in the library in *Who's Who*."

He stared at her for a moment longer, then threw back his head and laughed. "God, what a trusting soul. Find anything else that interested you?"

"Only things that would fill your ego. You still have my hand."

"I know. Tell me, Natasha, did you dislike me on general principles, or only because you thought I was a married man and had no business flirting with you?"

"Flirting?" She nearly choked on the word. "There was nothing so innocent in the way you looked at me. As if..."

"As if—?" he prompted.

As if we were already lovers, she thought, and felt her skin heat. "I didn't like it," she said shortly.

"Because you thought I was married?"

"Yes. No," she said, correcting herself when she realized where that could lead. "I just didn't like it." He brought her hand to his lips. "Don't," she managed.

"How would you like me to look at you?"

"It isn't necessary for you to look at all."

"But it is." He could feel it again, that high-strung passion, just waiting to burst free from whatever cell she had locked it in. "You'll be sitting right in front of me tomorrow night in class."

"I'm going to transfer."

"No, you won't." He brushed a finger over the small gold hoop in her ear. "You enjoyed it too much. I could see the wheels turning in that fabulous head of yours. And if you did," he continued before she could sputter out a response, "I'd just make a nuisance of myself in your shop."

"Why?"

"Because you're the first woman I've wanted in longer than I can remember."

Excitement rippled up her spine like chain lightning. Before she could prevent it, the memory of that stormy kiss curved back to weaken her. Yes, that had been a man who had wanted. And had, no matter how she had resisted, made her want, too.

But that had only been one kiss, fueled by lust despite the moonlight and soft air. She knew heartbreakingly well where such desires could lead.

"That's nonsense."

"Simple honesty," he murmured, fascinated by the emotions that came and went in her dark eyes. "I thought it best, since we'd gotten off to such a shaky beginning. Since you've determined for yourself that

I'm not married, knowing I'm attracted to you shouldn't insult you.''

"I'm not insulted," she said carefully. "I'm just not interested.''

"Do you always kiss men you're not interested in?''

"I didn't kiss you." She jerked her hand free. "You kissed me.''

"We can fix that." He gathered her close. "This time kiss me back.''

She could have pulled away. His arms weren't banding her as they had before, but were wrapped loosely, coaxingly around her. His lips were soft this time, soft, persuasive, patient. She could feel the warmth seep into her bloodstream like a drug. With a little moan, she slipped her hands up his back and held on.

It was like holding a candle and feeling the wax slowly melt as the fire burned at its center. He could feel her yield degree by degree until her lips parted for his own, accepting, inviting. But even as she gave, he could sense some strong, hard core that resisted, held back. She didn't want to feel whatever he was making her feel.

Impatient, he dragged her closer. Though her body molded itself to his and her head fell back in erotic surrender, there was still a part of her standing just out of his reach. What she gave him only stirred his appetite for more.

She was breathless when he released her. It took an effort, too much of an effort, Natasha thought, to level herself. But once she had, her voice was steady.

"I don't want to be involved.''

"With me, or with anyone?"

"With anyone."

"Good." He brushed a hand over her hair. "It'll be simpler to change your mind."

"I'm very stubborn," she muttered.

"Yes, I've noticed. Why don't you stay for dinner?"

"No."

"All right. I'll take you to dinner Saturday night."

"No."

"Seven-thirty. I'll pick you up."

"No."

"You wouldn't want me to come by the shop Saturday afternoon and embarrass you."

Out of patience, she stalked to the door. "I can't understand how a man that could play music with such sensitivity could be such a clod."

Just lucky, I guess, he thought when the door slammed. Alone again, he caught himself whistling.

Chapter Four

Saturdays in a toy store were noisy, crowded and chaotic. They were supposed to be. To a child even the word Saturday was magic—it meant a magic twenty-four hours when school was too faraway to be a problem. There were bikes to be ridden, games to be played, races to be won. For as long as Natasha had been running The Fun House, she had enjoyed Saturdays as much as her pint-size clientele.

It was one more black mark against Spence that he was the reason she couldn't enjoy this one.

She'd told him no, she reminded herself as she rang up sales on a set of jacks, three plastic dinosaurs and a pint of blowing bubbles. And she'd meant no.

The man didn't seem to understand plain English.

Why else would he have sent her the single red rose? And to the shop, of all places? she thought now, trying to scowl at it. Annie's romantic enthusiasm had been impossible to hold off. Even when Natasha had ignored the flower, Annie had rescued it, running across the street to buy a plastic bud vase so that it could have a place of honor on the checkout counter.

Natasha did her best not to look at it, not to stroke the tightly closed petals, but it wasn't as easy to ignore the fragile scent that wafted toward her every time she rang up a sale.

Why did men think they could soften up a woman with a flower?

Because they could, Natasha admitted, biting off a sigh as she glanced toward it.

That didn't mean she was going out to dinner with him. Tossing back her hair, Natasha counted out the pile of sweaty pennies and nickels the young Hampston boy passed her for his monthly comic-book purchase. Life should be so simple, she thought as the boy rushed out with the latest adventures of Commander Zark. Damn it, it was that simple. On a deep breath she steeled her determination. Her life was exactly that simple, no matter how Spence tried to complicate it. To prove it, she intended to go home, soak in a hot tub, then spend the rest of her evening stretched out on the sofa, watching an old movie and eating popcorn.

He'd been clever. She left the counter to go into the next aisle to referee a huffy disagreement between the Freedmont brothers about how they should spend their pooled resources. She wondered if the esteemed professor looked at their relationship—their nonrelationship, she corrected—as a chess match. She'd always been too reckless too succeed at that particular game, but she had a feeling Spence would play it patiently and well. All the same, if he thought she would be easily checkmated, he had a surprise coming.

Spence had led her second class brilliantly, never looking at her any longer than he had looked at any of his other students, answering her questions in the same tone he used with others. Yes, a very patient player.

Then, just when she'd relaxed, he'd passed her that first red rose as she walked out of class. A very smart move to endanger her queen.

If she'd had any spine at all, Natasha thought now, she would have dropped it onto the floor and ground it under her heel. But she hadn't, and now had to scramble to keep one play ahead of him. Because it had caught her off guard, Natasha told herself. Just like the one that had been delivered to the shop this morning.

If he kept it up, people were going to begin to talk. In a town this size, news items like red roses bounced from shop to pub, from pub to front stoop and from front stoop to backyard gossip sessions. She needed to find a way to stop it. At the moment, she couldn't come up with anything better than ignoring it. Ignoring Spence, she added. How she wished she could.

Bringing herself back to the problem at hand, Natasha hooked an arm around each of the squabbling Freedmont boys in a mock headlock.

"Enough. If you keep calling each other names like nerd and...what was the other?"

"Dork," the taller of the boys told her with relish.

"Yes, dork." She couldn't resist committing it to

memory. "That's a good one. If you keep it up, I'll tell your mother not to let you come in for two weeks."

"Aw, Tash."

"That means everyone else will see all the creepy things I get in for Halloween before either of you." She let that threat hang, giving the two little necks a quick squeeze. "So, I'll make a suggestion. Flip a coin and decide whether to buy the football or the magic set. Whatever you don't get now, you ask for for Christmas. Good idea?"

The boys grimaced at each other from either side of her. "Pretty good."

"No, you have to say it's very good, or I'll knock your heads together."

She left them arguing over which coin to use for the fatal flip.

"You missed your calling," Annie commented when the brothers raced off with the football.

"How's that?"

"You should be working for the UN." She nodded out the front window; the boys were practicing passing on their way down the street. "There aren't many tougher nuts than the Freedmont brothers."

"I make them afraid of me first, then offer them a dignified way out."

"See? Definitely UN material."

With a laugh, Natasha shook her head. "Other people's problems are the easiest to solve." Weakening, she glanced toward the rose again. If she had one wish at the moment, it would be for someone to come along and solve her own.

An hour later she felt a tug on the hem of her skirt.

"Hi."

"Freddie, hello." She flicked her finger over a bow that was trying to hold back Freddie's flyaway hair. It was tied from the blue ribbon Natasha had given her on her first visit. "Don't you look pretty today."

Freddie beamed, female to female. "Do you like my outfit?"

Natasha surveyed the obviously new blue denim overalls, parade stiff with sizing. "I like it very much. I have a pair just like them."

"You do?" Nothing, since Freddie had decided to make Natasha her newest heroine, could have pleased her more. "My daddy got them for me."

"That's nice." Despite her better judgment, Natasha scanned the shop for him. "Did he, ah, bring you in today?"

"No, Vera did. You said it was all right just to look."

"Sure it is. I'm glad you came in." And she was, Natasha realized. Just as she was stupidly disappointed that Freddie hadn't brought her daddy.

"I'm not supposed to touch anything." Freddie tucked her itchy fingers into her pockets. "Vera said I should look with my eyes and not with my hands."

"That's very good advice." And some Natasha wouldn't have minded others passing along to nimble-fingered children. "But some things are okay to touch. You just ask me."

"Okay. I'm going to join the Brownies and get a uniform and everything."

"That's wonderful. You'll come in and show it to me?"

Delight nearly split Freddie's face in two. "Okay.

It has a hat, and I'm going to learn how to make pillows and candle holders and all kinds of things. I'll make you something.''

''I'd like that.'' She tidied Freddie's lopsided bow.

''Daddy said you were going to eat dinner with him in a restaurant tonight.''

''Well, I—''

''I don't like restaurants very much, except for pizza, so I'm going to stay home, and Vera's going to fix tortillas for me and JoBeth. We get to eat in the kitchen.''

''That sounds nice.''

''If you don't like the restaurant, you can come back and have some. Vera always makes a lot.''

Uttering a helpless little sigh, Natasha bent to tie Freddie's left shoelace. ''Thank you.''

''Your hair smells pretty.''

Half in love, Natasha leaned closer to sniff Freddie's. ''So does yours.''

Fascinated by Natasha's tangle of curls, Freddie reached out to touch. ''I wish my hair was like yours,'' she said. ''It's straight as a pin,'' she added, quoting her Aunt Nina.

Smiling, Natasha brushed at the fragile wisps over Freddie's brow. ''When I was a little girl, we put an angel on top of the Christmas tree every year. She was very beautiful, and she had hair just like yours.''

Pleasure came flushing into Freddie's cheeks.

''Ah, there you are.'' Vera shuffled down the crowded aisle, straw carryall on one arm, a canvas bag on the other. ''Come, come, we must get back home before your father thinks we are lost.'' She held out a hand for Freddie and nodded to Natasha. "Good afternoon, miss."

"Good afternoon." Curious, Natasha raised a brow. She was being summed up again by the little dark eyes, and definitely being found wanting, Natasha thought. "I hope you'll bring Freddie back to visit soon."

"We will see. It is as hard for a child to resist a toy store as it is for a man to resist a beautiful woman."

Vera led Freddie down the aisle, not looking back when the girl waved and grinned over her shoulder.

"Well," Annie murmured as she stuck her head around the corner. "What brought that on?"

With a humorless smile, Natasha shoved a pin back into her hair. "At a guess, I would say the woman believes I have designs on her employer."

Annie gave an unladylike snort. "If anything, the employer has designs on you. I should be so lucky." Her sigh was only a little envious. "Now that we know the new hunk on the block isn't married, all's right with the world. Why didn't you tell me you were going out with him?"

"Because I wasn't."

"But I heard Freddie say—"

"He asked me out," Natasha clarified. "I said no."

"I see." After a brief pause, Annie tilted her head. "When did you have the accident?"

"Accident?"

"Yes, the one where you suffered brain damage."

Natasha's face cleared with a laugh, and she started toward the front of the shop.

"I'm serious," Annie said as soon as they had five

free minutes. "Dr. Spencer Kimball is gorgeous, un-attached and..." She leaned over the counter to sniff at the rose. "Charming. Why aren't you taking off early to work on real problems, like what to wear tonight?"

"I know what I'm wearing tonight. My bathrobe."

Annie couldn't resist the grin. "Aren't you rushing things just a tad? I don't think you should wear your robe until at least your third date."

"There's not going to be a first one." Natasha smiled at her next customer and rang up a sale.

It took Annie forty minutes to work back to the subject at hand. "Just what are you afraid of?"

"The IRS."

"Tash, I'm serious."

"So am I." When her pins worked loose again, she gave up and yanked them out. "Every American business person is afraid of the IRS."

"We're talking about Spence Kimball."

"No," Natasha corrected. "You're talking about Spence Kimball."

"I thought we were friends."

Surprised by Annie's tone, Natasha stopped tidying the racetrack display her Saturday visitors had wrecked. "We are. You know we are."

"Friends talk to each other, Tash, confide in each other, ask advice." Puffing out a breath, Annie stuffed her hands into the pockets of her baggy jeans. "Look, I know that things happened to you before you came here, things you're still carrying around but never talk about. I figured I was being a better friend by not asking you about it."

Had she been so obvious? Natasha wondered. All

this time she'd been certain she had buried the past and all that went with it—deeply. Feeling a little helpless, she reached out to touch Annie's hand. "Thank you."

With a dismissive shrug, Annie turned to flick the lock on the front door. The shop was empty now, the bustle of the afternoon only an echo. "Remember when you let me cry on your shoulder after Don Newman dumped me?"

Natasha pressed her lips into a thin line. "He wasn't worth crying over."

"I enjoyed crying over him," Annie returned with a quick, amused smile. "I needed to cry and yell and moan and get a little drunk. You were right there for me, saying all those great, nasty things about him."

"That was the easy part," Natasha remembered. "He was a dork." It pleased her tremendously to use the young Freedmont boy's insult.

"Yeah, but he was a terrific-looking dork." Annie allowed herself a brief reminiscence. "Anyway, you helped me over that rough spot until I convinced myself I was better off without him. You've never needed my shoulder, Tash, because you've never let a guy get past this." She lifted a hand, pressing her palm against empty air.

Amused, Natasha leaned back against the counter. "And what is that?"

"The Great Stanislaski Force Field," Annie told her. "Guaranteed to repel all males from the age of twenty-five to fifty."

Natasha lifted a brow, not quite sure if she was amused any longer. "I'm not certain if you're trying to flatter or insult me."

"Neither. Just listen to me a minute, okay?" Annie took a deep breath to keep herself from rushing through something she thought should be taken step-by-step. "Tash, I've seen you brush off guys with less effort than you'd swat away a gnat. And just as automatically," she added when Natasha remained silent. "You're very pleasant about it, and also very definite. I've never seen you give any man a second's thought once you've politely shown him the door. I've even admired you for it, for being so sure of yourself, so comfortable with yourself that you didn't need a date on Saturday night to keep your ego out of the dirt."

"Not sure of myself," Natasha murmured. "Just apathetic about relationships."

"All right." Annie nodded slowly. "I'll accept that. But this time it's different."

"What is?" Natasha skirted the counter and began to tally the day's sales.

"You see? You know I'm going to mention his name, and you're nervous."

"I'm not nervous," Natasha lied.

"You've been nervous, moody and distracted since Kimball walked into the shop a couple of weeks ago. In over three years, I've never seen you give a man more than five minutes' thought. Until now."

"That's only because this one is more annoying than most." At Annie's shrewd look, Natasha gave up. "All right, there is...something," she admitted. "But I'm not interested."

"You're afraid to be interested."

Natasha didn't like the sound of that, but forced herself to shrug it off. "It's the same thing."

"No, it's not." Annie put a hand over Natasha's and squeezed. "Look, I'm not pushing you toward this guy. For all I know, he could have murdered his wife and buried her in the rose garden. All I'm saying is, you're not going to be comfortable with yourself until you stop being afraid."

Annie was right, Natasha thought later as she sat on her bed with her chin on her hand. She was moody, she was distracted. And she was afraid. Not of Spence, Natasha assured herself. No man would ever frighten her again. But she was afraid of the feelings he stirred up. Forgotten, unwanted feelings.

Did that mean she was no longer in charge of her emotions? No. Did that mean she would act irrationally, impulsively, just because needs and desires had pried their way back into her life? No. Did that mean she would hide in her room, afraid to face a man? A most definite no.

She was only afraid because she had yet to test herself, Natasha thought, moving toward her closet. So tonight she would have dinner with the persistent Dr. Kimball, prove to herself that she was strong and perfectly capable of resisting a fleeting attraction, then get back to normal.

Natasha frowned at her wardrobe. With a restless move of her shoulders she pulled out a deep blue cocktail dress with a jeweled belt. Not that she was dressing for him. He was really irrelevant. It was one of her favorite dresses, Natasha thought as she stripped off her robe, and she rarely had the opportunity to wear anything but work clothes.

He knocked at precisely seven twenty-eight.

Natasha detested herself for anxiously watching the clock. She had reapplied her lipstick twice, checked and rechecked the contents of her purse and fervently wished that she had delayed taking her stand.

She was acting like a teenager, Natasha told herself as she walked to the door. It was only dinner, the first and last dinner she intended to share with him. And he was only a man, she added, pulling the door open.

An outrageously attractive man.

He looked wonderful, was all she could think, with his hair swept back from his face, and that half smile in his eyes. It had never occurred to her that a man could be gut-wrenchingly sexy in a suit and a tie.

"Hi." He held out another red rose.

Natasha nearly sighed. It was a pity the smoke-gray suit didn't make him seem more professorial. Giving in a little, she tapped the blossom against her cheek. "It wasn't the roses that changed my mind."

"About what?"

"About having dinner with you." She stepped back, deciding that she had no choice but to let him in while she put the flower into water.

He smiled then, fully, and exasperated her by looking charming and cocky at the same time. "What did?"

"I'm hungry." She set her short velvet jacket on the arm of the sofa. "I'll put this in water. You can sit if you like."

She wasn't going to give him an inch, Spence thought as he watched her walk away. Oddly enough, that only made her more interesting. He took a deep breath, shaking his head. Incredible. Just when he was convinced that nothing smelled sexier than soap, she put something on that made him think of midnight and weeping violins.

Deciding that he was safer thinking of something else, he studied the room. She preferred vivid colors, he mused, noting the emerald and teal slashes of the pillows on a sapphire-blue couch. There was a huge brass urn beside it, stuffed with silky peacock feathers. Candles of varying sizes and shades were set around the room so that it smelled, romantically, of vanilla and jasmine and gardenia. A shelf in the corner was crammed with books that ran the gamut from popular fiction to classic literature by way of home improvements for the novice.

The table surfaces were crowded with mementos, framed pictures, dried bouquets, fanciful statuettes inspired by fairy tales. There was a gingerbread house no bigger than his palm, a girl dressed as Red Riding Hood, a pig peeking out of the window of a tiny straw house, a beautiful woman holding a single glass slipper.

Practical tips on plumbing, passionate colors and fairy tales, he mused, touching a fingertip to the tiny crystal slipper. It was as curious and as intriguing a combination as the woman herself.

Hearing her come back into the room, Spence turned. "These are beautiful," he said, gesturing to one of the figures. "Freddie's eyes would pop out."

"Thank you. My brother makes them."

"Makes them?" Fascinated, Spence picked up the gingerbread house to study it more closely. It was carved from polished wood, then intricately painted so that each licorice whip and lollipop looked good enough to eat. "It's incredible. You rarely see work-manship like this."

Whatever her reservations, she warmed toward him and crossed the room to join him. "He's been carving and sculpting since he was a child. One day his art will be in galleries and museums."

"It should be already."

The sincerity in his voice hit her most vulnerable spot, her love of family. "It's not so easy. He's young and hardheaded and proud, so he keeps his job, hammering wood, instead of carving it to bring in money for the family. But one day..." She smiled at the collection. "He makes these for me, because I struggled so hard to learn to read English from this book of fairy tales I found in the boxes of things the church gave us when we came to New York. The pictures were so pretty, and I wanted so badly to know the stories that went with them."

She caught herself, embarrassed to have said anything. "We should go."

He only nodded, having already decided to pry gently until she told him more. "You should wear your jacket." He lifted it from the sofa. "It's getting chilly."

The restaurant he'd chosen was only a short drive away and sat on one of the wooded hills that over-looked the Potomac. If Natasha had been given a guess, she would have been on target with his pref-erence for a quiet, elegant backdrop and discreetly speedy service. Over her first glass of wine, she told herself to relax and enjoy.

"Freddie was in the shop today."

"So I heard." Amused, Spence lifted his own glass. "She wants her hair curled."

Natasha's puzzled look became a smile; she lifted a hand to her own. "Oh. That's sweet."

"Easy for you to say. I've just gotten the hang of pigtails."

To her surprise, Natasha could easily picture him patiently braiding the soft, flaxen tresses. "She's beautiful." The image of him holding the girl on his lap at the piano slipped back into her mind. "She has your eyes."

"Don't look now," Spence murmured, "but I believe you've given me a compliment."

Feeling awkward, Natasha lifted the menu. "To soften the blow," she told him. "I'm about to make up for skipping lunch this afternoon."

True to her word, she ordered generously. As long as she was eating, Natasha figured, the interlude would go smoothly. Over appetizers she was careful to steer the conversation toward subjects they had touched on in class. Comfortably they discussed late fifteenth-century music with its four-part harmonies and traveling musicians. Spence appreciated her genuine curiosity and interest, but was equally determined to explore more personal areas.

"Tell me about your family."

Natasha slipped a hot, butter-drenched morsel of lobster into her mouth, enjoying the delicate, almost decadent flavor. "I'm the oldest of four," she began, then became abruptly aware that his fingertips were playing casually with hers on the tablecloth. She slid her hand out of reach.

Her maneuver had him lifting his glass to hide a smile. "Are you all spies?"

A flicker of temper joined the lights that the candle brought to her eyes. "Certainly not."

"I wondered, since you seem so reluctant to talk about them." His face sober, he leaned toward her. "Say 'Get moose and squirrel.'"

Her mouth quivered before she gave up and laughed. "No." She dipped her lobster in melted butter again, coating it slowly, enjoying the scent, then the taste and texture. "I have two brothers and a sister. My parents still live in Brooklyn."

"Why did you move here, to West Virginia?"

"I wanted a change." She lifted a shoulder. "Didn't you?"

"Yes." A faint line appeared between his brows as he studied her. "You said you were about Freddie's age when you came to the States. Do you remember much about your life before that?"

"Of course." For some reason she sensed he was thinking more of his daughter than of her own memories of the Ukraine. "I've always believed impressions made on us in those first few years stay the longest. Good or bad, they help form what we are." Concerned, she leaned closer, smiling. "Tell me, when you think about being five, what do you remember?"

"Sitting at the piano, doing scales." It came so clearly that he nearly laughed. "Smelling hothouse roses and watching the snow outside the window. Being torn between finishing my practice and getting to the park to throw snowballs at my nanny."

"Your nanny," Natasha repeated, but with a

chuckle rather than a sneer he noted. She cupped her chin in her hands, leaning closer, alluring him with the play of light and shadow over her face. "And what did you do?"

"Both."

"A responsible child."

He ran a fingertip down her wrist and surprised a shiver out of her. Before she moved her hand away, he felt her pulse scramble. "What do you remember about being five?"

Because her reaction annoyed her, she was determined to show him nothing. She only shrugged. "My father bringing in wood for the fire, his hair and coat all covered with snow. The baby crying—my youngest brother. The smell of the bread my mother had baked. Pretending to be asleep while I listened to Papa talk to her about escape."

"Were you afraid?"

"Yes." Her eyes blurred with the memory. She didn't often look back, didn't often need to. But when she did, it came not with the watery look of old dreams, but clear as glass. "Oh, yes. Very afraid. More than I will ever be again."

"Will you tell me?"

"Why?"

His eyes were dark, and fixed on her face. "Because I'd like to understand."

She started to pass it off, even had the words in her mind. But the memory remained too vivid. "We waited until spring and took only what we could carry. We told no one, no one at all, and set off in the wagon. Papa said we were going to visit my mother's sister who lived in the west. But I think there were some who knew, who watched us go with tired faces and big eyes. Papa had papers, badly forged, but he had a map and hoped we would avoid the border guards.''

"And you were only five?"

"Nearly six by then.'' Thinking, she ran a fingertip around and around the rim of her glass. "Mikhail was between four and five, Alex just two. At night, if we could risk a fire, we would sit around it and Papa would tell stories. Those were good nights. We would fall asleep listening to his voice and smelling the smoke from the fire. We went over the mountains and into Hungary. It took us ninety-three days.''

He couldn't imagine it, not even when he could see it reflected so clearly in her eyes. Her voice was low, but the emotions were all there, bringing it richness. Thinking of the little girl, he took her hand and waited for her to go on.

"My father had planned for years. Perhaps he had dreamed it all of his life. He had names, people who would help defectors. There was war, the cold one, but I was too young to understand. I understood the fear, in my parents, in the others who helped us. We were smuggled out of Hungary into Austria. The church sponsored us, brought us to America. It was a long time before I stopped waiting for the police to come and take my father away.''

She brought herself back, embarrassed to have spoken of it, surprised to find her hand caught firmly in his.

"That's a lot for a child to deal with."

"I also remember eating my first hot dog.'' She smiled and picked up her wine again. She never spoke of that time, never. Not even with family. Now that she had, with him, she felt a desperate need to change the subject. "And the day my father brought home our first television. No childhood, even one with nannies, is ever completely secure. But we grow up. I'm a businesswoman, and you're a respected composer. Why don't you write?" She felt his fingers tense on hers. "I'm sorry," she said quickly. "I had no business asking that."

"It's all right." His fingers relaxed again. "I don't write because I can't."

She hesitated, then went on impulse. "I know your music. Something that intense doesn't fade."

"It hasn't mattered a great deal in the past couple of years. Just lately it's begun to matter again."

"Don't be patient."

When he smiled, she shook her head, at once impatient and regal. Her hand was gripping his now, hard and strong.

"No, I mean it. People always say when the time is right, when the mood is right, when the place is right. Years are wasted that way. If my father had waited until we were older, until the trip was safer, we might still be in the Ukraine. There are some things that should be grabbed with both hands and taken. Life can be very, very short."

He could feel the urgency in the way her hands gripped his. And he could see the shadow of regret in her eyes. The reason for both intrigued him as much as her words.

"You may be right," he said slowly, then brought the palm of her hand to his lips. "Waiting isn't always the best answer."

"It's getting late." Natasha pulled her hand free, then balled it into a fist on her lap. But that didn't stop the heat from spearing her arm. "We should go."

She was relaxed again when he walked her to her door. During the short drive home he had made her laugh with stories of Freddie's ploys to interest him in a kitten.

"I think cutting pictures of cats from a magazine to make you a poster was very clever." She turned to lean back against her front door. "You are going to let her have one?"

"I'm trying not to be a pushover."

Natasha only smiled. "Big old houses like yours tend to get mice in the winter. In fact, in a house of that size, you'd be wise to take two of JoBeth's kittens."

"If Freddie pulls that one on me, I'll know exactly where she got it." He twirled one of Natasha's curls around his fingers. "And you have a quiz coming up next week."

Natasha lifted both brows. "Blackmail, Dr. Kimball?"

"You bet."

"I intend to ace your quiz, and I have a strong feeling that Freddie could talk you into taking the entire litter all by herself, if she put her mind to it."

"Just the little gray one."

"You've already been to see them."

"A couple of times. You're not going to ask me in?"

"No."

"All right." He slipped his arms around her waist.

"Spence—"

"I'm just taking your advice," he murmured as he skimmed his lips over her jaw. "Not being patient." He brought her closer; his mouth brushed her earlobe. "Taking what I want." His teeth scraped over her bottom lip. "Not wasting time."

Then he was crushing his mouth against hers. He could taste the faintest tang of wine on her lips and knew he could get drunk on that alone. Her flavors were rich, exotic, intoxicating. Like the hint of autumn in the air, she made him think of smoking fires, drifting fog. And her body was already pressed eagerly against his in an instantaneous acknowledgment.

Passion didn't bloom, it didn't whisper. It exploded so that even the air around them seemed to shudder with it.

She made him feel reckless. Unaware of what he murmured to her, he raced his lips over her face, coming back, always coming back to her heated, hungry mouth. In one rough stroke he took his hands over her.

Her head was spinning. If only she could believe it was the wine. But she knew it was he, only he who made her dizzy and dazed and desperate. She wanted to be touched. By him. On a breathless moan, she let her head fall back, and the urgent trail of his lips streaked down her throat.

Feeling this way had to be wrong. Old fears and doubts swirled inside her, leaving empty holes that begged to be filled. And when they were filled, with liquid, shimmering pleasure, the fear only grew.

"Spence." Her fingers dug into his shoulders; she

fought a war between the need to stop him and the impossible desire to go on. "Please."

He was as shaken as she and took a moment, burying his face in her hair. "Something happens to me every time I'm with you. I can't explain it."

She wanted badly to hold him against herself, but forced her arms to drop to her sides. "It can't continue to happen."

He drew away, just far enough to be able to take her face into both hands. The chill of the evening and the heat of passion had brought color to her cheeks. "If I wanted to stop it, which I don't, I couldn't."

She kept her eyes level with his and tried not to be moved by the gentle way he cradled her face. "You want to go to bed with me."

"Yes." He wasn't certain if he wanted to laugh or curse her for being so matter-of-fact. "But it's not quite that simple."

"Sex is never simple."

His eyes narrowed. "I'm not interested in having sex with you."

"You just said—"

"I want to make love with you. There's a difference."

"I don't choose to romanticize it."

The annoyance in his eyes vanished as quickly as it had appeared. "Then I'm sorry I'll have to disappoint you. When we make love, whenever, wherever, it's going to be very romantic." Before she could evade, he closed his mouth over hers. "That's a promise I intend to keep."

Chapter Five

"Natasha! Hey, ah, Natasha!"

Broken out of thoughts that weren't particularly productive, Natasha glanced over and spied Terry. He was wearing a long yellow-and white-striped scarf in defense against a sudden plunge in temperature that had sprinkled frost on the ground. As he raced after her, it flapped awkwardly behind him. By the time he reached her, his glasses had slipped crookedly down to the tip of his reddening nose.

"Hi, Terry."

The hundred-yard dash had winded him. He dearly hoped it wouldn't aggravate his asthma. "Hi. I was—I saw you heading in." He'd been waiting hopefully for her for twenty minutes.

Feeling a bit like a mother with a clumsy child, she straightened his glasses, then wrapped the scarf more securely around his skinny neck. His rapid breathing fogged his lenses. "You should be wearing gloves," she told him, then patting his chilled hand, led him up the steps.

Overwhelmed, he tried to speak and only made a strangled sound in his throat.

"Are you catching a cold?" Searching through her purse, she found a tissue and offered it.

He cleared his throat loudly. "No." But he took the tissue and vowed to keep it until the day he died. "I was just wondering if tonight—after class—you know, if you don't have anything to do... You've probably got plans, but if you don't, then maybe...we could have a cup of coffee. Two cups," he amended desperately. "I mean you could have your own cup, and I'd have one." So saying, he turned a thin shade of green.

The poor boy was lonely, Natasha thought, giving him an absent smile. "Sure." It wouldn't hurt to keep him company for an hour or so, she decided as she walked into class. And it would help her keep her mind off...

Off the man standing in front of the class, Natasha reflected with a scowl; the man who had kissed the breath out of her two weeks before and who was currently laughing with a sassy little blonde who couldn't have been a day over twenty.

Her mood grim, she plopped down at her desk and poked her nose into a textbook.

Spence knew the moment she walked into the room. He was more than a little gratified to have seen the huffy jealousy on her face before she stuck a book in front of it. Apparently fate hadn't been dealing him such a bad hand when it kept him up to his ears in professional and personal problems for the last couple of weeks. Between leaky plumbing, PTA and Brownie meetings and a faculty conference, he hadn't had an hour free. But now things were running smoothly again. He studied the top of Natasha's head. He intended to make up for lost time.

Sitting on the edge of his desk, he opened a discussion of the distinctions between sacred and secular music during the baroque period.

She didn't want to be interested. Natasha was sure he knew it. Why else would he deliberately call on her for an opinion—twice?

Oh, he was clever, she thought. Not by a flicker, not by the slightest intonation did he reveal a more personal relationship with her. No one in class would possibly suspect that this smooth, even brilliant lecturer had kissed her senseless, not once, not twice, but three times. Now he calmly talked of early seventeenth-century operatic developments.

In his black turtleneck and gray tweed jacket he looked casually elegant and totally in charge. And of course, as always, he had the class in the palms of those beautiful hands he eloquently used to make a point. When he smiled over a student's comment, Natasha heard the little blonde two seats behind her sigh. Because she'd nearly done so herself, Natasha stiffened her spine.

He probably had a whole string of eager women. A man who looked like him, talked like him, kissed like him was bound to. He was the type that made promises to one woman at midnight and snuggled up to another over breakfast in bed.

Wasn't it fortunate she no longer believed in promises?

Something was going on inside that fabulous head of hers, Spence mused. One moment she was listening to him as if he had the answers to the mysteries of the universe on the tip of his tongue. The next, she was sitting rigidly and staring off into space, as though she wished herself somewhere else. He would swear that she was angry, and that the anger was directed squarely at him. Why was an entirely different matter.

Whenever he'd tried to have a word with her after class over the last couple of weeks, she'd been out of the building like a bullet. Tonight he would have to outmaneuver her.

She stood the moment class was over. Spence watched her smile at the man sitting across from her. Then she bent down to pick up the books and pencils the man scattered as he rose.

What was his name? Spence wondered. Maynard. That was it. Mr. Maynard was in several of his classes, and managed to fade into the background in each one. Yet at the moment the unobtrusive Mr. Maynard was crouched knee to knee with Natasha.

"I think we've got them all." Natasha gave Terry's glasses a friendly shove back up his nose.

"Thanks."

"Don't forget your scarf—" she began, then looked up. A hand closed over her arm and helped her to her feet. "Thank you, Dr. Kimball."

"I'd like to talk to you, Natasha."

"Would you?" She gave the hand on her arm a brief look, then snatched up her coat and books. Feeling as though she were on a chessboard again, she decided to aggressively counter his move. ''I'm sorry, it'll have to wait. I have a date.''

''A date?'' he managed, getting an immediate picture of someone dark, dashing and muscle-bound.

''Yes. Excuse me.'' She shook off his hand and stuck an arm into the sleeve of her coat. Since the men on either side of her seemed equally paralyzed, she shifted the books to her other arm and struggled to find the second sleeve. ''Are you ready, Terry?''

''Well, yeah, sure. Yeah.'' He was staring at Spence with a mixture of awe and trepidation. ''But I can wait if you want to talk to Dr. Kimball first.''

''There's no need.'' She scooped up his arm and pulled him to the door.

Women, Spence thought as he sat down at a desk. He'd already accepted the fact that he had never understood them. Apparently he never would.

''Jeez, Tash, don't you think you should have seen what Dr. Kimball wanted?''

''I know what he wanted,'' she said between her teeth as she pushed open the main doors. The rush of autumn air cooled her cheeks. ''I wasn't in the mood to discuss it tonight.'' When Terry tripped over the uneven sidewalk, she realized she was still dragging him and slowed her pace. ''Besides, I thought we were going to have some coffee.''

''Right.'' When she smiled at him, he tugged on his scarf as if to keep from strangling.

They walked into a small lounge where half the little square tables were empty. At the antique bar two men were muttering over their beers. A couple in the corner were all but sitting on each other's laps and ignoring their drinks.

She'd always liked this room with its dim lighting and old black-and-white posters of James Dean and Marilyn Monroe. It smelled of cigarettes and jug wine. There was a big portable stereo on a shelf above the bar that played an old Chuck Berry number loudly enough to make up for the lack of patrons. Natasha felt the bass vibrate through her chair as she sat down.

"Just coffee, Joe," she called to the man behind the bar before she leaned her elbows on the table. "So," she said to Terry, "How's everything going?"

"Okay." He couldn't believe it. He was here, sitting with her. On a date. She'd called it a date herself.

It would take a little prodding. Patient, she shrugged out of her coat. The overheated room had her pushing the sleeves of her sweater past her elbows. "It must be different for you here. Did you ever tell me where you were going to college before?"

"I graduated from Michigan State." Because his lenses were fogged again, Natasha seemed to be shrouded by a thin, mysterious mist. "When I, ah, heard that Dr. Kimball would be teaching here, I decided to take a couple years of graduate study."

"You came here because of Spence—Dr. Kimball?"

"I didn't want to miss the opportunity. I went to New York last year to hear him lecture." Terry lifted a hand and nearly knocked over a bowl of sugar. "He's incredible."

"I suppose," she murmured as their coffee was served.

"Where you been hiding?" the bartender asked, giving her shoulder a casual squeeze. "I haven't seen you in here all month."

"Business is good. How's Darla?"

"History." Joe gave her a quick, friendly wink. "I'm all yours, Tash."

"I'll keep it in mind." With a laugh, she turned back to Terry. "Is something wrong?" she asked when she saw him dragging at his collar.

"Yes. No. That is… Is he your boyfriend?"

"My…" To keep herself from laughing in Terry's face, she took a sip of coffee. "You mean Joe? No." She cleared her throat and sipped again. "No, he's not. We're just…" She searched for a word. "Pals."

"Oh." Relief and insecurity warred. "I just thought, since he… Well."

"He was only joking." Wanting to put Terry at ease again, she squeezed his hand. "What about you? Do you have a girl back in Michigan?"

"No. There's nobody. Nobody at all." He turned his hand over, gripping hers.

Oh, my God. As realization hit, Natasha felt her mouth drop open. Only a fool would have missed it, she thought as she stared into Terry's adoring, myopic eyes. A fool, she added, who was so tied up with her own problems that she missed what was happening under her nose. She was going to have to be careful, Natasha decided. Very careful.

"Terry," she began. "You're very sweet—"

That was all it took to make his hand shake. Coffee spilled down his shirt. Moving quickly, Natasha shifted chairs so that she was beside him. Snatching paper napkins from the dispenser, she began to blot the stain.

"It's a good thing they never serve it hot in this place. If you soak this in cold water right away, you should be all right."

Overcome, Terry grabbed both of her hands. Her head was bent close, and the scent of her hair was making him dizzy. "I love you," he blurted, and took aim with his mouth; his glasses slid down his nose.

Natasha felt his lips hit her cheekbone, cold and trembly. Because her heart went out to him, she decided that being careful wasn't the right approach. Firmness was called for, quickly.

"No, you don't." Her voice was brisk, she pulled back far enough to dab at the spill on the table.

"I don't?" Her response threw him off. It was nothing like any of the fantasies he'd woven. There was the one where he'd saved her from a runaway truck. And another where he'd played the song he was writing for her and she had collapsed in a passionate, weeping puddle into his arms. His imagination hadn't stretched far enough to see her wiping up coffee and calmly telling him he wasn't in love at all.

"Yes, I do." He snatched at her hand again.

"That's ridiculous," she said, and smiled to take the sting out of the words. "You like me, and I like you, too."

"No, it's more than that. I—"

"All right. Why do you love me?"

"Because you're beautiful," he managed, losing his grip as he stared into her face again. "You're the most beautiful woman I've ever seen."

"And that's enough?" Disengaging her hand from

his, she linked her fingers to rest her chin on them. "What if I told you I was a thief—or that I liked to run down small, furry animals with my car? Maybe I've been married three times and have murdered all my husbands in their sleep."

"Tash—"

She laughed, but resisted the temptation to pet his cheek. "I mean, you don't know me enough to love me. If you did, what I looked like wouldn't matter."

"But—but I think about you all the time."

"Because you've told yourself it would be nice to be in love with me." He looked so forelorn that she took a chance and laid one hand upon his. "I'm very flattered."

"Does this mean you won't go out with me?"

"I'm out with you now." She pushed her cup of coffee in front of him. "As friends," she said before the light could dawn again in his eyes. "I'm too old to be anything but your friend."

"No, you're not."

"Oh, yes." Suddenly she felt a hundred. "Yes, I am."

"You think I'm stupid," he muttered. In place of confused excitement came a crushing wave of humiliation. He could feel his cheeks sting with it.

"No, I don't." Her voice softened, and she reached once more for his hands. "Terry, listen—"

Before she could stop him, he pushed back his chair. "I've got to go."

Cursing herself, Natasha picked up his striped scarf. There was no use in following him now. He needed time, she decided. And she needed air.

The leaves were beginning to turn, and a few that

had fallen early scraped along the sidewalk ahead of the wind. It was the kind of evening Natasha liked best, but now she barely noticed it. She'd left her coffee untouched to take a long, circular walk through town.

Heading home, she thought of a dozen ways she could have handled Terry's infatuation better. Through her clumsiness she had wounded a sensitive, vulnerable boy. It could have been avoided, all of it, if she had been paying attention to what was happening in front of her face.

Instead she'd been blinded by her own unwelcome feelings for someone else.

She knew too well what it was to believe yourself in love, desperately, hopelessly in love. And she knew how it hurt to discover that the one you loved didn't return those feelings. Cruel or kind, the rejection of love left the heart bruised.

Uttering a sigh, she ran a hand over the scarf in her pocket. Had she ever been so trusting and defenseless? Yes, she answered herself. That and much, much more.

It was about damn time, Spence thought as he watched her start up the walk. Obviously her mind was a million miles away. On her date, he decided and tried not to grind his teeth. Well, he was going to see to it that she had a lot more to think about in very short order.

"Didn't he walk you home?"

Natasha stopped dead with an involuntary gasp. In the beam of her porch light she saw Spence sitting on her stoop. That was all she needed, she thought

while she dragged a hand through her hair. With
Terry she'd felt as though she'd kicked a puppy. Now
she was going to have to face down a large, hungry
wolf.

"What are you doing here?"

"Freezing."

She nearly laughed. His breath was puffing out in
white steam. With the wind chill, she imagined that
the effective temperature was hovering around
twenty-five degrees Fahrenheit. After a moment, Natasha decided she must be a very poor sport to be
amused at the thought of Spence sitting on cold concrete for the past hour.

He rose as she continued down the walk. How
could she have forgotten how tall he was? "Didn't
you invite your friend back for a drink?"

"No." She reached out and twisted the knob. Like
most of the doors in town, it was unlocked. "If I had,
you'd be very embarrassed."

"That's not the word for it."

"I'm suppose I'm lucky I didn't find you waiting
up for me inside."

"You would have," he muttered, "if it had occurred to me to try the door."

"Good night."

"Wait a damn minute." He slapped his palm on
the door before she could close it in his face. "I didn't
sit out here in the cold for my health. I want to talk
to you."

There was something satisfying in the brief, fruitless push-push they played with the door. "It's late."

"And getting later by the second. If you close the

door, I'm just going to beat on it until all your neighbors poke their heads out their windows."

"Five minutes," she said graciously, because she had planned to grant him that in any case. "I'll give you a brandy, then you'll go."

"You're all heart, Natasha."

"No." She laid her coat over the back of the couch. "I'm not."

She disappeared into the kitchen without another word. When she returned with two snifters of brandy, he was standing in the center of the room, running Terry's scarf through his fingers.

"What kind of game are you playing?"

She set down his brandy, then sipped calmly at her own. "I don't know what you mean."

"What are you doing, going out on dates with some college kid who's still wet behind the ears?"

Both her back and her voice stiffened. "It's none of your business whom I go out with."

"It is now," Spence replied, realizing it now mattered to him.

"No, it's not. And Terry's a very nice young man."

"Young's the operative word." Spence tossed the scarf aside. "He's certainly too young for you."

"Is that so?" It was one thing for her to say it, and quite another to have Spence throw it at her like an accusation. "I believe that's for me to decide."

"Hit a nerve that time," Spence muttered to himself. There had been a time—hadn't there?—when he had been considered fairly smooth with women. "Maybe I should have said you're too old for him."

"Oh, yes." Despite herself, she began to see the

humor of it. "That's a great deal better. Would you like to drink this brandy or wear it?"

"I'll drink it, thanks." He lifted the glass, but instead of bringing it to his lips, took another turn around the room. He was jealous, Spence realized. It was rather pathetic, but he was jealous of an awkward, tongue-tied grad student. And while he was about it, he was making a very big fool of himself. "Listen, maybe I should start over."

"I don't know why you would want to start something over you should never have begun."

But like a dog with a bone, he couldn't stop gnawing. "It's just that he's obviously not your type."

Fire blazed again. "Oh, and you'd know about my type?"

Spence held up his free hand. "All right, one straight question before my foot is permanently lodged in my mouth. Are you interested in him?"

"Of course I am." Then she cursed herself; it was impossible to use Terry and his feelings as a barricade against Spence. "He's a very nice boy."

Spence almost relaxed, then spotted the scarf again, still spread over the back of her couch. "What are you doing with that?"

"I picked it up for him." The sight of it, bright and a little foolish on the jewel colors of her couch, made her feel like the most vicious kind of femme fatale. "He left it behind after I broke his heart. He thinks he's in love with me." Miserable, she dropped into a chair. "Oh, go away. I don't know why I'm talking to you."

The look on her face made him want to smile and stroke her hair. He thought better of it and kept his tone brisk. "Because you're upset, and I'm the only one here."

"I guess that'll do." She didn't object when Spence sat down across from her. "He was very sweet and nervous, and I had no idea what he was feeling— or what he thought he was feeling. I should have realized, but I didn't until he spilled his coffee all over his shirt, and... Don't laugh at him."

Spence continued to smile as he shook his head. "I'm not. Believe me, I know exactly how he must have felt. There are some women who make you clumsy."

Their eyes met and held. "Don't flirt with me."

"I'm past flirting with you, Natasha."

Restless, she rose to pace the room. "You're changing the subject."

"Am I?"

She waved an impatient hand as she paced. "I hurt his feelings. If I had known what was happening, I might have stopped it. There is nothing," she said passionately, "nothing worse than loving someone and being turned away."

"No." He understood that. And he could see by the shadows haunting her eyes that she did, too. "But you don't really believe he's in love with you."

"He believes it. I ask him why he thinks it, and do you know what he says?" She whirled back, her hair swirling around her shoulders with the movement. "He says because he thinks I'm beautiful. That's it." She threw up her hands and started to pace again. Spence only watched, caught up in her movements and by the musical cadence that agitation brought to her voice. "When he says it, I want to slap him and say—what's wrong with you? A face is nothing but a face. You don't know my mind or my heart. But he has big, sad eyes, so I can't yell at him.''

"You never had a problem yelling at me.''

"You don't have big, sad eyes, and you're not a boy who thinks he's in love.''

"I'm not a boy,'' he agreed, catching her by the shoulders from behind. Even as she stiffened, he turned her around. "And I like more than your face, Natasha. Though I like that very much.''

"You don't know anything about me, either.''

"Yes, I do. I know you lived through experiences I can hardly imagine. I know you love and miss your family, that you understand children and have a natural affection for them. You're organized, stubborn and passionate.'' He ran his hands down her arms, then back to her shoulders. "I know you've been in love before.'' He tightened his grip before she could pull away. "And you're not ready to talk about it. You have a sharp, curious mind and caring heart, and you wish you weren't attracted to me. But you are.''

She lowered her lashes briefly to veil her eyes. "Then it would seem you know more of me than I of you.''

"That's easy to fix.''

"I don't know if I want to. Or why I should.''

His lips brushed hers, then retreated before she could respond or reject. "There's something there,'' he murmured. "That's reason enough.''

"Maybe there is,'' she began. "No.'' She drew back when he would have kissed her again. "Don't. I'm not very strong tonight.''

"A good way to make me feel guilty if I press my advantage."

She felt twin rushes of disappointment and relief when he released her. "I'll make you dinner," she said on impulse.

"Now?"

"Tomorrow. Just dinner," she added, wondering if she should already be regretting the invitation. "If you bring Freddie."

"She'd like that. So would I."

"Good. Seven o'clock." Natasha picked up his coat and held it out. "Now you have to go."

"You should learn to say what's on your mind." With a half laugh, Spence took the coat from her. "One more thing."

"Only one?"

"Yeah." He swung her back into his arms for one long, hard, mind-numbing kiss. He had the satisfaction of seeing her sink weakly onto the arm of the sofa when he released her.

"Good night," he said, then stepping outside, gulped in a deep breath of cold air.

It was the first time Freddie had been asked out to a grown-up dinner, and she waited impatiently while her father shaved. Usually she enjoyed watching him slide the razor through the white foam on his face. There were even times when she secretly wished she were a boy, so that she could look forward to the ritual. But tonight she thought her father was awfully slow.

"Can we go now?"

Standing in his bathrobe, Spence rinsed off the

traces of lather. "It might be a better idea if I put some pants on."

Freddie only rolled her eyes. "When are you going to?"

Spence scooped her up to bite gently at her neck. "As soon as you beat it."

Taking him at his word, she raced downstairs to prowl the foyer and count to sixty. Around the fifth round, she sat on the bottom step to play with the buckle of her left shoe.

Freddie had it all figured out. Her father was going to marry either Tash or Mrs. Patterson, because they were both pretty and had nice smiles. Afterward, the one he married would come and live in their new house. Soon she would have a new baby sister. A baby brother would do in a pinch, but it was definitely a second choice. Everybody would be happy, because everybody would like each other a lot. And her daddy would play his music late at night again.

When she heard Spence start down, Freddie jumped up and whirled around to face him. "Daddy, I counted to sixty a jillion times."

"I bet you left out the thirties again." He took her coat from the hall closet and helped bundle her into it.

"No, I didn't." At least she didn't think she had. "You took forever." With a sigh, she pulled him to the door.

"We're still going to be early."

"She won't mind."

At that moment, Natasha was pulling a sweater over her head and wondering why she had invited anyone to dinner, particularly a man every instinct told her to avoid. She'd been distracted all day, worrying if the food would be right, if she'd chosen the most complimentary wine. And now she was changing for the third time.

Totally out of character, she told herself as she frowned at her reflection in the mirror. The casual blue sweater and leggings calmed her. If she looked at ease, Natasha decided she would be at ease. She fastened long silver columns at her ears, gave her hair a quick toss, then hurried back to the kitchen. She had hardly checked her sauce when she heard the knock.

They were early, she thought, allowing herself one mild oath before going to the door.

They looked wonderful. Agitation vanished in a smile. The sight of the little girl with her hand caught firmly in her father's went straight to her heart. Because it came naturally, she bent to kiss Freddie on both cheeks. "Hello."

"Thank you for asking me to dinner." Freddie recited the sentence, then looked at her father for approval.

"You're welcome."

"Aren't you going to kiss Daddy, too?"

Natasha hesitated, then caught Spence's quick, challenging grin. "Of course." She brushed her lips formally against his cheeks. "That is a traditional Ukrainian greeting."

"I'm very grateful for *glasnost*." Still smiling, he took her hand and brought it to his lips.

"Are we going to have borscht?" Freddie wanted to know.

"Borscht?" Natasha lifted a brow as she helped Freddie out of her coat.

"When I told Mrs. Patterson that me and Daddy were going to have dinner at your house, she said that borscht was Russian for beet soup." Freddie managed not to say she thought it sounded gross, but Natasha got the idea.

"I'm sorry I didn't make any," she said, straight faced. "I made another traditional dish instead. Spaghetti and meatballs."

It was easy, surprisingly so. They ate at the old gateleg table by the window, and their talk ranged from Freddie's struggles with arithmetic to Neapolitan opera. It took only a little prodding for Natasha to talk of her family. Freddie wanted to know everything there was about being a big sister.

"We didn't fight very much," Natasha reflected as she drank after-dinner coffee and balanced Freddie on her knee. "But when we did, I won, because I was the oldest. And the meanest."

"You're not mean."

"Sometimes when I'm angry I am." She looked at Spence, remembering—and regretting—telling him he didn't deserve Freddie. "Then I'm sorry."

"When people fight, it doesn't always mean they don't like each other," Spence murmured. He was doing his best not to think how perfect, how perfectly right his daughter looked cuddled on Natasha's lap. Too far, too fast, he warned himself. For everyone involved.

Freddie wasn't sure she understood, but she was only five. Then she remembered happily that she would soon be six. "I'm going to have a birthday."

"Are you?" Natasha looked appropriately impressed. "When?"

"In two weeks. Will you come to my party?"

"I'd love to." Natasha looked at Spence as Freddie recited all the wonderful treats that were in store.

It wasn't wise to get so involved with the little girl, she warned herself. Not when the little girl was attached so securely to a man who made Natasha long for things she had put behind her. Spence smiled at her. No, it wasn't wise, she thought again. But it was irresistible.

Chapter Six

"Chicken pox." Spence said the two words again. He stood in the doorway and watched his little girl sleep. "It's a hell of a birthday present, sweetie."

In two days his daughter would be six, and by then, according to the doctor, she'd be covered with the itchy rash that was now confined to her belly and chest.

It was going around, the pediatrician had said. It would run its course. Easy for him to say, Spence thought. It wasn't his daughter whose eyes were teary. It wasn't his baby with a hundred-and-one-degree temperature.

She'd never been sick before, Spence realized as he rubbed his tired eyes. Oh, the sniffles now and again, but nothing a little TLC and baby aspirin hadn't put right. He dragged a hand through his hair;

Freddie moaned in her sleep and tried to find a cool spot on her pillow.

The call from Nina hadn't helped. He'd had to come down hard to prevent her from catching the shuttle and arriving on his doorstep. That hadn't stopped her telling him that Freddie had undoubtedly caught chicken pox because she was attending public school. That was nonsense, of course, but when he looked at his little girl, tossing in her bed, her face flushed with fever, the guilt was almost unbearable.

Logic told him that chicken pox was a normal part of childhood. His heart told him that he should be able to find a way to make it go away.

For the first time he realized how much he wanted someone beside him. Not to take things over, not to smooth over the downside of parenting. Just to be there. To understand what it felt like when your child was sick or hurt or unhappy. Someone to talk to in the middle of the night, when worries or pleasures kept you awake.

When he thought of that someone, he thought only of Natasha.

A big leap, he reminded himself and walked back to the bedside. One he wasn't sure he could make again and land on both feet.

He cooled Freddie's forehead with the damp cloth Vera had brought in. Her eyes opened.

"Daddy."

"Yes, funny face. I'm right here."

Her lower lip trembled. "I'm thirsty."

"I'll go get you a cold drink."

Sick or not, she knew how to maneuver. "Can I have Kool Aid?"

He pressed a kiss on her cheek. "Sure. What kind?"

"The blue kind."

"The blue kind." He kissed her again. "I'll be right back." He was halfway down the stairs when the phone rang simultaneously with a knock on the door. "Damn it. Vera, get the phone, will you?" Out of patience, he yanked open the front door.

The smile Natasha had practiced all evening faded. "I'm sorry. I've come at a bad time."

"Yeah." But he reached out to pull her inside. "Hang on a minute. Vera—oh good," he added when he saw the housekeeper hovering. "Freddie wants some Kool Aid, the blue kind."

"I will make it." Vera folded her hands in front of her apron. "Mrs. Barklay is on the phone."

"Tell her—" Spence broke off, swearing as Vera's mouth pruned. She didn't like to tell Nina anything. "All right, I'll get it."

"I should go," Natasha put in, feeling foolish. "I only came by because you weren't at class tonight, and I wondered if you were well."

"It's Freddie." Spence glanced at the phone and wondered if he could strangle his sister over it. "She has the chicken pox."

"Oh. Poor thing." She had to smother the automatic urge to go up and look in on the child herself. Not your child, Natasha reminded herself. Not your place. "I'll get out of your way."

"I'm sorry. Things are a little confused."

"Don't be. I hope she's well soon. Let me know if I can do anything."

At that moment Freddie called for her father in a voice that was half sniffle and half croak.

It was Spence's quick helpless glance up the stairs that had Natasha ignoring what she thought was her better judgment. "Would you like me to go up for a minute? I could sit with her until you have things under control again."

"No. Yes." Spence blew out a long breath. If he didn't deal with Nina now, she'd only call back. "I'd appreciate it." Reaching the end of his rope, he yanked up the phone receiver. "Nina."

Natasha followed the glow of the night-light into Freddie's room. She found her sitting up in bed, surrounded by dolls. Two big tears were sliding down her cheeks. "I want my daddy," she said obviously miserable.

"He'll be right here." Her heart lost, Natasha sat down on the bed and drew Freddie into her arms.

"I don't feel good."

"I know. Here, blow your nose."

Freddie complied, then settled her head on Natasha's breast. She sighed, finding it pleasantly different from her father's hard chest or Vera's cushy one. "I went to the doctor and got medicine, so I can't go to my Brownie meeting tomorrow."

"There'll be other meetings, as soon as the medicine makes you well."

"I have chicken pox," Freddie announced, torn between discomfort and pride. "And I'm hot and itchy."

"It's a silly thing, the chicken pox," Natasha said soothingly. She tucked Freddie's tousled hair behind one ear. "I don't think chickens get it at all."

Freddie's lips turned up, just a little. "JoBeth had it last week, and so did Mikey. Now I can't have a birthday party."

"You'll have a party later, when everyone's well again."

"That's what Daddy said." A fresh tear trailed down her cheek. "It's not the same."

"No, but sometimes not the same is even better."

Curious, Freddie watched the light glint off the gold hoop in Natasha's ear. "How?"

"It gives you more time to think about how much fun you'll have. Would you like to rock?"

"I'm too big to rock."

"I'm not." Wrapping Freddie in a blanket, Natasha carried her to the white wicker rocker. She cleared it of stuffed animals, then tucked one particularly worn rabbit in Freddie's arms. "When I was a little girl and I was sick, my mother would always rock me in this big, squeaky chair we had by the window. She would sing me songs. No matter how bad I felt, when she rocked me I felt better."

"My mother didn't rock me." Freddie's head was aching, and she wanted badly to pop a comforting thumb into her mouth. She knew she was too old for that. "She didn't like me."

"That's not true." Natasha instinctively tightened her arms around the child. "I'm sure she loved you very much."

"She wanted my daddy to send me away."

At a loss, Natasha lowered her cheek to the top of Freddie's head. What could she say now? Freddie's words had been too matter-of-fact to dismiss as a fantasy. "People sometimes say things they don't mean, and that they regret very much. Did your daddy send you away?"

"No."

"There, you see?"

"Do you like me?"

"Of course I do." She rocked gently, to and fro. "I like you very much."

The movement, the soft female scent and voice lulled Freddie. "Why don't you have a little girl?"

The pain was there, deep and dull. Natasha closed her eyes against it. "Perhaps one day I will."

Freddie tangled her fingers in Natasha's hair, comforted. "Will you sing, like your mother did?"

"Yes. And you try to sleep."

"Don't go."

"No, I'll stay awhile."

Spence watched them from the doorway. In the shadowed light they looked achingly beautiful, the tiny, flaxen-haired child in the arms of the dark, golden-skinned woman. The rocker whispered as it moved back and forth while Natasha sang some old Ukrainian folk song from her own childhood.

It move him as completely, as uniquely as holding the woman in his own arms had moved him. And yet so differently, so quietly that he wanted to stand just as he was, watching through the night.

Natasha looked up and saw him. He looked so frazzled that she had to smile.

"She's sleeping now."

If his legs were weak, he hoped it was because he'd climbed up and down the stairs countless times in the last twenty-four hours. Giving in to them, he sat down on the edge of the bed.

He studied his daughter's flushed face, nestled peacefully in the crook of Natasha's arm. "It's supposed to get worse before it gets better."

"Yes, it does." She stroked a hand down Freddie's hair. "We all had it when we were children. Amazingly, we all survived."

He blew out a long breath. "I guess I'm being an idiot."

"No, you're very sweet." She watched him as she continued to rock, wondering how difficult it had been for him to raise a baby without a mother's love. Difficult enough, she decided, that he deserved credit for seeing that his daughter was happy, secure and un- afraid to love. She smiled again.

"Whenever one of us was sick as children, and still today, my father would badger the doctor, then he would go to church to light candles. After that he would say this old gypsy chant he'd learned from his grandmother. It's covering all the bases."

"So far I've badgered the doctor." Spence managed a smile of his own. "You wouldn't happen to remember that chant?"

"I'll say it for you." Carefully she rose, lifting Freddie in her arms. "Should I lay her down?"

"Thanks." Together they tucked in the blankets. "I mean it."

"You're welcome." She looked over the sleeping child, and though her smile was easy, she was beginning to feel awkward. "I should go. Parents of sick children need their rest."

"At least I can offer you a drink." He held up the glass. "How about some Kool Aid? It's the blue kind."

"I think I'll pass." She moved around the bed toward the door. "When the fever breaks, she'll be bored. Then you'll really have your work cut out for you."

"How about some pointers?" He took Natasha's hand as they started down the steps.

"Crayons. New ones. The best is usually the simplest."

"How is it someone like you doesn't have a horde of children of her own?" He didn't have to feel her stiffen to know he'd said the wrong thing. He could see the sorrow come and go in her eyes. "I'm sorry."

"No need." Recovered, she picked up her coat from where she'd laid it on the newel post. "I'd like to come and see Freddie again, if it's all right."

He took her coat and set it down again. "If you won't take the blue stuff, how about some tea? I could use the company."

"All right."

"I'll just—" He turned and nearly collided with Vera.

"I will fix the tea," she said after a last look at Natasha.

"Your housekeeper thinks I have designs on you."

"I hope you won't disappoint her," Spence said as he led Natasha into the music room.

"I'm afraid I must disappoint both of you." Then she laughed and wandered to the piano. "But you should be very busy. All the young women in college talk about Dr. Kimball." She tucked her tongue into her cheek. "You're a hunk, Spence. Popular opinion is equally divided between you and the captain of the football team."

"Very funny."

"I'm not joking. But it's fun to embarrass you."
She sat and ran her fingers over the keys. "Do you
compose here?"

"I did once."

"It's wrong of you not to write." She played a
series of chords. "Art's more than a privilege. It's a
responsibility." She searched for the melody, then
with a sound of impatience shook her head. "I can't
play. I was too old when I tried to learn."

He liked the way she looked sitting there, her hair
falling over her shoulders, half curtaining her face,
her fingers resting lightly on the keys of the piano he
had played since childhood.

"If you want to learn, I'll teach you."

"I'd rather you write a song." It was more than
impulse, she thought. Tonight he looked as though he
needed a friend. She smiled and held out a hand.
"Here, with me."

He glanced up as Vera carried in a tray. "Just set
it there, Vera. Thank you."

"You will want something else?"

He looked back at Natasha. Yes, he would want
something else. He wanted it very much. "No. Good
night." He listened to the housekeeper's shuffling
steps. "Why are you doing this?"

"Because you need to laugh. Come, write a song
for me. It doesn't have to be good."

He did laugh. "You want me to write a bad song
for you?"

"It can be a terrible song. When you play it for
Freddie, she'll hold her ears and giggle."

"A bad song's about all I can do these days." But

he was amused enough to sit down beside her. "If I do this, I have to have your solemn oath that it won't be repeated for any of my students."

"Cross my heart."

He began to noodle with the keys, Natasha breaking in now and then to add her inspiration. It wasn't as bad as it might have been, Spence considered as he ran through some chords. No one would call it brilliant, but it had a certain primitive charm.

"Let me try." Tossing back her hair, Natasha struggled to repeat the notes.

"Here." As he sometimes did with his daughter, he put his hands over Natasha's to guide them. The feeling, he realized, was entirely different. "Relax." His murmur whispered beside her ear.

She only wished she could. "I hate to do poorly at anything," she managed. With his palms firmly over her hands, she struggled to concentrate on the music.

"You're doing fine." Her hair, soft and fragrant, brushed his cheek.

As they bent over the keys, it didn't occur to him that he hadn't played with the piano in years. Oh, he had played—Beethoven, Gershwin, Mozart and Bernstein, but hardly for fun.... It had been much too long since he had sat before the keys for entertainment.

"No, no an A minor maybe."

Natasha stubbornly hit a B major again. "I like this better."

"It throws it off."

"That's the point."

He grinned at her. "Want to collaborate?"

"You do better without me."

"I don't think so." His grin faded; he cupped her face in one hand. "I really don't think so."

This wasn't what she had intended. She had wanted to lighten his mood, to be his friend. She hadn't wanted to stir these feelings in both of them, feelings they would be wiser to ignore. But they were there, pulsing. No matter how strong her will, she couldn't deny them. Even the light touch of his fingers on her face made her ache, made her yearn, made her remember.

"The tea's getting cold." But she didn't pull away, didn't try to stand. When he leaned over to touch his mouth to hers, she only shut her eyes. "This can't go anywhere," she murmured.

"It already has." His hand moved up her back, strong, possessive, in contrast with the light play of his lips. "I think about you all the time, about being with you, touching you. I've never wanted anyone the way I want you." Slowly he ran a hand down her throat, over her shoulder, along her arm until their fingers linked over the piano keys. "It's like a thirst, Natasha, a constant thirst. And when I'm with you like this, I know it's the same for you."

She wanted to deny it, but his mouth was roaming hungrily over her face, taunting hers to tremble with need. And she did need, to be held like this, wanted like this. It had been easy in the past to pretend that being desired wasn't necessary. No, she hadn't had to pretend. Until now, until him, it had been true.

Now, suddenly, like a door opening, like a light being switched on, everything had changed. She yearned for him, and her blood swam faster, just knowing he wanted her. Even for a moment, she told herself as her hands clutched at his hair to pull his mouth to hers. Even for this moment.

It was there again, that whirlwind of sensation that erupted the instant they came together. Too fast, too hot, too real to be borne. Too stunning to be resisted.

It was as though he were the first, though he was not. It was as though he were the only one, though that could never be. As she poured herself into the kiss, she wished desperately that her life could begin again in that moment, with him.

There was more than passion here. The emotions that swirled inside her nearly swallowed him. There was desperation, fear and a bottomless generosity that left him dazed. Nothing would ever be simple again. Knowing it, a part of him tried to pull back, to think, to reason. But the taste of her, hot, potent, only drew him closer to the flame.

"Wait." For the first time she admitted her own weakness and let her head rest against his shoulder. "This is too fast."

"No." He combed his fingers through her hair. "It's taken years already."

"Spence." Struggling for balance, she straightened. "I don't know what to do," she said slowly, watching him. "It's important for me to know what to do."

"I think we can figure it out." But when he reached for her again, she rose quickly and stepped away.

"This isn't simple for me." Unnerved, she pushed back her hair with both hands. "I know it might seem so, because of the way I respond to you. I know that it's easier for men, less personal somehow."

He rose very carefully, very deliberately. "Why don't you explain that?"

"I only mean that I know that men find things like this less difficult to justify."

"Justify," he repeated, rocking back on his heels. How could he be angry so quickly, after being so bewitched? "You make this sound like some kind of crime."

"I don't always find the right words," she snapped. "I'm not a college professor. I didn't speak English until I was eight, couldn't read it for longer than that."

He checked his temper as he studied her. Her eyes were dark with something more than anger. She was standing stiffly, head up, but he couldn't tell if her stand was one of pride or self-defense. "What does that have to do with anything?"

"Nothing. And everything." Frustrated, she whirled back into the hallway to snatch up her coat. "I hate feeling stupid—hate being stupid. I don't belong here. I shouldn't have come."

"But you did." He grabbed her by her shoulders, so that her coat flew out to fall onto the bottom step. "Why did you?"

"I don't know. It doesn't matter why."

He gave her an impatient squeeze. "Why do I feel as if I'm having two conversations at the same time? What's going on in that head of yours, Natasha?"

"I want you," she said passionately. "And I don't want to."

"You want me." Before she could jerk away, he pulled her against himself. There was no patience in this kiss, no persuasion. It took and took, until she was certain she could have nothing left to give. "Why does that bother you?" he murmured against her lips.

Unable to resist, she ran her hands over his face, memorizing the shape. "There are reasons."

"Tell me about them."

She shook her head, and this time when she pulled back, he released her. "I don't want my life to change. If something happened between us, yours would not, but mine might. I want to be sure it doesn't."

"Does this lead back to that business about men and women thinking differently?"

"Yes."

That made him wonder who had broken her heart, and he didn't smile. "You look more intelligent than that. What I feel for you has already changed my life."

That frightened her, because it made her want to believe it. "Feelings come and go."

"Yes, they do. Some of them. What if I told you I was falling in love with you?"

"I wouldn't believe you." Her voice shook, and she bent to pick up her coat. "And I would be angry with you for saying it."

Maybe it was best to wait until he could make her believe. "And if I told you that until I met you, I didn't know I was lonely?"

She lowered her eyes, much more moved by this than she would have been by any words of love. "I would have to think."

He touched her again, just a hand to her hair. "Do you think everything through?"

Her eyes were eloquent when she looked at him. "Yes."

"Then think about this. It wasn't my intention to seduce you—not that I haven't given that a great deal of thought on my own, but I didn't see it happening with my daughter sick upstairs."

"You didn't seduce me."

"Now she's taking potshots at my ego."

That made her smile. "There was no seduction. That implies planned persuasion. I don't want to be seduced."

"I'll keep that in mind. All the same, I don't think I want to dissect all this like a Music major with a Beethoven concerto. It ruins the romance in much the same way."

She smiled again. "I don't want romance."

"That's a pity." And a lie, he thought, remembering the way she'd looked when he'd given her a rose. "Since chicken pox is going to be keeping me busy for the next week or two, you'll have some time. Will you come back?"

"To see Freddie." She shrugged into her coat, then relented. "And to see you."

She did. What began as just a quick call to bring Freddie a get-well present turned into the better part of an evening, soothing a miserable, rash-ridden child and an exhausted, frantic father. Surprisingly she enjoyed it, and made a habit over the next ten days of dropping in over her lunch break to spell a still-suspicious Vera, or after work to give Spence a much-needed hour of peace and quiet.

As far as romance went, bathing an itchy girl in

corn starch left a lot to be desired. Despite it, Natasha found herself only more attracted to Spence and more in love with his daughter.

She watched him do his best to cheer the miserably uncomfortable patient on her birthday, then helped him deal with the pair of kittens that were Freddie's favored birthday gift. As the rash faded and boredom set in, Natasha pumped up Spence's rapidly fading imagination with stories of her own.

"Just one more story."

Natasha smoothed Freddie's covers under her chin. "That's what you said three stories ago."

"You tell good ones."

"Flattery will get you nowhere. It's past my bedtime." Natasha lifted a brow at the big red alarm clock. "And yours."

"The doctor said I could go back to school on Monday. I'm not 'fectious."

"Infectious," Natasha corrected. "You'll be glad to see your friends again."

"Mostly." Stalling, Freddie played with the edge of her blanket. "Will you come and see me when I'm not sick?"

"I think I might." She leaned over to make a grab and came up with a mewing kitten. "And to see Lucy and Desi."

"And Daddy."

Cautious, Natasha scratched the kitten's ears. "Yes, I suppose."

"You like him, don't you?"

"Yes. He's a very good teacher."

"He likes you, too." Freddie didn't add that she had seen her father kiss Natasha at the foot of her bed just the night before, when they'd thought she was asleep. Watching them had given her a funny feeling in her stomach. But after a minute it had been a good funny feeling. "Will you marry him and come and live with us?"

"Well, is that a proposal?" Natasha managed to smile. "I think it's nice that you'd want me to, but I'm only friends with your daddy. Like I'm friends with you."

"If you came to live with us, we'd still be friends."

The child, Natasha reflected, was as clever as her father. "Won't we be friends if I live in my own house?"

"I guess." The pouty lower lip poked out. "But I'd like it better if you lived here, like JoBeth's mom does. She makes cookies."

Natasha leaned toward her, nose to nose. "So, you want me for my cookies."

"I love you." Freddie threw her arms around Natasha's neck and clung. "I'd be a good girl if you came."

Stunned, Natasha hugged the girl tight and rocked. "Oh, baby, I love you, too."

"So you'll marry us."

Put like that, Natasha wasn't sure whether to laugh or cry. "I don't think getting married right now is the answer for any of us. But I'll still be your friend, and come visit and tell you stories."

Freddie gave a long sigh. She knew when an adult was evading, and realized that it would be smart to retreat a step. Particularly when she had already made up her mind. Natasha was exactly what she wanted for a mother. And there was the added bonus that

Natasha made her daddy laugh. Freddie decided then and there that her most secret and solemn Christmas wish would be for Natasha to marry her father and bring home a baby sister.

"Promise?" Freddie demanded.

"Cross my heart." Natasha gave her a kiss on each cheek. "Now you go to sleep. I'll find your daddy so he can come up and kiss you good-night."

Freddie closed her eyes, her lips curved with her own secret smile.

Carrying the kitten, Natasha made her way downstairs. She'd put off her monthly books and an inventory to visit tonight. More than a little midnight oil would be burned, she decided, rubbing the kitten against her cheek.

She would have to be careful with Freddie now, and with herself. It was one thing for her to have fallen in love with the youngster, but quite another for the girl to love her enough to want her for a mother. How could she expect a child of six to understand that adults often had problems and fears that made it impossible for them to take the simple route?

The house was quiet, but a light was shining from the music room. She set down the kitten, knowing he would unerringly race to the kitchen.

She found Spence in the music room, spread on the two-cushion sofa so that his legs hung over one end. In sloppy sweats and bare feet he looked very little like the brilliant composer and full professor of music. Nor had he shaved. Natasha was forced to admit that the shadow of stubble only made him more attractive, especially when combined with tousled hair a week or two late for the barber.

He was sleeping deeply, a throw pillow crunched under his head. Natasha knew, because Vera had unbent long enough to tell her that Spence had stayed up throughout two nights during the worst of his daughter's fever and discomfort.

She was aware, too, that he had juggled his schedule at the college with trips home during the day. More than once during her visits she'd found him up to his ears in paperwork.

Once she had thought him pampered, a man who'd come by his talents and his position almost by birth. Perhaps he had been born with his talent, she thought now, but he worked hard, for himself and for his child. There was nothing she could admire more in a man.

I'm falling in love with him, she admitted. With his smile and his temper, his devotion and his drive. Perhaps, just perhaps they could give something to each other. Cautiously, carefully, with no promises between them.

She wanted to be his lover. She had never wanted such a thing before. With Anthony it had just happened, overwhelming her, sweeping her up and away, then leaving her shattered. It wouldn't be that way with Spence. Nothing would ever hurt her that deeply again. And with him there was a chance, just a chance of happiness.

Shouldn't she take it? Moving quietly, she unfolded the throw of soft blue wool that was draped along the back of the couch to spread it over him. It had been a long time since she'd taken a risk. Perhaps the time was here. She bent to brush her lips over his brow. And the man.

Chapter Seven

The black cat screeched a warning. A rushing gust
of wind blew open the door with an echoing slam and
maniacal laughter rolled in. What sounded like ooze
dripped down the walls, plunking dully onto the bare
concrete floor as the prisoners rattled their chains.
There was a piercing scream followed by a long, desperate moan.

"Great tunes," Annie commented and popped a
gum ball into her mouth.

"I should have ordered more of those records."
Natasha took an orange fright wig and turned a harmless stuffed bear into a Halloween ghoul. "That's the
last one."

"After tonight you'll have to start thinking Christmas, anyway." Annie pushed back her pointed black
hat, then grinned, showing blackened teeth. "Here

come the Freedmont boys.'' She rubbed her hands together and tried out a cackle. "If this costume's worth anything, I should be able to turn them into frogs.''

She didn't quite manage that, but sold them fake blood and and latex scars.

"I wonder what those little dears have in store for the neighborhood tonight,'' Natasha mused.

"Nothing good.'' Annie ducked under a hanging bat. "Shouldn't you get going?''

"Yes, in a minute.'' Stalling, Natasha fiddled with her dwindling supply of masks and fake noses. "The pig snouts sold better than I'd imagined. I didn't realize so many people would want to dress up as livestock.'' She picked one up to hold it over her nose. "Maybe we should keep them out year round.''

Recognizing her friend's tactics, Annie ran her tongue over her teeth to keep from grinning. "It was awfully nice of you to volunteer to help decorate for Freddie's party tonight.''

"It's a little thing,'' Natasha said and hated herself for being nervous. She replaced the snout, then ran her finger over a wrinkled elephant trunk attached to oversize glasses. "Since I suggested the idea of her having a Halloween party to make up for her missed birthday, I thought I should help.''

"Uh-huh. I wonder if her daddy's going to come as Prince Charming.''

"He is not Prince Charming.''

"The Big Bad Wolf?'' On a laugh, Annie held up her hands in a gesture of peace. "Sorry. It's just such a kick to see you unnerved.''

"I'm not unnerved.'' That was a big lie, Natasha

admitted while she packed up some of her contributions to the party. "You know, you're welcome to come."

"And I appreciate it. I'd rather stay home and guard my house from preadolescent felons. And don't worry," she added before Natasha could speak again. "I'll lock up."

"All right. Maybe I'll just—" Natasha broke off as the door jingled open. Another customer, she thought, would give her a little more time. When she spotted Terry, there was no way of saying who was more surprised. "Hello."

He swallowed over the huge lump in his throat and tried to look beyond her costume. "Tash?"

"Yes." Hoping he'd forgiven her by now, she smiled and held out a hand. He'd changed his seat in class, and every time she had tried to approach him, he'd darted off. Now he stood trapped, embarrassed and uncertain. He touched her outstretched hand, then stuck his own into his pocket.

"I didn't expect to see you here."

"No?" She tilted her head. "This is my shop." She wondered if it would strike him that she had been right when she'd said how little he knew her, and her voice softened. "I own it."

"You own it?" He looked around, unable to hide the impression it made on him. "Wow. That's something."

"Thank you. Did you come to buy something or just to look?"

Instantly he colored. It was one thing to go into a store, and another to go into one where the owner was a woman he'd professed to love. "I just...ah..."

"Something for Halloween?" she prompted. "They have parties at the college."

"Yeah, well, I kind of thought I might slip into a couple. I guess it's silly really, but..."

"Halloween is very serious business here at The Fun House," Natasha told him solemnly. As she spoke, another scream ripped from the speakers. "You see?"

Embarrassed that he'd jumped, Terry managed a weak smile. "Yeah. Well, I was thinking, maybe a mask or something. You know." His big, bony hands waved in space, then retreated to his pockets.

"Would you like to be scary or funny?"

"I don't, ah, I haven't thought about it."

Understanding, Natasha resisted the urge to pat his cheek. "You might get some ideas when you look at what we have left. Annie, this is my friend, Terry Maynard. He's a violinist."

"Hi." Annie watched his glasses slide down his nose after his nervous nod of greeting and thought him adorable. "We're running low, but we've still got some pretty good stuff. Why don't you come over and take a look? I'll help you pick one out."

"I have to run." Natasha began gathering up her two shopping bags, hoping that the visit had put them back on more solid ground. "Have a good time at your party, Terry."

"Thanks."

"Annie, I'll see you in the morning."

"Right. Don't bob for too many apples." Pushing her pointed hat out of her eyes again, Annie grinned at Terry. "So, you're a violinist."

"Yeah." He gave Natasha's retreating back one

last look. When the door closed behind her he felt a pang, but only a small one. "I'm taking some graduate classes at the college."

"Great. Hey, can you play 'Turkey in the Straw'?"

Outside Natasha debated running home to get her car. The cool, clear air changed her mind. The trees had turned. The patchwork glory of a week before, with its scarlets and vivid oranges and yellows, had blended into a dull russet. Dry, curling leaves spun from the branches to crowd against the curbs and scatter on the sidewalks. They crackled under her feet as she began the short walk.

The hardiest flowers remained, adding a spicy scent so different from the heavy fragrances of summer. Cooler, cleaner, crisper, Natasha thought as she drew it in.

She turned off the main street to where hedges and big trees shielded the houses. Jack-o'-lanterns sat on stoops and porches, grinning as they waited to be lighted at dusk. Here and there effigies in flannel shirts and torn jeans hung from denuded branches. Witches and ghosts stuffed with straw sat on steps, waiting to scare and delight the wandering trick-or-treaters.

If anyone had asked her why she had chosen a small town in which to settle, this would have been one of her answers. People here took the time—the time to carve a pumpkin, the time to take a bundle of old clothes and fashion it into a headless horseman. Tonight, before the moon rose, children could race along the streets, dressed as fairies or goblins. Their goody bags would swell with store-bought candy and homemade cookies, while adults pretended not to recognize the miniature hoboes, clowns and demons. The only thing the children would have to fear was make-believe.

Her child would have been seven.

Natasha paused for a moment, pressing a hand to her stomach until the grief and the memory could be blocked. How many times had she told herself the past was past? And how many times would that past sneak up and slice at her?

True, it came less often now, but still so sharply and always unexpectedly. Days could go by, even months, then it surfaced, crashing over her, leaving her a little dazed, a little tender, like a woman who had walked into a wall.

A car engine was gunned. A horn blasted. "Hey, Tash."

She blinked and managed to lift a hand in passing salute, though she couldn't identify the driver, who continued on his way.

This was now, she told herself, blinking to focus again on the swirl of leaves. This was here. There was never any going back. Years before she had convinced herself that the only direction was forward. Deliberately she took a long, deep breath, relieved when she felt her system level. Tonight wasn't the time for sorrows. She had promised another child a party, and she intended to deliver.

She had to smile when she started up the steps of Spence's home. He had already been working, she noted. Two enormous jack-o'-lanterns flanked the porch. Like Comedy and Tragedy, one grinned and the other scowled. Across the railing a white sheet had been shaped and spread so that the ghost it became seemed to be in full flight. Cardboard bats with red eyes swooped down from the eaves. In an old rocker beside the door sat a hideous monster who held his laughing head in his hand. On the door was a full-size cutout of a witch stirring a steaming cauldron.

Natasha knocked under the hag's warty nose. She was laughing when Spence opened the door. "Trick or treat," she said.

He couldn't speak at all. For a moment he thought he was imagining things, had to be. The music-box gypsy was standing before him, gold dripping from her ears and her wrists. Her wild mane of hair was banded by a sapphire scarf that flowed almost to her waist with the corkscrew curls. More gold hung around her neck, thick, ornate chains that only accented her slenderness. The red dress was snug, scooped at the bodice and full in the skirt, with richly colored scarfs tied at the waist.

Her eyes were huge and dark, made mysterious by some womanly art. Her lips were full and red, turned up now as she spun in a saucy circle. It took him only seconds to see it all, down to the hints of black lace at the hem. He felt as though he'd been standing in the doorway for hours.

"I have a crystal ball," she told him, reaching into her pocket to pull out a small, clear orb. "If you cross my palm with silver, I'll gaze into it for you."

"My God," he managed. "You're beautiful."

She only laughed and stepped inside. "Illusions. Tonight is meant for them." With a quick glance around, she slipped the crystal back into her pocket. But the image of the gypsy and the mystery remained. "Where's Freddie?"

His hand had gone damp on the knob. "She's..." It took a moment for his brain to kick back into gear. "She's at JoBeth's. I wanted to put things together when she wasn't around."

"A good idea." She studied his gray sweats and dusty sneakers. "Is this your costume?"

"No. I've been hanging cobwebs."

"I'll give you a hand." Smiling, she held up her bags. "I have some tricks and I have some treats. Which would you like first?"

"You have to ask?" he said quietly, then hooking an arm around her waist, brought her up hard against himself. She threw her head back, words of anger and defiance in her eyes and on the tip of her tongue. Then his mouth found hers. The bags slipped out of her hands. Freed, her fingers dived into his hair.

This wasn't what she wanted. But it was what she needed. Without hesitation her lips parted, inviting intimacy. She heard his quiet moan of pleasure merge with her own. It seemed right, somehow it seemed perfectly right to be holding him like this, just inside his front door, with the scents of fall flowers and fresh polish in the air, and the sharp-edged breeze of autumn rushing over them.

It was right. He could taste and feel the rightness with her body pressed against his own, her lips warm and agile. No illusion this. No fantasy was she, despite the colorful scarfs and glittering gold. She was real, she was here, and she was his. Before the night was over, he would prove it to both of them.

"I hear violins," he murmured as he trailed his lips down her throat.

"Spence." She could only hear her heartbeat, like

thunder in her head. Struggling for sanity, she pushed away. "You make me do things I tell myself I won't." After a deep breath she gave him a steady look. "I came to help you with Freddie's party."

"And I appreciate it." Quietly he closed the door. "Just like I appreciate the way you look, the way you taste, the way you feel."

She shouldn't have been so aroused by only a look. Couldn't be, not when the look told her that whatever the crystal in her pocket promised, he already knew their destiny. "This is a very inappropriate time."

He loved the way her voice could take on that regal tone, czarina to peasant. "Then we'll find a better one."

Exasperated, she hefted the bags again. "I'll help you hang your cobwebs, if you promise to be Freddie's father—and only Freddie's father while we do."

"Okay." He didn't see any other way he'd survive an evening with twenty costumed first-graders. And the party, he thought, wouldn't last forever. "We'll be pals for the duration."

She liked the sound of it. Choosing a bag, she reached inside. She held up a rubber mask of a bruised, bloodied and scarred face. Competently she slipped it over Spence's head. "There. You look wonderful."

He adjusted it until he could see her through both eyeholes, and had a foolish and irresistible urge to look at himself in the hall mirror. Behind the mask he grinned. "I'll suffocate."

"Not for a couple of hours yet." She handed him the second bag. "Come on. It takes time to build a haunted house."

* * *

It took them two hours to transform Spence's elegantly decorated living room into a spooky dungeon, fit for rats and screams of torture. Black and orange crepe paper hung on the walls and ceiling. Angel-hair cobwebs draped the corners. A mummy, arms folded across its chest leaned in a corner. A black-caped witch hung in the air, suspended on her broom. Thirsty and waiting for dusk, an evil-eyed Dracula lurked in the shadows, ready to pounce.

"You don't think it's too scary?" Spence asked as he hung up a Pin-the-Nose-on-the-Pumpkin game. "They're first-graders."

Natasha flicked a finger over a rubber spider that hung by a thread and sent him spinning. "Very mild. My brothers made a haunted house once. They blindfolded Rachel and me to take us through. Milkhail put my hand in a bowl of grapes and told me it was eyes."

"Now that's disgusting," Spence decided.

"Yes." It delighted her to remember it. "Then there was this spaghetti—"

"Never mind," he interrupted. "I get the idea."

She laughed, adjusting her earring. "In any case, I had a wonderful time and have always wished I'd thought of it first. The children tonight would be very disappointed if we didn't have some monsters waiting for them. After they've been spooked, which they desperately want to be, you turn on the lights, so they see it's all pretend."

"Too bad we're out of grapes."

"It's all right. When Freddie's older, I'll show you how to make a bloodied severed hand out of a rubber glove."

"I can't wait."

"What about food?"

"Vera's been a Trojan." With his mask on top of his head, Spence stood back to study the whole room. It felt good, really good to look at the results, and to know that he and Natasha had produced them together. "She's made everything from deviled eggs to witch's brew punch. You know what would have been great? A fog machine."

"That's the spirit." His grin made her laugh and long to kiss him. "Next year."

He liked the sound of that, he realized. Next year, and the year after. A little dazed at the speed with which his thoughts were racing, he only studied her.

"Is something wrong?"

"No." He smiled. "Everything's just fine."

"I have the prizes here." Wanting to rest her legs, Natasha sat on the arm of a chair beside a lounging ghoul. "For the games and costumes."

"You didn't have to do that."

"I told you I wanted to. This is my favorite." She pulled out a skull, then flicking a switch, set it on the floor where it skimmed along, disembodied, its empty eyes blinking.

"Your favorite." Tongue in cheek, Spence picked it up where it vibrated in his hand.

"Yes. Very gruesome." She tilted her head. "Say 'Alas, poor Yorick!'"

He only laughed and switched it off. Then he pulled down his mask. "'O, that this too, too solid flesh would melt.'" She was chuckling when he came over and lifted her to her feet. "Give us a kiss."

"No," she decided after a moment. "You're ugly."

"Okay." Obligingly he pushed the mask up again. "How about it?"

"Much worse." Solemnly she slid the mask down again.

"Very funny."

"No, but it seemed necessary." Linking her arm with his, she studied the room. "I think you'll have a hit."

"We'll have a hit," he corrected. "You know Freddie's crazy about you."

"Yes." Natasha gave him an easy smile. "It's mutual."

They heard the front door slam and a shout. "Speaking of Freddie."

Children arrived first in trickles, then in a flood. When the clock struck six, the room was full of ballerinas and pirates, monsters and superheroes. The haunted house brought gasps and shrieks and shudders. No one was brave enough to make the tour alone, though many made it twice, then a third time. Occasionally a stalwart soul was courageous enough to poke a finger into the mummy or touch the vampire's cape.

When the lights were switched on there were moans of disappointment and a few relieved sighs. Freddie, a life-size Raggedy Ann, tore open her belated birthday presents with abandon.

"You're a very good father," Natasha murmured.

"Thanks." He linked his fingers with hers, no longer questioning why it should be so right for them to stand together and watch over his daughter's party. "Why?"

"Because you haven't once retreated for aspirin, and you hardly winced when Mikey spilled punch on your rug."

"That's because I have to save my strength for when Vera sees it." Spence dodged, in time to avoid collision with a fairy princess being chased by a goblin. There were squeals from every corner of the room, punctuated by the crashing and moaning of the novelty record on the stereo. "As for the aspirin... How long can they keep this up?"

"Oh, a lot longer than we can."

"You're such a comfort."

"We'll have them play games now. You'll be surprised how quickly two hours can pass."

She was right. By the time the numbered noses had all been stuck in the vicinity of the pumpkin head, when musical chairs was only a fond memory, after the costume parade and judging, when the last apple bobbed alone and the final clothespin had clunked into a mason jar, parents began to trail in to gather up their reluctant Frankensteins and ghoulies. But the fun wasn't over.

In groups and clutches, trick-or-treaters canvassed the neighborhood for candy bars and caramel apples. The wind-rushed night and crackling leaves were things they would remember long after the last chocolate drop had been consumed.

It was nearly ten before Spence managed to tuck an exhausted and thrilled Freddie into bed. "It was the best birthday I ever had," she told him. "I'm glad I got the chicken pox."

Spence rubbed a finger over a smeared orange freckle the cold cream had missed. "I don't know if I'd go that far, but I'm glad you had fun."

"Can I have—?"

"No." He kissed her nose. "If you eat one more piece of candy you'll blow up."

She giggled, and because she was too tired to try any strategy, snuggled into her pillow. Memories were already swirling in her head. "Next year I want to be a gypsy like Tash. Okay?"

"Sure. Go to sleep now. I'm going to take Natasha home, but Vera's here."

"Are you going to marry Tash soon, so she can stay with us?"

Spence opened his mouth, then closed it again as Freddie yawned hugely. "Where do you get these ideas?" he muttered.

"How long does it take to get a baby sister?" she asked as she drifted off.

Spence rubbed a hand over his face, grateful that she had fallen asleep and saved him from answering.

Downstairs he found Natasha cleaning up the worst of the mess. She flicked back her hair as he came in. "When it looks as bad as this, you know you've had a successful party." Something in his expression had her narrowing her eyes. "Is something wrong?"

"No. No, it's Freddie."

"She has a tummy ache," Natasha said, instantly sympathetic.

"Not yet." He shrugged it off with a half laugh. "She always manages to surprise me. Don't," he said and took the trash bag from her. "You've done enough."

"I don't mind."

"I know."

Before he could take her hand, she linked her own. "I should be going. Tomorrow's Saturday—our busiest day."

He wondered what it would be like if they could simply walk upstairs together, into his bedroom. Into his bed. "I'll take you home."

"That's all right. You don't have to."

"I'd like to." The tension was back. Their eyes met, and he understood that she felt it as well. "Are you tired?"

"No." It was time for some truths, she knew. He had done what she'd asked and been only Freddie's father during the party. Now the party was over. But not the night.

"Would you like to walk?"

The corners of her lips turned up, then she put her hand into his. "Yes. I would."

It was colder now, with a bite in the air warning of winter. Above, the moon was full and chillingly white. Clouds danced over it, sending shadows shifting. Over the rustle of leaves they heard the echoing shouts and laughter of lingering trick-or-treaters. Inevitably the big oak on the corner had been wrapped in bathroom tissue by teenagers.

"I love this time," Natasha murmured. "Especially at night when there's a little wind. You can smell smoke from the chimneys."

On the main street, older children and college students still stalked in fright masks and painted faces. A poor imitation of a wolf howl bounced along the storefronts, followed by a feminine squeal and laughter. A car full of ghouls paused long enough for them to lean out the windows and screech.

Spence watched the car turn a corner, its passengers still howling. "I can't remember being anywhere that Halloween was taken so seriously."

"Wait until you see what happens at Christmas."

Natasha's own pumpkin was glowing on her stoop beside a bowl half-filled with candy bars. There was a sign on her door. Take Only One. Or Else.

Spence shook his head at it. "That really does it?"

Natasha merely glanced at the sign. "They know me."

Leaning over, Spence plucked one. "Can I have a brandy to go with it?"

She hesitated. If she let him come in, it was inevitable that they would pick up where the earlier kiss had left off. It had been two months, she thought, two months of wondering, of stalling, of pretending. They both knew it had to stop sooner or later.

"Of course." She opened the door and let him in.

Wound tight, she went into the kitchen to pour drinks. It was yes or it was no, she told herself. She had known the answer long before this night, even prepared for it. But what would it be like with him? What would she be like? And how, when she had shared herself with him in that most private way, would she be able to pretend she didn't need more?

Couldn't need more, Natasha reminded herself. Whatever her feelings for him, and they were deeper, much deeper than she dared admit, life had to continue as it was. No promises, no vows. No broken hearts.

He turned when she came back into the room, but

didn't speak. His own thoughts were mixed and confused. What did he want? Her, certainly. But how much, how little could he accept? He'd been sure he'd never feel this way again. More than sure that he would never want to. Yet it seemed so easy to feel, every time he looked at her.

"Thanks." He took the brandy, watching her as he sipped. "You know, the first time I lectured, I stood at the podium and my mind went completely blank. For one terrible moment I couldn't think of anything I'd planned to say. I'm having exactly the same problem now."

"You don't have to say anything."

"It's not as easy as I thought it would be." He took her hand, surprised to find it cold and unsteady. Instinctively he lifted it to press his lips to the palm. It helped, knowing she was as nervous as he. "I don't want to frighten you."

"This frightens me." She could feel sensation spear her. "Sometimes people say I think too much. Maybe it's true. If it is, it's because I feel too much. There was a time...." She took her hand from his, wanting to be strong on her own. "There was a time," she repeated, "when I let what I felt decide for me. There are some mistakes that you pay for until you die."

"This isn't a mistake." He set down the brandy to take her face between his hands.

Her fingers curled around his wrists. "I don't want it to be. There can't be any promises, Spence, because I'd rather not have them than have them broken. I don't need or want pretty words. They're too easily said." Her grip tightened. "I want to be your lover, but I need respect, not poetry."

"Are you finished?"

"I need for you to understand," she insisted.

"I'm beginning to. You must have loved him a great deal."

She dropped her hands, but steadied herself before she answered. "Yes."

It hurt, surprising him. He could hardly be threatened by someone from her past. He had a past, as well. But he *was* threatened, and he *was* hurt. "I don't care who he was, and I don't give a damn what happened." That was a lie, he realized, and one he'd have to deal with sooner or later. "But I don't want you thinking of him when you're with me."

"I don't, not the way you mean."

"Not in any way."

She raised a brow. "You can't control my thoughts or anything else about me."

"You're wrong." Fueled by impotent jealousy, he pulled her into his arms. The kiss was angry, demanding, possessive. And tempting. Tempting her so close to submission that she struggled away.

"I won't be taken." Her voice was only more defiant because she was afraid she was wrong.

"Your rules, Natasha?"

"Yes. If they're fair."

"To whom?"

"Both of us." She pressed her fingers against her temples for a moment. "We shouldn't be angry," she said more quietly. "I'm sorry." She offered a shrug and a quick smile. "I'm afraid. It's been a long time since I've been with anyone—since I've wanted to be.''

He picked up his brandy, staring into it as it swirled. "You make it hard for me to stay mad.''

"I'd like to think we were friends. I've never been friends with a lover.''

And he'd never been in love with a friend. It was a huge and frightening admission, and one he was certain he couldn't make out loud. Perhaps, if he stopped being clumsy, he could show her.

"We are friends." He held out a hand, then curled his fingers around hers. "Friends trust each other, Natasha.''

"Yes.''

He looked at their joined hands. "Why don't we—?" A noise at the window had him breaking off and glancing over. Before he could move, Natasha tightened her hold. It took only a moment to see that she wasn't frightened, but amused. She brought a finger from her free hand to her lips.

"I think it's a good idea to be friends with my professor," she said, lifting her voice and making a go-ahead gesture to Spence.

"I, ah, I'm glad Freddie and I have found so many nice people since we've moved." Puzzled, he watched Natasha root through a drawer.

"It's a nice town. Of course, sometimes there are problems. You haven't heard about the woman who escaped from the asylum.''

"What asylum?" At her impatient glance, he covered himself. "No, I guess not.''

"The police are keeping very quiet about it. They know she's in the area and don't want people to panic." Natasha flicked on the flashlight she'd uncovered and nodded in approval as the batteries proved strong. "She's quite insane, you know, and likes to kidnap small children. Especially young boys. Then she tortures them, hideously. On a night with a full moon she creeps up on them, so silently, so evilly. Then before they can scream, she grabs them around the throat."

So saying, she whipped up the shade on the window. With the flashlight held under her chin, she pressed her face against the glass and grinned.

Twin screams echoed. There was a crash, a shout, then the scramble of feet.

Weak from laughter, Natasha leaned against the windowsill. "The Freedmont boys," she explained when she'd caught her breath. "Last year they hung a dead rat outside Annie's door." She pressed a hand to her heart as Spence came over to peer out the window. All he could see was two shadows racing across the lawn.

"I think the tables are well-turned."

"Oh, you should have seen their faces." She dabbed a tear from her lashes. "I don't think their hearts will start beating again until they pull the covers over their heads."

"This should be a Halloween they don't forget."

"Every child should have one good scare they remember always." Still smiling, she stuck the light under her chin again. "What do you think?"

"It's too late to scare me away." He took the flashlight and set it aside. Closing his hand over hers, he drew her to her feet. "It's time to find out how much is illusion, how much is reality." Slowly he pulled the shade down.

Chapter Eight

It was very real. Painfully real. The feel of his mouth against hers left no doubt that she was alive and needy. The time, the place, meant nothing. Those could have been illusions. But he was not. Desire was not. She felt it spring crazily inside her at only a meeting of lips.

No, it wasn't simple. She had known since she had first tasted him, since she had first allowed herself to touch him that whatever happened between them would never be simple. Yet that was what she had been so certain she'd wanted. Simplicity, a smooth road, an easy path.

Not with him. And not ever again.

Accepting, she twined her arms around him. Tonight there would be no past, no future. Only one moment taken in both hands, gripped hard and enjoyed.

Answer for answer, need for need, they clung together. The low light near the door cast their silhouettes onto the wall, one shadow. It shifted when they did, then stilled.

When he swept her into his arms, she murmured a protest. She had said she wouldn't be taken and had meant it. Yet cradled there she didn't feel weak. She felt loved. In gratitude and in acceptance she pressed her lips to his throat. As he carried her toward the bedroom, she allowed herself to yield.

Then there was only moonlight. It crept through the thin curtain, softly, quietly, as a lover might creep through the window to find his woman. Her lover said nothing as he set her on her feet by the bed. His silence told her everything.

He'd imagined her like this. It seemed impossible, yet he had. The image had been clear and vivid. He had seen her with her hair in wild tangles around her face, with her eyes dark and steady, her skin gleaming like the gold she wore. And in his imaginings, he'd seen much, much more.

Slowly he reached up to slip the scarf from her hair, to let it float soundlessly to the floor. She waited. With his eyes on hers he loosened another and another of the slashes of color—sapphire, emerald, amber—until they lay like jewels at her feet. She smiled. With his fingertips he drew the dress off her shoulders, then pressed his lips to the skin he'd bared.

A sigh and a shudder. Then she reached for him, struggling to breathe while she pulled his shirt over his head. His skin was taut and smooth under her palms. She could feel the quiver of muscle at the passage of her hands. As her eyes stayed on his, she could see the flash and fury of passion that darkened them.

He had to fight every instinct to prevent himself from tearing the dress from her, ripping aside the barriers and taking what she was offering. She wouldn't stop him. He could see it in her eyes, part challenge, part acknowledgment and all desire.

But he had promised her something. Though she claimed she wanted no promises, he intended to keep it. She would have romance, as much as he was capable of giving her.

Fighting for patience, he undid the range of buttons down her back. Her lips were curved when she pressed them to his chest. Her hands were smooth when she slipped his pants over his hips. As the dress slid to the floor, he brought her close for a long, luxurious kiss.

She swayed. It seemed foolish to her, but she was dizzy. Colors seemed to dance in her head to some frantic symphony she couldn't place. Her bracelets jingled when he lifted her hand to press a small circle of kisses upon her wrist. Material rustled, more notes to the song, when he slipped petticoat after colorful petticoat over her hips.

He hadn't believed she could be so beautiful. But now, standing before him in only a thin red chemise and the glitter of gold, she was almost more than a man could bear. Her eyes were nearly closed, but her head was up—a habit of pride that suited her well. Moonlight swam around her.

Slowly she lifted her arms, crossing them in front of her to push the slender straps from her shoulders. The material trembled over her breasts, then clung for

a fleeting instant before it slithered to the floor at their
feet. Now there was only the glitter of gold against
her skin. Exciting, erotic, exotic. She waited, then
lifted her arms again—to him.

"I want you," she said.

Flesh met flesh, drawing twin moans from each of
them. Mouth met mouth, sending shock waves of
pleasure and pain through both. Desire met desire,
driving out reason.

Inevitable. It was the only thought that filtered
through the chaos in her mind as her hands raced over
him. No force this strong, no need this deep could be
anything but inevitable. So she met that force, met
that need, with all of her heart.

Patience was forgotten. She was a hunger in him
already too long denied. He wanted all, everything
she was, everything she had. Before he could demand,
she was giving. When they tumbled onto the bed, his
hands were already greedily searching to give and to
take pleasure.

Could he have known it would be so huge, so consuming? Everything about her was vivid and honed
sharp. Her taste an intoxicating mix of honey and
whiskey, both heated. Her skin as lush as a rose petal
drenched in evening dew. Her scent as dark as his
own passion. Her need as sharp as a freshly whetted
blade.

She arched against him, offering, challenging, crying out when he sought and found each secret. Pleasure arrowed into him as her small, agile body pressed
against his. Strong, willful, she rolled over him to
exploit and explore until his breath was a fire in his
lungs and his body a mass of sensation. Half-mad, he

tumbled with her over the bed and spread a tangle of sheets around them. When he lifted himself over her, he could see the wild curtain of her hair like a dark cloud, the deep, rich glow of her eyes as they clung to his. Her breathing was as hurried as his own, her body as willing.

Never before, he realized, and never again would he find anyone who matched him so perfectly. Whatever he needed, she needed, whatever he wanted, she wanted. Before he could ask, she was answering. For the first time in his life, he knew what it was to make love with mind and heart and soul as well as body.

She thought of no one and of nothing but him. When he touched her, it was as though she'd never been touched before. When he said her name, it was the first time she'd heard it. When his mouth sought hers, it was a first kiss, the one she'd been waiting for, wishing for all of her life.

Palm to palm their hands met, fingers gripping hard like one soul grasping another. They watched each other as he filled her. And there was a promise, felt by both. In a moment of panic she shook her head. Then he was moving in her, and she with him.

"Again," was all he said as he pulled her against him.

"Spence."

"Again." His mouth covered hers, waking her out of a half dream and into fresh passion.

He wanted her just as much, now that he knew what they could make between them, but with a fire that held steady on slow burn. This time, though desire was still keen, the madness was less intense. He could appreciate the subtle curves, the soft angles, the lazy sighs he could draw out of her with only a touch. It was like making love to some primitive goddess, naked but for the gold draped over her skin. After so long a thirst he quenched himself slowly, leisurely after that first, greedy gulp.

How had she ever imagined she had known what it was to love a man, or to be loved by one? There were pleasures here that as a woman she knew she had never tasted before. This was what it was to be steeped, to be drowned, to be sated. She ran her hands over him, absorbing the erotic sensations of the flick of his tongue, the scrape of his teeth, the play of those clever fingertips. No, these were new pleasures, very new. And their taste was freedom.

As the moon soared high into the night, so did she.

"I thought I had imagined what it would be like to be with you." Her head resting on his shoulder, Spence trailed his fingers up and down her arm. "I didn't even come close."

"I thought I would never be here with you." She smiled into the dark. "I was very wrong."

"Thank God. Natasha—"

With a quick shake of her head, she put a finger to his lips. "Don't say too much. It's easy to say too much in the moonlight." And easy to believe it, she added silently.

Though impatient, he bit back the words he wanted to say. He had made a mistake once before by wanting too much, too quickly. He was determined not to make mistakes with Natasha. "Can I tell you that I'll never look at gold chains in quite the same way again?''

With a little chuckle she pressed a kiss to his shoulder. "Yes, you can tell me that."

He toyed with her bracelets. "Can I tell you I'm happy?"

"Yes."

"Are you?"

She tilted her head to look at him. "Yes. Happier than I thought I could be. You make me feel..." She smiled, making a quick movement with her shoulders. "Like magic."

"Tonight was magic."

"I was afraid," she murmured. "Of you, of this. Of myself," she admitted. "It's been a very long time for me."

"It's been a long time for me, too." At her restless movement, he caught her chin in his hand. "I haven't been with anyone since before my wife died."

"Did you love her very much? I'm sorry," she said quickly and closed her eyes tight. "I have no business asking that."

"Yes, you do." He kept his fingers firm. "I loved her once, or I loved the idea of her. That idea was gone long before she died."

"Please. Tonight isn't the time to talk about things that were."

When she sat up, he went with her, cupping her forearms in his hands. "Maybe not. But there are things I need to tell you, things we will talk about."

"Is what happened before so important?"

He heard the trace of desperation in her voice and

wished he could find the reason. "I think it could be."

"This is now." She closed her hands over his. It was as close to a promise as she dared make. "Now I want to be your friend and your lover."

"Then be both."

She calmed herself with a deliberate effort.

"Perhaps I don't want to talk about other women while I'm in bed with you."

He could feel that she was braced and ready to argue. In a move that threw her off, he leaned closer to touch his lips to her brow. "We'll let you use that one for now."

"Thank you." She brushed a hand through his hair. "I'd like to spend this night with you, all night." With a half smile, she shook her head. "You can't stay."

"I know." He caught her hand to bring it to his lips. "Freddie would have some very awkward questions for me if I wasn't around for breakfast in the morning."

"She's a very lucky girl."

"I don't like leaving this way."

She smiled and kissed him. "I understand, as long as the other woman is only six."

"I'll see you tomorrow." Bending closer, he deepened the kiss.

"Yes." On a sigh she wrapped her arms around him. "Once more," she murmured, drawing him down to the bed. "Just once more."

In her cramped office at the back of the shop, Natasha sat at her desk. She had come in early to catch up on the practical side of business. Her ledger was up-to-date, her invoices had been filled. With Christmas less than two months away, she had completed her orders. Early merchandise was already stacked wherever room could be found. It made her feel good to be surrounded by the wishes of children, and to know that on Christmas morning what was now stored in boxes would cause cries of delight and wonder.

But there were practicalities as well. She had only begun to think of displays, decorations and discounts. She would have to decide soon whether she wanted to hire part-time help for the seasonal rush.

Now, at midmorning, with Annie in charge of the shop, she had textbooks and notes spread out. Before business there were studies, and she took both very seriously.

There was to be a test on the baroque era, and she intended to show her teacher—her lover—that she could hold her own.

Perhaps it shouldn't have been so important to prove she could learn and retain. But there had been times in her life, times she was certain Spence could never understand, when she had been made to feel inadequate, even stupid. The little girl with broken English, the thin teenager who'd thought more about dance than schoolbooks, the dancer who'd fought so hard to make her body bear the insults of training, the young woman who had listened to her heart, not her head.

She was none of those people any longer, and yet she was all of them. She needed Spence to respect her intelligence, to see her as an equal, not just as the woman he desired.

She was being foolish. On a sigh, Natasha leaned back in her chair to toy with the petals of the red rose that stood at her elbow. Even more than foolish, she was wrong. Spence was nothing like Anthony. Except for the vaguest of physical similarities, those two men were almost opposites. True, one was a brilliant dancer, the other a brilliant musician, but Anthony had been selfish, dishonest, and in the end cowardly.

She had never known a man more generous, a man kinder than Spence. He was compassionate and honest. Or was that her heart talking? To be sure. But the heart, she thought, didn't come with a guarantee like a mechanical toy. Every day she was with him, she fell deeper and deeper in love. So much in love, she thought, that there were moments, terrifying moments, when she wanted to toss aside everything and tell him.

She had offered her heart to a man before, a heart pure and fragile. When it had been given back to her, it had been scarred.

No, there were no guarantees.

How could she dare risk that again? Even knowing that what was happening to her now was different, very different from what had happened to the young girl of seventeen, how could she possibly take the chance of leaving herself open again to that kind of pain and humiliation?

Things were better as they were, she assured herself. They were two adults, enjoying each other. And they were friends.

Taking the rose out of its vase, she stroked it along

her cheek. It was a pity that she and her friend could only find a few scattered hours to be alone. There was a child to consider, then there were schedules and responsibilities. But in those hours when her friend became her lover, she knew the true meaning of bliss.

Bringing herself back, she slipped the flower into the vase and shifted her concentration to her studies. Within five minutes the phone rang.

"Good morning, Fun House."

"Good morning, business person."

"Mama!"

"So, you are busy or you have a moment to talk to your mother?"

Natasha cradled the phone in both hands, loving the sound of her mother's voice. "Of course I have a moment. All the moments you like."

"I wondered, since you have not called me in two weeks."

"I'm sorry." For two weeks a man had been the center of her life. But she could hardly tell that to her mother. "How are you and Papa and everyone?"

"Papa and me and everyone are good. Papa gets a raise."

"Wonderful."

"Mikhail doesn't see the Italian girl anymore." Nadia gave thanks in Ukrainian and made Natasha laugh. "Alex, he sees all the girls. Smart boy, my Alex. And Rachel has time for nothing but her studies. What of Natasha?"

"Natasha is fine. I'm eating well and getting plenty of sleep," she added before Nadia could ask.

"Good. And your store?"

"We're about to get ready for Christmas, and I expect a better year than last."

"I want you to stop sending your money."

"I want you to stop worrying about your children."

Nadia's sigh made Natasha smile. It was an old argument. "You are a very stubborn woman."

"Like my mama."

That was true enough, and Nadia clearly didn't intend to concede. "We will talk about this when you come for Thanksgiving."

Thanksgiving, Natasha thought. How could she have forgotten? Clamping the receiver between ear and shoulder, she flipped through her calendar. It was less than two weeks away. "I can't argue with my mother on Thanksgiving." Natasha made a note for herself to call the train station. "I'll be up late Wednesday evening. I'll bring the wine."

"You bring yourself."

"Myself and the wine." Natasha scribbled another note to herself. It was a difficult time to take off, but she had never missed—and would never miss—a holiday at home. "I'll be so glad to see all of you again."

"Maybe you bring a friend."

It was another old routine, but this time, for the first time, Natasha hesitated. No, she told herself with a shake of her head. Why would Spence want to spend Thanksgiving in Brooklyn?

"Natasha?" Nadia's well-honed instincts had obviously picked up her daughter's mental debate. "You have friend?"

"Of course. I have a lot of friends."

"Don't be smart with your mama. Who is he?"

"He's no one." Then she rolled her eyes as Nadia began tossing out questions. "All right, all right. He's a professor at the college, a widower," she added. "With a little girl. I was just thinking they might like company for the holiday, that's all."

"Ah."

"Don't give me that significant ah, Mama. He's a friend, and I'm very fond of the little girl."

"How long you know him?"

"They just moved here late this summer. I'm taking one of his courses, and the little girl comes in the shop sometimes." It was all true, she thought. Not all the truth, but all true. She hoped her tone was careless. "If I get around to it, I might ask him if he'd like to come up."

"The little girl, she can sleep with you and Rachel."

"Yes, if—"

"The professor, he can take Alex's room. Alex can sleep on the couch."

"He may already have plans."

"You ask."

"All right. If it comes up."

"You ask," Nadia repeated. "Now go back to work."

"Yes, Mama. I love you."

Now she'd done it, Natasha thought as she hung up. She could almost see her mother standing beside the rickety telephone table and rubbing her hands together.

What would he think of her family, and they of him? Would he enjoy a big, rowdy meal? She thought of the first dinner they had shared, the elegant table, the quiet, discreet service. He probably has plans anyway, Natasha decided. It just wasn't something she was going to worry about.

Twenty minutes later the phone ran again. It was probably her mother, Natasha thought, calling with a dozen questions about this "friend." Braced, Natasha picked up the receiver. "Good morning, Fun House."

"Natasha."

"Spence?" Automatically she checked her watch. "Why aren't you at the university? Are you sick?"

"No. No. I came home between classes. I've got about an hour. I need you to come."

"To your house?" There was an urgency in his voice, but it had nothing to do with disaster and everything to do with excitement. "Why? What is it?"

"Just come, will you? It's nothing I can explain. I have to show you. Please."

"Yes, all right. Are you sure you're not sick?"

"No." She heard his laugh and relaxed. "No, I'm not sick. I've never felt better. Hurry up, will you?"

"Ten minutes." Natasha snatched up her coat. He'd sounded different. Happy? No, elated, ecstatic. What did a man have to be ecstatic about in the middle of the morning? Perhaps he was sick. Pulling on her gloves, she dashed into the shop.

"Annie, I have to—" She stopped, blinked, then stared at the image of Annie being kissed, soundly, by Terry Maynard. "I...excuse me."

"Oh, Tash, Terry just... Well, he..." Annie blew the hair out of her eyes and grinned foolishly. "Are you going out?"

"Yes, I have to see someone." She bit her lip to

keep from grinning back. "I won't be more than an hour. Can you manage?"

"Sure." Annie smoothed down her hair, while Terry stood beside her, turning various shades of red. "It has been a quiet morning. Take your time."

Perhaps the world had decided to go crazy today, Natasha thought as she rushed down the street. First her mother calling, already preparing to kick Alex out of his bed for a stranger. Spence demanding she come to his house and see…something in the middle of the day. And now Annie and Terry, kissing each other beside the cash register. Well, she could only deal with one at a time. It looked as though Spence was first on the list.

She took his steps two at time, convinced he was suffering from some sort of fever. When he pulled open the door before she reached it, she was certain of it. His eyes were bright, his color up. His sweater was rumpled and his tie unknotted.

"Spence, are you—?"

Before she could get the words out, he was snatching her up, crushing his mouth to hers as he swung her around and around. "I thought you'd never get here."

"I came as quickly as I could." Instinctively she put a hand to his cheek. Then the look in his eyes had her narrowing her own. No, it wasn't a fever, she decided. At least it wasn't the kind that required medical attention. "If you had me run all the way over here for that, I'm going to hit you very hard."

"For—no," he answered on a laugh. "Though it's a wonderful idea. A really wonderful idea." He kissed her again until she thoroughly agreed with him.

"I feel like I could make love with you for hours, days, weeks."

"They might miss you in class," she murmured. Steadying herself, she stepped back. "You sounded excited. Did you win the lottery?"

"Better. Come here." Remembering the door, he slammed it shut, then pulled her into the music room. "Don't say anything. Just sit."

She obliged, but when he went to the piano, she started to stand again. "Spence, I'd enjoy a concert, but—"

"Don't talk," he said impatiently. "Just listen."

And he began to play.

It took only moments for her to realize it was nothing she'd heard before. Nothing that had been written before. A tremor ran through her body. She clasped her hands tightly in her lap.

Passion. Each note swelled with it, soared with it, wept with it. She could only stare, seeing the intensity in his eyes and the fluid grace of his fingers on the keys. The beauty of it ripped at her, digging deep into heart and into soul. How could it be that her feelings, her most intimate feelings could be put to music?

As the tempo built, her pulse beat thickly. She couldn't have spoken, could hardly breathe. Then the music flowed into something sad and strong. And alive. She closed her eyes as it crashed over her, unaware that tears had began to spill onto her cheeks.

When it ended, she sat very still.

"I don't have to ask you what you think," Spence murmured. "I can see it."

She only shook her head. She didn't have the words to tell him. There were no words. "When?"

"Over the last few days." The emotion the song had wrenched from him came flooding back. Rising, he went to her to take her hands and pulled her to her feet. As their fingers met, she could feel the intensity he'd poured into his music. "It came back." He pressed her hands to his lips. "At first it was terrifying. I could hear it in my head, the way I used to. It's like being plugged into heaven, Natasha. I can't explain it."

"No. You don't have to. I heard it."

She understood, he thought. Somehow he'd been sure she would. "I thought it was just wishful thinking, or that when I sat down there…" He looked back at the piano. "That it would vanish. But it didn't. It flowed. God, it's like being given back your hands or your eyes."

"It was always there." She lifted her hands to his face. "It was just resting."

"No, *you* brought it back. I told you once, my life had changed when I met you. I didn't know how much. It's for you, Natasha."

"No, it's for you. Very much for you." Wrapping her arms around him, she pressed her mouth to his. "It's just the beginning."

"Yes." He dragged his hands through her hair so that her face was tilted to his. "It is." His grip only tightened when she would have pulled away. "If you heard that, if you understood that, you know what I mean. And you know what I feel."

"Spence, it would be wrong for you to say anything now. Your emotions are all on the surface. What you feel about your music is easily confused with other things."

"That's nonsense. You don't want to hear me tell you that I love you."

"No." Panic skidded up her spine. "No, I don't. If you care for me at all, you won't."

"It's a hell of a position you put me in."

"I'm sorry. I want you to be happy. As long as things go on as they are—"

"And how long can things go on as they are?"

"I don't know. I can't give you back the words you want to give to me. Even feeling them, I can't." Her eyes lifted again to meet his. "I wish I could."

"Am I still competing against someone else?"

"No." Quickly she reached out to take his hands. "No. What I felt for—before," she corrected, "was a fantasy. A girl's make-believe. This is real. I'm just not strong enough to hold onto it."

Or too strong to give in to it, he thought. And it was hurting her. Perhaps because he wanted her so badly, his impatience was adding pressure that would break them apart instead of bring them together.

"Then I won't tell you that I love you." He kissed her brow. "And that I need you in my life." He kissed her lips, lightly. "Not yet." His fingers curled tightly over hers. "But there'll come a time, Natasha, when I will tell you. When you'll listen. When you'll answer me."

"You make it sound like a threat."

"No, it's one of those promises you don't want to hear." He kissed her on both cheeks, casually enough to confuse her. "I have to get back."

"Yes, so do I." She picked up her gloves, only to run them restlessly through her hands. "Spence, it meant a very great deal that you wanted to share this with me. I know what it's like to lose part of yourself. I'm very proud of you and for you. And I'm glad that you celebrated this with me.''

"Come back, have dinner with me. I haven't begun to celebrate.''

She smiled again. "I'd like that.''

She didn't often buy champagne, but it seemed appropriate. Even necessary. A bottle of wine was little enough to offer for what he had given her that morning. The music itself was a gift she would always treasure. With it, he'd given her time and a glimpse of hope.

Perhaps he did love her. If she believed it, she could allow herself time to let it strengthen. If she believed it, she would have to tell him everything. It was that, even more than her own fears that still held her back.

She needed time for that, as he did.

But tonight was for celebrating.

She knocked and tried a sober smile for Vera. "Good evening.''

"Miss.'' With this noncommital greeting, Vera opened the door wider. She kept her thoughts on Natasha very much to herself. True, the woman made the *señor* happy and seemed very fond of Freddie. But after more than three years of having them to herself, Vera was very cautious of sharing. "Dr. Kimball is in the music room with Freddie.''

"Thank you. I brought some wine.''

"I will take it.''

With only a little sigh, Natasha watched Vera walk

away. The more the housekeeper held firm, the more determined Natasha was to win her over.

She heard Freddie's giggles as she approached the music room. And others, she realized. When she reached the door, she spotted Freddie and JoBeth clinging to each other and squealing. And why not? Natasha thought with a grin. Spence was wearing a ridiculous helmet and aiming a cardboard spool like a weapon.

"Stowaways aboard my ship are fed to the Beta Monster," he warned them. "He has six-foot teeth and bad breath."

"No!" Eyes wide, heart pounding with delight and dread, Freddie scrambled for cover. "Not the Beta Monster."

"He likes little girls best." With an evil laugh, he scooped the squealing JoBeth under one arm. "He swallows little boys whole, but he chews and chews and chews when I feed him girls."

"That's gross." JoBeth covered her mouth with both hands.

"You bet." So saying, Spence made a dive and came up with a squirming Freddie. "Say your prayers, you're about to be the main course." Then with a muffled "Oomph," he tumbled onto the couch with both of them.

"We vanquished you!" Freddie announced, climbing over him. "The Wonder Sisters vanquished you."

"This time, but next time it's the Beta Monster." As he blew the hair out of his eyes, he spotted Natasha in the doorway. "Hi." She thought his smile was adorably sheepish. "I'm a space pirate."

"Oh. Well, that explains it." Before she could step

into the room, both girls deserted the space pirate to launch themselves at her.

"We always beat him," Freddie told her. "Always, always."

"I'm glad to hear it. I wouldn't want anyone I know to be eaten by the Beta Monster."

"He just made it up," JoBeth said wisely. "Dr. Kimball makes things up real good."

"Yes, I know."

"JoBeth's going to stay for dinner, too. You're going to be Daddy's guest and she's going to be mine. You get to have seconds first."

"That's very polite." She bent to kiss Freddie's cheeks, then JoBeth's. "How is your mama?"

"She's going to have a baby." JoBeth screwed up her face and shrugged her shoulders.

"I heard." Natasha smoothed JoBeth's hair. "Are you taking care of her?"

"She doesn't get sick in the mornings anymore, but Daddy says she'll be fat soon."

Miserably envious, Freddie shifted from one foot to the other. "Let's go up to my room," she told JoBeth. "We can play with the kittens."

"You will wash your hands and faces," Vera told them as she came in with the ice bucket and glasses. "Then you will come down to dinner, walking like ladies, not running like elephants." She nodded to Spence. "Miss Stanislaski brought champagne."

"Thank you, Vera." Belatedly he remembered to remove his helmet.

"Dinner in fifteen minutes," she stated, then went out.

"Now she knows I have designs on you," Natasha

muttered. "And is certain I'm after your great wealth."

With a laugh, he pried the cork free. "That's all right, I know you're only after my body." Wine frothed to the lip of the glasses, then receded.

"I like it very much. Your body." With a smile she accepted the flute of champagne.

"Then maybe you'd like to enjoy it later." He touched the rim of his glass to hers. "Freddie twisted my arm and got me to agree to a sleep-over at the Rileys'. So I don't feel left out, maybe I can stay with you tonight. All night."

Natasha took her first sip of wine, letting the taste explode on her tongue. "Yes," she said, and smiled at him.

Chapter Nine

Natasha watched the shadows dancing from the lights the candles tossed around the room. Soothing, they played over the curtains, the top rung of the old ladder-back chair in the corner, over the coxcomb she had impulsively slipped into an empty milk bottle and set on her dresser. Her room, she thought. It had always been very much hers. Until...

With a half sigh she let her hand rest on Spence's heart.

It was no longer quiet; the wind had risen to toss a late, cold rain against the panes. Outside it was a chilled, gusty night that promised a chilled, frosty morning. Winter often came early to the little town snuggled in the foothills of the Blue Ridge. But she was warm, beautifully warm, in Spence's arms.

The silence between them was easy, as the loving

had been. Curled close, they lay still, content to let the hours pass, one lazy second at a time. Each of them quietly celebrated the knowledge that in the morning they wouldn't wake alone. His hand skimmed over her thigh, her hip, until it linked with hers.

There was music playing inside her head—the song he had given her that morning. She knew she would remember each note, each chord, for the rest of her life. And it was only the beginning for him, or a new beginning. The idea of that delighted her. In the years to come she would hear his music and remember the time they had had together. On hearing it she would celebrate again, even if his music took him away.

Still, she had to ask.

"Will you go back to New York?"

He brushed his lips through her hair. "Why?"

"You're composing again." She could imagine him there, in evening dress, attending the opening of his own symphony.

"I don't need to be in New York to compose. And if I did, there are more reasons to stay here."

"Freddie."

"Yes, there's Freddie. And there's you."

Her restless movement rustled the sheets. She could see him after the symphony at some small intimate party, the Rainbow Room perhaps, or a private club. He would be dancing with a beautiful woman.

"The New York you lived in is different from mine."

"I imagine." He wondered why that should matter to her. "Do you ever think of going back?"

"To live, no. But to visit." It was silly, she

thought, to be nervous about asking such a simple thing. "My mother called me today."

"Is everything all right?"

"Yes. She only called to remind me about Thanksgiving. I'd almost forgotten. Every year we have a big dinner and eat too much. Do you go home for the holiday?"

"I am home."

"I mean to your family." She shifted to watch his face.

"I only have Freddie. And Nina," he added. "She always goes out to the Waldorf."

"Your parents. I've never asked you if you still have them, or where they live."

"They're in Cannes." Or was it Monte Carlo? It occurred to him suddenly that he didn't know for certain. The ties there were loose, comfortably so for everyone involved.

"Won't they come back for the holidays?"

"They never come to New York in the winter."

"Oh." Try as she might, she couldn't picture the holidays without family.

"We never ate at home on Thanksgiving. We always went out, were usually traveling." His memories of his childhood were more of places than people, more of music than words. "When I was married to Angela, we usually met friends at a restaurant and went to the theater."

"But—" She caught herself and fell silent.

"But what?"

"Once you had Freddie."

"Nothing changed." He shifted onto his back to stare at the ceiling. He'd wanted to tell her about his marriage, about himself—the man he had been—but had put it off. For too long, he reflected. How could he expect to build, when he had yet to clear away the emotional rubble of his past? "I've never explained to you about Angela."

"It's not necessary." She took his hand again. She'd wanted to invite him to a meal, not dredge up old ghosts.

"It is for me." Sitting up, he reached for the bottle of champagne they had brought back with them. Filling both glasses, he handed her one.

"I don't need explanations, Spence."

"But you'll listen?"

"Yes, if it's important to you."

He took a moment to gather his thoughts. "I was twenty-five when I met her. On top of the world as far as my music went, and to be honest, at twenty-five, very little else mattered to me. I had spent my life traveling, doing exactly what I pleased and being successful in what was most important to me. I don't believe anyone had ever told me, 'No, you can't have that. No, you can't do that.' When I saw her, I wanted her."

He paused to sip, to look back. Beside him Natasha stared into her glass, watching bubbles rise. "And she wanted you."

"In her way. The pity was that her attraction for me was as shallow as mine for her. And in the end just as destructive. I loved beautiful things." With a half laugh he tilted his glass again. "And I was used to having them. She was exquisite, like a delicate porcelain doll. We moved in the same circles, attended the same parties, preferred the same literature and music.''

Natasha shifted her glass from one hand to the other, wishing his words didn't make her feel so miserable. ''It's important to have things in common.''

''Oh, we had plenty in common. She was as spoiled and as pampered as I, as self-absorbed and as ambitious. I don't think we shared any particularly admirable qualities.''

''You're too hard on yourself.''

''You didn't know me then.'' He found himself profoundly grateful for that. ''I was a very rich young man who took everything I had for granted, because I had always had it. Things change,'' he murmured.

''Only people who are born with money can consider it a disadvantage.''

He glanced over to see her sitting cross-legged, the glass cupped in both hands. Her eyes were solemn and direct, and made him smile at himself. ''Yes, you're right. I wonder what might have happened if I had met you when I was twenty-five.'' He touched her hair, but didn't dwell on the point. ''In any case, Angela and I were married within a year and bored with each other only months after the ink had dried on the marriage certificate.''

''Why?''

''Because at that time we were so much alike. When it started to fall apart, I wanted badly to fix it. I'd never failed at anything. The worst of it was, I wanted the marriage to work more for my own ego than because of my feelings for her. I was in love with the image of her and the image we made together.''

"Yes." She thought of herself and her feelings for Anthony. "I understand."

"Do you?" The question was only a murmur. "It took me years to understand it. In any case, once I did, there were other considerations."

"Freddie," Natasha said again.

"Yes, Freddie. Though we still lived together and went through the motions of marriage, Angela and I had drifted apart. But in public and in private we were...civilized. I can't tell you how demeaning and destructive a civilized marriage can be. It's a cheat, Natasha, to both parties. And we were equally to blame. Then one day she came home furious, livid. I remember how she stalked over to the bar, tossing her mink aside so that it fell on the floor. She poured a drink, drank it down, then threw the glass against the wall. And told me she was pregnant."

Her throat dry, Natasha drank. "How did you feel?"

"Stunned. Rocked. We'd never planned on having children. We were much too much children, spoiled children ourselves. Angela had had a little more time to think it all through and had her answer. She wanted to go to Europe to a private clinic and have an abortion."

Something tightened inside Natasha. "Is that what you wanted?"

He wished, how he wished he could have answered unequivocally no. "At first I didn't know. My marriage was falling apart, I'd never given a thought to having children. It seemed sensible. And then, I'm not sure why, but I was furious. I guess it was because it was the easy way again, the easy way out for both of us. She wanted me to snap my fingers and get rid of this…inconvenience.''

Natasha stared down at her own balled fist. His words were hitting much too close to home. ''What did you do?''

''I made a bargain with her. She would have the baby, and we would give the marriage another shot. She would have the abortion and I would divorce her, and make certain that she didn't get what she considered her share of the Kimball money.''

''Because you wanted the child.''

''No.'' It was a painful admission, one that still cost him. ''Because I wanted my life to run the way I'd imagined it would. I knew if she had an abortion, we would never put the pieces back. I thought perhaps if we shared this, we'd pull it all together again.''

Natasha remained silent for a moment, absorbing his words and seeing them reflected in her own memories. ''People sometimes think a baby will fix what's broken.''

''And it doesn't,'' he finished. ''Nor should it have to. By the time Freddie was born, I was already losing my grip on my music. I couldn't write. Angela had delivered Freddie, then passed her over to Vera, as though she were no more than a litter of kittens. I was little better.''

''No.'' She reached out to take his wrist. ''I've seen you with her. I know how you love her.''

''Now. What you said to me that night on the steps of the college, about not deserving her. It hurt because it was true.'' He saw Natasha shake her head but went on. ''I'd made a bargain with Angela, and for more than a year I kept it. I barely saw the child, because

I was so busy escorting Angela to the ballet or the theater. I'd stopped working completely. I did nothing. I never fed her or bathed her or cuddled her at night. Sometimes I'd hear her crying in the other room and wonder—what is that noise? Then I'd remember.''

He picked up the bottle to top off his glass. ''Sometime before Freddie was two I stepped back and looked at what I'd done with my life. And what I hadn't done. It made me sick. I had a child. It took more than a year for it to sink in. I had no marriage, no wife, no music, but I had a child. I decided I had an obligation, a responsibility, and it was time to pull myself up and deal with it. That's how I thought of Freddie at first, when I finally began to think of her. An obligation.'' He drank again, then shook his head. ''That was little better than ignoring her. Finally I looked, really looked at that beautiful little girl and fell in love. I picked her up out of her crib, scared to death, and just held her. She screamed for Vera.''

He laughed at that, then stared once more into his wine. ''It took months before she was comfortable around me. By that time I'd asked Angela for a divorce. She'd snapped up my offer without a blink. When I told her I was keeping the child, she wished me luck and walked out. She never came back to see Freddie, not once in all the months the lawyers were battling over a settlement. Then I heard that she'd been killed. A boating accident in the Mediterranean. Sometimes I'm afraid Freddie remembers what her mother was like. More, I'm afraid she'll remember what I was like.''

Natasha remembered how Freddie had spoken of

her mother when they had rocked. Setting aside her glass, she took Spence's face in her hand. "Children forgive," she told him. "Forgiveness is easy when you're loved. It's harder, so much harder to forgive yourself. But you must."

"I think I've begun to."

Natasha took his glass and set it aside. "Let me love you," she said simply, and enfolded him.

It was different now that passion had mellowed. Slower, smoother, richer. As they knelt on the bed, their mouths met dreamily—a long, lazy exploration of tastes that had become hauntingly familiar. She wanted to show him what he meant to her, and that what they had together, tonight, was worlds apart from what had been. She wanted to comfort, excite and cleanse.

A sigh, then a murmur, then a low, liquid moan. The sounds were followed by a light, breezy touch. Fingertips trailing on flesh. She knew his body now as well as her own, every angle, every plane, every vulnerability. When his breath caught on a tremble, her laughter came quietly. Watching him in the shifting candlelight, she brushed kisses at his temple, his cheek, the corner of his mouth, his throat. There a pulse beat for her, heavy and fast.

She was as erotic as any fantasy, her body swaying first to, then away from his. Her eyes stayed on him, glowing, aware, and her hair fell in a torrent of dark silk over her naked shoulders.

When he touched her, skimming his hands up and over, her head fell back. But there was nothing of submission in the gesture. It was a demand. Pleasure me.

On a groan he lowered his mouth to her throat and felt the need punch like a fist through his gut. His open mouth growing greedy, he trailed down her, pausing to linger at the firm swell of her breast. He could feel her heart, almost taste it, as its beat grew fast and hard against his lips. Her hands came to his hair, gripping tight while she arched like a bow.

Before he could think he reached for her and sent her spiraling over the first crest.

Breathless, shuddering, she clung, managing only a confused murmur as he laid her back on the bed. She struggled for inner balance, but he was already destroying will and mind and control.

This was seduction. She hadn't asked for it, hadn't wanted it. Now she welcomed it. She couldn't move, couldn't object. Helpless, drowning in her own pleasure, she let him take her where he willed. His mouth roamed freely over her damp skin. His hands played her as skillfully as they might a fine-tuned instrument. Her muscles went lax.

Her breath began to rush through her lips. She heard music. Symphonies, cantatas, preludes. Weakness became strength and she reached for him, wanting only to feel his body fit against her own.

Slowly, tormentingly, he slid up her, leaving trails of heat and ice, of pleasure and pain. His own body throbbed as she moved under him. He found her mouth, diving deep, holding back even when her fingers dug into his hips.

Again and again he brought them both shivering to the edge, only to retreat, prolonging dozens of smaller pleasures. Her throat was a long white column he could feast on as she rose to him. Her arms wrapped themselves fast around him like taut silk. Her breath rushed along his cheek, then into his mouth, where it formed his own name like a prayer against his lips.

When he slipped into her, even pleasure was shattered.

Natasha awoke to the scent of coffee and soap, and the enjoyable sensation of having her neck nuzzled.

"If you don't wake up," Spence murmured into her ear, "I'm going to have to crawl back into bed with you."

"All right," she said on a sigh and snuggled closer.

Spence took a long, reluctant look at her shoulders, which the shifting sheets had bared. "It's tempting, but I should be home in an hour."

"Why?" Her eyes still closed, she reached out. "It's early."

"It's nearly nine."

"Nine? In the morning?" Her eyes flew open. She shot up in bed, and he wisely moved the cup of coffee out of harm's way. "How can it be nine?"

"It comes after eight."

"But I never sleep so late." She pushed back her hair with both hands, then managed to focus. "You're dressed."

"Unfortunately," he agreed, even more reluctantly when the sheets pooled around her waist. "Freddie's due home at ten. I had a shower." Reaching out, he began to toy with her hair. "I was going to wake you, see if you wanted to join me, but you looked so terrific sleeping I didn't have the heart." He leaned over to nip at her bottom lip. "I've never watched you sleep before."

The very idea of it had the blood rushing warm under her skin. "You should have gotten me up."

"Yes." With a half smile he offered her the coffee. "I can see I made a mistake. Easy with the coffee," he warned. "It's really terrible. I've never made it before."

Eyeing him, she took a sip, then grimaced. "You really should have wakened me." But she valiantly took another sip, thinking how sweet it was of him to bring it to her. "Do you have time for breakfast? I'll make you some."

"I'd like that. I was going to grab a doughnut from the bakery down the street."

"I can't make pastries like Ye Old Sweet Shoppe, but I can fix you eggs." Laughing, she set the cup aside. "And coffee."

In ten minutes she was wrapped in a short red robe, frying thin slices of ham. He liked watching her like this, her hair tousled, eyes still heavy with sleep. She moved competently from stove to counter, like a woman who had grown up doing such chores as a matter of course.

Outside a thin November rain was falling from a pewter sky. He heard the muffled sound of footsteps from the apartment above, then the faint sound of music. Jazz from the neighbor's radio. And there was the sizzle of meat grilling, the hum of the baseboard heater under the window. Morning music, Spence thought.

"I could get used to this," he said, thinking aloud.

"To what?" Natasha popped two slices of bread into the toaster.

"To waking up with you, having breakfast with you."

Her hands fluttered once, as if her thoughts had suddenly taken a sharp turn. Then, very deliberately they began to work again. And she said nothing at all.

"That's the wrong thing to say again, isn't it?"

"It isn't right or wrong." Her movements brisk, she brought him a cup of coffee. She would have turned away once more, but he caught her wrist. When she forced herself to look at him, she saw that the expression in his eyes was very intense. "You don't want me to fall in love with you, Natasha, but neither one of us have a choice about it."

"There's always a choice," she said carefully. "It's sometimes hard to make the right one, or to know the right one."

"Then it's already been made. I am in love with you."

He saw the change in her face, a softening, a yielding, and something in her eyes, something deep and shadowed and incredibly beautiful. Then it was gone. "The eggs are going to burn."

His hand balled into a fist as she walked back to the stove. Slowly, carefully he flexed his fingers. "I said I love you, and you're worried about eggs burning."

"I'm a practical woman, Spence. I've had to be." But it was hard to think, very hard, when her mind and heart were dragging her in opposing directions. She fixed the plates with the care she might have given to a state dinner. Going over and over the words in her head, she set the plates on the table, then sat down across from him.

"We've only known each other a short time."

"Long enough."

She moistened her lips. What she heard in his voice was more hurt than anger. She wanted nothing less than to hurt him. "There are things about me you don't know. Things I'm not ready to tell you."

"They don't matter."

"They do." She took a deep breath. "We have something. It would be ridiculous to try to deny it. But love—there is no bigger word in the world. If we share that word, things will change."

"Yes."

"I can't let them. From the beginning I told you there could be no promises, no plans. I don't want to move my life beyond what I have now."

"Is it because I have a child?"

"Yes, and no." For the first time since he'd met her, nerves showed in the way she linked and unlinked her fingers. "I would love Freddie even if I hated you. For herself. Because I care for you, I only love her more. But for you and me to take what we have and make something more from this would change even that. I'm not ready to take on the responsibilities of a child." Under the table she pressed her hand hard against her stomach. "But with or without Freddie, I don't want to take the next step with you. I'm sorry, and I understand if you don't want to see me again."

Torn between frustration and fury, he rose to pace to the window. The rain was still falling thinly, coldly upon the dying flowers outside. She was leaving something out, something big and vital. She didn't trust him yet, Spence realized. After everything they'd shared, she didn't yet trust him. Not enough.

"You know I can't stop seeing you, any more than I can stop loving you."

You could stop being in love, she thought, but found herself afraid to tell him. It was selfish, hideously so, but she wanted him to love her. "Spence, three months ago I didn't even know you."

"So I'm rushing things."

She moved her shoulder and began to poke at her eggs.

He studied her from behind, the way she held herself, how her fingers moved restlessly from her fork to her cup, then back again. He wasn't rushing a damn thing, and they both knew it. She was afraid. He leaned against the window, thinking it through. Some jerk had broken her heart, and she was afraid to have it broken again.

All right, he thought. He could get around that. A little time and the most subtle kind of pressure. He would get around it, he promised himself. For the first part of his life, he'd thought nothing would ever be as important to him as his music. In the last few years he'd learned differently. A child was infinitely more important, more precious and more beautiful. Now he'd been taught in a matter of weeks that a woman could be as important, in a different way, but just as important.

Freddie had waited for him, bless her. He would wait for Natasha.

"Want to go to a matinee?"

She'd been braced for anger, so only looked blankly over her shoulder. "What?"

"I said would you like to go to a matinee? The movies." Casually he walked back to the table to join her. "I promised Freddie I'd take her to the movies this afternoon."

"I—yes." A cautious smile bloomed. "I'd like to go with you. You're not angry with me?"

"Yes, I am." But he returned her smile as he began to eat. "I figured if you came along, you'd buy the popcorn."

"Okay."

"The jumbo size."

"Ah, now I begin to see the strategy. You make me feel guilty, so I spend all my money."

"That's right, and when you're broke, you'll have to marry me. Great eggs," he added when her mouth dropped open. "You should eat yours before they get cold."

"Yes." She cleared her throat. "Since you've offered me an invitation, I have one for you. I was going to mention it last night, but you kept distracting me."

"I remember." He rubbed his foot over hers. "You're easily distracted, Natasha."

"Perhaps. It was about my mother's phone call and Thanksgiving. She asked me if I wanted to bring someone along." She frowned at her eggs. "I imagine you have plans."

His smile was slow and satisfied. Perhaps the wait wouldn't be as long as he'd thought. "Are you asking me to Thanksgiving dinner at your mother's?"

"My mother asked," Natasha said precisely. "She

always makes too much food, and she and Papa enjoy company. When it came up, I thought about you and Freddie.''

"I'm glad to know that you think about us."

"It's nothing," she said, annoyed with herself for stringing out what should have been a simple invitation. "I always take the train up on Wednesday after work and come back Friday evening. Since there is no school, it occurred to me that you both might enjoy the trip."

"Do we get borscht?"

The corners of her lips curved. "I could ask." She pushed her plate aside when she saw the gleam in his eyes. He wasn't laughing, she thought, as much as planning. "I don't want you to get the wrong idea. It's simply an invitation from friend to friend."

"Right."

She frowned at him. "I think Freddie would enjoy a big family meal."

"Right again."

His easy agreement had her blowing out a frustrated breath. "Just because it's at my parents' home doesn't mean I'm taking you there for..." She waved her hand as she searched for an appropriate phrase. "For approval, or to show you off."

"You mean your father won't take me into the den and ask me my intentions?"

"We don't have a den," she muttered. "And no. I'm a grown woman." Because Spence was grinning, she lifted a brow. "He will, perhaps, study you discreetly."

"I'll be on my best behavior."

"Then you'll come?"

He sat back, sipping his coffee and smiling to himself. "I wouldn't miss it."

Chapter Ten

Freddie sat in the back seat with a blanket tucked up to her chin and clutched her Raggedy Ann. Because she wanted to drift with her own daydreams she pretended to sleep, and pretended so well that she actually dozed from time to time. It was a long drive from West Virginia to New York, but she was much too excited to be bored.

There was soft music on the car radio. She was enough of her father's daughter to recognize Mozart, and child enough to wish there were words to sing along to. Vera had already been dropped off at her sister's in Manhattan, where the housekeeper would holiday until Sunday. Now Spence was directing the big, quiet car through the traffic toward Brooklyn.

Freddie was only a little disappointed that they hadn't taken the train, but liked snuggling up and listening to her father and Natasha talk. She didn't pay much attention to what they said. Their voices were enough.

She was almost sick with excitement at the idea of meeting Natasha's family and sharing a big turkey dinner. Though she didn't like turkey very much, Natasha had told her that there would be plenty of cranberry sauce and succotash. Freddie had never eaten succotash, but the name was so funny, she knew it would be good. Even if it wasn't, even if it was disgusting, she was determined to be polite and clean her plate. JoBeth had told her that her grandmother got upset if JoBeth didn't eat all her vegetables, so Freddie wasn't taking any chances.

Lights flickered over her closed lids. Her lips curved a little as she heard Natasha's laugh merging with her father's. In her imaginings they were already a family. Instead of Raggedy Ann, Freddie was carefully tending to her baby sister as they all drove through the night to her grandparents' house. It was just like the song, she thought, but she didn't know if they were going over any rivers. And she didn't think they would pass through the woods.

Her baby sister's name was Katie, and she had black, curly hair like Natasha. Whenever Katie cried, Freddie was the only one who could make her happy again. Katie slept in a white crib in Freddie's room, and Freddie always made sure she was covered with a pink blanket. Babies caught colds, Freddie knew. When they did, you had to give them medicine out of a little dropper. They couldn't blow their noses themselves. Everyone said that Katie took her medicine best from Freddie.

Delighted with herself, Freddie snuggled the doll closer. "We're going to Grandmother's," she whispered, and began to build a whole new fantasy around the visit.

The trouble was, Freddie wasn't sure that the people she was pretending were her grandparents would like her. Not everyone liked kids, she thought. Maybe they wished she wasn't coming to visit. When she got there, they would want her to sit in a chair with her hands folded on her lap. That was the way Aunt Nina told her young ladies sat. Freddie hated being a young lady. But she would have to sit for just hours, not interrupting, not talking too loud, and never, never running in the house.

They would get mad and frown at her if she spilled something on the floor. Maybe they would yell. She'd heard JoBeth's father yell, especially when JoBeth's big brother, who was in third grade already and was supposed to know better, had taken one of his father's golf clubs to hit at rocks in the backyard. One of the rocks had crashed right through the kitchen window.

Maybe she would break a window. Then Natasha wouldn't marry her daddy and come to stay with them. She wouldn't have a mother or a baby sister, and Daddy would stop playing his music at night again.

Almost paralyzed by her thoughts, Freddie shrank against the seat as the car slowed.

"Yes, turn right here." At the sight of her old neighborhood, Natasha's spirits rose even higher. "It's about halfway down, on the left. You might be able to find a space...yes, there." She spotted a parking space behind her father's ancient pickup. Obviously the Stanislaskis had put out the word that their daughter and friends were coming, and the neighbors had cooperated.

It was like that here, she thought. The Poffenbergers had lived on one side, the Andersons on the other for as long as Natasha could remember. One family would bring food when there was illness, another would mind a child after school. Joys and sorrows were shared. And gossip abounded.

Mikhail had dated the pretty Anderson girl, then had ended up as best man at her wedding, when she'd married one of his friends. Natasha's parents had stood as godparents for one of the Poffenberger babies. Perhaps that was why, when Natasha had found she'd needed a new place and a new start, she had picked a town that had reminded her of home. Not in looks, but in ties.

"What are you thinking?" Spence asked her.

"Just remembering." She turned her head to smile at him. "It's good to be back." She stepped onto the curb, shivered once in the frosty air, then opened the back door for Freddie while Spence popped the trunk. "Freddie, are you asleep?"

Freddie kept herself balled tight, but squeezed her eyes open. "No."

"We're here. It's time to get out."

Freddie swallowed, clutching the doll to her chest. "What if they don't like me?"

"What's this?" Crouching, Natasha brushed the hair from Freddie's cheeks. "Have you been dreaming?"

"They might not like me and wish I wasn't here.

They might think I'm a pest. Lots of people think kids're pests.''

"Lots of people are stupid then," Natasha said briskly, buttoning up Freddie's coat.

"Maybe. But they might not like me, anyway."

"What if you don't like them?"

That was something that hadn't occurred to her. Mulling it over, Freddie wiped her nose with the back of her hand before Natasha could come up with a tissue. "Are they nice?"

"I think so. After you meet them, you can decide. Okay?"

"Okay."

"Ladies, maybe you could pick another time to have a conference." Spence stood a few feet away, loaded down with luggage. "What was that all about?" he asked when they joined him on the sidewalk.

"Girl talk," Natasha answered with a wink that made Freddie giggle.

"Great." He started up the worn concrete steps behind Natasha. "Nothing I like better than to stand in the brisk wind holding three hundred pounds of luggage. What did you pack in here? Bricks?"

"Only a few, along with some essentials." Delighted with him, she turned and kissed his cheek—just as Nadia opened the door.

"Well." Pleased, Nadia folded her arms across her chest. "I told Papa you would come before Johnny Carson was over."

"Mama." Natasha rushed up the final steps to be enfolded in Nadia's arms. There was the scent she always remembered. Talc and nutmeg. And, as always, there was the strong, sturdy feel of her mother's body. Nadia's dark and sultry looks were just as strong, more so, perhaps, with the lines etched by worry, laughter and time.

Nadia murmured an endearment, then drew Natasha back to kiss her cheeks. She could see herself as she had been twenty years before. "Come on, you leave our guests standing in the cold."

Natasha's father bounded into the hall to pluck her off the floor and toss her into the air. He wasn't a tall man, but the arms beneath his work shirt were thick as cinder blocks from his years in the construction trade. He gave a robust laugh as he kissed her.

"No manners," Nadia declared as she shut the door. "Yuri, Natasha brings guests."

"Hello." Yuri thrust out a callused hand and pumped Spence's. "Welcome."

"This is Spence and Freddie Kimball." As she made introductions, Natasha noticed Freddie slip her hand into her father's.

"We are happy to meet you." Because warmth was her way, Nadia greeted them both with kisses. "I will take your coats, and you please come in and sit. You will be tired."

"We appreciate you having us," Spence began. Then, sensing that Freddie was nervous, he picked her up and carried her into the living room.

It was small, the wallpaper old and the furniture worn. But there were lace doilies on the arms of the chairs, the woodwork gleamed in the yellow lamplight from vigorous polishing, and here and there were exquisitely worked pillows. Framed family pictures fought for space among the potted plants and knicknacks.

A husky wheeze had Spence glancing down. There was an old gray dog in the corner. His tail began to thump when he saw Natasha. With obvious effort he rose and waddled to her.

"Sasha." She crouched to bury her face in the dog's fur. She laughed as he sat down again and leaned against her. "Sasha is a very old man," she explained to Freddie. "He likes best now to sleep and eat."

"And drink vodka," Yuri put in. "We will all have some. Except you," he added and flicked a finger down Freddie's nose. "You would have some champagne, huh?"

Freddie giggled, then bit her lip. Natasha's father didn't look exactly like she'd imagined a grandfather. He didn't have snow-white hair and a big belly. Instead his hair was black and white at the same time, and he had no belly at all. He talked funny, with a deep, rumbly kind of voice. But he smelled good, like cherries. And his smile was nice.

"What's vodka?"

"Russian tradition," Yuri answered her. "A drink we make from grain."

Freddie wrinkled her nose. "That sounds yucky," she said, then immediately bit her lip again. But at Yuri's burst of laughter she managed a shy smile.

"Natasha will tell you that her papa always teases little girls." Nadia poked an elbow into Yuri's ribs. "It's because he is really just little boy at heart. You would like hot chocolate?"

Freddie was torn between the comfort of her

father's hand and one of her favorite treats. And Nadia was smiling at her, not with that goofy look grown-ups sometimes put on when they had to talk to kids. It was a warm smile, just like Natasha's.

"Yes, ma'am."

Nadia gave a nod of approval at the child's manners. "Maybe you would like to come with me. I show you how to make it with big, fat marshmallows."

Forgetting shyness, Freddie took her hand from Spence's and put it into Nadia's. "I have two cats," she told Nadia proudly as they walked into the kitchen. "And I had chicken pox on my birthday."

"Sit, sit," Yuri ordered, gesturing toward the couch. "We have a drink."

"Where are Alex and Rachel?" With a contented sigh, Natasha sank into the worn cushions.

"Alex takes his new girlfriend to the movies. Very pretty," Yuri said, rolling his bright, brown eyes. "Rachel is at lecture. Big-time lawyer from Washington, D.C. comes to college."

"And how is Mikhail?"

"Very busy. They remodel apartment in Soho." He passed out glasses, tapping each before he drank. "So," he said to Spence as he settled in his favorite chair, "you teach music."

"Yes. Natasha's one of my best students in Music History."

"Smart girl, my Natasha." He settled back in his chair and studied Spence. But not, as Natasha had hoped, discreetly. "You are good friends."

"Yes," Natasha put in, uneasy about the gleam in her father's eyes. "We are. Spence just moved into town this summer. He and Freddie used to live in New York.''

"So. This is interesting. Like fate.''

"I like to think so,'' Spence agreed, enjoying himself. "It was especially fortunate that I have a little girl and Natasha owns a very tempting toy store. Added to that, she signed up for one of my classes. It made it difficult for her to avoid me when she was being stubborn.''

"She is stubborn,'' Yuri agreed sadly. "Her mother is stubborn. Me, I am very agreeable.''

Natasha gave a quick snort.

"Stubborn and disrespectful women run in my family.'' Yuri took another healthy drink. "It is my curse.''

"Perhaps one day I'll be fortunate enough to say the same.'' Spence smiled over the rim of his glass. "When I convince Natasha to marry me.''

Natasha sprang up, ignoring her father's grin. "Since the vodka's gone to your head so quickly, I'll see if Mama has any extra hot chocolate.''

Yuri pushed himself out of his chair to reach for the bottle as Natasha disappeared. "We'll leave the chocolate to the women.''

Natasha awoke at first light with Freddie curled in her arms. She was in the bed of her childhood, in a room where she and her sister had spent countless hours talking, laughing, arguing. The wallpaper was the same. Faded roses. Whenever her mother had threatened to paint it, both she and Rachel had objected. There was something comforting about waking up to the same walls from childhood through adolescence to adulthood.

Turning her head, she could see her sister's dark hair against the pillow of the next bed. The sheets and blankets were in tangles. Typical, Natasha thought with a smile. Rachel had more energy asleep than most people had fully awake. She had come in the night before after midnight, bursting with enthusiasm over the lecture she had attended, full of hugs and kisses and questions.

Natasha brushed a kiss over Freddie's hair, then carefully shifted her. The child snuggled into the pillow without making a sound. Quietly Natasha rose. She took a moment to steady herself when the floor tilted. Four hours' sleep, she decided, was bound to make anyone light-headed. Gathering her clothes, she went off to shower and dress.

Arriving downstairs, she caught the scent of coffee brewing. It didn't seem to appeal to her, but she followed it into the kitchen.

"Mama." Nadia was already at the counter, busily rolling out piecrusts. "It's too early to cook."

"On Thanksgiving it's never too early." She lifted her cheek for a kiss. "You want coffee?"

Natasha pressed a hand to her uneasy stomach. "No. I don't think so. I assume that bundle of blankets on the couch is Alex."

"He gets in very late." Nadia pursed her lips briefly in disapproval, then shrugged. "He's not a boy anymore."

"No. You'll just have to face it, Mama, you have grown children—and you raised them very well."

"Not so well that Alex learns to pick up his

socks.'' But she smiled, hoping her youngest son wouldn't deprive her of that last vestige of motherhood too soon.

"Did Papa and Spence stay up very late?"

"Papa likes talking to your friend. He's a nice man.'' Nadia laid a circle of dough on a pie plate, then took up another chunk to roll out. "Very handsome.''

"Yes,'' Natasha agreed, but cautiously.

"He has good job, is responsible, loves his daughter.''

"Yes,'' Natasha said again.

"Why don't you marry him when he wants you to?"

She'd figured on this. Biting back a sigh, Natasha leaned on the kitchen table. "There are a lot of nice, responsible and handsome men, Mama. Should I marry them all?''

"Not so many as you think.'' Smiling to herself, Nadia started on a third crust. "You don't love him?'' When Natasha didn't answer, Nadia's smile widened. "Ah.''

"Don't start. Spence and I have only known each other for a few months. There's a lot he doesn't know about me.''

"So tell him.''

"I don't seem to be able to.''

Nadia put down her rolling pin to cup her daughter's face in two floury hands. "He is not like the other one.''

"No, he's not. But—''

Impatient, Nadia shook her head. "Holding on to

something that's gone only makes a sickness inside. You have a good heart, Tash. Trust it."

"I want to." She wrapped her arms around her mother and held tight. "I do love him, Mama, but it still scares me. And it still hurts." On a long breath she drew back. "I want to borrow Papa's truck."

Nadia didn't ask where she was going. Didn't need to. "Yes. I can go with you."

Natasha only kissed her mother's cheek and shook her head.

She'd been gone an hour before Spence made his bleary-eyed way downstairs. He and the gray dog exchanged glances of sympathy. Yuri had been generous with the vodka the night before, to guests and pets. At the moment, Spence felt as though a chain gang were chipping rock in his head. Operating on automatic, he found the kitchen, following the scents of baking, and blissfully, coffee.

Nadia took one look, laughed broadly and gestured to the table. "Sit." She poured a cup of coffee, strong and black. "Drink. I fix you breakfast."

Like a dying man, Spence clutched the cup in both hands. "Thanks. I don't want to put you out."

Nadia merely waved a hand as she reached for a cast-iron skillet. "I know a man with a hangover. Yuri poured you too much vodka."

"No. I took care of that all on my own." He opened the aspirin bottle she set on the table. "Bless you, Mrs. Stanislaski."

"Nadia. You call me Nadia when you get drunk in my house."

"I don't remember feeling like this since college."

So saying he downed three aspirins. "I can't imagine why I thought it was fun at the time." He managed a weak smile. "Something smells wonderful."

"You will like my pies." She pushed fat sausages around in the skillet. "You met Alex last night."

"Yes." Spence didn't object when she filled his cup a second time. "That was cause enough for one more drink. You have a beautiful family, Nadia."

"They make me proud." She laughed as the sausage sizzled. "They make me worry. You know, you have daughter."

"Yes." He smiled at her, picturing what Natasha would look like in a quarter of a century.

"Natasha is the only one who moves far away. I worry most for her."

"She's very strong."

Nadia only nodded as she added eggs to the pan. "Are you patient, Spence?"

"I think so."

Nadia glanced over her shoulder. "Don't be too patient."

"Funny. Natasha once told me the same thing."

Pleased, Nadia popped bread into the toaster. "Smart girl."

The kitchen door swung open. Alex, dark, rumpled and heavy-eyed, grinned. "I smelled breakfast."

The first snow was falling, small, thin flakes that swirled in the wind and vanished before they hit the ground. There were some things, Natasha knew, that were beautiful and very precious, and here for only such a short time.

She stood alone, bundled against the cold she

didn't feel. Except inside. The light was pale gray, but not dreary, not with the tiny, dancing snowflakes. She hadn't brought flowers. She never did. They would look much too sad on such a tiny grave.

Lily. Closing her eyes, she let herself remember how it had felt to hold that small, delicate life in her arms. Her baby. *Milaya.* Her little girl. Those beautiful blue eyes, Natasha remembered, those exquisite miniature hands.

Like the flower she had been named for, Lily had been so lovely, and had lived such a brief, brief time. She could see Lily, small and red and wrinkled, her little hands fisted when the nurse had first laid her in Natasha's arms. She could feel even now that sweet ache that tugged when Lily had nursed at her breast. She remembered the feel of that soft, soft skin and the smell of powder and lotion, the comfort of rocking late at night with her own baby girl on her shoulder.

So quickly gone, Natasha thought. A few precious weeks. No amount of time, no amount of prayer would ever make her understand it. Accept, perhaps, but never understand.

"I love you, Lily. Always." She bent to press her palm against the cold grass. Rising again, she turned and walked away through the lightly dancing snow.

Where had she gone? There could be a dozen places, Spence assured himself. It was foolish to be worried. But he couldn't help it. Some instinct was at work here, heightened by the certainty that Natasha's family knew exactly where she was, but refused to say.

The house was already filled with noise, laughter,

and the smells of the celebrational meal to come. He tried to shake off the feeling that wherever Natasha was, she needed him.

There was so much she hadn't told him. That had become crystal clear when he saw the pictures in the living room. Natasha in tights and dance shoes, in ballet skirts and toe shoes. Natasha with her hair streaming behind her, caught at the apex of a grand jeté.

She'd been a dancer, quite obviously a professional, but had never mentioned it.

Why had she given it up? Why had she kept something that had been an important part of her life a secret from him?

Coming out of the kitchen, Rachel saw him with one of the photographs in his hand. She kept silent for a moment, studying him. Like her mother, she approved of what she saw. There was a strength here and a gentleness. Her sister needed and deserved both.

"It's a beautiful picture."

He turned. Rachel was taller than Natasha, more willowy. Her dark hair was cut short in a sleek cap around her face. Her eyes, more gold than brown, dominated. "How old was she?"

Rachel dipped her hands into the pockets of her trousers as she crossed the room. "Sixteen, I think. She was in the corps de ballet then. Very dedicated. I always envied Tash her grace. I was a klutz." She smiled and gently changed the subject. "Always taller and skinnier than the boys, knocking things over with my elbows. Where's Freddie?"

Spence set down the picture. Without saying it, Rachel had told him that if he had questions, they were for Natasha. "She's upstairs, watching the Macy's parade with Yuri."

"He never misses it. Nothing disappointed him more than when we grew too old to want to sit in his lap and watch the floats."

A laughing squeal from the second floor had them both turning toward the stairs. Feet clomped. A pink whirlwind in her jumpsuit, Freddie came dashing down to launch herself at Spence. "Daddy, Papa makes bear noises. *Big* bear noises."

"Did he rub his beard on your cheek?" Rachel wanted to know.

"It's scratchy." She giggled, then wriggled down to run upstairs once more, hoping he'd do it again.

"She's having the time of her life," Spence decided.

"So's Papa. How's your head?"

"Better, thanks." He heard the sound of the truck pulling up outside, and glanced toward the window.

"Mama needs my help." Rachel slipped back into the kitchen.

He was at the door waiting for her. Natasha looked very pale, very tired, but she smiled when she saw him. "Good morning." Because she needed him, she slipped her arms around his waist and held tight.

"Are you all right?"

"Yes." She was now, she realized, when he was holding her like this. Stronger, she pulled back. "I thought you might sleep late."

"No, I've been up awhile. Where have you been?"

She unwound her scarf. "There was something I needed to do." After peeling off her coat, she hung it in the narrow closet. "Where is everyone?"

"Your mother and Rachel are in the kitchen. The last time I looked, Alex was on the phone."

This time the smile came easily. "Sweet-talking a girl."

"Apparently. Freddie's up with your father, watching the parade."

"And putting him in heaven." She touched her fingertips to Spence's cheek. "Will you kiss me?"

There was some need here, he thought as he bent toward her. Some deep, private need she still refused to share. Her lips were cold when his met them, but they softened, then warmed. At last they curved.

"You're very good for me, Spence."

"I was hoping you'd catch on to that." He gave her bottom lip a playful nip. "Better?"

"Much. I'm glad you're here." She squeezed his hand. "How do you feel about some of Mama's hot chocolate?"

Before he could answer, Freddie came sprinting down the steps again, one shoelace trailing, to throw her arms around Natasha's waist. "You're back!"

"So I am." Natasha bent to kiss the top of Freddie's head. "What have you been up to?"

"I'm watching the parade with Papa. He can talk just like Donald Duck, and he lets me sit on his lap."

"I see." Leaning closer, Natasha took a sniff. There was the telltale fragrance of gumdrops lingering on Freddie's breath. "Does he still hog all the yellow ones?"

Freddie giggled, casting a quick, cautious look at her father. Spence had a much different view of gumdrops than Yuri. "It's okay. I like the red ones best."

"How many red ones?" Spence asked her.

Freddie lifted her shoulders and let them fall. It was, Spence noted with some amusement, almost a mirror image of Natasha's habitual gesture. "Not too many. Will you come up and watch with us?" She tugged at Natasha's hand. "It's almost time for Santa Claus."

"In a little while." Out of habit, Natasha crouched to tie Freddie's shoelace. "Tell Papa that I won't mention the gumdrops to Mama. If he saves me some."

"Okay." She dashed up the stairs.

"He's made quite an impression on her," Spence observed.

"Papa makes impressions on everyone." She started to rise, and felt the room spin. Before she could sink to the floor again, Spence had her arms.

"What is it?"

"Nothing." She pressed a hand to her head, waiting for the dizziness to pass. "I stood up too fast, that's all."

"You're pale. Come sit down." He had an arm hooked around her waist, but she shook her head.

"No, I'm fine, really. Just a little tired." Relieved that the room had steadied, she smiled at him. "Blame it on Rachel. She would have talked through the night if I hadn't fallen asleep on her in self-defense."

"Have you eaten anything?"

"I thought you were a doctor of music." She smiled again and patted his cheek. "Don't worry, the minute I go into the kitchen, Mama will start feeding me."

Just then the front door opened. Spence watched

Natasha's face light up. ''Mikhail!'' With a laugh, she threw herself into the arms of her brother.

He had the dark, blinding good looks that ran in the family. The tallest of the brood, he had to bend to gather Natasha close. His hair curled over his ears and collar. His coat was worn, his boots were scarred. His hands, as they stroked Natasha's hair, were wide-palmed and beautiful.

It took Spence only seconds to see that while Natasha loved all of her family deeply, there was a separate and special bond here.

''I've missed you.'' She drew back just far enough to kiss his cheeks, then hugged him close again. ''I've really missed you.''

''Then why don't you come more often?'' He pushed her away, wanting a good long look. He didn't care for the pallor in her cheeks, but since her hands were still cold, he realized she'd been out. And he knew where she'd spent that morning. He murmured something in Ukrainian, but she only shook her head and squeezed his hands tight. With a shrug very like her own, he put the subject aside.

''Mikhail, I want you to meet Spence.''

As he took off his coat, Mikhail turned to study Spence. Unlike Alex's friendly acceptance or Rachel's subtle measuring, this was an intense and prolonged stare that left Spence in no doubt that if Mikhail didn't approve, he wouldn't hesitate to say so.

''I know your work,'' he said at length. ''It's excellent.''

''Thank you.'' Spence met look for look. ''I can say the same about yours.'' When Mikhail lifted one dark brow, Spence continued. "I've seen the figures you carved for Natasha."

"Ah." A glimmer of a smile curved Mikhail's mouth. "My sister always was fond of fairy tales." There was a squeal from upstairs, followed by rumbling laughter.

"That's Freddie," Natasha explained. "Spence's daughter. She's making Papa's day."

Mikhail slipped a thumb through one belt loop. "You are a widower."

"That's right."

"And now you teach at college."

"Yes."

"Mikhail," Natasha interrupted. "Don't play big brother. I'm older than you."

"But I'm bigger." Then with a quick, flashing grin, he tossed an arm around her shoulder. "So what's to eat?"

Too much, Spence decided as the family gathered around the table late that afternoon. The huge turkey in the center of the hand-crocheted tablecloth was only the beginning. Faithful to her adopted country's holiday, Nadia had prepared a meal that was an American tradition from the chestnut dressing to the pumpkin pies.

Wide-eyed, Freddie gawked, staring at platter after platter. The room was full of noise as everyone talked over and around everyone else. The china was mismatched. Old Sasha lay sprawled under the table near her feet, hoping for a few unobtrusive handouts. She was sitting on a wobbly chair and the New York Yellow Pages. As far as she was concerned, it was the best day of her life.

Alex and Rachel began to argue over some childhood infraction. Mikhail joined in to tell them they were both wrong. When her opinion was sought, Natasha just laughed and shook her head, then turned to Spence and murmuring something into his ear that made him chuckle.

Nadia, her cheeks rosy with the pleasure of having her family together, slipped a hand into Yuri's as he lifted his glass.

"Enough," he said, and effectively silenced the table. "You can argue later about who let white mice loose in science lab. Now we toast. We are thankful for this food that Nadia and my girls have fixed for us. And more thankful for the friends and family who are here together to enjoy it. We give thanks, as we did on our first Thanksgiving in our country, that we are free."

"To freedom," Mikhail said as he lifted his glass.

"To freedom," Yuri agreed. His eyes misted and he looked around the table. "And to family."

Chapter Eleven

That evening, with Freddie dozing in his lap, Spence listened to Yuri tell stories of the old country. While the meal had been a noisy competition for conversation, this hour was one of quiet and content. Across the room Rachel and Alex played a trivia game. They argued often, but without heat.

In the corner, Natasha and Mikhail sat close, dark heads together. Spence could hear their murmurs and noted that one often reached to touch the other's hand, to touch a cheek. Nadia sat smiling, interrupting Yuri occasionally to correct or comment as she worked another pillow cover.

"Woman." Yuri pointed at his wife with the stem of his after-dinner pipe. "I remember like yesterday."

"You remember as you like to remember."

"*Tak.*" He stuck the pipe back into his mouth. "And what I remember makes better story."

When Freddie stirred, Spence shifted her. "I'd better put her to bed."

"I will do it." Nadia set her needlework aside and rose. "I would like to." Making soothing noises, she lifted Freddie. Sleepy and agreeable, Freddie snuggled into her neck.

"Will you rock me?"

"Yes." Touched, Nadia kissed her hair as she started toward the steps. "I will rock you in the chair where I rocked all my babies."

"And sing?"

"I will sing you a song my mother sang to me. You would like that?"

Freddie gave a yawn and a drowsy nod.

"You have a beautiful daughter." Like Spence, Yuri watched them turn up the steps. "You must bring her back often."

"I think I'll have a hard time keeping her away."

"She is always welcome, as you are." Yuri took a puff on his pipe. "Even if you don't marry my daughter."

That statement brought on ten seconds of humming silence until Alex and Rachel bent back over their game, smothering grins. Spence didn't bother to smother his own as Natasha rose.

"There isn't enough milk for the morning," she decided on the spot. "Spence, why don't you walk with me to get some?"

"Sure."

A few moments later they stepped outside, wrapped in coats and scarves. The air had a bite that Natasha welcomed. Overhead the sky was clear as black glass and icy with stars.

"He didn't mean to embarrass you," Spence began.

"Yes, he did."

Spence didn't bother to hold back the chuckle, and draped an arm over her shoulders. "I suppose he did. I like your family."

"So do I. Most of the time."

"You're lucky to have them. Watching Freddie here has made me realize how important family is. I don't suppose I've really tried to get closer to Nina or my parents."

"They're still family. Perhaps we're as close as we are, because when we came here we only had each other."

"It's true my family never crossed the mountains into Hungary in a wagon."

That made her laugh. "Rachel was always jealous that she hadn't been born yet. When she was little, she would get back by saying she was more American, because she'd been born in New York. Then not long ago, someone said to her that if she wanted to be a lawyer, she should think of changing or shortening her name." With a new laugh, Natasha looked up at him. "She became very insulted and very Ukrainian."

"It's a good name. You could always keep it professionally after you marry me."

"Don't start."

"Must be your father's influence." He glanced at the dark shop, where a Closed sign hung on the door. "The store's closed."

"I know." She turned into his arms. "I just wanted

to walk. Now that we're standing here in a dark doorway, alone, I can kiss you."

"Good point." Spence lowered his mouth to hers.

Natasha was annoyed with herself for dozing off and on during the drive home. She felt as though she'd spent a week mountain climbing, rather than less than forty-eight hours in her family home. By the time she shook herself awake for the last time, they were crossing the Maryland border into West Virginia.

"Already." She straightened in her seat and cast an apologetic glance at Spence. "I didn't help you drive."

"It's all right. You looked like you needed the rest."

"Too much food, too little sleep." She looked back at Freddie, who was sleeping soundly. "We've been poor company for you."

"You can make up for it. Come home with me for a while."

"All right." It was the least she could do, Natasha thought. With Vera away until Sunday, she could help him tuck Freddie into bed and fix him a light meal.

When they pulled up in front of the house, they managed the suitcases and the sleeping child between them. "I'll take her up," he murmured. "It won't take long."

Natasha waited in the kitchen, brewing tea and making sandwiches. It was ridiculous, she thought. She not only was exhausted but starving. By the time Spence came down again, she had Vera's worktable set.

"She's sleeping like a rock." He scanned the table. "You read my mind."

"With two unconscious passengers you couldn't stop and eat."

"What have we got?"

"Old Ukrainian tradition." She pulled back her chair. "Tuna fish."

"Wonderful," Spence decided after the first bite.

It was more than the sandwich. He liked having her there, sitting across from him in the glare of the kitchen light with the house quiet around them. "I guess you'll open the shop tomorrow."

"Absolutely. It'll be a madhouse from now until Christmas. I've hired a college student part-time, and he starts tomorrow." She lifted her cup and grinned at him over the rim. "Guess who it is."

"Melony Trainor," he said, naming one of his most attractive students and earning a punch on the shoulder.

"No. She's too busy flirting with men to work. Terry Maynard."

"Maynard? Really?"

"Yes. He can use the money to buy a new muffler for his car. And..." She paused dramatically. "He and Annie are an item."

"No kidding?" He was grinning as he sat back. "Well, he certainly got over having his life shattered quickly."

Natasha lifted a brow. "It wasn't shattered, only shaken. They've been seeing each other almost every night for three weeks."

"Sounds serious."

"I think it is. But Annie's worried she's too old for him."

"How much older is she?"

Natasha leaned forward and lowered her voice. "Oh, very much older. Nearly an entire year."

"Cradle robber."

With a laugh she leaned back again. "It's nice to see them together. I only hope they don't forget to wait on customers because they're mooning at each other." She shrugged, and went back to her tea. "I think I'll go in early and start on the decorations."

"You'll be tired at the end of the day. Why don't you come here for dinner?"

Curious, she tilted her head. "You cook?"

"No." He grinned and polished off his sandwich. "But I do great takeout. You can get a whole box of chicken or pizza with the works. I've even been known to come up with oriental seafood."

"I'll leave the menu to you." She rose to clear the table, but he took her hand.

"Natasha." He stood, using his free hand to stroke her hair. "I want to thank you for sharing the last couple of days with me. It meant a lot."

"To me too."

"Still, I've missed being alone with you." He bent to brush his lips over hers. "Come upstairs with me. I want very much to make love with you in my bed."

She didn't answer. Nor did she hesitate. Slipping an arm around his waist, she went with him.

He left the bedside light on low. She could just see the dark, masculine colors he'd chosen for his room. Midnight blue, forest green. An oil painting in a heavy, ornate frame dominated one wall. She could see the silhouettes of exquisite antiques. The bed was big, a generous private space covered by a thick, soft quilt. A special space, Natasha realized, knowing he had never brought another woman to this bed, to this room.

In the mirror over the bureau she caught their reflections as they stood side by side and saw herself smile when he touched a hand to her cheek.

There was time, time to savor. The fatigue she had felt earlier had vanished. Now she felt only the glow that came from loving and being loved. Words were too difficult, but when she kissed him, her heart spoke for her.

Slowly they undressed each other.

She slipped his sweater over his head. He undid the buttons of her cardigan, then pushed it from her shoulders. Keeping her eyes on his, she unfastened his shirt. He slid up the cotton sweater, letting his fingers trail until she was free of it. She unhooked his trousers. He flipped the three snaps that held her slacks at the waist. Keeping his hands light, he drew the teddy down her body as she tugged away the last barrier between them.

Quietly they moved together, her palms pressing against his back, his skimming up her sides. Heads tilting first this way, then that, they experimented with long, lingering kisses. Enjoyment. Their bodies warming, their mouths seeking, it seemed so easy here.

They drew back in unspoken agreement. Spence pulled down the quilt. They slipped under it together.

Intimacy had no rival, Natasha thought. There was nothing to compare with this. Their bodies rubbed against each other, so that the sheets whispered with each movement. Her sigh answered his murmurs. The flavor and fragrance of his skin was familiar, personal. His touch, gentle, then persuasive, then demanding, was everything she wanted.

She was simply beautiful. Not just her body, not just that exquisite face, but her spirit. When she moved with him, there was a harmony more intense than any he could create with music. She was his music—her laugh, her voice, her gestures. He knew of no way to tell her. Only to show her.

He made love with her as though it were the first and the only time. Never had she felt so elegant, so graceful. Never had she felt so strong or so sure.

When he rose over her, when she rose to meet him, it was perfect.

"I'd like you to stay."

Natasha turned her face into his throat. "I can't. Freddie would ask questions in the morning I don't know how to answer."

"I have a very simple answer. I'll tell her the truth. I'm in love with you."

"That's not simple."

"It is the truth." He shifted so that he could look at her. Her eyes were shadowed in the dim light. "I do love you, Natasha."

"Spence—"

"No. No logic or excuses. We're past that. Tell me if you believe me."

She looked into his eyes and saw what she already knew. "Yes, I believe you."

"Then tell me what you feel. I need to know."

He had a right to know, she thought, though she could all but taste the panic on her tongue. "I love you. And I'm afraid."

He brought her hand to his lips to press a kiss firmly against her fingers. "Why?"

"Because I was in love before, and nothing, nothing could have ended as badly."

There was that shadow again, he thought impatiently. The shadow from her past that he could neither fight nor conquer because it was nameless.

"Neither of us have come into this without a few bruises, Natasha. But we have a chance to make something new, something important."

She knew he was right, felt he was right, yet still held back. "I wish I were so sure. Spence, there are things you don't know about me."

"That you were a dancer."

She shifted then, to gather the sheets to her breast and sit up. "Yes. Once."

"Why haven't you mentioned it?"

"Because it was over."

He drew the hair away from her face. "Why did you stop?"

"I had a choice to make." The ache came back, but briefly. She turned to him and smiled. "I was not so good. Oh, I was adequate, and perhaps in time I would have been good enough to have been a principal dancer. Perhaps... It was something I wanted very badly once. But wanting something doesn't always make it happen."

"Will you tell me about it?"

It was a beginning, one she knew she had to make. "It's not very exciting." She lifted her hands, then let them fall onto the sheet. "I started late, after we came here. Through the church my parents met Martina Latovia. Many years ago she was an important Soviet dancer who defected. She became friends with my mother and offered to give me classes. It was good for me, the dance. I didn't speak English well, so it was hard to make friends. Everything was so different here, you see."

"Yes, I can imagine."

"I was nearly eight by that time. It becomes difficult to teach the body, the joints, to move as they weren't meant to move. But I worked very hard. *Madame* was kind and encouraging. My parents were so proud." She laughed a little, but warmly. "Papa was sure I would be the next Pavlova. The first time I danced *en pointe*, Mama cried. Dance is obsession and pain and joy. It's a different world, Spence. I can't explain. You have to know it, be a part of it."

"You don't have to explain."

She looked over at him. "No, not to you," she murmured. "Because of the music. I joined the corps de ballet when I was almost sixteen. It was wonderful. Perhaps I didn't know there were other worlds, but I was happy."

"What happened?"

"There was another dancer." She shut her eyes. It was important to take this slowly, carefully. "You've heard of him, I imagine. Anthony Marshall."

"Yes." Spence had an immediate picture of a tall, blond man with a slender build and incredible grace. "I've seen him dance many times."

"He was magnificent. Is," she corrected. "Though it's been years since I've seen him dance. We became involved. I was young. Too young. And it was a very big mistake."

Now the shadow had a name. "You loved him."

"Oh yes. In a naive and idealistic kind of way. The only way a girl can love at seventeen. More, I thought he loved me. He told me he did, in words, in actions. He was very charming, romantic…and I wanted to believe him. He promised me marriage, a future, a partnership in dance, all the things I wanted to hear. He broke all those promises, and my heart."

"So now you don't want to hear promises from me."

"You're not Anthony," she murmured, then lifted a hand to his cheek. Her eyes were dark and beautiful, her voice only more exotic as emotions crowded. "Believe me, I know that. And I don't compare, not now. I'm not the same woman who built dreams on a few careless words."

"What I've said to you hasn't been careless."

"No." She leaned closer to rest her cheek against his. "Over the past months I've come to see that, and to understand that what I feel for you is different from anything I've felt before." There was more she wanted to tell him, but the words clogged her throat. "Please, let that be enough for now."

"For now. It won't be enough forever."

She turned her mouth to his. "Just for now."

How could it be? Natasha asked herself. How could it be that when she was just beginning to trust herself, to trust her heart, that this should happen? How could she face it again?

It was like a play run backward and started again,

when her life had changed so drastically and completely. She sat back on her bed, no longer concerned about dressing for work, about starting a normal day. How could things be normal now? How could she expect them to be normal ever again?

She held the little vial in her hand. She had followed the instructions exactly. Just a precaution, she had told herself. But she'd known in her heart. Since the visit to her parents two weeks before she'd known. And had avoided facing the reality.

It was not the flu that made her queasy in the mornings. It was not overwork or stress that caused her to be so tired, or that brought on the occasional dizzy spells. The simple test that she'd bought over the counter in the drugstore had told her what she'd already known and feared.

She was carrying a child. Once again she was carrying a child. The rush of joy and wonder was totally eclipsed by the bone-deep fear that froze her.

How could it be? She was no longer a foolish girl and had taken precautions. Romance aside, she had been practical enough, responsible enough to visit her doctor and begin taking those tiny little pills, when she had realized where her relationship with Spence was bound to go. Yet she was pregnant. There was no denying it.

How could she tell him? Covering her face with her hands, Natasha rocked back and forth to give herself some small comfort. How could she go through all of it again, when that time years before was still so painfully etched on her memory?

She had known Anthony no longer loved her, if he had ever. But when she'd learned she was carrying his child, she had been thrilled. And so certain that he would share her delight. When she'd gone to him, almost bubbling over, glowing with the joy of it, his cruelty had all but cut her in two.

How grudgingly he'd let her into his apartment, Natasha remembered. How difficult it had been for her to continue to smile when she'd seen his table set for two, the candles lighted, the wine chilling—as he'd so often prepared the stage when he'd loved her. Now he'd set that stage for someone else. But she'd persuaded herself that it didn't matter. Once she'd told him, everything would change.

Everything had.

"What the hell are you talking about?" She remembered the fury in his eyes as he'd stared at her.

"I went to the doctor this afternoon. I'm pregnant, almost two months." She reached out for him. "Anthony—"

"That's an old game, Tash." He'd said it casually, but perhaps he'd been shaken. He'd stalked to the table to pour a glass of wine.

"It's not a game."

"No? Then how could you be so stupid?" He'd grabbed her arm and given her a quick shake, his magnificent mane of hair flying. "If you've gotten yourself in trouble, don't expect to come running to me to fix it."

Dazed, she'd lifted a hand to rub her arm where his fingers had bit in. It was only that he didn't understand, she'd told herself. "I'm having a child. Your child. The doctor says the baby will come in July."

"Maybe you're pregnant." He'd shrugged as he'd downed the wine. "It doesn't concern me."

"It must."

He'd looked at her then, his glass held aloft, his eyes cool. "How do I know it's mine?"

At that she'd paled. As she'd stood there, she'd remembered how it had felt when she'd almost stepped in front of a bus on her first trip to New York City. "You know. You have to know."

"I don't have to know anything. Now, if you'll excuse me, I'm expecting someone."

In desperation she'd reached out for him. "Anthony, don't you understand? I'm carrying our baby."

"Your baby," he corrected. "Your problem. If you want some advice, get rid of it."

"Get—" She hadn't been so young or so naive that she hadn't understood his meaning. "You can't mean it."

"You want to dance, Tash? Try picking classes back up after taking off nine months to give birth to some brat you're going to end up giving away in any case. Grow up."

"I have grown up." She'd laid a hand on her stomach, in protection and defense. "And I will have this child."

"Your choice." He'd gestured with his wineglass. "Don't expect to pull me into it. I've got a career to think of. You're probably better off," he decided. "Talk some loser into marrying you and set up housekeeping. You'd never be any better than mediocre at dance anyway."

So she had had the child and loved it—for a brief, brief time. Now there was another. She couldn't bear to love it, couldn't bare to want it. Not when she knew what it was like to lose.

Frantic, she threw the vial across the room and began pulling clothes out of her closet. She had to get away. She had to think. She would get away, Natasha promised herself, then pressed her fingers against her eyes until she calmed. But she had to tell him.

This time she drove to his house, struggling for calm as the car brought her closer. Because it was Saturday, children were playing in yards and on the sidewalk. Some called out to her as she passed, and she managed to lift a hand in a wave. She spotted Freddie wrestling with her kittens on the grass.

"Tash! Tash!" Lucy and Desi darted for cover, but Freddie raced to the car. "Did you come to play?"

"Not today." Summoning a smile, Natasha kissed her cheeks. "Is your daddy home?"

"He's playing music. He plays music a lot since we came here. I drew a picture. I'm going to send it to Papa and Nana."

Natasha struggled to keep the smile in place at Freddie's names for her parents. "They will like that very much."

"Come on, I'll show you."

"In a little while. I need to speak to your father first. By myself."

Freddie's bottom lip threatened. "Are you mad at him?"

"No." She pressed a finger to Freddie's nose. "Go find your kittens. I'll talk to you before I go."

"Okay." Reassured, Freddie raced off, sending out

whoops that would have the kittens cowering in the bushes, Natasha reflected.

It was better to keep her mind a blank, she decided as she knocked on the front door. Then she would take it slowly, logically, like an adult.

"Miss." Vera opened the door, her expression less remote than usual. Freddie's description of the Thanksgiving holiday in Brooklyn had done a great deal to win her over.

"I'd like to see Dr. Kimball if he's not busy."

"Come in." She found herself frowning a bit as she studied Natasha. "Are you all right, miss? You're very pale."

"Yes, I'm fine. Thank you."

"Would you like tea?"

"No—no, I can't stay long."

Though Vera privately thought Natasha looked like a cornered rabbit, she nodded. "You'll find him in the music room. He's been up half the night working."

"Thank you." Clutching her bag, Natasha started down the hall. She could hear the music he was playing, something weepy. Or perhaps it was her own mood, she thought; she blinked back tears.

When she saw him, she remembered the first time she had walked into that room. Perhaps she had started to fall in love with him that day, when he had sat there with a child on his lap, surrounded by sunlight.

She pulled off her gloves, running them through her nervous hands as she watched him. He was lost in it, both captor and captive of the music. Now she would change his life. He hadn't asked for this, and they both knew that loving wasn't always enough.

"Spence." She murmured his name when the music stopped, but he didn't hear. She could see the intensity was still on him as he scribbled on staff paper. He hadn't shaved. It made her want to smile, but instead her eyes filled. His shirt was rumpled and open at the collar. His hair was tousled. As she watched, he ran a hand through it. "Spence," she repeated.

He looked up-annoyed at first. Then he focused and smiled at her. "Hi. I didn't expect to see you today."

"Annie's watching the shop." She knit her hands. "I needed to see you."

"I'm glad you did." He rose, though the music was still filling his head. "What time is it anyway?" Absently he glanced at his watch. "Too early to ask you for lunch. How about some coffee?"

"No." Even the thought of coffee made her stomach roll. "I don't want anything. I needed to tell you...." Her fingers knotted. "I don't know how. I want you to know I never intended—this isn't intended to put you under obligation...."

The words trailed off again, he shook his head and started toward her. "If something's wrong, why don't you tell me?"

"I'm trying to."

He took her hand to lead her to the couch. "The best way's often straight out."

"Yes." She put her hand to her spinning head. "You see, I..." She saw the concern in his eyes, then everything went black....

She was lying on the sofa, and Spence was kneeling beside her, chafing her wrists. "Take it easy," he murmured. "Just lie still. I'll call a doctor."

"No. There's no need." Carefully she pushed herself up. "I'm all right."

"The hell you are." Her skin was clammy under his hand. "You're like ice, and pale as a ghost. Damn it, Natasha, why didn't you tell me you weren't well? I'll take you to the hospital."

"I don't need the hospital or the doctor." Hysteria was bubbling under her heart. She fought it back and forced herself to speak. "I'm not sick, Spence. I'm pregnant."

ing beside her, taking her wrist. "Take it easy," he murmured, "and lie still. I'll call a doctor."

"No, don't." To reassure, she carefully she got to her feet and—"I'm all right."

"You look pale." Her skin was clammy under his hand. "You're shaken, and half in shock. Dammit, Natasha, why did I always let you wear yourself—"

"I'll take you to the hospital."

"I don't need the hospital, or the doctor." Nerves bubbling close beneath, she forced herself at back and forced herself to speak. "I'm up—with Joshua. I'm pregnant."

Chapter Twelve

"What?" It was the best he could do; he sank back onto his heels and stared at her. "What did you say?"

She wanted to be strong, had to be. He looked as though she'd hit him with a blunt instrument. "I'm pregnant," she repeated, then made a helpless gesture. "I'm sorry."

He only shook his head, waiting for it to sink in. "Are you sure?"

"Yes." It was best to be matter-of-fact, Natasha told herself. He was a civilized man. There would be no accusations, no cruelty. "This morning I took a test. I suspected before, for a couple of weeks, but…"

"Suspected." His hand curled into a fist on the cushion. She didn't look furious, as Angela had. She looked destroyed. "And you didn't mention it."

"I saw no need until I knew. There was no point in upsetting you."

"I see. Is that what you are, Natasha? Upset?"

"What I am is pregnant," she said briskly. "And I felt it was only right to tell you. I'm going away for a few days." Though she still felt shaky, she managed to stand.

"Away?" Confused, afraid she would faint again, furious, he caught her. "Now just a damn minute. You drop in, tell me you're pregnant, and now you calmly tell me you're going away?" He felt something sharp punch into his gut. Its name was fear. "Where?"

"Just away." She heard her own voice, snappish and rude, and pressed a hand to her head. "I'm sorry, I'm not handling this well. I need some time. I need to go away."

"What you need to do is sit down until we talk this out."

"I can't talk about it." She felt the pressure inside her build like floodwaters against a dam. "Not yet—not until I...I only wanted to tell you before I left."

"You're not going anywhere." He grabbed her arm to pull her back. "And you damn well will talk about it. What do you want from me? Am I supposed to say, 'Well, that's interesting news, Natasha. See you when you get back'?"

"I don't want anything." When her voice rose this time, she couldn't control it. Passions, griefs, fears, poured out even as the tears began. "I never wanted anything from you. I didn't want to fall in love with you, I didn't want to need you in my life. I didn't want your child inside me."

"That's clear enough." His grip tightened, and he let his own temper free. "That's crystal clear. But you do have my child inside you, and now we're going to sit down and talk about what we're going to do about it.''

"I tell you I need time.''

"I've already given you more than enough time, Natasha. Apparently fate's taken a hand again, and you're going to have to face it.''

"I can't go through this again. I won't.''

"Again? What are you talking about?''

"I had a child.'' She jerked away to cover her face with her hands. Her whole body began to quake. "I had a child. Oh, God.''

Stunned, he put a gentle hand upon her shoulder. "You have a child?''

"Had.'' The tears seemed to be shooting up, hot and painful, from the center of her body. "She's gone.''

"Come sit down, Natasha. Talk to me.''

"I can't. You don't understand. I lost her. My baby. I can't bear the thought of going through it all again.'' She tore herself away. "You don't know, you can't know, how much it hurts.''

"No, but I can see it.'' He reached for her again. "I want you to tell me about this, so I can understand.''

"What would that change?''

"We'll have to see. It isn't good for you to get so upset now.''

"No.'' She swiped a hand over her cheek. "It doesn't do any good to be upset. I'm sorry I'm behaving like this.''

"Don't apologize. Sit down. I'll get you some tea.

We'll talk." He led her to a chair and she went unre-
sistingly. "I'll only be a minute."

He was away for less than that, he was sure, but
when he came back, she was gone.

Mikhail carved from a block of cherry wood and
listened to the blast of rock and roll through his ear-
phones. It suited the mood he could feel from the
wood. Whatever was inside—and he wasn't sure just
what that was yet—was young and full of energy.
Whenever he carved, he listened, whether it was to
blues or Bach or simply the rush and whoosh of traffic
four floors below his window. It left his mind free to
explore whatever medium his hands were working in.

Tonight his mind was too cluttered, and he knew
he was stalling. He glanced over his worktable and
across his cramped and cluttered two-room apartment.
Natasha was curled in the overstuffed, badly sprung
chair he'd scavaged off the street the previous summer. She had a book in her hands, but Mikhail didn't
think she'd turned a page in more than twenty
minutes. She, too, was stalling.

As annoyed with himself as with her, he pulled off
the headphones. He only had to turn to be in the
kitchen. Saying nothing, he put a pot onto one of the
two temperamental gas burners and brewed tea.
Natasha made no comment. When he brought over
two cups, setting hers on the scarred surface of a
nearby table, she glanced up blankly.

"Oh. *Dyakuyu.*"

"It's time to tell me what's going on."

"Mikhail—"

"I mean it." He dropped onto the mismatched hassock at her feet. "You've been here nearly a week, Tash."

She managed a small smile. "Ready to kick me out?"

"Maybe." But he put a hand over hers, rubbing lightly. "I haven't asked any questions, because that was what you wanted. I haven't told Mama and Papa that you arrived at my door one evening, looking pale and frightened, because you asked me to say nothing."

"And I appreciate it."

"Well, stop appreciating it." He made one of his characteristically abrupt gestures. "Talk to me."

"I told you I needed to get away for a little while, and I didn't want Mama and Papa to fuss over me." She moved her shoulders, then reached for her tea. "You don't fuss."

"I'm about to. Tell me what's wrong." He leaned over and cupped her chin in one hand. "Tash, tell me."

"I'm pregnant," she blurted out, then shakily set the tea down again.

He opened his mouth, but when the words didn't come, he simply wrapped his arms around her. Taking a long, labored breath, she held on.

"You're all right? You're well?"

"Yes. I went to the doctor a couple days ago. He says I'm fine. We're fine."

He drew back to study her face. "The college professor?"

"Yes. There hasn't been anyone but Spence."

Mikhail's dark eyes kindled. "If the bastard's treated you badly—"

"No." She found it odd that she was able to smile and caught Mikhail's fisted hands in hers. "No, he's never treated me badly."

"So he doesn't want the child." When Natasha merely looked down at their joined hands, Mikhail narrowed his eyes. "Natasha?"

"I don't know." She pulled away to stand and pace through Mikhail's collection of beat-up furniture and blocks of wood and stone.

"You haven't told him?"

"Of course I told him." As she moved, her hands clasped and unclasped. To calm herself, she stopped by Mikhail's Christmas tree—a one-foot evergreen in a pot that she'd decorated with bits of colored paper. "I just didn't give him much of a chance to say anything when I did. I was too upset."

"You don't want the child."

She turned at that, her eyes wide. "How can you say that? How could you think that?"

"Because you're here, instead of working things out with the college professor."

"I needed time to think."

"You think too much."

It wasn't anything he hadn't said before. Natasha's jaw set. "This isn't a matter of deciding between a blue dress and a red one. I'm having a child."

"*Tak.* Why don't you sit down and relax before you give it wrinkles."

"I don't want to sit down." She began to prowl again, shoving a box out of her way with one foot. "I didn't want to get involved with him in the first place. Even when I did, when he made it impossible for me to do otherwise, I knew it was important to keep some distance. I wanted to make sure I didn't make the same mistakes again. And now..." She made a helpless gesture.

"He isn't Anthony. This baby isn't Lily." When she turned around, her eyes were so drenched with emotion that he rose to go to her. "I loved her, too."

"I know."

"You can't judge by what's gone, Tash." Gently he kissed her cheeks. "It isn't fair to you, your professor or the child."

"I don't know what to do."

"Do you love him?"

"Yes, I love him."

"Does he love you?"

"He says—"

He caught her restless hands in his own. "Don't tell me what he says, tell me what you know."

"Yes, he loves me."

"Then stop hiding and go home. You should be having this conversation with him, not with your brother."

He was slowly going out of his mind. Every day Spence went by Natasha's apartment, certain that this time she would answer the door. When she didn't, he stalked over to harass Annie in the shop. He barely noticed the Christmas decorations in shop windows, the fat, cheerful Santas, the glittery angels, the colored lights strung around the houses. When he did, it was to scowl at them.

It had taken all of his efforts to make a show of holiday spirit for Freddie. He'd taken her to pick out a tree, spent hours decorating it with her and complimenting her crumbling popcorn strings. Dutifully he'd listened to her ever-growing Christmas list, and had taken her to the mall to sit in Santa's lap. But his heart wasn't in it.

It had to stop, he told himself and he stared out the window at the first snowfall. Whatever crisis he was facing, whatever chaos his life was in, he wouldn't see Freddie's Christmas spoiled.

She asked about Natasha every day. It only made it more difficult because he had no answers. He'd watched Freddie play an angel in her school's Christmas pageant and wished Natasha had been with him.

And what of their child? He could hardly think of anything else. Even now Natasha might be carrying the baby sister Freddie so coveted. The baby, Spence had already realized, that he desperately wanted. Unless... He didn't want to think of where she had gone, what she had done. How could he think of anything else?

There had to be a way to find her. When he did, he would beg, plead, browbeat and threaten until she came back to him.

She'd had a child. The fact left him dazed. A child she had lost, Spence remembered. But how, and when? Questions that needed answering crowded his mind. She had said she loved him, and he knew that saying it had been difficult for her. Even so, she had yet to trust him.

"Daddy." Freddie bounced into the room, her mind full of the Christmas that was only six days away. "We're making cookies."

He glanced over his shoulder to see Freddie grinning, her mouth smeared with red and green sugar.

Spence swooped her up to hold her close. "I love you, Freddie."

She giggled, then kissed him. "I love you, too. Can you come make cookies with us?"

"In a little while. I have to go out first." He was going to go to the shop, corner Annie and find out where Natasha had gone. No matter what the redhead said, Spence didn't believe that Natasha would have left her assistant without a number where she could be reached.

Freddie's lip poked out while she fiddled with Spence's top button. "When will you come back?"

"Soon." He kissed her again before he set her down. "When I come back, I'll help you bake cookies. I promise."

Content, Freddie rushed back to Vera. She knew her father always kept his promises.

Natasha stood outside the front door as the snow fell. There were lights strung along the roof and around the posts. She wondered how they would look when they were lighted. There was a full-size Santa on the door, his load of presents making him bend from the waist. She remembered the witch that had stood there on Halloween. On that first night she and Spence had made love. On that night, she was certain, their child had been conceived.

For a moment she almost turned back, telling herself she should go to her apartment, unpack, catch her breath. But that would only be hiding again. She'd hidden long enough. Gathering her courage, she knocked.

The moment Freddie opened the door, the little

girl's eyes shone. She let out a squeal and all but jumped into Natasha's arms. "You're back, you're back! I've been waiting for you forever."

Natasha held her close, swaying back and forth. This was what she wanted, needed, she realized as she buried her face in Freddie's hair. How could she have been such a fool? "It's only been a little while."

"It's been days and days. We got a tree and lights, and I already wrapped your present. I bought it myself at the mall. Don't go away again."

"No," Natasha murmured. "I won't." She set Freddie down to step inside and close out the cold and snow.

"You missed my play. I was an angel."

"I'm sorry."

"We made the halos in school and got to keep them, so I can show you how I looked."

"I'd like that."

Certain everything was back to normal, Freddie took her hand. "I tripped once, but I remembered all my lines. Mikey forgot his. I said 'A child is born in Bethlehem,' and 'Peace on Earth,' and sang 'Gloria in selfish Deo.'"

Natasha laughed for the first time in days. "I wish I had heard that. You will sing it for me later?"

"Okay. We're baking cookies." Still holding Natasha's hand, she began to drag her toward the kitchen.

"Is your daddy helping you?"

"No, he had to go out. He said he'd come back soon and bake some. He promised."

Torn between relief and disappointment, Natasha followed Freddie into the kitchen.

"Vera, Tash is back."

"I see." Vera pursed her lips. Just when she'd thought Natasha *might* be good enough for the *señor* and her baby, the woman had gone off without a word. Still, she knew her duty. "Would you like some coffee or tea, miss?"

"No, thank you. I don't want to be in your way."

"You have to stay." Freddie tugged at Natasha's hand again. "Look, I've made snowmen and reindeers and Santas." She plucked what she considered one of her best creations from the counter. "You can have one."

"It's beautiful." Natasha looked down at the snowman with red sugar clumped on his face and the brim of his hat broken off.

"Are you going to cry?" Freddie asked.

"No." She managed to blink back the mist of tears. "I'm just glad to be home."

As she spoke, the kitchen door opened. Natasha held her breath when Spence stepped into the room. He didn't speak. His hand still on the door, he stopped to stare. It was as if he'd conjured her up out of his own chaotic thoughts. There was snow melting in her hair and on the shoulders of her coat. Her eyes were bright, teary.

"Daddy, Tash is home," Freddie announced, running to him. "She's going to bake cookies with us."

Vera briskly untied her apron. Whatever doubts she'd had about Natasha were eclipsed by the look on her face. Vera knew a woman in love when she saw her. "We need more flour. Come, Freddie, we will go buy some."

"But I want to—"

"You want to bake, we need flour to bake. Come, we'll get your coat." Businesslike, Vera bustled Freddie out of the room.

Alone, Spence and Natasha stood where they were; the moment stretched out. The heat in the kitchen was making her dizzy. Natasha stripped off her coat and laid it over the back of a chair. She wanted to talk to him, reasonably. That couldn't be done if she fainted at his feet.

"Spence." The word seemed to echo off the walls, and she took a deep breath. "I was hoping we could talk."

"I see. Now you've decided talking's a good idea."

She started to speak, then changed her mind. When the oven timer went off behind her, she turned automatically to take up the hot mitt and remove the latest batch of cookies from the oven. She took her time setting them on the cooling rack.

"You're right to be angry with me. I behaved very badly toward you. Now I have to ask you to listen to me, and hope you can forgive me."

He studied her for one long, silent moment. "You certainly know how to defuse an argument."

"I didn't come to argue with you. I've had time to think, and I realize that I chose a very poor way to tell you about the baby, then to leave as I did." She looked down at her hands, her tightly laced fingers. "To just run away was inexcusable. I can only tell you that I was afraid and confused and too emotional to think clearly."

"One question," he interjected, then waited until

she lifted her head. He needed to see her face. "Is there still a baby?"

"Yes." The blank puzzlement in her eyes became awareness. Awareness became regret. "Oh, Spence, I'm sorry, so sorry to have caused you to think that I might have..." She blinked away tears, knowing her emotions were still too close to the surface. "I'm sorry. I went to Mikhail's to stay with him a few days." She let out a shaky breath. "May I sit?"

He only nodded, then moved to the window as she slid behind the table. Laying his palms upon the counter, he looked out at the snow. "I've been going out of my mind, wondering where you were, how you were. The state you were in when you left, I was terrified you'd do something rash before we could talk it through."

"I could never do what you thought, Spence. This is our baby."

"You said you didn't want it." He turned again. "You said you wouldn't go through it again."

"I was afraid," Natasha admitted. "And it's true I hadn't wanted to get pregnant, not now. Not ever. I'd like to tell you everything."

He wanted badly, much too badly, just to reach out to her, to hold her and tell her that nothing mattered. Because he knew it did matter, he busied himself at the stove. "Do you want some coffee?"

"No. It makes me sick now." She smiled a little when he fumbled with the pot. "Please, would you sit down?"

"All right." He sat down across from her, then spread his hands. "Go ahead."

"I told you that I had been in love with Anthony

while I was with the corps de ballet. I was just seventeen when we became lovers. He was the first for me. There's been no one for me until you.''

''Why?''

The answer was much easier than she'd believed. ''I'd never loved again until you. The love I feel for you is much different from the fantasies I had for Anthony. With you it isn't dreams and knights and princes. With you it's real and solid. Day-to-day. Ordinary—ordinary in the most beautiful way. Can you understand?''

He looked at her. The room was quiet, insulated by the snow. It smelled of warm cookies and cinnamon. ''Yes.''

''I was afraid to feel this strongly for you, for anyone, because what happened between Anthony and me...'' She waited a moment, surprised that there was no pain now, only sadness. ''I had believed him, everything he said, everything he promised me. When I discovered he made many of the same promises to other women, I was crushed. We argued, and he sent me away like a child who had displeased him. A few weeks later I discovered I was pregnant. I was thrilled. I could only think that I was carrying Anthony's child and that when I told him, he would see that we belonged together. Then I told him.''

Spence reached for her hand without a word.

''It was not as I had imagined. He was angry. The things he said.... It doesn't matter,'' she went on. ''He didn't want me, he didn't want the child. In those few moments I grew up years. He wasn't the man I had wanted him to be, but I had the child. I wanted that baby." Her fingers tightened on his. "I so desperately wanted that baby."

"What did you do?"

"The only thing I could. There could be no dancing now. I left the company and went home. I know it was a burden for my parents, but they stood by me. I got a job in a department store. Selling toys." She smiled at that.

"It must have been difficult for you." He tried to imagine her, a teenager, pregnant, deserted by the father of her child, struggling to hold it all together.

"Yes, it was. It was also a wonderful time. My body changed. After the first month or two when I felt so fragile, I began to feel strong. So strong. I would sit in bed at night and read books on babies and birthing. I would ask Mama dozens of questions. I knit—badly," she said with a quiet laugh. "Papa built a bassinet, and Mama sewed a white skirt with pink and blue ribbons. It was beautiful." She felt the tears well up and shook her head. "Could I have some water?"

He rose, and filling a glass from the tap, set it beside her. "Take your time, Natasha." Because he knew they both needed it, he stroked her hair. "You don't have to tell me everything at once."

"I need to." She sipped slowly, waiting for him to sit down again. "I called her Lily," she murmured. "She was so lovely, so tiny and soft. I had no idea it was possible to love anything, anyone, the way you love a child. I would watch her sleep for hours, so thrilled, so awed that she had come from me."

The tears were falling now, soundlessly. One fell onto the back of her hand. "It was hot that summer, and I would take her out in this little carriage to get air and sunshine. People would stop to look at her. She hardly cried, and when I nursed her, she would put a hand on my breast and watch me with those big eyes. You know what it is. You have Freddie.''

"I know. There's nothing like having a child.''

"Or losing one,'' Natasha said softly. "It was so quick. She was only five weeks old. I woke up in the morning, surprised that she had slept through the night. My breasts were full of milk. The bassinet was by my bed. I reached down for her, picked her up. At first I didn't understand, didn't believe....'' She broke off to press her hands to her eyes. "I remember screaming and screaming—Rachel rushing up out of the next bed, the rest of the family running in—Mama taking her from me.'' The silent tears turned to weeping. Her face now covered by her hands, she let go in a way she usually only allowed herself in private.

There was nothing he could say, nothing to be said. Instead of searching for meaningless words, he rose to crouch beside her and gather her into his arms. The passion of her grief held sway. Then on a half sob, she turned and clung to him, accepting comfort.

Her hands were fisted against his back. Gradually they relaxed as he kept her close. The hot tears slowed, and the pain, now shared, eased.

"I'm all right,'' she managed at length. Pulling away, she began to fumble in her bag for a tissue. Spence took it from her to dry her cheeks himself. "The doctor called it crib death. No reason,'' she said as she closed her eyes once more. "That was somehow worse. Not knowing why, not being sure if I could have stopped it.''

"No." He took both her hands and she opened her eyes. "Don't do that. Listen to me. I can only imagine what it would be like to go through what you went through, but I know that when truly horrible things happen, it's usually out of our control."

"It took me a long time to accept what I can never understand." She turned over her hands in his. "A long time to start living again, going back to work, finally moving here, starting my business. I think I would have died without my family." She gave herself a moment, sipping the water to cool her dry throat. "I didn't want to love anyone again. Then there was you. And Freddie."

"We need you, Natasha. And you need us."

"Yes." She took his hand to press it to her lips. "I want you to understand. Spence, when I learned I was pregnant, it all came flying back at me. I tell you, I don't think I could survive going through that again. I'm so afraid to love this child. And I already do."

"Come here." He lifted her to her feet, keeping her hands locked tight in his. "I know that you loved Lily, and that you'll always love her and grieve for her. So will I now. What happened before can't be changed, but this is a different place, a different time. A different child. I want you to understand that we're going to go through this pregnancy, the birth and the rearing together. Whether you want me or not."

"I'm afraid."

"Then we'll be afraid together. And when this baby is eight and rides a two-wheeler for the first time, we'll be afraid together."

Her lips trembled into a smile. "When you say it, I can almost believe it."

"Believe it." He bent to kiss her. "Because it's a promise."

"Yes, it's time for promises." Her smile grew. "I love you." It was so easy to say it now. So easy to feel it. "Will you hold me?"

"On one condition." He rubbed away a drying tear with his thumb. "I want to tell Freddie she's expecting a baby brother or sister. I think it would make a great Christmas present for her."

"Yes." She felt stronger, surer. "I want us to tell her."

"All right, you've got five days."

"Five days for what?"

"To make whatever plans you want to make, to arrange to have your family come down, buy a dress, whatever you need to do to get ready for the wedding."

"But—"

"No buts." He framed her face with his hands and silenced her. "I love you, I want you. You're the best thing to come into my life since Freddie, and I don't intend to lose you. We've made a child, Natasha." Watching her, he laid a hand on her stomach, gently possessive. "A child I want. A child I already love."

In a gesture of trust, she placed her hand on his. "I won't be afraid if you're with me."

"We have a date here Christmas Eve. I'm going to wake up Christmas morning with my wife."

She steadied herself by putting her hands on his forearms. "Just like that?"

"Just like that."

With a laugh, she threw her arms around his neck and said one word. "Yes."

Epilogue

Christmas Eve was the most beautiful day in the year as far as Natasha was concerned. It was a time to celebrate life and love and family.

The house was quiet when she came in. She was drawn to the tree and the light. She sent an angel spinning on one branch, then turned to study the room.

On the table there was a papier-mâché reindeer with only one ear. Compliments of Freddie's second-grade art class. Beside it stood a pudgy snowman holding a lantern. An exquisite porcelain crèche was displayed on the mantel. Beneath it hung four stockings. A fire crackled in the grate.

A year before she had stood before the fire and promised to love, honor and cherish. They had been the easiest promises she had ever had to keep. Now this was her home.

Home. She took a deep breath to draw in the scents of pine and candles. It was so good to be home. Last-minute shoppers had crowded The Fun House until late in the afternoon. Now there was only family.

"Mama." Freddie raced in, trailing a bright red ribbon. "You're home."

"I'm home." Laughing, Natasha scooped her up to spin her around.

"We took Vera to the airport so she can spend Christmas with her sister, then we watched the planes. Daddy said when you got home we'd have dinner, then sing Christmas carols."

"Daddy's absolutely right." Natasha draped the ribbon over Freddie's shoulder. "What's this?"

"I'm wrapping a present, all by myself. It's for you."

"For me? What is it?"

"I can't tell you."

"Yes, you can. Watch." She dropped onto the couch to run her fingers along Freddie's ribs. "It'll be easy," she said as Freddie squealed and squirmed.

"Torturing the child again," Spence commented from the doorway.

"Daddy!" Springing up, Freddie raced to him. "I didn't tell."

"I knew I could count on you, funny face. Look who woke up." He bounced a baby on his hip.

"Here, Brandon." Madly in love, Freddie passed up the ribbon so that he could play with it. "It's pretty, just like you."

At six months, young Brandon Kimball was chubby, rosy-cheeked and delighted with the world in general. He clutched the ribbon in one hand and reached for Freddie's hair with the other.

Walking over, Natasha held out her arms. "Such a big boy," she murmured as her son reached for her. Gathering him close, she pressed a kiss to his throat. "So beautiful."

"He looks just like his mother." Spence stroked a hand over Brandon's thick, black curls. As if he approved of the statement, Brandon let out a gurgling laugh. When he wriggled, Natasha set him down to crawl on the rug.

"It's his first Christmas." Natasha watched him scoot over to torment one of the cats and saw Lucy dart under the sofa. She's no fool, Natasha thought happily.

"And our second." He turned Natasha into his arms. "Happy anniversary."

Natasha kissed him once, then twice. "Have I told you today that I love you?"

"Not since I called you this afternoon."

"Much too long ago." She slipped her arms around his waist. "I love you. Thank you for the most wonderful year of my life."

"You're very welcome." He glanced over her head only long enough to see that Freddie had prevented Brandon from pulling an ornament from a low branch. "But it's only going to get better."

"Do you promise?"

He smiled and lowered his mouth to hers again. "Absolutely."

Freddie stopped crawling with Brandon to watch them. A baby brother had turned out to be nice, after

all, but she was still holding out for that baby sister.
She smiled as she saw her parents embrace.

Maybe next Christmas.

*   *   *   *   *

FALLING FOR RACHEL

Mary Kay, here's one just for you

Prologue

Nick couldn't figure out how he'd been so damn stupid. Maybe it was more important to be part of the gang than he liked to admit. Maybe he was mad at the world in general and figured it was only right to get his licks in when he had the chance. And certainly he'd have lost face if he'd backed out when Reece and T.J. and Cash were so fired up.

But he'd never actually broken the law before.

Not quite true, he reminded himself as he pulled himself through the broken window and into the back of the electronics store. But they'd only been little laws. Setting up a three-card monte scam over on Madison for suckers and tourists, hawking hot watches or Gucci knockoffs up on Fifth, forging a couple of ID's so that he could buy a beer. He'd worked in a chop shop for a while, but it wasn't as if *he'd* stolen the cars. He'd just broken them down for parts. He'd gotten stung a few times for fighting with the Hombres, but that was a matter of honor and loyalty.

Breaking into a store and stealing calculators and portable stereos was a big leap. While it had seemed like a lark over a couple of beers, the reality of it was setting those brews to churning in his stomach.

The way Nick saw it, he was trapped, as he'd always been. There was no easy way out.

"Hey, man, this is better than swiping candy bars, right?" Reece's eyes, dark and surly, scanned the storeroom shelves. He was a short man with a rough complexion who'd spent several of his twenty years in Juvenile Hall. "We're gonna be rich."

T.J. giggled. It was his way of agreeing with anything Reece said. Cash, who habitually kept his own counsel, was already shoving boxes of video games in the black duffel he carried.

"Come on, Nick." Reece tossed him an army-surplus bag. "Load it up."

Sweat began to roll down Nick's back as he shoved radios and minirecorders into the sack. What the hell was he doing here? he asked himself. Ripping off some poor slob who was just trying to make a living? It wasn't like fleecing tourists or selling someone else's heat. This was stealing, for God's sake.

"Listen, Reece, I—" He broke off when Reece turned and shined the flashlight in Nick's eyes.

"Got a problem, bro?"

Trapped, Nick thought again. Copping out now wouldn't stop the others from taking what they'd come for. And it would only bring him humiliation.

"No. No, man, no problem." Anxious to get it all

over with, he shoved more boxes in without bothering to look at them. "Let's not get too greedy, okay? I mean, we got to get the stuff out, then we got to fence it. We don't want to take more than we can handle."

His lips pulled back in a sneer, Reece slapped Nick on the back. "That's why I keep you around. Your practical mind. Don't worry about turning the stuff. I told you, I got a connection."

"Right." Nick licked his dry lips and reminded himself he was a Cobra. It was all he'd ever been, all he ever would be.

"Cash, T.J., take that first load out to the car." Reece flipped the keys. "Make sure you lock it. Wouldn't want any bad guys stealing anything, would we?"

T.J.'s giggles echoed off the ceiling as he wiggled out the window. "No, sir." He pushed his wraparound sunglasses back on his nose. "Thieves everywhere these days. Right, Cash?"

Cash merely grunted and wrestled his way out the window.

"That T.J.'s a real idiot." Reece hefted a boxed VCR. "Give me a hand with this, Nick."

"I thought you said we were just going for the small stuff."

"Changed my mind." Reece pushed the box into Nick's arms. "My old lady's been whining for one of these." Reece tossed back his hair before climbing through the window. "You know your problem, Nick? Too much conscience. What's it ever gotten you? Now, the Cobras, we're family. Only time you got to have a conscience is with your family." He held out his arms. When Nick put the VCR into them, Reece slipped off into the dark.

Family, Nick thought. Reece was right. The Cobras were his family. You could count on them. He'd had to count on them. Pushing all his doubts aside, Nick shouldered his bag. He had to think of himself, didn't he? His share of tonight's work would keep a roof over his head for another month or two. He could have paid for his room the straight way if he hadn't gotten laid off from the delivery-truck job.

Lousy economy, he decided. If he had to steal to make ends meet, he could blame the government. The idea made him snicker as he swung one leg out of the window. Reece was right, he thought. You had to look out for number one.

"Need a hand with that?"

The unfamiliar voice had Nick freezing halfway out the window. In the shadowy light he saw the glint of a gun, the flash of a badge. He gave one fleeting, panicky thought to shoving the bag at the silhouette and making a run for it. Shaking his head, the cop stepped closer. He was young, dark, with a weary kind of resignation in the eyes that warned Nick that he'd been this route before.

"Do yourself a favor," the cop suggested. "Just chalk it up to bad luck."

Resigned, Nick slipped out of the window, set the bag down, faced the wall and assumed the position. "Is there any other kind?" he muttered, and let his mind wander as he was read his rights.

Chapter One

With a briefcase in one hand and a half-eaten bagel in the other, Rachel raced up the courthouse steps. She hated to be late. Detested it. Knowing she'd drawn Judge Hatchet-Face Snyder for the morning hearing only made her more determined to be inside and at the defense table by 8:59. She had three minutes to spare, and would have had twice that if she hadn't stopped by the office first.

How could she have known that her boss would be lying in wait with another case file?

Two years of working as a public defender, she reminded herself as she hit the doors at a run. That was how she should have known.

She scanned the elevators, gauged the waiting crowd and opted for the stairs. Cursing her heels, she took them two at a time and swallowed the rest of the bagel. There was no use fantasizing about the coffee she craved to wash it down with.

She screeched to a halt at the courtroom doors and took a precious ten seconds to straighten her blue serge jacket and smooth down her tousled, chin-length black hair. A quick check showed her that her earrings were still in place. She looked at her watch and let out a deep breath.

Right on time, Stanislaski, she told herself as she moved sedately through the doors and into the courtroom. Her client, a twenty-three-year-old hooker with a heart of flint, was being escorted in as Rachel took her place. The solicitation charges would probably have earned her no more than a light fine and time served, but stealing the john's wallet had upped the ante.

As Rachel had explained to her bitter client, not all customers were too embarrassed to squawk when they lost two hundred in cash and a gold card.

"All rise!"

Hatchet-Face strode in, black robes flapping around all six-foot-three and two hundred and eighty pounds of him. He had skin the color of a good cappuccino and a face as round and unfriendly as the pumpkins Rachel remembered carving with her siblings every Halloween.

Judge Snyder tolerated no tardiness, no sass and no excuses in his courtroom. Rachel glanced over at the assistant district attorney who would be the opposing counsel. They exchanged looks of sympathy and got to work.

Rachel got the hooker off with ninety days. Her client was hardly brimming with gratitude as the bai-

man in handcuffs and the uniformed cop behind him. She managed to snag a cup of coffee, and took it with her into a small room that boasted one barred window, a single long table and four scarred chairs. Taking a seat, she flipped open her briefcase and dug out the paperwork on Nicholas LeBeck.

It seemed her client was nineteen and unemployed and rented a room on the Lower East Side. She let out a little sigh at his list of priors. Nothing cataclysmic, she mused, but certainly enough to show a bent for trouble. The attempted burglary had taken him up a step, and it left her little hope of having him treated as a minor. There had been several thousand dollars' worth of electronic goodies in his sack when Detective Alexi Stanislaski collared him.

She'd be hearing from Alex, no doubt, Rachel thought. There was nothing her brother liked better than to rub her nose in it.

When the door of the conference room opened, she continued to sip her coffee as she took stock of the man being led in by a bored-looking policeman.

Five-ten, she estimated. A hundred and forty. Needed some weight. Dark blond hair, shaggy and nearly shoulder-length. His lips were quirked in what looked like a permanent smirk. It might have been an attractive mouth otherwise. A tiny peridot stud that nearly matched his eyes gleamed in his earlobe. The eyes, too, would have been attractive if not for the bitter anger she read there.

"Thank you, Officer." At her slight nod, the cop uncuffed her client and left them alone. "Mr. LeBeck, I'm Rachel Stanislaski, your lawyer."

"Yeah?" He dropped into a chair, then tipped it

back. "Last PD I had was short and skinny and had a bald spot. Looks like I got lucky this time."

"On the contrary. You were apprehended crawling out of a broken window of a storeroom of a locked store, with an estimated six thousand dollars' worth of merchandise in your possession."

"The markup on that crap is incredible." It wasn't easy to keep the sneer in place after a miserable night in jail, but Nick had his pride. "Hey, you got a cigarette on you?"

"No. Mr. LeBeck, I'd like to get your hearing set as soon as possible so that we can arrange for bail. Unless, of course, you prefer to spend your nights in jail."

He shrugged his thin shoulders and tried to look unconcerned. "I'd just as soon not, sweetcakes. I'll leave that to you."

"Fine. And it's Stanislaski," she said mildly. "*Ms.* Stanislaski. I'm afraid I was only given your file this morning on my way to court, and had time for no more than a brief conversation with the DA assigned to your case. Because of your previous record, and the type of crime involved here, the state had decided to try you as an adult. The arrest was clean, so you won't get a break there."

"Hey, I don't expect breaks."

"People rarely get them." She folded her hands over his file. "Let's cut to the chase, Mr. LeBeck. You were caught, and unless you want to weave some fairy tale about seeing the broken window and going in to make a citizen's arrest..."

He had to grin. "Not bad."

"It stinks. You're guilty, and since the arresting of-

ficer didn't make any mistakes, and you have an un-
fortunate list of priors, you're going to pay. How much
you pay is going to depend on you.''

He continued to rock in his chair, but a fresh line
of sweat was sneaking down his spine. A cell. This
time they were going to lock him in a cell—not just
for a few hours, but for months, maybe years.

''I hear the jails are overcrowded—costs the taxpayers a lot of money. I figure the DA would spring
for a deal.''

''It was mentioned.'' Not just bitterness, Rachel realized. Not just anger. She saw fear in his eyes now,
as well. He was young and afraid, and she didn't know
how much she would be able to help him. ''About
fifteen thousand in merchandise was taken out of the
store, over and above what was in your possession.
You weren't alone in that store, LeBeck. You know
it, I know it, the cops know it. And so does the DA.
You give them some names, a lead on where that merchandise might be sitting right now, and I can cut you
a deal.''

His chair banged against the floor. ''The hell with
that. I never said anybody was with me. Nobody can
prove it, just like nobody can prove I took more than
what I had in my hands when the cop took me.''

Rachel leaned forward. It was a subtle move, but
one that had Nick's eyes locking on hers. ''I'm your
lawyer, LeBeck, and the one thing you're not going
to do is lie to me. You do, and I'll leave you twisting
in the wind, just like your buddies did last night.'' Her
voice was flat, passionless, but he heard the anger simmering beneath. He had to fight to keep from squirming in his chair. ''You don't want to cut a deal,'' she

continued, "that's your choice. So you'll serve three to five instead of the six months in and two years probation I can get you. Either way, I'll do my job. But don't sit there and insult me by saying you pulled this alone. You're penny-ante, LeBeck." It pleased her to see the anger back in his face. The fear had begun to soften her. "Con games and sticky fingers. This is the big leagues. What you tell me stays with me unless you want it different. But you play it straight with me, or I walk."

"You can't walk. You were assigned."

"And I can get reassigned. Then you'll go through this with somebody else." She began to pile papers back in her briefcase. "That would be your loss. Because I'm good. I'm real good."

"If you're so good, how come you're working for the PD's office."

"Let's just say I'm paying off a debt." She snapped her briefcase closed. "So what's it going to be?"

Indecision flickered over his face for just a moment, making him look young and vulnerable, before he shook his head. "I'm not going to turn in my friends. No deal."

She let out a short, impatient breath. "You were wearing a Cobra jacket when you were collared."

They'd taken that when they booked him—just as they'd taken his wallet, his belt, and the handful of change in his pocket. "So what?"

"They're going to go looking for your *friends*, those same friends who are standing back and letting you take the heat all alone. The DA can push this to burglary and hang a twenty-thousand-dollar theft over your head."

"No names," he said again. "No deal."

"Your loyalty's admirable, and misplaced. I'll do what I can to have the charges reduced and have bail set. I don't think it'll be less than fifty thousand. Can you scrape ten percent together?"

Not a chance in hell, he thought, but he shrugged. "I can call in some debts."

"All right, then, I'll get back to you." She rose, then slipped a card out of her pocket. "If you need me before the hearing, or if you change your mind about the deal, give me a call."

She rapped on the door, then swung through when it opened. An arm curled around her waist. She braced instinctively, then let out a little hiss of breath when she looked up and saw her brother grinning at her.

"Rachel, long time no see."

"Yeah, it must be a day and a half."

"Grumpy." His grin widened as he pulled her out of the corridor and into the squad room. "Good sign." His gaze skimmed over her shoulder and locked briefly on LeBeck. "So, they tied you up with that one. Tough break, sweetheart."

She gave him a sisterly elbow in the ribs. "Stop gloating and get me a decent cup of coffee." Resting a hip against the corner of his desk, she rapped her fingertips against her briefcase. Nearby a short, round man was holding a bandanna to his temple and moaning slightly as he gave a statement to another cop. Someone was talking in loud and rapid Spanish. A woman with a bruise on her cheek was weeping and rocking a fat toddler.

The squad room smelled of all of it—the despair, the anger, the boredom. Rachel had always thought that if your senses were very keen you could just barely scent the justice beneath it all. It was very much the same in her offices, a few blocks away.

For a moment, Rachel pictured her sister, Natasha, having breakfast with her family in her pretty kitchen in the big, lovely house in West Virginia. Or opening her colorful toy shop for the day. The image made her smile a bit, just as it did to imagine her brother Mikhail carving something passionate or fanciful out of wood in his sun-washed new studio, perhaps having a hasty cup of coffee with his gorgeous wife before she hurried off to her midtown office.

And here she was, waiting for a cup of what would certainly be very bad coffee in a downtown precinct house filled with the sight and smells and sounds of misery.

Alex handed her the coffee, then eased down on the desk beside her.

"Thanks." She sipped, winced, and watched a couple of hookers strut out of the holding cells. A tall, bleary-eyed man with a night's worth of stubble shifted around them and followed a uniform through the door that led down to the cells. Rachel gave a little sigh.

"What's wrong with us, Alexi?"

He grinned again and slipped an arm around her. "What? Just because we like slogging through the dregs for a living, for little pay and less gratitude? Nothing. Not a thing."

She chuckled and fueled her system with the motor oil disguised as coffee. "At least you just got a promotion. Detective Stanislaski."

"Can't help it if I'm good. You, on the other hand,

are spinning your wheels putting criminals back on the streets I'm risking life and limb to keep clean.''

She snorted, scowling at him over the brim of the paper cup. ''Most of the people I represent aren't doing anything more than trying to survive.''

''Sure—by stealing, cheating, and assaulting.''

Her temper began to heat. ''I went to court this morning to represent an old man who'd copped some disposable razors. A real desperate case, that one. I guess they should have locked him up and thrown away the key.''

''So it's okay to steal as long as what you take isn't particularly valuable?''

''He needed help, not a jail sentence.''

''Like that creep you got off last month who terrorized two old shopkeepers, wrecked their store and stole the pitiful six hundred in the till?''

She'd hated that one, truly hated it. But the law was clear, and had been made for a reason. ''Look, you guys blew that one. The arresting officer didn't read him his rights in his native language or arrange for a translator. My client barely understood a dozen words of English.'' She shook her head before Alex could jump into one of his more passionate arguments. ''I don't have time to debate the law with you. I need to ask you about Nicholas LeBeck.''

''What about him? You got the report.''

''You were the arresting officer.''

''Yeah—so? I was on my way home, and I happened to see the broken window and the light inside. When I went to investigate, I saw the perpetrator coming through the window carrying a sackful of electronics. I read him his rights and brought him in.''

"What about the others?"

Alex shrugged and finished off the last couple of swallows of Rachel's coffee. "Nobody around but LeBeck."

"Come on, Alex, twice as much was taken from the store as what my client allegedly had in his bag."

"I figure he had help, but I didn't see anyone else. And your client exercised his right to remain silent. He has a healthy list of priors."

"Kid stuff."

Alex sneered. "You could say he didn't spend his childhood in the Boy Scouts."

"He's a Cobra."

"He had the jacket," Alex agreed. "And the attitude."

"He's a scared kid."

With a sound of disgust, Alex chucked the empty cup into a wastebasket. "He's no kid, Rach."

"I don't care how old he is, Alex. Right now he's a scared kid sitting in a cell and trying to pretend he's tough. It could have been you, or Mikhail—even Tash or me—if it hadn't been for Mama and Papa."

"Hell, Rachel."

"It could have been," she insisted. "Without the family, without all the hard work and sacrifices, any one of us could have gotten sucked into the streets. You know it."

He did. Why did she think he'd become a cop? "The point is, we didn't. It's a basic matter of what's right and what's wrong."

"Sometimes people make bad choices because there's no one around to help them make good ones."

They could have spent hours debating the many

shades of justice, but he had to get to work. "You're too softhearted, Rachel. Just make sure it doesn't lead to being softheaded. The Cobras are one of the roughest gangs going. Don't start thinking your client's a candidate for Boys' Town."

Rachel straightened, pleased that her brother remained slouched against the desk. It meant they were eye to eye. "Was he carrying a weapon?"

Alex sighed. "No."

"Did he resist arrest?"

"No. But that doesn't change what he was doing, or what he is."

"It might not change what he was doing—allegedly—but it might very well say something about what he is. Preliminary hearing's at two."

"I know."

She smiled again and kissed him. "See you there."

"Hey, Rachel." She turned at the doorway and looked back. "Want to catch a movie tonight?"

"Sure." She'd made it to the outside in two steps when her name was called again, more formally this time.

"Ms. Stanislaski!"

She paused, flipping her hair back with one hand as she looked over her shoulder. It was the tired-eyed, stubble-faced man she'd noticed before. Hard to miss, she reflected as he hurried toward her. He was over six feet by an inch or so, and his baggy sweatshirt was held up by a pair of broad shoulders. Faded jeans, frayed at the cuffs, white at the stress points, fit well over long legs and narrow hips.

It would have been hard not to miss the anger, too.

It radiated from him, and it was reflected in steel-blue eyes set deep in a rough, hollow-cheeked face.

"Rachel Stanislaski?"

"Yes."

He caught her hand and, in the process of shaking it, dragged her down a couple of steps. He might look lean and mean, Rachel thought, but he had the grip of a bear trap.

"I'm Zackary Muldoon," he said, as if that explained everything.

Rachel only lifted a brow. He certainly looked fit to spit nails, and after that brief taste of his strength she wouldn't have put the feat past him. But she wasn't easily intimidated, particularly when she was standing in an area swarming with cops.

"Can I help you, Mr. Muldoon?"

"I'm counting on it." He dragged a big hand through a tousled mop of hair as dark as her own. He swore and took her elbow to pull her down the rest of the steps. "What's it going to take to get him out? And why the hell did he call you and not me? And why in God's name did you let him sit in a cell all night? What kind of lawyer are you?"

Rachel shook her arm free—no easy task—and prepared to use her briefcase as a weapon if it became necessary. She'd heard about the black Irish and their tempers. But Ukrainians were no slouches, either.

"Mr. Muldoon, I don't know who you are or what you're talking about. And I happen to be very busy." She'd managed two steps when he whirled her around. Rachel's tawny eyes narrowed dangerously. "Look, Buster—"

"I don't care how busy you are, I want some answers. If you don't have time to help Nick, then we'll get another lawyer. God knows why he chose some fancy broad in a designer suit in the first place.'' His blue eyes shot fire, the Irish poet's mouth hardening into a sneer.

She sputtered, angry color flagging both cheeks. She jabbed one stiffened, clear-tipped finger in his chest. *"Broad?* You just watch who you call *broad,* pal, or—''

''Or you'll get your boyfriend to lock me in a cell?'' Zack suggested. Yeah, that was definitely a fancy face, he thought in disgust. Butter-soft skin in pale gold, and eyes like good Irish whiskey. What he needed was a street fighter, and he'd gotten society. ''I don't know what kind of defense Nick expects from some woman who spends her time kissing cops and making dates when she's supposed to be working.''

''It's none of your business what I—'' She took a deep breath. Nick. ''Are you talking about Nicholas LeBeck?''

''Of course I'm talking about Nicholas LeBeck. Who the hell do you think I'm talking about?'' His black brows drew together over his furious eyes. ''And you'd better come up with some answers, lady, or you're going to be off his case and out on your pretty butt.''

''Hey, Rachel!'' An undercover cop dressed like a wino sidled up behind her. He eyed Zack. ''Any problem here?''

''No.'' Though her eyes were blazing, she offered him a half smile. ''No, I'm fine, Matt. Thanks.'' She edged over to one side and lowered her voice. ''I don't owe you any answers, Muldoon. And insulting me is a poor way to gain my cooperation."

"You're paid to cooperate," he told her. "Just how much are you hosing the boy for?"

"Excuse me?"

"What's your fee, sugar?"

Her teeth set. The way she saw it, *sugar* was only a marginal step up from *broad.* "I'm a public defender, Muldoon, assigned to LeBeck's case. That means he doesn't owe me a damn thing. Just like I don't owe you."

"A PD?" He all but backed her off the sidewalk and into the building. "What the devil does Nick need a PD for?"

"Because he's broke and unemployed. Now, if you'll excuse me..." She set a hand on his chest and shoved. She'd have been better off trying to shove away the brick building at her back.

"He lost his job? But..." The words trailed off. This time Rachel read something other than anger in his eyes. Weariness, she thought. A trace of despair. Resignation. "He could have come to me."

"And who the hell are you?"

Zack rubbed a hand over his face. "I'm his brother."

Rachel pursed her lips, lifted a brow. She knew how the gangs worked, and though Zack looked rough-and-ready enough to fit in with the Cobras, he also looked too old to be a card-carrying member.

"Don't the Cobras have an age limit?"

"What?" He let his hand drop and focused on her again with a fresh oath. "Do I look like I belong to a street gang?"

With her head tilted, Rachel ran her gaze from his battered high-tops to his shaggy dark head. He had the look of a street tough, certainly of a man who could bulldoze his way down alleys, pounding rivals with those big-fisted hands. The hard, hollowed face and hot eyes made her think he'd enjoy cracking skulls, particularly hers. "Actually, you could pass. And your manners certainly reflect the code. Rude, abrasive, and rough."

He didn't give a damn what she thought of his appearance, or his manners, but it was time they set the record straight. "I'm Nick's brother—stepbrother, if you want to be technical. His mother married my father. Get it?"

Her eyes remained wary, but there was some interest there now. "He said he didn't have any relatives."

For an instant, she thought she saw hurt in those steel-blue depths. Then it was gone, hardened away. "He's got me, whether he likes it or not. And I can afford a real lawyer, so why don't you fill me in, and I'll take it from there."

This time she didn't merely set her teeth, she practically snarled. "I happen to be a *real* lawyer, Muldoon. And if LeBeck wants other counsel, he can damn well ask for it himself."

He struggled to find the patience that always seemed to elude him. "We'll get into that later. For now, I want to know what the hell's going on."

"Fine." She snapped the word out as she looked at her watch. "You can have fifteen minutes of my time, providing you take it while I eat. I have to be back in court in an hour."

Chapter Two

From the way she looked—elegant sex in a three-piece suit—Zack figured her for one of the trendy little restaurants that served complicated pasta dishes and white wine. Instead, she stalked down the street, her long legs eating up the sidewalk so that he didn't have to shorten his pace to keep abreast.

She stopped at a vendor and ordered a hot dog—loaded—with a soft drink, then stepped aside to give Zack room to make his selection. The idea of eating anything that looked like a hot dog at what he considered the crack of dawn had his stomach shriveling. Zack settled for a soft drink—the kind loaded with sugar and caffeine—and a cigarette.

Rachel took the first bite, licked mustard off her thumb. Over the scent of onions and relish, Zack caught a trace of her perfume. It was like walking through the jungle, he thought with a frown. All those ripe, sweaty smells, and then suddenly, unexpectedly, you could come across some exotic, seductive vine tangled with vivid flowers.

"He's charged with burglary," Rachel said with her mouth full. "Not much chance of shaking it. He was apprehended climbing out of the window with several thousand dollars' worth of stolen merchandise in his possession."

"Stupid." Zack downed half the soft drink in a swallow. "He doesn't have to steal."

"That's neither here nor there. He was caught, he was charged, and he doesn't deny the act. The DA's willing to deal, offer probation and community service, if Nick cooperates."

Zack chuffed out smoke. "Then he'll cooperate."

Rachel's left brow lifted, then settled. She had no doubt Zackary Muldoon thought he could prod, push or punch anybody into anything. "I sincerely doubt it. He's scared, but he's stubborn. And he's loyal to the Cobras."

Zack said something foul about the Cobras. Rachel was forced to agree. "Well, that may be, but it doesn't change the bottom line. His record is fairly lengthy, and it won't be easy to get around it. It's also mostly hustle and jive. The fact that this is his first step into the big leagues might help reduce his sentence. I think I can get him off with three years. If he behaves, he'll only serve one."

Zack's fingers dug into the aluminum can, crushing it. Fear settled sickly in his stomach. "I don't want him to go to prison."

"Muldoon, I'm a lawyer, not a magician."

"They got back the stuff he took, didn't they?"

"That doesn't negate the crime, but yes. Of course, there's several thousand more outstanding."

"I'll make it good." Somehow. Zack heaved the can toward a waste can. It tipped the edge, joggled, then fell inside. "Listen, I'll make restitution on what was stolen. Nick's only nineteen. If you can get the DA to try him as a minor, it would go easier."

"The state's tough on gang members, and with his record I don't think it would happen."

"If you can't do it, I'll find someone who can." Zack threw up a hand before she could tear into him. "I know I came down on you before. Sorry. I work nights, and I'm not my best in the morning." Even that much of an apology grated on him, but he needed her. "I get a call an hour ago from one of Nick's friends telling me he's been in jail all night. When I get down here and see him, it's the same old story. I don't need you. I don't need anybody. I'm handling it." He tossed down his cigarette, crushed it out, lit another. "And I know he's scared down to the bone." With something close to a sigh, he jammed his hands in his pockets. "I'm all he's got, Ms. Stanislaski. Whatever it takes, I'm not going to see him go to prison."

It was never easy for her to harden her heart, but she tried. She wiped her hands carefully on a paper napkin. "Have you got enough money to cover the losses? Fifteen thousand?"

He winced, but nodded. "I can get it."

"It'll help. How much influence do you have over Nick?"

"Next to none." He smiled, and Rachel was surprised to note that the smile held considerable charm. "But that can change. I've got an established business, and a two-bedroom apartment. I can get you professional and character references, whatever you need. My record's clean— Well, I did spend thirty days in the brig when I was in the navy. Bar fight." He shrugged it off. "I don't guess they'd hold it against me, since it was twelve years ago."

Rachel turned the possibilities over in her mind. "If I'm reading you right, you want me to try to get the court to turn Nick over to your care."

"The probation and community service. A responsible adult to look out for him. All the damages paid."

"You might not be doing him any favor, Muldoon."

"He's my brother."

That she understood perfectly. Rachel cast her eyes skyward as the first drop of rain fell. "I've got to get back to the office. If you've got the time, you can walk with me. I'll make some calls, see what I can do."

A bar, Rachel thought with a sigh as she tried to put together a rational proposition for the hearing that afternoon. Why did the man have to own a bar? She supposed it suited him—the big shoulders, the big hands, the crooked nose that she assumed had been broken. And, of course, the rough, dark Irish looks that matched his temper.

But it would have been so much nicer if she could tell the judge that Zackary Muldoon owned a nice men's shop in midtown. Instead, she was going to ask a judge to hand over the responsibility and the guardianship of a nineteen-year-old boy—with a record and an attitude—to his thirty-two-year-old stepbrother, who ran an East Side bar called Lower the Boom.

There was a chance, a slim one. The DA was still pushing for names, but the shop owner had been greatly mollified with the promise of settlement. No doubt he'd inflated the price of his merchandise, but that was Muldoon's problem, not hers.

She didn't have much time to persuade the DA that he didn't want to try Nick as an adult. Taking what information she'd managed to pry out of Zack, she snagged opposing counsel and settled into one of the tiny conference rooms in the courthouse.

"Come on, Haridan, let's clean this mess up and save the court's time and the taxpayers' money. Putting this kid in jail isn't the answer."

Haridan, balding on top and thick through the middle, eased his bulk into a chair. "It's my answer, Stanislaski. He's a punk. A gang member with a history of antisocial behavior."

"Some tourist scams and some pushy-shovey."

"Assault."

"Charges were dropped. Come on, we both know it's minor-league. *He's* minor-league. We've got a scared, troubled kid looking for his place with a gang. We want him out of the gang, no question. But jail isn't the way." She held up a hand before Haridan could interrupt. "Look, his stepbrother is willing to help—not only by paying for property you have absolutely no proof my client stole, but by taking responsibility. Giving LeBeck a job, a home, supervision. All you have to do is agree to handling LeBeck as a minor."

"I want names."

"He won't give them." Hadn't she gone back down and harassed Nick for nearly an hour to try to pry one loose? "You can put him away for ten years, and you still won't get one. So what's the point? You haven't got a hardened criminal here—yet. Let's not make him one."

They knocked that back and forth, and Haridan softened. Not out of the goodness of his heart, but because his plate was every bit as full as Rachel's. He had neither the time nor the energy to pursue one punk kid through the system.

"I'm not dropping it down from burglary to nighttime breaking and entering." On that he was going to stand firm, but he would throw her a crumb. "Even if we agree to handle him as a juvie, the judge isn't going to let him walk with probation."

Rachel gathered up her briefcase. "Just leave the judge to me. Who'd we pull?"

Haridan grinned. "Beckett."

Marlene C. Beckett was an eccentric. Like a magician, she pulled unusual sentences out of her judge's robes as if they were little white rabbits. She was in her midforties, dashingly attractive, with a single streak of white hair that swept through a wavy cap of fire-engine red.

Personally, Rachel liked her a great deal. Judge Beckett was a staunch feminist and former flower child who had proven that a woman—an unmarried, career-oriented woman—could be successful and intelligent without being abrasive or whiny. She might have been in a man's world, but Judge Beckett was all woman. Rachel respected her, admired her, even hoped to follow in her footsteps one day.

She just wished she'd been assigned to another judge.

As Beckett listened to her unusual plea, Rachel felt her stomach sinking down to her knees. Beckett's lips were pursed. A bad sign. One perfectly manicured nail was tapping beside the gavel. Rachel caught the judge studying the defendant, and Zack, who sat in the front row behind him.

"Counselor, you're saying the defendant will make restitution for all properties lost, and that though the state is agreeable that he be tried as a minor, you don't want him bound over for trial."

"I'm proposing that trial may be waived, Your Honor, given the circumstances. Both the defendant's mother and stepfather are deceased. His mother died five years ago, when the defendant was fourteen, and his stepfather died last year. Mr. Muldoon is willing and able to take responsibility for his stepbrother. If it please the court, the defense suggests that once restitution is made, and a stable home arranged, a trial would be merely an unproductive way of punishing my client for a mistake he already deeply regrets."

With what might have been a snort, Beckett cast a look at Nick. "Do you deeply regret bungling your attempt at burglary, young man?"

Nick lifted one shoulder and looked surly. A sharp rap on the back of the head from his stepbrother had him snarling. "Sure, I—" He glanced at Rachel. The warning in her eyes did more to make him subside than the smack. "It was stupid."

"Undoubtedly," Judge Beckett agreed. "Mr. Haridan, what is your stand on this?"

"The district attorney's office is not willing to drop charges, Your Honor, though we will agree to regard the defendant as a juvenile. An offer to lessen or drop charges was made—if the defendant would provide the names of his accomplices."

"You want him to squeal on those he—mistakenly, I'm sure—considers friends?" Beckett lifted a brow at Nick. "No dice?"

"No, ma'am."

She made some sound that Rachel couldn't interpret, then pointed at Zack. "Stand up…Mr. Muldoon, is it?"

Ill at ease, Zack did so. "Ma'am? Your Honor?"

"Where were you when your young brother was getting himself mixed up with the Cobras?"

"At sea. I was in the navy until two years ago, when I came back to take over my father's business."

"What rank?"

"Chief petty officer, ma'am."

"Mm-hmm…" She took his measure, as a judge and as a woman. "I've been in your bar—a few years back. You used to serve an excellent manhattan."

Zack grinned. "We still do."

"Are you of the opinion, Mr. Muldoon, that you can keep your brother out of trouble and make a responsible citizen of him?"

"I…I don't know, but I want a chance to try."

Beckett tapped her fingers and sat back. "Have a seat. Ms. Stanislaski, the court is not of the opinion that a trial would be out of place in this matter—"

"Your Honor—"

Beckett cut Rachel off with a single gesture. "I haven't finished. I'm going to set bail at five thousand dollars."

This brought on an objection from the DA that was dealt with in exactly the same manner.

"I'm also going to grant the defendant what we'll call a provisionary probation. Two months," Beckett said, folding her hands. "I will set the trial date for two months from today. If during that two-month period the defendant is found to be walking the straight and narrow, is gainfully employed, refrains from associating with known members of the Cobras and has not committed any crime, this court will be amenable to extending that probation, with the likelihood of a suspended sentence."

"Your Honor," Haridan puffed out, "how can we be certain the defendant won't waltz in here in two months and claim to have upheld the provisions?"

"Because he will be supervised by an officer of the court, who will serve as co-guardian with Mr. Muldoon for the two-month period. And I will receive a written report on Mr. LeBeck from that officer." Beckett's lips curved. "I think I'm going to enjoy this. Rehabilitation, Mr. Haridan, does not have to be accomplished in prison."

Rachel restrained herself from giving Haridan a smug grin. "Thank you, Your Honor."

"You're quite welcome, Counselor. Have your report to me every Friday afternoon, by three."

"My..." Rachel blinked, paled, then gaped. "My report? But, Your Honor, you can't mean for me to supervise Mr. LeBeck."

"That is precisely what I mean, Ms. Stanislaski. I

believe having a male and a female authority figure will do our Mr. LeBeck a world of good.''

"Yes, Your Honor, I agree. But…I'm not a social worker."

"You're a public servant, Ms. Stanislaski. So serve." She rapped her gavel. "Next case."

Stunned speechless by the judge's totally unorthodox ruling, Rachel moved to the back of the courtroom. "Good going, champ," her brother muttered in her ear. "Now you've got yourself hooked good."

"How could she do that? I mean, how could she just *do* that?"

"Everybody knows she's a little crazy." Furious, he swung Rachel out in the hall by an elbow. "There's no way in holy hell I'm letting you play baby-sitter for that punk. Beckett can't force you to."

"No, of course she can't." After dragging a hand through her hair, she shook Alex off. "Stop pulling at me and let me think."

"There's nothing to think about. You've got your own family and your own life. Watching over LeBeck is out of the question. And for all you know, that brother of his is just as dangerous. It's bad enough I have to watch you defend these creeps. No way I'm having you play big sister to one of them."

If he'd sympathized with her predicament, she might not have been quite as hasty. If he'd told her she'd gotten a raw deal, she probably would have agreed and set the wheels in motion to negate it. But…

"You don't have to watch me do anything, Alexi, and I can play big sister to whomever I choose. Now why don't you take that big bad badge of yours and go arrest some harmless vagrant."

His blood boiled every bit as quickly as hers. "You're not doing this."

"I'll decide what I'm going to do. Now back off."

He cupped a hand firmly on her chin just as she poked it out. "I've got a good mind to—"

"The lady asked you to back off." Zack's voice was quiet, like a snake before it strikes. Alex whipped his head around, eyes hot and ready. It took all of his training to prevent himself from throwing the first punch.

"Keep out of our business."

Zack planted his feet and prepared. "I don't think so."

They looked like two snarling dogs about to go for the throat. Rachel pushed her way between them.

"Stop it right now. This is no way to behave outside a courtroom. Muldoon, is this how you're going to show Nick responsibility? By picking fights?"

He didn't even glance at her, but kept his eyes on Alex. "I don't like to see women pushed around."

"I can take care of myself." She rounded on her brother. "You're supposed to be a cop, for heaven's sake. And here you are acting like a rowdy schoolboy. You think about this. The court believes this is a viable solution, so I'm obligated to try it."

"Damn it, Rachel—" Alex's eyes went flat and cold when Zack stepped forward again. "Pal, you mess with me, or my sister, you'll be wearing your teeth in a glass by your bedside."

"Sister?" Thoughtfully Zack examined one face, then the other. Oh, yes, the family resemblance was strong enough when you took a minute to study them. They both had those wild good looks that came through the blood. His anger cooled instantly. That changed things. He gave Rachel another speculative look. It changed a lot of things.

"Sorry. I didn't realize it was a family argument. You go ahead and yell at her all you want."

Alex had to fight to keep his lips from twitching. "All right, Rachel, you're going to listen to me."

She had to sigh. Then she had to take his face in her hands and kiss him. "Since when have I ever listened to you? Go away, Alexi. Chase some bad guys. And I'll have to take a rain check on that movie tonight."

There was no arguing with her. There never was. Changing tactics, Alex stared down Zack. "You watch out for her, Muldoon, and watch good. Because while you're at it, I'm going to be watching you."

"Sounds fair. Come by the bar anytime, Officer. First one's on the house."

Muttering under his breath, Alex stalked away. He turned once when Rachel called something out to him in Ukrainian. With a reluctant smile, he shook his head and kept walking.

"Translation?" Zack asked.

"Just that I would see him Sunday. Did you pay the bond?"

"Yeah, they're going to release him in a minute." Zack took a moment to reevaluate now that he realized she'd been kissing her brother that morning, not a lover. "I take it your brother isn't too thrilled to see you tangled up with me and Nick."

She gave Zack a long, bland look. "Who is, Muldoon? But since that's the court ruling, let's go get started."

"Get started?"

"We're going to pick up our charge, and you're going to move him into your apartment."

After spending the better part of a decade sharing close quarters with a couple hundred sailors. Zack gave one last wistful thought to the dissolution of his privacy. "Right." He took Rachel by the arm—a gesture she tried not to resent. "I don't suppose you've got any rope in that briefcase of yours."

It wasn't necessary to tie Nick up to gain his cooperation. But it was close. He sulked. He argued. He swore. By the time they'd walked out of the courthouse to hail a cab, Zack was biting down on fury and Nick had switched his resentment to Rachel.

"If this is the best deal you could cut, you'd better go back to law school. I've got rights, and the first one is to fire you."

"Your privilege, LeBeck," Rachel said, idly checking her watch. "You're certainly free to seek other counsel, but you can't fire me as your court-appointed guardian. We're stuck with each other for the next two months."

"That's bull. If you and that crazy judge think you can cook up—"

Zack made his move first, but Rachel merely elbowed him out of the way and went toe-to-toe with Nick. "You listen to me, you sorry, spoiled, sulky little jerk. You've got two choices—pretending to be a human being for the next eight weeks or going to prison for three years. I don't give a damn which way you go, but I'll tell you this. You think you're tough? You think you've got all the answers? You go inside for a week, and with that pretty face of yours the cons will be on you like dogs on fresh meat. You'd be willing to deal then, pal. Believe me, you'd be willing to deal.''

That shut him up, and Rachel had the added satisfaction of seeing his angry flush die to a sickly pallor. She gestured when a cab swung to the curb. ''Your choice, tough guy,'' she said, and turned to Zack. ''I've got work to do. I should be able to clear things up by around seven, then I'll be by to see how things are going.''

''I'll keep dinner warm,'' he said with a smirk, then caught her hand before she could walk away. ''Thanks. I mean it.'' She would have shrugged it off. His hand was hard as rock, calluses over calluses. He grinned. ''You're all right, Counselor. For a broad.'' He climbed into the cab behind his brother, sent her a quick salute as they pulled away. ''She's right about you being a jerk, Nick,'' Zack said easily. ''But you sure as hell picked a lawyer with first-class legs.''

Nick said nothing, but he did sneak a look out the rear window. He'd noticed Rachel's legs himself.

When they arrived at Nick's room ten minutes later, Zack had to swallow another bout of temper. It wouldn't do any good to yell at the kid every five minutes. But why in the hell had he picked such a neighborhood?

Hoods loitering on street corners. Drug deals negotiated out in broad daylight. Hookers already slicked up and stalking their prey. He could smell the stench of overripe garbage and unwashed humanity. His feet crunched on broken glass as they crossed the heaving sidewalk and entered the scarred and graffiti-laden brick building.

The smells were worse here, trapped inside, where even the fitful September breeze couldn't reach. Zack maintained his silence as they climbed up three floors, ignoring the shouted arguments behind closed doors and the occasional crash and weeping.

Nick unlocked the door and stepped into a single room furnished with a sagging iron bed, a broken dresser and a rickety wooden chair braced with a torn phone book. A few heavy-metal posters had been tacked to the stained walls in a pitiful attempt to give the room some personality. Helpless against the rage that geysered inside him, Zack let loose with a string of curses that turned the stale air blue.

"And what the hell have you been doing with the money I sent home every month when I was at sea? With the salary you were supposed to be earning from the delivery job? You're living in garbage, Nick. What's worse, you chose to live in it."

Not for a second would Nick have admitted that most of his money had gone into the Cobra treasury. Nor would he have admitted the shame he felt at having Zack see how he lived. "It's none of your damn business," he shot back. "This is my place, just like it's my life. You were never around, were you? Just because you got tired of cruising around on some stupid destroyer doesn't give you the right to come back here and take over."

"I've been back two years," Zack pointed out wearily. "And I spent a year of that watching the old man die. You didn't bother to come around much, did you?"

Nick felt a fresh wash of shame, and a deep, desperate sorrow that he was certain Zack could never understand. "He wasn't my old man."

Zack's head jerked up. Nick's hands fisted. Violent temper snapped and sizzled in the room. The slightest move would have sparked it into flame. Slowly, effortfully, Zack forced his body to relax.

"I'm not going to waste my time telling you he did the best he could."

"How the hell do you know?" Nick tossed back. "You weren't here. You got out your way, *bro.* I got out mine."

"Which brings us full circle. Pack up what you want, and let's go."

"This is my place—" Zack moved so quickly that the snarl caught in Nick's throat. He was up against the wall, Zack's big hands holding him in place while his thin body quivered with rage. Zack's face was so close to his, all Nick could see were those dark, dangerous eyes.

"For the next two months, like it or not, your place is with me. Now cut the crap and get some clothes together. Your free ride's over." He released Nick, knowing he had the strength and skill to snap his defiant young brother in half. "You got ten minutes, kid. You're working tonight."

By seven, Rachel was indulging a fantasy about a steamy bubble bath, a glass of crisp white wine and an hour with a good book. It helped ease the discomfort of the crowded subway car. She braced her feet against the swaying, kept her gaze focused on the middle distance. There were a few rough-looking characters scattered through the car whom she'd assessed and decided to ignore. A wino was snoring in the seat behind her, his face hidden under a newspaper.

At her stop, she bulled her way out, then started up the steps into the wet, windy evening. Hunched in her jacket, she fought with her umbrella, then slogged the two blocks to Lower the Boom.

The beveled glass door was heavy. She tugged it open and stepped out of the chill into the warmth, sounds and scents of an established neighborhood bar. It wasn't the dive she'd been expecting, but a wide wood-paneled room with a glossy mahogany bar trimmed in brass. The stools were burgundy leather, and every one was occupied. Neat tables were set around the room to accommodate more customers. There were the scents of whiskey and beer, cigarette smoke and grilled onions. A jukebox played the blues over the hum of conversation.

She spotted two waitresses winding their way through the patrons. No fishnet stockings and cleavage, Rachel mused. Both women were dressed in white slacks with modified sailor tops. There was a great deal of laughter, and she caught snatches of an argument as to whether the Mets still had a chance to make the play-offs.

Zack was in the center of the circular bar, drawing a beer for a customer. He'd exchanged his sweatshirt for a cable-knit turtleneck in navy blue. Oh, yes, she could see him on the deck of a ship, Rachel realized. Braced against the rolling, face to the wind. The bar's nautical theme, with its ship's bells and anchors, suited him.

She conjured up an image of him in uniform, found it entirely too attractive, and blinked it away.

She wasn't the fanciful type, she reminded herself. She was certainly no romantic. Above all, she was not the kind of woman who walked into a bar and found herself attracted to some land-locked sailor with shaggy hair, big shoulders and rough hands.

The only reason she was here was to uphold the court's ruling. However distasteful it might be to be hooked up with Zackary Muldoon for two months, she would do her duty.

But where was Nick?

"Would you like a table, miss?"

Rachel glanced around at a diminutive blonde hefting a large tray laden with sandwiches and beer. "No, thanks. I'll just go up to the bar. Is this place always crowded?"

The waitress's gray eyes brightened as she looked around the room. "Is it crowded? I didn't notice." With a laugh, she moved off while Rachel walked to the bar. She eased her way between two occupied stools, rested a foot on the brass rail and waited to catch Zack's eye.

"Well, darling..." The man on her left had a plump, pleasant face. He shifted on his stool to get a better look. "Don't think I've seen you in here before."

"No." Since he looked old enough to be her father, Rachel granted him a small smile. "You haven't."

"Pretty young girl like you shouldn't be here all alone." He leaned back—his stool creaking dangerously—and slapped the man on her other side on the shoulder. "Hey, Harry, we ought to buy this lady a drink."

Harry, who continued to sip his beer and work a crossword puzzle in the dim light, merely nodded. "Sure thing, Pete. Set it up. I need a five-letter word for the possibility of danger or pain."

Rachel glanced up. Zack was watching her, his blue eyes dark and steady, his bony face set and unsmiling. She felt something hot streak up her spine. *"Peril,"* she murmured, and fought off a shudder.

"Yeah! Hey, thanks!" Pleased, Harry pushed up his reading glasses and smiled at her. "First drink's on me. What'll you have, honey?"

"Pouilly-Fumé." Zack set a glass of pale gold wine in front of her. "And the first one's on the house." He lifted a brow. "That suit you, Counselor?"

"Yes." She let out the breath she hadn't been aware of holding. "Thank you."

"Zack always gets the prettiest ones," Pete said with a sigh. "Tip me another, kid. Least you can do, since you stole my girl." He shot Rachel a wink that had her relaxing with a smile again.

"And how often does he steal your girls, Pete?"

"Once, twice a week. It's humiliating." He grinned at Zack over a fresh beer. "Old Zack did date one of my girls once. Remember that time you were home on leave, Zack, you took my Rosemary to the movies, out to Coney Island? She's married and working on her second kid now."

Zack mopped up the bar with a cloth. "She broke my heart."

"There isn't a female alive who's scratched your heart, much less broken it." This from the blond waitress, who slapped an empty tray on the bar. "Two house wines, white. A Scotch, water back, and a draft. Harry, you ought to buy yourself one of those little clip-on lights before you ruin what's left of your eyes."

"*You* broke my heart, Lola." Zack put some glasses on the tray. "Why do you think I ran off and joined the navy?"

"Because you knew how good you'd look in dress whites." She laughed, hefted the tray, then glanced at Rachel. "You watch out for that one, sweetie. He's dangerous."

Rachel sipped at her wine and tried to pretend the scents slipping out from the kitchen weren't making her stomach rumble. "Have you got a minute?" she asked Zack. "I need to see where you're living."

Pete let out a hoot and rolled his eyes. "What's the guy got?" he wanted to know.

"More than you'll ever have." Zack grinned at him and signaled to another bartender to cover for him. "I just seem to attract aggressive women. Can't keep their hands off me."

Rachel finished off her wine before sliding from the stool. "I can restrain myself if I put my mind to it. Though it pains me to mar his reputation," she said to Pete, "I'm his brother's lawyer."

"No fooling?" Impressed, Pete took a closer look. "You the one who got the kid out of jail?"

"For the time being. Muldoon?"

"Right this way for the tour." He flipped up a section of the bar and stepped through. Again he took her arm. "Try to keep up."

"You know, I don't need you to hold on to me. I've been walking on my own for some time."

He pushed open a heavy swinging door that led to the kitchen. "I like holding on to you."

Rachel got the impression of gleaming stainless steel and white porcelain, the heavy scent of frying potatoes and grilling meat, before her attention was absorbed by an enormous man. He was dressed all in white, and his full apron was splattered and stained. Because he towered over Zack, Rachel estimated him at halfway to seven feet and a good three-fifty. If he'd played football, he would have been the entire defensive line.

His face was shiny from the kitchen heat, and the color of india ink. There was a scar running from one coal-black eye down to his massive chin. His hamlike hands were delicately building a club sandwich.

"Rio, this is Rachel Stanislaski, Nick's lawyer."

"How-de-do." She caught the musical cadence of the West Indies in his voice. "Got that boy washing dishes like a champ. Only broke him five or six all night."

Standing at a huge double sink, up to the elbows in soapy water, Nick turned his head and scowled. "If you call cleaning up someone else's slop a job, you can just—"

"Now don't you be using that language around this lady here." Rio picked up a cleaver and brought it down with a *thwack* to cut the sandwich in two, then four. "My mama always said nothing like washing dishes to give a body plenty of time for searching the soul. You keep washing and searching, boy."

Nick would have liked to have said more. Oh, he'd

have loved to. But it was hard to argue with a seven-foot man holding a meat cleaver. He went back to muttering.

Rio smiled, and noted that Rachel was eyeing the sandwich. "How 'bout I fix you some hot meal? You can eat after you finish your business."

"Oh, I..." Her mouth was watering. "I really should get home."

"Zack, he's going to see you home after you're done. It's too late for a woman to go walking the streets by herself."

"I don't need—"

"Dish her up some of your chili, Rio," Zack suggested as he pulled Rachel toward a set of stairs. "This won't take long."

Rachel found herself trapped, hip to hip with him in a narrow staircase. He smelled of the sea, she realized, of that salty, slightly electric scent that meant a storm was brewing beyond the horizon. "It's very kind of you to offer, Muldoon, but I don't need a meal, or an escort."

"You'll get both, need them or not." He turned, effectively trapping her against the wall. It felt good to have his body brush hers. As good as he'd imagined it would. "I never argue with Rio. I met him in Jamaica about six years ago—in a little bar tussle. I watched him pick up a two-hundred-pound man and toss him through a wall. Now, Rio's mostly a peaceful sort of man, but if you get him riled, there's no telling what he might do." Zack lifted a hand and wound a lock of Rachel's hair around his finger. "Your hair's wet."

She slapped his hand away and tried to pretend her heart wasn't slamming in her throat. "It's raining."

"Yeah. I can smell it on you. You sure are something to look at, Rachel."

She couldn't move forward, couldn't move back, so she did the only thing open to her. She bristled like a cornered cat. "You're in my way, Muldoon. My advice is to move your butt and save the Irish charm for someone who'll appreciate it."

"In a minute. Was that Russian you yelled after your brother today?"

"Ukrainian," she said between her teeth.

"Ukrainian." He considered that, and her. "I never made it to the Soviet Union."

She lifted a brow. "Neither have I. Now can we save this discussion until after I've seen the living arrangements?"

"All right." He started up the steps again, his hand on the small of her back. "It's not much, but I can guarantee it's a large step up from the dump Nick was living in. I don't know why he—" He cut himself off and shrugged. "Well, it's done."

Rachel had a feeling it was just beginning.

Chapter Three

Though it brought on all manner of headaches, Rachel took her new charge seriously. She could handle the inconvenience, the extra time sliced out of her personal life, Nick's surly and continued resentment. What gave her the most trouble was the enforced proximity with Zackary Muldoon.

She couldn't dismiss him and she couldn't work around him. Having to deal with him on what was essentially a day-to-day basis was sending her stress level through the roof.

If only she could pigeonhole him, she thought as she walked from the subway to her apartment after a Sunday dinner with her family, it would somehow make things easier. But after nearly a week of trying, she hadn't even come close.

He was rough, impatient, and, she suspected, potentially violent. Yet he was concerned enough about his stepbrother to shell out money and—much more vital—time and energy to set the boy straight. In his off hours, he dressed in clothes more suited to the rag basket than his tall, muscled frame. Yet when she'd walked through his apartment over the bar, she'd found everything neat as a pin. He was always putting his hands on her—her arm, her hair, her shoulder— but he had yet to make the kind of move she was forever braced to repel.

He flirted with his female customers, but as far as Rachel had been able to glean, it stopped at flirtation. He'd never been married, and though he'd left his family for months, even years, at a time, he'd given up the sea and had landlocked himself when his father became too ill to care for himself.

He irritated her on principle. But on some deeper, darker level, the very things about him that irritated her fanned little flames in her gut that Rachel could only describe as pure lust.

She'd tried to cool them by reminding herself that she wasn't the lusty type. Passionate, yes. When it came to her work, her family and her ambitions. But men, though she enjoyed their companionship and their basic maleness, had never been at the top of her list of priorities.

Sex was even lower than that. And it was very annoying to find herself itchy.

So who was Zackary Muldoon, and would she be better off not knowing?

When he stepped out of the shadows into the glow of a streetlight, she jolted and choked back a scream.

"Where the hell have you been?"

"I— Damn it, you scared me to death." She brought a trembling hand back out of her purse, where it had shot automatically toward a bottle of Mace. Oh, she hated to be frightened. Detested having to admit she could be vulnerable. "What are you doing lurking out here in front of my building?"

"Looking for you. Don't you ever stay home?"

"Muldoon, with me it's party, party, party." She stalked up the steps and jammed her key in the outer door. "What do you want?"

"Nick took off."

She stopped halfway through the door, and he bumped solidly into her. "What do you mean, took off?"

"I mean he slipped out of the kitchen sometime this afternoon, when Rio wasn't looking. I can't find him." He was so furious—with Nick, with Rachel, with himself—that it took all of his control not to punch his fist through the wall. "I've been at it almost five hours, and I can't find him."

"All right, don't panic." Her mind was already clicking ahead as she walked through the tiny lobby to the single gate-fronted elevator. "It's early, just ten o'clock. He knows his way around."

"That's the trouble." Disgusted with himself, Zack stepped in the car with her. "He knows his way around too well. The rule was, he'd tell me when he was going, and where. I've got to figure he's hanging out with the Cobras."

"Nick's not going to break that kind of tie overnight." Rachel continued to think as the elevator creaked its way up to the fourth floor. "We can drive ourselves crazy running around the city trying to hunt him down, or we can call in the cavalry.''

"The cavalry?''

She shoved the gate open and walked into the hallway. "Alex.''

"No cops,'' Zack said quickly, grabbing her arms. "I'm not setting the cops on him.''

"Alex isn't just a cop. He's my brother.'' Struggling to hold on to her own patience, she pried his fingers from her arms. "And I'm an officer of the court, Zack. If Nick's breaking the provisions, I can't ignore it.''

"I'm not going to see him tossed back in a cell barely a week after I got him out.''

"*We* got him out,'' she corrected, then unlocked her door. "If you didn't want my help and advice, you shouldn't have come.''

Zack shrugged and stepped inside. "I guess I figured we could go out looking together.''

The room was hardly bigger than the one Nick had rented, but it was all female. Not flouncy, Zack thought. Rachel wouldn't go for flounce. There were vivid colors in the plump pillows tossed over a low-armed sofa. The scented candles were burned down to various lengths, and mums were just starting to fade in a china vase.

There was a huge bronze-framed oval mirror on one wall. Its glass needed resilvering. A three-foot sculpture in cool white marble dominated one corner. It reminded Zack of a mermaid rising up out of the sea. There were smaller sculptures, as well, all of them passionate, some of them bordering on the ferocious. A timber wolf rearing out of a slab of oak, twisted fingers of bronze and copper that looked like a fire just out of control, a smooth and sinuous malachite cobra ready to strike.

There were shelves of books, and dozens of framed photographs—and there was the unmistakable scent of woman.

Zack felt uncharacteristically awkward and clumsy, and completely out of place. He stuck his hands in his pockets, certain he'd knock over one of those slender tapers. His mother had liked candles, he remembered. Candles and flowers and blue china bowls.

"I'll make coffee." Rachel tossed her purse aside and walked into the adjoining kitchen.

"Yeah. Good." Restless, Zack roamed the room, checked out the view through the cheerful striped curtains, frowned over the photographs that were obviously of her family, paced back to the sofa. "I don't know what I'm doing. What makes me think I can play daddy to a kid Nick's age? I wasn't around for half his life. He hates me. He's got a right."

"You've been doing fine," Rachel countered, taking out cups and saucers. "You're not playing daddy, you're being his brother. If you weren't around for half his life, it's because you had a life of your own. And he doesn't hate you. He's angry and full of resentment which is a long way from hate—which he wouldn't have any right to. Now stop feeling sorry for yourself, and get out the milk."

"Is that how you cross-examine?" Not sure whether he was amused or annoyed, Zack opened the refrigerator.

"No, I'm much tougher than that in court."

"I bet." He shook his head at the contents of her

refrigerator. Yogurt, a package of bologna, another of cheese, several diet soft drinks, a jug of white wine, two eggs, and half a stick of butter. "You're out of milk."

She swore, then sighed. "So we drink it black. Did you and Nick have a fight?"

"No— I mean no more than usual. He snarls, I snarl back. He swears, I swear louder. But we actually had what could pass for a conversation last night, then watched an old movie on the tube after the bar closed."

"Ah, progress..." She handed him his coffee in a dainty cup and saucer that felt like a child's tea set in his hands.

"We get a lot of families in for lunch on Sundays." Zack ignored the china handle and wrapped his fingers around the bowl of the cup. "He was down in the kitchen at noon. I figured he might like to knock off early, you know, take some time for himself. I went into the kitchen around four. Rio didn't want to rat on him, so he'd been covering for him for an hour or so. I hoped he'd just taken a breather, but... Then I went out looking." Zack finished off the coffee, then helped himself to more. "I've been pretty hard on him the last few days. It seemed like the best way. On my first ship, my CO was a regular Captain Bligh. I hated the bastard until I realized he'd turned us into a crew." Zack grinned a little. "Hell, I still hated him, but I never forgot him."

"Stop beating yourself up." She couldn't prevent herself from reaching out, touching his arm. "It isn't as if you hanged him from the yardarm or whatever. Now sit down and try to relax. Let me talk to Alex."

He did sit, though he wasn't happy about it. Because he felt like an idiot trying to balance the delicate saucer on his knee, he set it down on the table. There wasn't an ashtray in sight, so he clamped down on the urge for a cigarette.

He paid little attention to Rachel until her voice rose in frustration. Then he smiled a little. She was certainly full of fire, punching out requests and orders with the aplomb of a seasoned seaman. Lord, he'd gotten so he looked forward to hearing that throaty, impatient voice. How many times over the past few days had he made up excuses to call her?

Too many, he admitted. Something about the lady had hooked him, and Zack wasn't sure whether he wanted to pry himself loose or be reeled in.

And the last thing he should be doing now was thinking of his libido, he reminded himself. He had to think about Nick.

Obviously Rachel's brother was resisting, but she wasn't taking no for an answer. When she switched to heated Ukrainian, Zack reached over to toy with the spitting cobra in the center of the coffee table. It drove him crazy when she talked in Ukrainian.

"Tak," she said, satisfied that she'd worn Alex down. "I owe you one, Alexi." She laughed, a rich, and full-blooded laugh that sent heat straight to Zack's midsection. "All right, all right, so I'll owe you two." Zack watched her hang up and cross long legs covered in a hunter-green material that was silky enough to whisper seductively when her thighs brushed together. "Alex and his partner are going to cruise around, check out some of the Cobras' known haunts. They'll let us know if they see him."

"So we wait?"

"We wait." She rose and took a fresh legal pad from a drawer. "To pass the time, you can fill me in a little more on Nick's background. You said his mother died when he was about fifteen. What about his father?"

"His mother wasn't married before." Zack reached automatically for a cigarette, then remembered. Recognizing the gesture, Rachel rose again and found a chipped ashtray. "Thanks." Relieved, he lit a cigarette, cupping his fingers around the tip out of habit. "Nadine was about eighteen when she got pregnant, and the guy wasn't interested in family. He took off and left her to fend for herself. So she had Nick and did what she could. One day she came into the bar looking for work. Dad hired her."

"How old was Nick?"

"Four or five. Nadine was barely making ends meet. Sometimes she couldn't get a sitter for him, so Dad told her to bring the kid along and I'd watch him. He was okay," Zack said with a half smile. "I mean, he was real quiet. Most of the time he'd just watch you like he was expecting to get dumped on. But he was smart. He'd just started school, but he could already read, and he could print some, too. Anyway, a couple months later, Nadine and my father got married. Dad was about twenty years older than she was, but I guess they were both lonely. My mother'd been dead for more than ten years. Nadine and the kid moved in."

"How did you...how did Nick adjust?"

"It seemed okay. Hell, I was a kid myself." Restless again, he rose to pace. "Nadine bent over backward trying to please everyone. That's the way she was. My father...he wasn't always easy, you know, and he put a lot of time into the bar. We weren't a Norman Rockwell kind of family, but we did okay.'' He glanced back at her photographs, surprised at the quick twinge of envy. ''I didn't mind the kid hanging around me. Much. Then I joined the navy, right out of high school. It was kind of a family tradition. When Nadine died, it was hard on Nick. Hard on my father. I guess you could say they took it out on each other.''

''Is that when Nick started to get into trouble?''

''I'd say he got into his share before that, but it got worse. Whenever I'd get back, my father would be full of complaints. The boy wouldn't do this, he did that. He was hanging around with punks. He was looking for trouble. And Nick would skulk off or slam out. If I said anything, he'd tell me to kiss his—'' He shrugged. ''You get the picture.''

She thought she did. A young boy unwanted by his father. He begins to admire his new brother, and then feels deserted by him, as well. He loses his mother and finds himself alone with a man old enough to be his grandfather, a man who couldn't relate to him.

Nothing permanent in his life—except rejection.

''I'm not a psychologist, Zack, but I'd say he needs time to trust that you mean to stay part of his life this time around. And I don't think taking a firm hand is wrong. In fact, I think that's just what he'd understand from you, and respect in the long run. Maybe that just needs to be balanced a bit.'' She sighed and set her notes aside. ''Which is where I come in. So far, I've been just as rough on him. Let's try a little good-cop-bad-cop. I'll be the sympathetic ear. Believe me, I understand hotheads and bad boys. I grew up with them. We can start by—'' The phone rang and she snagged it. ''Hello. Uh-huh. Good. That's good. Thanks, Alex.'' She could see the relief in Zack's eyes before she hung up. ''They spotted him on his way back to the bar.''

Relief sparked quickly into anger. ''When I get my hands on him—''

''You'll ask, in a very reasonable fashion, where he was,'' Rachel told him. ''And to make certain you do, I'm going with you.''

Nick let himself into Zack's apartment. He figured he'd been pretty clever. He'd managed to slip in and out of the kitchen without setting off Rio's radar. The way they were watching him around here, he thought, he might as well be doing time.

Everything was going wrong, anyway. He ducked into the kitchen and, since Zack wasn't around to say any different, opened a beer. He'd just wanted to check in with the guys, see what was happening on the street.

And they'd treated him like an outsider.

They didn't trust him, Nick thought resentfully as he swigged one long swallow, then two. Reece had decided that since he'd gotten out so quickly, he must have ratted. He thought he'd convinced most of the gang that he was clean, but when he'd spilled the whole story—from how he'd been caught to how he'd ended up washing dishes in Zack's bar, they'd laughed at him.

It hadn't been the good, communal laughter he'd shared with the Cobras in the past. It had been snide and nasty, with T.J. giggling like a fool and Reece smirking and playing with his switchblade. Only Cash had been the least bit sympathetic, saying how it was a raw deal.

Not one of them had bothered to explain why they'd left him hanging when the cop showed up.

When he'd left them, he'd gone by Marla's place. They'd been seeing each other steadily for the past couple of months, and he'd been sure he'd find a sympathetic ear, and a nice warm body. But she'd been out—with somebody else.

Looked as though he'd been dumped again, all around. Nothing new, Nick told himself. But the sting of rejection wasn't any easier to take this time.

Damn it, they were supposed to be his family. They were supposed to stick up for him, stand by him, not shake him loose at the first hint of trouble. He wouldn't have done it to them, he told himself, and heaved the empty beer bottle into the trash, where it smashed satisfactorily. No, by God, he wouldn't have done it to them.

When he heard the door open, he set his face into bored lines and sauntered out of the kitchen. He'd expected Zack, but he hadn't expected Rachel. Nick felt a heat that was embarrassment and something more try to creep up into his cheeks.

Zack peeled off his jacket, hoping he had a firm grip on his temper. "I guess you've got a good reason why you skipped out this afternoon."

"I wanted some air." Nick pulled out a cigarette, struck a match. "There a law against it?"

"We had an agreement," Zack said evenly. "You

were supposed to check with me before you went out, and tell me your plans.''

"No, man. You had an agreement. Last I looked it was a free country and people could go for a walk when they felt like it.'' He gestured toward Rachel. "You bring the lawyer to sue me, or what?''

"Listen, kid—''

"I'm not a kid,'' Nick shot back. "You came and went as you damn well pleased when you were my age.''

"I wasn't a thief at your age.'' Incensed, Zack took two steps forward. Rachel snagged his arm.

"Why don't you go down and get me a glass of wine, Muldoon? The kind you served me the other night will do just fine.'' When he tried to shake her off, she tightened her grip. "I want a moment alone with my client, so take your time.''

"Fine.'' He bit off the word before he stalked to the door. "Whatever she says, pal, you're on double KP next week. And if you try to sneak off again, I'll have Rio chain you to the sink.'' He gave himself the sweet satisfaction of slamming the door.

Nick took another puff on his cigarette and dropped onto the couch. "Big talk,'' he muttered. "He's always figured he could boss me around. I've been on my own for years, and it's time he got that straight.''

Rachel sat down beside him. She didn't bother to mention that she could smell the beer on his breath and he was underage. Why hadn't Zack seen the raw need in Nick's eyes? Why hadn't *she* seen it before?

"It's tough, having to move in here after having a place of your own.''

Her voice was mild, and without censure. Nick

squinted through the smoke. "Yeah," he said, cautiously. "I can hack it for a couple of months, I guess."

"When I first moved out, I was a little older than you—not much. I was excited, and scared, and lonely. I wouldn't have admitted to lonely if my life had depended on it. I've got two older brothers. They checked up on me constantly." She laughed a little. Nick didn't crack a smile. "It infuriated me, and it made me feel safe. They still get on my back, but I can usually find a way around them."

Nick stared hard at the tip of his cigarette. "He's not my real brother."

Oh, Lord, he looked young, she thought. And so terribly sad. "I suppose that would depend on your definition of real." She laid a hand on his knee, prepared for him to shrug her off, but he only switched his gaze from his cigarette to her fingers. "It'd be easier for you to believe he doesn't care, but you're not stupid, Nick."

There was a hot ball in his throat that he refused to believe was tears. "Why should he care? I'm nothing to him."

"If he didn't care, he wouldn't yell at you so much. Take it from me—I come from a family where a raised voice is a sign of unswerving love. He wants to look out for you."

"I can look out for myself."

"And have been," she agreed. "But most of us can use a hand now and again. He won't thank me for telling you all this, but I think you should know." She waited until he raised his eyes again. "He's had to take out a loan to pay for the stolen property and the damages.''

''That's bull,'' Nick shot back, appalled. ''Did he lay that trip on you?''

''No, I checked on it myself. It seems old Mr. Muldoon's illness drained quite a bit of his savings, and Zack's. Zack's gotten the bar back on a pretty solid footing again, but he didn't have enough to swing the costs. A man doesn't put himself out like that for someone he doesn't care about.''

The sick feeling in Nick's gut had him crushing out the cigarette. ''He just feels obligated, that's all.''

''Maybe. Either way, it seems to me you owe him something, Nick. At least you owe him a little cooperation over the next few weeks. He was scared when he came looking for me tonight. You probably don't want to believe that, either.''

''Zack's never been scared of anything.''

''He didn't come right out and say it, but I think he believed you'd taken off for good, that he wasn't going to see you again.''

''Where the hell would I go?'' he demanded. ''There's nobody—'' He broke off, ashamed to admit there was no one to go to. ''We made a deal,'' he muttered, ''I'm not going to skip.''

''I'm glad to hear it. And I'm not going to ask you where you went,'' she added with a faint smile. ''If I did, I'd have to put it in my report to Judge Beckett, and I'd rather not. So we'll just say you went out for some air, lost track of the time. Maybe the next time you feel like you've got to get out, you could call me.''

''Why?''

"Because I know how it feels when you need to break loose." He looked so lost that Rachel skimmed a hand through his hair, brushing it back from his face. "Lighten up, Nick. It's not a crime to be friends with your lawyer, either. So what do you say? You give me a break and try a little harder to get along with Zack, and I'll do what I can to keep him off your back? I know all kinds of tricks for handling nosy older brothers."

Her scent was clouding his senses. He didn't know why he hadn't noticed before how beautiful her eyes were. How deep and wide and soft. "Maybe you and I could go out sometime."

"Sure." She saw the suggestion only as a break-through in trust, and she smiled. "Rio's a terrific cook, but once in a while you just got to have pizza, right?"

"Yeah. So I can call you?"

"Absolutely." She gave his hand a quick squeeze. When his hand tightened over hers, she was only mildly surprised. Before she could comment, Zack was pushing the door open again. Nick jumped up as if he were on a string.

Zack passed Rachel her wine, then handed Nick the ginger-ale bottle he had hooked under one finger. Taking his time, he twisted off the top of the beer he had hooked under another. "So, did you two finish your consultation?"

"For now." Rachel sipped her wine and lifted a brow at Nick.

It wasn't easy, especially after what she'd told him Zack had done, but Nick met his brother's eyes. "I'm sorry I took off."

The surprise was so great that Zack had to swallow

quickly or choke on his beer. "Okay. We can work out a schedule so you can have more free time." What the hell did he do now? "Uh...Rio could use some help swabbing down the kitchen. Things usually break up early on Sunday nights."

"Sure, no problem." Nick started for the door. "See you, Rachel."

When the door closed, Zack dropped down beside her, shaking his head. "What'd you do, hypnotize him?"

"Not exactly."

"Well, what the hell did you say to him?"

She sighed, tremendously pleased with herself, and settled back. "That's privileged information. He just needs someone to stroke his bruised ego now and again. You two may not be biological brothers, but your temperament's very similar."

"Oh." He settled back, as well, swinging an arm around the top of the couch so that he could play with her hair. "How's that."

"You're both hotheaded and stubborn—which is easy for me to recognize, as I come from a long line of the same." Enjoying the wine and the quiet, she let her eyes close. "You don't like to admit you made a mistake, and you'd rather punch your way out of a problem than reason it through."

"Are you trying to say those are faults?"

She had to laugh. "We'll just call them personality traits. My family is ripe with passionate natures. And what a passionate nature requires is an outlet. My sister Natasha had dance, then her own business and her family. My brother Mikhail has his art. Alexi has his quest to right wrongs, and I have the law. As I see it, you had the navy, and now this bar. Nick hasn't found his yet.''

He brushed a finger lightly over the nape of her neck, felt the quick quiver that ran through her. ''Do you really consider the law enough of an outlet for passion?''

''The way I play it.'' She opened her eyes, but the smile that had started to curve her lips died away. He'd shifted, and his face was close—much too close—and his hands had slipped down to her shoulders. The warning bell that rang in her brain had come too late. ''I've got to get home,'' she said quickly. ''I've got a nine-o'clock hearing.''

''I'll take you in a minute.''

''I know the way, Muldoon.''

''I'll take you,'' he said again, and something in his tone made it quite clear that he wasn't talking about walking her to her door. He tugged the wineglass out of her hand and set it aside. ''We were talking about passionate natures.'' His fingers skimmed up through her hair, fisted in it. ''And outlets.''

In an automatic defensive gesture, her hand slammed against his chest, but he continued to draw her closer. ''I came here to help you, Muldoon,'' she reminded him as his mouth hovered dangerously above hers. ''Not to play games.''

''Just testing your theory, Counselor.'' He nipped lightly at her lower lip, once, twice. When that teasing sample stirred the juices, he crushed his mouth to hers and devoured.

She could stop him. Of course she would stop him, Rachel told herself. She knew how to defend herself against unwanted advances. The trouble was, she hadn't a clue as to how to defend herself against advances she didn't want to want.

His mouth was so…avid. So impatient. So greedy. She wondered if he would swallow her whole. He used lips and tongue and teeth devastatingly. If there was an instant, some fraction of a heartbeat, when she could have resisted, it passed unnoticed, and she was swamped by the hot wave that was his need, or hers. Or what they made together. On one long, throaty moan, she went under for the third time, dragging him with her.

He'd been prepared for her to slap or scratch. And he would have accepted it, would have forced himself to be satisfied with that quick, tempting taste. He was a man with large appetites, but he had never been one to take what wasn't offered willingly.

She didn't offer. She exploded. In that blink of time before his mouth covered hers, he'd seen the fire come into her eyes, that dark, liquid fire that equaled passion. When the kiss had gone from teasing to fevered, she had answered, pulling him far deeper into that hot well of desires than he'd intended to go.

And that moan. It sprinted along his spine, that glorious feline sound that was both surrender and demand. Even as it died away, she was wrapping herself around him, pressing that incredibly lean and limber body against his in a way that had a chain of explosions rioting through his system.

She heard his breathy oath, felt the long cushions of the couch press into her back as he shifted her. For one wild moment, all she could think was Yes! This was what she wanted, this wild flurry of sensations, this crazed, mindless mating of flesh. As his mouth raced down to savage her throat, she arched against him, craving the possession.

Then he said her name. Groaned it. The shock of hearing it ripped her back to reality. She was grappling on a couch in a strange apartment with a man she barely knew.

"No." His hands were moving over her, and they nearly dragged her back into the whirlwind. Desperate to pull away, she shoved and struggled. "Stop. I said no."

He couldn't get his breath. If someone had held a gun to his head, he wouldn't have moved. But the *no* stopped him. He managed to lift his head, and the reckless light in his eyes had her fighting against a shudder. "Why?"

"Because this is insane." God, she could still taste him on her lips, and the churning for more of him was making her crazy. "Get off me."

He could have strangled her for making him want to beg. "Your call, lady." Because his hands were unsteady, he balled them into fists. "I thought you said you didn't play games."

She was humiliated, furious, and frustrated beyond belief. As she saw it, the best disguise was full-blown anger. "I don't. You're the one who pushed yourself on me. The simple fact is, I'm not interested."

"I guess that's why you were kissing me so hard my teeth are loose."

"You kissed me." She jabbed a finger at him. "And you're so damn big I couldn't stop you."

"A simple no did," he reminded her, and lit a cigarette. "Let's keep it honest, Counselor. I wanted to kiss you. I've been wanting to do that, and more, ever since I saw you sitting like a queen in that grubby station house. Now, maybe you didn't feel the same way, but when I kissed you, you kissed me right back.''

Sometimes retreat was the best defense. Rachel snatched up her purse and jacket. ''It's done, so there's nothing more to discuss.''

''Wrong.'' He was up and blocking her path. ''We can finish discussing it while I take you home.''

''I don't want you to take me home. I'm not having you take me home.'' Eyes blazing, she swung her jacket over her shoulders. ''And if you insist on following me there, I'll have you arrested for harassment.''

He merely grabbed her by the arm. ''Try it.''

She did something she wished she'd done the first time she laid eyes on him. She punched him in the stomach. He let out a little *whoosh* of air, and his eyes narrowed.

''First one's free. Now, we can walk to the subway, or I can carry you there.''

''What's wrong with you?'' she shouted. ''Can't you take no for an answer?''

His response was to shove her back against the door and kiss the breath out of her. ''If I didn't,'' he said between his teeth, ''we wouldn't be walking out of here right now when you've got me so wound up I'm going to have to live in a cold shower for the next week.'' He yanked open the door. ''Now...are you going to walk, or are you going to ride over my shoulder?''

She stuck out her chin and sailed past him.

She'd walk, all right. But she'd be damned if she'd speak to him.

Chapter Four

At the end of a harried ten-hour day, Rachel walked out of the courthouse. She should have been feeling great—her last client was certainly happy with the non-guilty verdict she'd gotten for him. But this time the victory hadn't managed to lift her spirits. The only solution she could see was to pick up a quart of ice cream on the way home and gorge herself into a sugar coma.

It usually worked, and since, as a law-abiding citizen, she couldn't relieve her tension by striding into Lower the Boom and shooting Zackary Muldoon through his thick skull, it was the safest alternative.

She almost tripped over her own feet when she saw him rise from his perch at the bottom of the steps.

"Counselor." He reached out a hand when she teetered. "Steady as she goes."

"What now?" she demanded, jerking away. "Doesn't it occur to you that—even though I've been appointed by the court as Nick's co-guardian—I'm entitled to an hour of personal time without you in my face?"

He studied that face, noting signs of fatigue, as well as temper, in those big, tawny eyes. "You know, honey, I figured you'd be in a better mood after winning a case like you just did. Let's try these." With a flourish, he brought his other hand from behind his back. It was filled with gold, bronze and rust-colored mums.

Refusing to be charmed, Rachel gave them one long, suspicious glare. "What are those for?"

"To replace the ones that are dying in your apartment." When she made no move to take them, he bit down on his impatience. He'd come to apologize, damn it, and it looked as though she was going to make him go through with it. "Okay, I'm sorry. I got pushy the other night. And after I got over wanting to choke you, I realized you'd gone out of your way to do me a favor, and I'd repaid it by..." Furious all over again, he thrust the flowers at her. "Hell, lady, all I did was kiss you."

All he did? she thought, tempted to toss the flowers down and grind them underfoot. Just kissing didn't jangle a woman's system for better than thirty-six hours. "Why don't you take your flowers, and your charming apology, and—"

"Hold on." He thought it better to stop her before she said something he'd regret. "I said I was sorry, and I meant it, but maybe I should be more specific." To ensure that she'd stay put until he was finished, he wrapped his fingers around the lapel of her plum-colored jacket. "I'm not sorry I kissed you, any more than I'm going to be sorry the next time I kiss you. I am sorry for the way I acted after you put on the brakes."

She lifted a brow. "The way you acted," she repeated. "You mean like a jerk."

It gave her a great deal of pleasure to see a muscle twitch in his jaw.

"Okay."

A smart attorney knew when to accept a compromise. Lips pursed, she studied the flowers. "Are these a bribe, Muldoon?"

The way she said his name, with just a hint of a sneer, told him he'd gotten over the first hurdle. "Yeah."

"All right, I'll take them."

"Gee, thanks." Now that his hands were free, he tucked his thumbs in his front pockets. "I slipped in the courtroom about an hour ago and watched you."

"Oh?" She couldn't tell him how glad she was she hadn't seen him. "And?"

"Not bad. Turning a vandalism charge around on the other guy—"

"The plaintiff," she explained. "My client was justifiably frustrated after he'd exhausted all reasonable attempts to have his landlord live up to the terms of his lease."

"And spray painting The Landlord from Hell all over the guy's brownstone on the Upper West Side was his way of relieving that frustration."

"He certainly made his point. My client had paid his rent on time and in good faith, and the landlord consistently refused to acknowledge each and every request for repair and maintenance. Under the terms of the lease—''

"Hey, babe." Zack raised a hand, palm out. "You don't have to sell me. By the time you got through, I was pulling for him. There were murmurs in the visitors' gallery about lynching the landlord." His mouth was sober enough, but his eyes danced with humor. The contrast was all but irresistible.

Her smile was quick and wicked. "I love justice."

Reaching out, he toyed with the tiny gold links circling her neck. "Maybe you'd like to celebrate your victory for the underdog. Want to go for a walk?"

Mistake. The word popped full-blown into her mind, but she could smell the spicy flowers, and the evening was beautifully balmy. "I guess I would, as long as it's to my apartment. I should put these in water."

"Let me take that." He'd tugged the briefcase out of her hand before she could object. Then—she should have expected it—he took her arm. "What do you carry in here, bricks?"

"The law's a weighty business, Muldoon." His grip on her forced her to slow her pace to his. He strolled when she would have strode. "So, how's it going with Nick?"

"It's better. At least I think it's better. He balked at the idea of Rio teaching him to cook, but the idea of busing tables didn't seem to bother him much. He still won't talk to me—I mean really talk to me. But it's only been a week."

"You've got seven more."

"Yeah." He let go of her arm long enough to reach

into his pocket and take out a handful of change. He dropped it into a panhandler's cup in a gesture so automatic that Rachel assumed he made a habit of it. "I figure if they could turn me from a green recruit into a sailor in about the same amount of time, I have a pretty good shot at this."

"Do you miss it?" She tilted her head up to his. "Being at sea?"

"Not so much anymore. Sometimes I still wake up at night and think I'm aboard ship." Then there were the nightmares, but that wasn't something a man shared with a woman. "Once things are stable, I'm planning on buying a boat, maybe taking a couple of months and sailing down to the Islands. Maybe a nice ketch, forty-two feet—not too fancy." He could already see it, a trim little honey, quick to the touch, brass and mahogany gleaming, white sails bulging in the wind. He imagined Rachel would look just fine standing at the bow. "You ever done any sailing?"

"Not unless you count taking the ferry over to Liberty Island."

"You'd like it." He skimmed his fingers lightly down her arm. "It's what you might call an outlet."

Rachel decided it was safer not to comment. When they reached her building, she turned to him, holding out a hand for her briefcase. "Thanks for the flowers, and the walk. I'll probably come by the bar tomorrow after work and look in on Nick."

Instead of giving her the briefcase, he closed his hand over hers. "I took the night off, Rachel. I want to spend it with you."

Her quick jolt of alarm both pleased and amused him. "Excuse me?"

"Maybe I should rephrase that. I'd like to spend the night with you—several nights running, in fact—but I'll settle for the evening." He managed to wind a lock of her hair around his finger before she remembered to bat his hand away. "Some food, some music. I know a place that does both really well. If the idea of a date makes you nervous..."

"I'm not nervous." Not exactly, she thought.

"Anyway, we can consider it a few hours between two people who have a mutual interest. It couldn't hurt if we got to know each other a little better." He pulled out his trump card. "For Nick's sake."

She studied him, much as she had the witness she'd so ruthlessly cross-examined earlier. "You want to spend the evening with me for Nick's sake?"

Giving up, he grinned. "Hell, no. There's bound to be some spillover benefit there, but I want to spend the evening with you for purely selfish reasons."

"I see. Well, since you didn't perjure yourself, I may be able to cut a deal. It has to be an early evening, somewhere I can dress comfortably. And you won't..." How had he phrased it? "Get pushy."

"You're a tough one, Counselor."

"You got it."

"Deal," he said, and gave her the briefcase.

"Fine. Come back in twenty minutes. I'll be ready."

A bar, Rachel thought a half hour later. She should have known Zack would spend his night off on a busman's holiday. Actually, she supposed it was more of a club. There was a three-piece band playing the blues on a small raised stage, and there were a handful of couples dancing on a tiny square of floor surrounded by tables. From the way he was greeted by the waitress, he was obviously no stranger.

Within moments they were settled at a table in a shadowy corner, with a glass of wine for her and a mug of beer for him.

"I come for the music," he explained. "But the food's good, too. That's not something I mention to Rio."

"Since I've seen the way he slices a club sandwich, I can't hold that against you." She squinted at the tiny menu. "What do you recommend?"

"Trust me." His thigh brushed hers as he shifted closer to toy with the stones dangling at her ear. He smiled at her narrowed eyes. "And try the grilled chicken."

She discovered he could be trusted, at least when it came to food. Enjoying every bite, lulled by the music, she began to relax. "You said the navy was a family tradition. Is that why you joined, really?"

"I wanted to get out." He nursed a second beer, appreciating the way she plowed through the meal. He'd always been attracted to a woman with an appetite. "I wanted to see the world. I only figured on the four years, but then I re-upped."

"Why?"

"I got used to being part of a crew, and I liked the life. Looking out and seeing nothing but water, or watching the land pull away when you headed out. Coming into port and seeing a place you'd never seen before."

"In nearly ten years I imagine you saw a lot of places."

"The Mediterranean, the South Pacific, the Indian Ocean, the Persian Gulf. Froze my…fingers off in the North Atlantic and watched sharks feed in the Coral Sea."

Both fascinated and amused, she propped her elbows on the table. "Did you know you didn't mention one land mass? Doesn't one body of water look pretty much like another from the deck of a ship?"

"No." He didn't think he could explain, knew he wasn't lyrical enough to describe the varying hues of the water, the subtle degrees of the power of the deep. What it felt like to watch dolphins run, or whales sound. "I guess you could say that a body of water has its own personality, just like a body of land does."

"You do miss it."

"It gets in your blood. How about you? Is the law a Stanislaski family tradition?"

"No." Under the table, her foot began to tap to the beat of the bass. "My father's a carpenter. So was his father."

"Why law?"

"Because I'd grown up in a family who'd known oppression. They escaped Ukraine with what they could carry in a wagon—in the winter through the mountains—eventually reaching Austria. I was born here, the first of my family to be born here."

"It sounds as though you regret it."

He was astute, she decided. More astute than she'd given him credit for. "I suppose I regret not being a part of both sides. They haven't forgotten what it was like to taste freedom for the first time. I've never known anything but freedom. Freedom and justice go hand in hand."

"Some might say you could be serving justice in a nice, cushy law firm."

"Some might."

"You had offers." When her brows lifted, he shrugged. "You're representing my brother. I checked on you. Graduated top of your class at NYCC, passed the bar first shot, then turned down three very lucrative offers from three very prestigious firms to work for peanuts as a public defender. I had to figure either you were crazy or dedicated."

She swallowed a little bubble of temper and nodded. "And you left the navy with a chestful of medals, including the Silver Star. Your file includes, along with a few reprimands for insubordination, a personal letter of gratitude from an admiral for your courage during a rescue at sea in a hurricane." Enjoying his squirm of embarrassment, she lifted her glass in toast. "I checked, too."

"We were talking about you," he began.

"No. You were." Smiling, she cupped her chin on her hand. "So tell me, Muldoon, why did you turn down a shot at officer candidate school?"

"Didn't want to be a damn officer," he muttered. Rising, he grabbed her hand and hauled her to her feet. "Let's dance."

She chuckled as he dragged her onto the crowded dance floor. "You're blushing."

"I am not. And shut up."

Rachel tucked her tongue in her cheek. "It must be hell being a hero."

"Here's the deal." Zack held her lightly by the arms on the edge of the dance floor. "You drop the stuff about medals and admirals, and I won't mention that you were class valedictorian.''

She thought it over. "Fair enough. But I think—"

He pulled her into his arms. "Stop thinking."

It did the trick, all right. The moment she found herself pressed hard against him, her mind clicked off. She could still hear the music, the low, seductive alto sax, the pulse of the bass, the slow rhythms of the piano notes, but rational thought vanished.

They weren't dancing. Rachel was certain no one would call this locked-hard, swaying embrace a dance. But it would be foolish to try to pull away when there was so little room. Breathing wasn't all that important, after all. Not when you could feel your own heart slamming against your ribs.

She hadn't intended to wind her arms quite so firmly around his neck, but now that they were there, there seemed little point in moving them. Besides, if she skimmed her fingers up just a bit, they could trail through his hair so that she could discover how fascinating that silky contrast was compared to the rock-hard body molded to hers.

"You fit." He bent his head so that his mouth was against her ear. "I was a little too wound up to be sure the other night. But I thought you would."

The subtle movements of his lips against her skin had her shivering before she could prevent it. "What?"

"Fit," he said again, letting his hands follow those curvy lines down to her hips and back again.

"That's only because I'm standing on my toes."

"Honey, height doesn't have a thing to do with it." He rubbed his cheek against her hair, filling himself with the scent, the texture. "You feel right, you smell right, you taste right."

Shaken, she turned her head before his mouth could finish its journey down the side of her face. "I could have you arrested for trying to seduce me in a public place."

"That's all right. I know a good lawyer." He trailed his fingers under the back of her soft wool sweater to the heated skin beneath.

Her breath caught, then released unsteadily. "They'll have us both arrested."

"I'll post bail." There was nothing but Rachel under the sweater, he was sure of it. His mouth went dry as dust. "I want you alone." Biting off a groan, he dipped his head to press his lips to her neck. "Do you know what I'd do to you right now if I had you alone?"

She shook her swimming head. "We should sit down. We shouldn't do this."

"I want to touch you, every inch of you. And taste you. I want to make you crazy."

He already was. If she didn't manage to slow things down, her overcharged system was likely to explode. "Two steps back," she said on a long breath, and took just that. His hands remained at her waist, but at least she could breathe again. At least she managed two gulps of air before she looked into his eyes and the breath backed up in her lungs again. "Too much, too fast, Muldoon. I'm not a spontaneous type of person."

What she *was* was a volcano ready to erupt. He was damn sure going to be there when the ground started to shake. But he didn't intend to scare her off, either.

"Hey, you want time. I can give you an hour. Two, if you really want me to suffer."

She shook her head, edging back to the table. "Let's just say I'll let you know if and when I'm ready to take this any further."

"She wants me to suffer," Zack said under his breath. When she didn't sit, he reached for his wallet. "I take it we're leaving."

"An early evening," she reminded him. And she wanted badly to get outside, where the air could cool her blood.

"A deal's a deal." He tossed bills onto the table. "Why don't we walk back? A little exercise might help us both sleep tonight."

A twenty-block hike, Rachel mused. It couldn't hurt.

"Cold?" he asked a short time later.

"No. It's nice." But he slipped an arm around her shoulders anyway. "I don't often get a chance to just walk. Mostly it's a dash from my place to the office, from the office to the courthouse."

"What do you do when you're not dashing?"

"Oh, I go to the movies, window-shop, visit the family. In fact, I was thinking it might be good for Nick to go with me one Sunday. Have some of Mama's home cooking, listen to one of Papa's stories, see how my brothers harass me."

"Just Nick?"

She slanted him a look. "I suppose we could make room for Nick's brother."

"It's been a long time since I—since either of us

had a family meal. How about the cop? I can't see him piping us aboard.''

"I'll handle Alex." Now that she'd suggested it, her mind began to turn quickly. "You know, Natasha and her family are due to visit in a couple of weeks. Things will be crowded and crazy. It might be the perfect opportunity to toss Nick into your not-so-average-family type of situation. I'll see what I can work out.''

"I know I thanked you before, but I don't think I know how to tell you how much I appreciate what you're doing for him.''

"The court—''

"That's bilge, Rachel." They reached the steps of her building, and he turned her to face him. "You're not just filing weekly reports or representing a client. You put yourself out for Nick right from the start.''

"Okay, so I've got a weak spot for bad boys. Don't let it get around.''

"No, what you've got is class, and a good heart." He liked the way she looked in the shadowy light, the vitality that pulsed from her like breath, the snap of energy and embarrassment in her eyes. "It's a tough combination to beat.''

She shrugged under his hands. "Now you're going to make me blush, Muldoon, so let's not get sloppy. If things work out the way we want, you can buy me more flowers at the end of the two months. We'll call it square." He let her back up one step, but then held her firm. She was uneasy, but she wasn't surprised. "Listen, it's been nice, but...''

"I don't figure you're going to ask me in.''

"No," she said definitely, remembering how her

body had reacted to him in a crowded club. "I'm not."

"So I'll just have to take care of this out here."

"Zack..."

"You know I'm not going to let you go without kissing you, Rachel." To tease them both, he skimmed his lips over her jaw. "Especially when I only have to touch you to know all the want's not on my side."

"This is never going to work," she murmured, but her arms were already sliding around him.

"Sure it will. We just put our lips together, and what happens happens."

This time she knew what to expect, and braced. It made no difference at all. The same heat, the same rush, the same power. The same reckless, unrelenting need. Had she said it was too much? No, it wasn't enough. She was afraid she could never get enough. How could she have lived her entire life without knowing what it was to be truly needy?

"I'm not getting involved this way," she murmured against his mouth. "Not with you. Not with anyone."

"Okay. Fine." Ruthlessly, he dragged her head back and plundered. A flash fire erupted between them until he felt singed down to the bone. He all but whimpered when she nipped impatiently at his lower lip. Images began to cartwheel in his head—him scooping her up and carrying her inside, falling with her into a big, soft bed. Making love with her on some white, deserted beach, with the sun beating down on her naked, golden skin. Waves pounding against the shore as she cried out his name.

"Hey, buddy."

The voice behind him was nothing more than an

irritating buzzing in his head. Zack would cheerfully have ignored it, but he felt the slight prick of a knife at his back. Keeping Rachel behind him, he turned and looked into the pale, sooty-eyed face of the mugger.

"How about I let you keep the babe, and you hand over your wallet? Hers, too." The mugger turned the knife so that the backwash of the streetlight caught the steel. "And let's make it fast."

Blocking Rachel with his body, Zack reached in his back pocket. He could hear Rachel's unsteady breathing as she unzipped her bag. It wasn't impulse, but instinct. The moment the mugger's eyes shifted, Zack lunged.

With a scream in her throat and the Mace in her hand, Rachel watched them struggle. She saw the knife flash, heard the awful crunch of fist against bone before the blade clattered to the sidewalk. Then the mugger was racing off into the dark, and she and Zack were as alone as they'd been seconds before.

He turned back to her. She noted that he wasn't even breathing hard, and that the gleam in his eyes had only sharpened. "Where were we?"

"You idiot." The words were little more than a whisper as she fought to get them out over the lump of fear in her throat. "Don't you know any better than to jump someone holding a knife? He could have killed you."

"I didn't feel like losing my wallet." He glanced down at the can in her hand. "What's that?"

"Mace." Disgusted by the fact she hadn't even popped off the safety top, she dropped it back in her purse. "I'd have given him a faceful if you hadn't gotten in the way."

"Next time I'll step aside and let you handle it." He frowned down at the trickle of blood on his wrist and swore without much heat. "I guess he nicked me."

She went pale as water. "You're bleeding."

"I thought it was his." Annoyed more than hurt, he poked a finger through the rip in the arm of his sweater. "I got this on Corfu, my last time through. Damn it." Eyes narrowed, he stared down the street, wondering if he had a chance of catching up with the mugger and taking the price of the sweater, if not its sentimental value, out of his hide.

"Let me see." Her fingers trembled as she pushed the sleeve up to examine the long, shallow slash. "Idiot!" she said again, and began to fumble in her purse for her keys. "You'll have to come inside and let me fix it. I can't believe you did something so stupid."

"It was the principle," he began, but she cut him off with a stream of Ukrainian as she stabbed her key at the lock.

"English," he said, pressing a hand to his stomach as it began to knot. "Use English. You don't know what it does to me when you talk in Russian."

"It's not Russian." Snatching his good arm, she pulled him inside. "You were just showing off, that's all. Oh, it's just like a man." Still pulling him, she stalked into the elevator.

"Sorry." He was fighting off a grin, trying to look humble. "I don't know what got into me." He certainly wasn't going to admit he'd had worse scratches shaving.

"Testosterone," she said between her teeth. "You can't help it." She kept her hand on him until she'd gotten them inside her apartment. "Sit," she ordered, and dashed into the bathroom.

He sat, making himself at home by propping his feet on her coffee table. "Maybe I should have a brandy," he called out. "In case I'm going into shock."

She hurried back out with bandages and a small bowl of soapy water. "Do you feel sick?" Scared all over again, she pressed a hand to his brow. "Are you dizzy?"

"Let's see." Always willing to take advantage of an opportunity, he grabbed a fistful of her hair and pulled her mouth to his. "Yeah," he said when he let her go. "You could say I'm feeling a little light-headed."

"Fool." She slapped his hand aside, then sat down to clean the wound. "This could have been serious."

"It was serious," he told her. "I hate having someone poke me in the back with a knife when I'm kissing a woman. Honey, if you don't stop shaking, I'm going to have to get *you* a brandy."

"I'm not shaking—or if I am, it's just because I'm mad." She tossed her hair back and glared at him. "Don't you ever do that again."

"Aye, aye, sir."

To pay him back for the smirk, she dumped iodine over the wound. When he swore, it was her turn to smile. "Baby," she said accusingly, but then took pity on him and blew the heat away. "Now hold still while I put a bandage on it."

He watched her work. It was very pleasant to feel her fingers on his skin. It seemed only natural that he should lean over to nibble at her ear.

Fire streaked straight up her spine. "Don't." Shifting out of reach, she pulled his sleeve down over the fresh bandage. "We're not going to pick things up now. Not here." Because if they did, she knew there would be no backing off.

"I want you, Rachel." He caught her hand in his before she could stand. "I want to make love with you."

"I know what you want. I have to know what I want."

"Before we were interrupted downstairs, I think that was pretty clear."

"To you, maybe." After a deep breath, she pulled her hand free and stood. "I told you, I don't do things spontaneously. And I certainly don't take a lover on impulse. If I act on the attraction I feel for you, I'll do so with a clear head."

"I don't think I've had a clear head since I laid eyes on you." He stood, as well, but because it suddenly seemed important to both of them he kept his distance. "I realize how the saying goes about guys like me and women in every port. That's not reality—not my reality, anyway. I'm not going to tell you I spent every liberty curled up with a good book, but..."

"It's not my business."

"I'm beginning to think it is, or could be." The look in his eyes kept her from arguing. "I've been on land for two years, and there hasn't been anybody important." He couldn't believe what he was saying, what he felt compelled to say, but the words just tumbled out. "I'll be damned if there's ever been anyone like you in my life."

"I have priorities..." she began. The words

sounded weak to her. "And I don't know if I want this kind of complication right now. We have Nick to think about, as well, and I'd rather we just take it slow."

"Take it slow," he repeated. "I can't give you any promises on that. I *can* promise that the first chance I get, when it's just you and me, I'm going to do whatever it takes to shake up those priorities of yours."

She jammed nervous hands in her pockets. "I appreciate the warning, Muldoon. And here's one for you. I don't shake easily."

"Good." His grin flashed before he walked to the door. "Winning's no fun if it's easy. Thanks for the first aid, Counselor. Lock your door." He shut it quietly behind him and decided to walk home.

At this rate, he was never going to get any sleep.

Chapter Five

She wasn't avoiding him. Exactly. She was busy, that was all. Her caseload didn't allow time for her to drop by Zack's bar night after night and chat with the regulars. It wasn't as if she were neglecting her duty. She had slipped in a time or two to talk with Nick in the kitchen. If she'd managed to get in and out without running into Zack, it was merely coincidence.

And a healthy survival instinct.

If she let her answering machine screen her calls at home, it was simply because she didn't want to be disturbed unnecessarily.

Besides, he hadn't called. The jerk.

At least she was making some progress where Nick was concerned. He had called her, twice. Once at her office, and once at home. She found his suggestion that they catch a movie together a hopeful sign. After all, if he spent an evening with her, he wouldn't be hanging out with the Cobras, looking for trouble.

After ninety minutes of car chases, gunplay and the assorted mayhem of the action-adventure he'd chosen, they settled down in a brightly lit pizzeria.

"Okay, Nick, so tell me how it's going." His answer was a shrug, but Rachel gave his arm a squeeze and pressed. "Come on, you've had two weeks to get used to things. How are you feeling about it?"

"It could be worse." He pulled out a cigarette. "It's not so bad having a little change in my pocket, and I guess Rio's not so bad. It's not like he's on my case all the time."

"But Zack is?"

Nick blew out a stream of smoke. He liked to watch her through the haze. It made her look more mysterious, more exotic. "Maybe he's laid off a little. But it's like tonight. I got the night off, right? But he wants to know where I'm going, who I'm going with, when I'll be back. That kind of sh—" He caught himself. "That kind of stuff. I mean, hey, I'm going to be twenty in a couple of months. I don't need a keeper."

"He's a pushy guy," Rachel said, trying to strike a balance between sympathy and sternness. "But he's not only responsible for you in the eyes of the law— he cares about you." Because his answering snort seemed more automatic than sincere, she smiled. "His style's a little rough, but I'd have to say his intentions are good."

"He's going to have to give me some room."

"You're going to have to earn it." She squeezed his hand to take the sting out of her words. "What did you tell him about tonight?"

"I said I had a date, and he should butt out." Nick grinned, pleased when he saw the answering humor in Rachel's eyes. He'd have been very disappointed if he'd realized she was amused at the term *date*. "It's like he's got his life and I got mine. You know what I'm saying?"

"Yes." She drew a deep appreciative breath as their pizza arrived. "And what do you want to do with your life, Nick?"

"I figure I'll take what comes."

"No ambitions?" She took the first bite, watching him. "No dreams?"

Something flickered in his eyes before he lowered them. "I don't want to be serving drinks for a living, that's for sure. Zack can have it." After crushing out his cigarette, he applied himself to the pizza. "And no way I'm going into the damn navy, either. He swung that one by me the other day, and I shot it down big-time."

"Well, you seem to know what you don't want. That's a step."

He reached out to toy with the little silver ring on her finger. "Did you always want to be a lawyer?"

"Pretty much. For a while I wanted to be a ballerina, like my sister. That's when I was five. It only took about three lessons for me to figure out it wasn't all tutus and toe shoes. Then I thought I might be a carpenter, like the men in my family, so I asked for a tool set for my birthday. I think I was eight. I managed to build a pretty fair book rack before I retired." She smiled, and his heart rate accelerated. "It took me a while to come to the conclusion that I couldn't be what Natasha was, or Papa or Mama or anyone else. I had to find my own way.'' She said it casually, hoping the concept would take root.

"So you went to law school.''

"Mmm...'' Her eyes brightened as she studied him. "Can you keep a secret?''

"Sure.''

"Perry Mason.'' Laughing at herself, she scooped up another slice. "I was fascinated by those old reruns. You know, how there would always be this murder, and Perry would take the case when his client looked doomed. Lieutenant Tragg would have all this evidence, and Perry would have Della and Paul Drake out looking for clues to prove his client's innocence. Then they'd go to court. Lots of objections, and 'Your Honor, as usual the counsel for the defense is turning this proceeding into a circus.' It would look bad for Perry. He'd be up against that smug-faced DA.''

"Hamilton Berger,'' Nick said, grinning.

"Right. Perry would play it real close to the vest, dropping little hints to Della, but never spilling the whole thing. You just knew he had all the answers, but he would string it out. Then, always at the eleventh hour, he'd get the real murderer up on the witness stand, and he'd just hammer the truth out of him, until the poor slob would crumble like a cookie and confess all.''

"Then he'd explain how he'd figured it all out in the epilogue,'' Nick finished for her. "And you wanted to be Perry Mason.''

"You bet,'' Rachel agreed over a bite of pizza. "By the time I realized it wasn't that black-and-white, and it certainly wasn't that tidy, I was hooked.''

"Ray Charles,'' Nick said, half to himself.

"What?"

"It just made me think how listening to Ray Charles made me want to play the piano."

Rachel rested her chin on her folded hands and tried to ease the door open a little farther. "Do you play?"

"Not really. I used to think it would be pretty cool. Sometimes I'd hang around this music store and fiddle around until they kicked me out." The twinge of embarrassment made him brush the rest aside. "I got over it."

But once she had a purpose, Rachel wasn't easily shaken. "I always wished I'd learned. Tash got my mother a piano a few months ago—when we found out she'd always wanted to play. All those years we were growing up, she never mentioned it. All those years..." Her words trailed off, and then she shook herself back to the matter at hand. "My sister married a musician. Spencer Kimball."

"Kimball?" Nick's eyes widened before he could prevent it. "The composer?"

"You know his work?"

"Yeah." He struggled to keep it cool. A guy couldn't admit he listened to longhair music—unless it was heavy metal. "Some."

Delighted with his reaction, Rachel continued, just as casually. "At one of our visits down to see Tash and her family, we caught Mama at the piano. She got all flustered and kept saying how she was too old to learn, and how foolish it was. But then Spence sat down with her to show her a few chords, and you could see, you could just see, how much she wanted to learn. So on Mother's Day, we worked out this big, elaborate plan to get her out of the house for a few hours. Anyway, when she came back, the piano was in the living room. She cried.'' Rachel blinked the mist out of her own eyes and sighed. ''She takes lessons twice a week now, and she's practicing for her first recital.''

''That's cool,'' Nick murmured, obscurely touched.

''Yeah, it's pretty cool.'' She smiled at him. ''I guess it proves it's never too late to try.'' When she offered a hand, she wanted him to take it as a gesture of friendship and support. ''What do you say we walk off some of this pizza?''

''Yeah.'' His fingers closed around hers, and Nicholas LeBeck was in heaven.

He was content to listen to her talk, to have her laugh shiver over him. Even the shadows of the girls who had weaved in and out of his life faded away. They were nothing compared to the woman who walked beside him, slim and soft and fragrant.

She listened when he talked. And she was interested in what he had to say. When she smiled up at him, those exotic eyes flashing with humor, his stomach tied itself into slippery knots.

He could have walked with her for hours.

''This is it.''

Nick pulled up short, standing in almost the exact spot his brother had a few nights before. As his gaze skimmed over the building at her back, he imagined what it would be like if she asked him in. They'd have coffee, and she'd slip off her shoes and curl those long legs up as they talked.

He'd be careful with her, even gentle. Once his nerves settled.

''I'm glad we could do this,'' she was saying, already taking out her keys. "I hope if you're feeling restless again, or just need to talk to someone, you'll call me. When I file my report with Judge Beckett tomorrow, I think she'll be pleased with the way things are working out."

"Are you?" His eyes locked on hers as he lifted a hand to her hair. "Pleased with the way things are working out?"

"Sure." A little alarm shrilled in Rachel's head, but she dismissed it as absurd. "I think you've taken a step in the right direction."

"Me too."

The alarm continued to beep as she backed up. "We'll have to do this again soon, but I've got to get in now. I have an early meeting."

"Okay. I'll call you."

She blinked as his hand slipped around to cup her neck. "Ah, Nick..."

His mouth closed over hers, very warm, very firm. Her eyes stayed open, registering shock, as her hand flew up to press against his shoulder. His fingers tensed against her neck, and she had the impression of a very lean, very hard body before she managed to pull away.

"Nick," she said again, groping.

"It's okay." He smiled, tucked her hair behind her ear in a gesture that reminded her vividly of his brother. "I'll be in touch."

He strolled away. No...good Lord, he was swaggering, Rachel thought as she stared after him. With her mind whirling, she let herself in. "Oh, boy," she sighed as she paced the elevator.

What now? What now? How could she have been

so stupid? Cursing herself, she stomped off the elevator and toward her apartment. This was great, just great. Here she'd been trying to make friends with Nick, and all the while he'd been thinking...

She didn't want to think about what he'd been thinking.

Without taking off her jacket, she paced the apartment. There had to be a reasonable, diplomatic way to handle this, she told herself. He was only nineteen, he just had a crush, she was overreacting.

Then she remembered those limber fingers on the back of her neck, the firm press of those lips, the smooth and practiced way he'd drawn her against him.

Wrong, Rachel thought, and closed her eyes. She wasn't dealing with a child's puppy love, but with a full-grown man's desire.

Dropping down onto the arm of the couch, she dragged her hands through her hair. She should have seen it coming, she told herself. She should have stopped it before it started. She should have done a lot of things.

After twenty minutes of kicking herself, she snatched up the phone. She might be hip-deep in quicksand, but she wasn't going to sink alone.

"Lower the Boom."

"Let me talk to Muldoon," Rachel snapped, scowling at the sound of laughter and bar chatter that hummed through the receiver. "It's Rachel Stanislaski."

"You got it. Hey, Zack, phone for you. It's the babe."

Babe? Rachel thought, narrowing her eyes.

"Babe?" she repeated out loud the moment Zack had answered.

"Hey, sugar, I'm not responsible for the opinions of my bartenders." He took a swallow of mineral water. "So you finally realized you couldn't keep away from me."

"Stuff it, Muldoon. We need to talk. Tonight."

He stopped grinning and shifted the phone. "Is there a problem?"

"Damn right."

"Nick breezed through a couple of minutes ago. He seemed fine when he headed upstairs."

"He's upstairs?" she said, calculating. "Just make sure he stays up there. I'm coming right over." She hung up before he could ask any questions.

It wasn't exactly the way he'd planned it, Zack thought as he mixed a couple of stingers. His strategy had been to lie back for a few days, let Rachel simmer. Until she came to a boil—and came looking for him.

She hadn't sounded lonely or aroused or vulnerable over the phone. She'd sounded mad as a hornet.

He cast his eyes up at the ceiling, picturing the apartment overhead, as he automatically added a twist to a glass of club soda. Obviously it had to do with Nick. Where the hell had the boy been all evening? he wondered.

What kind of trouble had he gotten himself into this time? With half an ear, Zack took an order for two drafts, a margarita on the rocks and a coffee, black. Damned if he'd thought the boy was in trouble, Zack reflected. Nick had looked relaxed, calm, even approachable, when he'd checked in. Zack remembered thinking that the date had been a rousing success. And he'd hoped to be able to ease the girl's name out of his brother—along with a bit more salient information.

He didn't figure Nick needed a course in the birds and bees, but he hoped to drop a few hints about responsibility, protection and respect.

A steady girl, a steady job, a stable home. They all seemed to be coming together. So what the hell...

His thoughts broke off as he looked up. Rachel walked in, cheeks flushed from the chilly evening, eyes snapping. As she crossed the room, she peeled off her jacket to reveal one of those soft sweaters she often wore. This one was the color of a good burgundy, with a wide cowl neck that draped softly over the swell of her breasts. It rode her hips, and under it she wore snug black leggings that showed off those first-class legs.

Zack checked to make sure his tongue wasn't hanging out.

She stopped at the bar only long enough to glare at him. "In your office." Without waiting for a response, she strode off.

"Well, well..." Lola watched Rachel swing Zack's office door open, then shut it behind her with a loud click. "Looks like the lady's got something on her mind."

"Yeah." Zack set the last glass on Lola's tray. All he could think was, there was definitely a fire in the hole. "If Nick comes back down, tell him I'm...tied up."

"You're the boss."

"Right." And he intended to remain the boss. He

swung through the bar and, taking one bracing breath, marched into his office.

Rachel had tossed her jacket and purse aside, and was pacing. When the door opened, she stopped, swung her hair back and leveled a killing gaze at him.

"Don't you ever talk to him?" she demanded. "Aren't you making any effort to find out what's going on in his head? What kind of a guardian are you, anyway?"

"What the hell is this?" He threw up his hands in disgust. "I don't see or hear from you in days, then you come stalking in here just so you can yell at me. Just simmer down, Counselor, and remember I'm not some felon on the witness stand."

"Don't tell me to simmer down," she tossed back. It felt good, really good, to assuage her guilt and frustration with a pitched battle. "I'm the one who's going to have to deal with him. And if you were any kind of a brother, you would have known. You could have warned me."

Because his confidence as a brother was still at low tide, he hissed out an oath. Rachel echoed it as he shoved her into a chair. "Just sit down and take it from the top. I assume we're talking about Nick."

"Of course we're talking about Nick." She popped up again, and was pushed right back down. "I don't have anything else to discuss with you."

"We'll bypass that for now. Just what is it I should have known and warned you about?"

"That he'd...he'd..." She blew out a breath, struggling for the proper phrase. "That he'd started to think of me as a woman."

"How the hell is he supposed to think of you? As a tuna?"

"I mean as a *woman*," she said between her teeth. "Do I have to spell it out?"

His brows shot up, then settled again as he reached for a cigarette. "Don't be stupid, Rachel. He's nineteen. I'm not saying he's blind and wouldn't appreciate the way you look. But he's got a girl. He was out with her tonight."

"You idiot." She sprang up again, and this time she thumped a fist on his chest. "He was out with *me* tonight."

"Out with you?" With a frown, Zack studied her. "What for?"

"We went to the movies, had a pizza. I wanted to get him to talk a little—informally—so when he called I said sure."

"One step at a time. Nick called you and asked you out on a date."

"It wasn't a date. I didn't think it was a damn date." Since she didn't see anything handy to kick other than Zack's shin, she stalked a circle around his office again. "It seemed to me if we could develop a relationship— A friendship," she corrected hastily. "It would make things easier all around."

Considering, Zack took a drag of his cigarette. "Sounds reasonable. So you took in a flick and had a pizza. What's the problem? Did he get into a fight, give you a hard time?" He stopped, alarmed. "You didn't run in to any of the Cobras?"

"No, no, no…" Incensed, she whirled around the room. "Aren't you listening to me? I said he was thinking about me as a woman...as a date. As a... Oh, boy." She let out a long breath. "He kissed me."

Zack's eyes turned into dark, dangerous slits. "Define *kiss*."

"You know damn well what a kiss is. You smack your lips up against somebody's." She spun away, then back. "I should have seen it coming, but I didn't. Then, before I realized what he was thinking, wham!"

"Wham," Zack repeated, trying to stay calm. He took his own turn around the room, bumping his shoulders against hers. "Okay, listen, I think you're making a big deal out of nothing. He kissed you goodnight. It's a gesture. He's just a kid."

"No," Rachel said, and her tone had Zack turning back to her. "He's not."

Temper was clawing to gain freedom. As a result, Zack's voice was deadly calm. "Did he try to—"

"No." Recognizing the signs, she cut him off. "Of course he didn't. He just kissed me. But it was the way... Listen, Zack, I know the difference between a casual kiss good-night between friends and—and, well, a move. And I can tell you Nick has a very smooth move."

"Glad to hear it," Zack said between his teeth.

Suddenly drained, she dropped down onto the corner of his desk. "I don't know what to do."

"I'll straighten him out."

"How?"

"I don't know how," he shot back, crushing out his cigarette. "I'll be damned if I'm going to be competing with my kid brother."

The muttered aside had her narrowing her eyes. "I'm not a trophy, Muldoon."

"I didn't mean—" With a shake of his head, he leaned on the desk beside her. "Look, this throws me off course, okay? I figured Nick was out making time with some pretty little teenager whose daddy would want her home by midnight, and now I find out he's coming on to you. If he wasn't my brother, I'd go knock him around a little."

"Typical," she muttered.

He ignored that and tried to think. "It's probably normal for him to develop—or think he's developed— feelings for you. Don't you think?"

"Maybe." She tilted her head to slant Zack a look. "I don't want to hurt him."

"Me either. You could back off, stay unavailable— the way you've tried to be with me."

"I've been busy." All dignity, she lifted her chin. "And we're not talking about you. In any case, I considered that, but I'm supposed to be his co-guardian. I can't do that long-distance. Besides, he talked to me tonight. He really talked, and relaxed, and showed me a little of what's underneath all that defiance. If I cut him off now, just when he's beginning to open up and trust me, I don't know what damage I might do."

"You can't string him along, Rachel."

"I know that." She wanted to lay her head on Zack's shoulder, just for a minute. She looked down at her hands instead. "I need to find a way to let him know I want to be his friend—just his friend—without crushing his ego."

Zack took her hand, and when she didn't pull it away he twined his fingers in hers. "I'll talk to him. Calmly," he added when Rachel frowned at him.

"Actually, I wanted to dump the whole business in

your lap, but the more I think about it, the more I'm sure he'd only resent it coming from you. How can you tell him I'm not interested without letting him know we discussed his feelings behind his back?'' She shut her eyes. ''And I'm not feeling very good about that, either.''

''You had to tell me.''

''Yeah, I think I did, just like I think I'm going to have to figure out what to do.''

He ran his thumb over her knuckles. ''We're in this together, remember?''

''How can I forget? But you and Nick are just getting your balance. This is bound to tilt the scales, Zack. I think it's best if I try to handle it.'' A smile played around the corners of her mouth. ''I guess I should apologize for coming here and jumping on you.''

''At least it got you here. We'll handle it.'' He brought her hand to his lips, enjoying the way her eyes darkened and became cautious. ''You let him down easy, and I'll let him take it out on me. After all, I can't blame the kid for trying, when I'm doing the same myself.''

''One has nothing to do with the other.'' She pushed away from the desk, but he continued to hold her hand.

''I'm glad to hear it. Feeling better?''

Her lips quirked. ''Fighting always makes me feel better.''

''Then, sugar, by the time we're through with each other, you should be feeling like a million bucks. I don't suppose you'd like to hang around for a couple of hours until I can close the bar.''

''No.'' Her heart picked up a beat at the thought.

A dark, empty bar, blues on the juke, the world locked outside. "No, I have to go."

"I'm shorthanded tonight, or I'd see you home. I'll put you in a cab."

"I can put myself in a cab."

"Okay. In a minute." He caught her by the hips, lifted her, then set her on the desk. "I've missed you," he murmured, nuzzling her neck.

Without thinking—he certainly had a way of making her stop thinking—she tilted her head to give him more access to her skin. "I've been busy."

"I don't doubt you've been busy." He moved up to nip at her earlobe. "But you've been stubborn. I like that about you, Rachel. Right now I can't think of a damn thing I don't like about you."

This was a mistake. Any minute she'd remember why it was a mistake. She was sure of it. "You just want to talk me into bed."

His lips curved before they came down on hers. "Oh, yeah..." He fisted his hands in her hair, and a deep sound of pleasure came from his throat when she arched against him. "How'm I doing?"

"You're making things very difficult for me."

"Good. That's good." He was very close to pressing her back on the desk and doing all the things he'd fantasized about during those long, dark nights he'd lain alone in bed, thinking of her. And she sighed. The soft, broken sound of it seemed to rip something inside his gut. Grinding out an oath, he buried his face in her hair. "I sure pick my spots," he muttered. "On the sidewalk with a mugger, in my office with a barful of customers outside the door. Every time I'm around you I start acting like a kid in the back seat of a parked car.''

She had to concentrate just to breathe. As he continued to hold her, just hold her, she found herself stroking his hair, counting his heartbeats, warming toward him in a way that was entirely different from the flash heat of a moment before.

She'd been right about the quicksand, she realized. And she'd been right about not sinking alone. ''We're not kids,'' she murmured.

''No, we're not.'' Not quite sure he could trust himself, he drew back, taking both her hands in his. ''I know it's moving fast, and I know it's complicated, but I want you. There's no getting around it.''

''I knew this would happen if I came here tonight. I came anyway.'' Muddled, she shook her head. ''I don't know what that says about me, or about us. I do know it's not smart, and I'm usually smart. The best thing for me to do is walk out the door and go home.''

He tugged on her hands, bringing her off the desk and close to him again. ''What are you going to do?''

She wavered, caught on the thin edge between temptation and common sense. Images of what could be swam giddily through her head and left her throat dry. Repercussions...she couldn't quite see them clearly, but she knew they existed. And she was afraid they would be severe indeed.

''I'm going to walk out the door and go home.'' She let out an unsteady breath when he said nothing. ''For now.''

She grabbed up her jacket, her purse. When she reached the door, his hand closed over hers on the knob. A quick thrill of panicked excitement raced through her at the thought that he would simply turn the lock.

She wouldn't permit it. Of course she wouldn't permit it.

Would she?

"Sunday" was all he said.

Her scattered thoughts scrambled to make sense of the word. "Sunday?"

"I can shift things around and take the day off. Spend it with me."

Relief. Confusion. Pleasure. She had no idea which emotion was uppermost. "You want to spend Sunday with me."

"Yeah. You know, take in a couple of museums, maybe an art gallery, a walk in the park, have a fancy lunch somewhere. I figure most of the time we've spent together so far's been after dark."

Odd...that hadn't occurred to her before. "I guess it has."

"Why don't we try a Sunday afternoon?"

"I..." She couldn't think of a single reason why not. "All right. Why don't you come by around eleven?"

"I'll be there."

She turned the knob, then glanced back at him. "Museums?" she said on a laugh. "Is this on the level, Muldoon?"

"I happen to appreciate art," he told her, leaning forward to touch his lips to hers in a quiet kiss that rocked her back on her heels. "And beauty."

She slipped out quickly. As she walked up to the corner to hail a cab, it occurred to her she hadn't yet decided how best to handle Nick. And she sure as hell hadn't figured out how to handle Nick's big brother.

Chapter Six

Rachel was cursing when her buzzer sounded promptly at eleven o'clock Sunday morning. Securing an earring, she pressed the intercom. "Muldoon?"

"You sound out of breath, sugar. Should I take that as a compliment?"

"Come on up," she said shortly. "And don't call me sugar."

After snapping off the intercom, she flipped off her three security locks, then gave herself one last look in the mirror. She'd forgotten her second earring. Grumbling, she went on a quick search until she found it lying on the kitchen counter beside her empty coffee cup.

It was her day off, damn it. And she resented having it interrupted for work. Not because she'd been looking forward to spending it with Zack. Particularly. It was just that it had been a long time since she'd had a day to wander through museums and galleries, and— She broke off her silent complaining at the knock on the door.

"Come in, it's open."

"Anxious?" Zack commented as he walked in. Then he lifted a brow and took one long look. She was standing in the center of the room, slim and lovely in a bronze-toned suede jacket and short skirt set off by a slightly mannish silk blouse in a flashy blue. She was barefoot, and he found his mouth watering as he watched her perform the feminine and oddly intimate task of securing a shiny gold knot to her ear. "You look nice."

"Thanks. You, too." No, what he looked was sexy, she thought, damn sexy, in snug black jeans, a midnight-blue sweater, and a bomber jacket in soft black leather. But *nice* would have to do. "Listen, Zack, I tried to catch you before you left the bar. I'm sorry I missed you."

"Is there a problem?" He watched as she wiggled one foot into a bronze-colored pump. By the time she'd wiggled into the second, his palms were sweaty and he'd missed what she'd said. "Sorry, what?"

"I said my boss called, about a half hour ago. I've got an attempted murder I have to deal with."

That cut his fantasy off as quickly as a faceful of ice water. "A what?"

"Attempted murder. Alexi's precinct. I can probably plead down to assault with a deadly weapon, but I have to see him today so I can meet with the DA in the morning." She spread her hands. "I'm really sorry I didn't catch you before you came all the way over."

"No problem. I'll go with you."

"With me?" She liked the idea, a little too much. "You don't want to spoil your day off spending it at a police station."

"I'm taking the day off to be with you," he reminded her, and picked up her coat where she'd tossed it over the back of the couch. "Besides, it won't take all day, will it?"

"No, probably no more than an hour, but—"

"So let's get started." He walked to her, then turned her around so that he could slip the coat slowly on one arm, then the other. Lowering his head, he sniffed at her neck. "Did you spray that stuff on for the felon, or for me?"

She shivered once before cautiously stepping away. "For me." Picking up her briefcase, she held it between them like a shield. "I have to go by the office first. We already have a file on the guy. He's been around."

"Okay." He tugged the briefcase away, took her hand. "Let's go, Counselor."

Alex spotted his sister the moment she walked into the station. Since he wasn't any happier than she to be spending his Sunday morning at work, he immediately brightened. Giving Rachel a hard time always lifted his spirits.

Grinning, he strolled over, a greeting on his lips. When he spotted the man hovering around her, the humor in his eyes turned instantly to suspicion. "Rach."

Still clipping her visitor's badge to her lapel, she glanced up. "Alex. They got you, too, huh?"

"Looks like. Muldoon, isn't it?"

"That's right." Zack returned the steady stare and nodded. "Nice to see you again, Officer."

"Detective," Alex corrected. "I didn't hear anything about LeBeck being pulled in."

"I'm not here about Nick." Rachel recognized Alex's unfriendly, aggressive stance. He'd assumed it with every boy and man she'd dated since she'd turned fifteen. "I'm representing Victor Lomez."

"Now that's real slime." But Alex wasn't nearly as concerned about Rachel's client as he was with the reason the big Irishman was carrying her briefcase. "So, did you two run into each other outside?"

"No, Alexi." Rachel commandeered the coffee he was carrying. Though she knew it was worthless, she shot him a warning glance. "Zack and I had plans for the day."

"What kind of plans?"

"The kind that aren't any of your business." She kissed his cheek as an excuse to get close enough to his ear to whisper, "Knock it off." Leaning back, she smiled at Zack. "Grab a seat, Muldoon, and some of this horrible coffee. Like I said, this shouldn't take too long."

"I got all day," he told her as she walked off to a conference room. He turned back to Alex and said blandly, "So, you want to take me down to interrogation?"

Alex told himself he wasn't particularly amused, and gestured with a jerk of his head. "In here'll do." It pleased him to be behind his desk while Zack sat in the chair used to grill witnesses. "What's the story, Muldoon?"

Casually Zack took out a cigarette. He offered one to Alex and lit up when Alex shook his head. "You want to know what I'm doing with your sister." He blew out a stream of smoke, considering. "If you're any kind of detective, you should be able to figure that one out. She's beautiful, she's smart. She's a soft heart in a tough, sexy shell." Taking another drag, he watched Alex's eyes narrow. "Listen, you want it straight, or do you want me to tell you I'm just interested in her legal services?"

"Watch your step."

Because he understood the need to protect what he loved, Zack leaned forward. "Stanislaski, if you know Rachel, you know *she's* been watching my step. Nobody, but nobody, pushes her into something she doesn't want."

"You figure you got her pegged?"

"Are you kidding?" Zack's smile came quickly, and was friendly enough to make Alex's shoulders relax. "There isn't a man alive who really understands a woman. Especially a smart one." When he saw Alex's eyes shift over his shoulder, Zack glanced around. He saw a short, wiry, oily-skinned man being hauled toward the conference room by a uniformed cop. "Is that the one?"

"Yeah, that's Lomez."

Zack hissed smoke through his teeth and swore roundly. Alex could only agree.

At the conference table, Rachel looked up. Though she'd represented Lomez on his last count of assault, she was going over his file. "Well, Lomez, we meet again."

"You took your sweet time getting here." He

dropped down in the seat and ignored the hovering cop. But he was sweating. Bungling the mugging meant he'd missed his connection. He hadn't had a fix in fourteen hours. "You bring me a smoke this time?"

"No. Thank you, Officer." Rachel waited until she was alone with her client, then folded her hands over his paperwork. "Well, you really pulled a prize this time out. The woman you attacked was sixty-three. I called the hospital this morning. You should be relieved to know they've bumped her condition up from critical to fair."

Lomez shrugged, his small black eyes gleaming at Rachel. He couldn't keep his hands still. He began to beat a tattoo on the table with his fingertips as he tapped his feet. His system was skidding to a much wilder rhythm. "Hey, if she'd handed over her purse like I told her, I wouldn't have had to get rough, you know?"

God, he sickened her, Rachel thought, fighting to remember she was a public servant. And Lomez, however revolting, was the public. "Knifing a senior citizen isn't going to win you the key to the city. It's sure as hell going to buy you a lock. Damn it, Lomez, she had twelve dollars."

His mouth was dry, and his skin was cold. "Then it wouldn't have cost her a lot to hand it over. You just get me out. That's your job." And the minute he was back on the street, he'd pressure one of the other Hombres to score for him. "I had to sit in that stinking cell all night."

"You're charged with attempted murder," Rachel said flatly.

Lomez tapped his damp hands against his thighs.

Even his bones were screaming. "I didn't kill the old bitch."

Rachel wished she hadn't finished the coffee. At least she could have used it to wash some of the disgust out of her mouth. "You stuck a knife in her, three times. The officer responding pursued you as you fled the scene—with the knife and the victim's purse. They've got you cold, Lomez, and your priors aren't going to make the judge think leniency. Your repertoire includes assault, assault and battery, breaking and entering and two counts of possession."

"I don't need a list. I need bail."

"Odds are slim the DA's going to agree to bail, and if he does, it'll be well out of your range. Now I'm going to do what I can to get him to toss the attempted murder. You plead guilty to—"

"Guilty, my butt."

"It's going to be your butt," she said evenly. "You're not going to walk away from this one, Lomez. No matter how many rabbits I pull out of my hat, you're not going to do short time this turn around. Plead guilty to assault with a deadly weapon, it's likely I can swing the judge for seven to ten."

Sweat popped cold on his brow, on his lips. "The hell with that."

Because she was fast running out of patience, she slapped his file closed. "It won't get any sweeter. You cooperate, and I should be able to keep you from spending the next twenty years in a cage."

He screamed at her, then leaped across the table and struck before she had a chance to dodge. The backhanded blow knocked her out of her chair and onto the floor, where he fell on her. "You get me out!" He squeezed his hands on her throat, too wired even to feel her nails rake his wrist. "You bitch, you get me out or I'll kill you!"

At first she could only see his face, the sick rage in it. Then it faded as red dots swam in front of her eyes. Choking, she struck out, smashing the heel of her hand against the bridge of his nose. His blood splattered over her, but his hands tightened.

A roaring filled her ears, buzzing over the wild curses he shouted at her. The red dots faded to gray as she bucked under him.

Then her windpipe was free and she was sucking air down her burning throat. Someone was calling her name, desperately, and she was being lifted, held tight. She thought she smelled the scent of the sea before she fell limply into it.

Cool fingers on her face. Wonderful. Strong hands clasped hard over hers. Comforting. A sigh before waking. Agony.

Rachel blinked her eyes open. Two faces were looming over hers, equally grim, with eyes that held both rage and fear. Woozily she lifted a hand to Zack's cheek, then Alex's. "I'm all right." Her voice was husky, bruises already forming on her throat.

"Just lie still," Alex murmured in Ukrainian, stroking her head with a hand that still throbbed from where it had connected with Lomez's face. "Can you drink some water?"

She nodded. "I want to sit up." As she focused on the room, she realized she was lying on the faded couch in the captain's office. Murmuring her thanks to her brother, she sipped from the paper cup he held to her lips. "Lomez?"

"In a cage, where he belongs." Fighting off the tremors of reaction, Alex lowered his brow to hers. He continued to speak in Ukrainian, kissing her brow, her cheeks, then sitting back on his heels to hold her hand. "You just relax. An ambulance is on the way."

"I don't need an ambulance." Reading the argument in his eyes, she shook her head. "I don't." She glanced down to see that her blouse was gaping open. It was ruined, of course, she thought in disgust. That and her suede skirt were spotted with blood. "His blood, not mine," she pointed out.

"You broke his slimy low-life nose," Alex snapped.

"I'm glad my self-defense class wasn't wasted." When he began to swear, she caught his hand. "Alexi," she began, her voice low, intense. "Do you know what it is for me to accept that you risk your life every day, every night? Do you know I accept only because I love you so much?"

"Don't turn this around on me," he said furiously. "That bastard nearly killed you. He was so far gone it took three of us to drag him off."

She didn't want to think about that just yet. She couldn't. "I played it wrong."

"You—"

"I did," she insisted. "But the point is, we can't change what we are. I won't change, not even for you. Now cancel the ambulance and do something for me."

He called her a name, a rude one, in their native language. It made her smile. "I'm no more of a horse's ass than you. I need to contact my office and explain. I won't be able to represent Lomez under the circumstances."

"Damn right you won't." It was small satisfaction, but he could hope for little more. Gently he touched his fingers to the bruise on her cheekbone. "He's going down, Rachel. I'll make damn sure he goes down for this, if nothing else. There's nothing you or anyone else can do."

"That's for the courts to decide." She got shakily to her feet. "And you will not call Mama and Papa." When he said nothing, she lifted a brow. "If you do, I'll have to tell them about your last undercover assignment. The one where you went through the second-story window."

"Go home," he said, giving up. "Get some rest." He turned away from her to study Zack. His opinion of him had changed a bit, since Zack had been one of the three who'd hauled Lomez off Rachel. Alex had been a cop long enough to recognize murder in a man's eyes, and it had shone darkly in Zack's. He assumed, correctly, that Zack would have dealt with Lomez himself, regardless of cops, if he hadn't been so busy cradling Rachel in his arms. "You'll get her there." It wasn't a question.

"Count on it." He said nothing else as Alex left them.

Unsteady, and far from sure of herself, Rachel tried to smile. "Some date, huh?"

A muscle jumped in his jaw as he studied her spattered blouse. "Can you walk?"

"Of course I can walk." She hoped. The little seed of annoyance his terse question planted helped her get across the room. "Look, I'm sorry things got messed up this way. You don't have to—"

"Do me a favor," he said as he took her arm and led her through the squad room. "Just shut up."

She obliged him, though she was sorely tempted to tell him how foolish it was to indulge in a cab for the few blocks to her building. It was better if she didn't talk, she realized. Not only did it hurt, but she was also afraid her voice would begin to shake as much as her body wanted to.

She'd be alone in a few minutes, she reminded herself. Then she'd be able to indulge in a nice bout of trembling and weeping if she wanted to. But not in front of Zack. Not in front of anybody.

With a drunk's exaggerated care, she stepped out of the cab and onto the sidewalk. Mild shock, she deduced. It would pass. She'd make it pass.

"Thanks," she began. "I'm sorry…"

"I'm taking you up."

"Look, I've already ruined your morning. It isn't necessary to—" But he was already half carrying her to the door.

"Didn't I tell you to shut up?" He pulled open her briefcase to look for her keys himself. White-hot rage had his fingers fumbling. Didn't she know how pale she was? Couldn't she understand what it did to him inside to hear the way her voice rasped?

He pulled her through the door, into the elevator, and jabbed his finger on the button.

"I don't know what you're so mad about," she muttered, wincing a little as she swallowed. "You lost a couple of hours, sure, but do you know what I paid for this suit? And I've only worn it twice." Tears sprang to her eyes, and she blinked them back furiously as he dragged her down the hall to her apartment. "A PD's salary isn't exactly princely." She rubbed ice-cold hands together as he unlocked her door. "I had to eat yogurt for a month to afford it, even on sale. And I don't even like yogurt."

The first tear spilled out. She dashed it away as she walked inside. "Even if I could get it cleaned, I wouldn't be able to wear it after—" She broke off and made an enormous effort to pull herself back. She was babbling about a suit, for God's sake. Maybe she was losing her mind.

"Okay." She let out what she thought was a slow, careful breath. It hitched as it came out. "You got me home. I appreciate it. Now go away."

He merely tossed her briefcase aside, then tugged the coat from her shoulders. "Sit down, Rachel."

"I don't want to sit down." Another tear. It was too late to stop it. "What I want is to be alone." When her voice broke, she pressed her hands to her face. "Oh, God, leave me alone."

He picked her up, moving to the couch to hold her in his lap. Stroking her back through the tremors, feeling her tears hot and damp on his neck. He forced his hands to be gentle, even as the rage and fear worked inside him. As she curled up against him, he closed his eyes and murmured the useless words that always seemed to comfort.

She cried hard, he realized. But she didn't cry long. She trembled violently, but the trembling was soon controlled. She didn't try to push away. If she had, he wouldn't have allowed it. Perhaps he was comforting her. But holding her, knowing she was safe, and with him, brought him tremendous comfort.

"Damn it." When the worst was over, she let her head lie weakly on his shoulder. "I told you to go away."

"We had a deal, remember? You're spending the day with me." His hands tightened once, convulsively, before he managed to gentle them again. "You scared me, big-time."

"Me, too."

"And if I go away, I'm going to have to go back down there, find a way to get to that son of a bitch, and break him in half."

It was odd how a threat delivered so matter-of-factly could seem twice as deadly as a shout. "Then I guess you'd better hang around until the impulse fades. I'm really all right," she told him, but she left her head cuddled against his shoulder. "This was just reaction."

There was still an ice floe of fury in his gut. That was his reaction, and he'd deal with it later. "It may be his blood, Rachel, but they're your bruises."

Frowning, she touched fingers gingerly to her cheek. "How bad does it look?"

Despite himself, he chuckled. "Lord, I didn't know you were that vain."

She bristled, pulling back far enough to scowl at him. "It has nothing to do with vanity. I have a meeting in the morning, and I don't need all the questions."

He cupped her chin, tilted her head to the side. "Take it from someone who's had his share of bruises, sugar. You're going to get the questions. Now forget about tomorrow." He touched his lips, very gently, to the bruise, and made her heart stutter. "Have you got any tea bags? Any honey?"

"Probably. Why?"

"Since you won't go to the hospital, you'll have to put up with Muldoon first aid." He shifted her from his lap and propped her against the pillows. Their vivid colors only made her appear paler. "Stay."

Since the bout of weeping had tired her, she didn't argue. When Zack came out of the kitchen five minutes later, tea steaming in the cup in his hands, she was out like a light.

She awakened groggy, her throat on fire. The room was dim and utterly quiet, disorienting her. Pushing herself up on her elbows, she saw that the curtains had been drawn. The bright afghan her mother had crocheted years before had been tucked around her.

Groaning only a little, she tossed it aside and stood up. Steady, she thought with some satisfaction. You couldn't keep a Stanislaski down.

But this one needed about a gallon of water to ease the flames in her throat. Rubbing her eyes, she padded into the kitchen, then let out a shriek that seared her abused throat when she spotted Zack bending over the stove.

"What the hell are you doing? I thought you were gone."

"Nope." He stirred the contents of the pot on the stove before turning to study her. Her color was back, and the glazed look had faded from her eyes. It would take a great deal longer for the bruises to disappear.

"I had Rio send over some soup. Do you think you can eat now?"

"I guess." She pressed a hand to her stomach. She was starving, but she wasn't sure how she was going to manage getting anything down her throbbing throat. "What time is it?"

"About three."

She'd slept nearly two hours, she realized, and found the idea of her dozing on the couch while Zack puttered in the kitchen both embarrassing and touching. "You didn't have to hang around."

"You know, your throat would feel better sooner if you didn't talk so much. Go in and sit down."

Since the scent of the soup was making her mouth water, she obliged him. After tugging the curtains open, she sat at the little gateleg table by the window. With some disgust, she shrugged out of her stained jacket and tossed it aside. As soon as she'd indulged herself with some of Rio's soup, she would shower and change.

Obviously Zack had found his way around her kitchen, Rachel mused as he came in carrying bowls and mugs on a tray.

"Thanks." She saw his gaze light briefly on the jacket, heat, then flatten.

"I pawed through some of your records while you were out." It pleased him that he could speak casually when he wanted to break something. Someone. "Mind if I put one on?"

"No, go ahead."

Watching the steam, she stirred her soup while he put an old B. B. King album on her stereo. "And they said we had nothing in common."

Relieved that he wasn't going to bring the incident up, she smiled. "I stole it from Mikhail. He has very eclectic taste in music." Once Zack was seated across from her, she spooned up soup and swallowed gingerly. Sighed. It soothed her fevered throat the way a mother soothes a fretful child. "Wonderful. What's in it?"

"I never ask. Rio never tells."

With a murmur of acknowledgment, she continued to eat. "I'll have to figure out how to bribe him. My mother would love the recipe for this." She switched to tea. After the first sip, her eyes opened wide.

"You didn't have honey," Zack said mildly. "But you had brandy."

She took another, more cautious sip. "It ought to dull the nerve endings."

"That's the idea." Reaching across the table, he took her hand. "Feel any better?"

"Lots. I really am sorry you had your Sunday wrecked."

"Don't make me tell you to shut up again."

She only smiled. "I'm starting to think you're not such a bad guy, Muldoon."

"Maybe I should have brought you soup before."

"The soup helped." She spooned up some more. "But not making me feel like an idiot when I was crying all over you did the trick."

"You had pretty good cause. Being tough's not always the answer."

"It usually works." She sipped more of the brandy-laced tea. "I didn't want to let go in front of Alex. He worries enough." Her lips curved. "You know how it is to have a younger sibling who refuses to see things the way you do.''

"You mean so you'd like to rap their head against the wall? Yeah, I know."

"Well, whether Alex likes to believe it or not, I can handle my own life. Nick will, too, when the time comes."

"He's not like that creep today," Zack said softly. "He never could be."

"Of course not." Concerned, she pushed her bowl aside. This time she took his hand. "You mustn't even think like that. Listen to me. For two years I've seen them come in and go out. Some are twisted beyond redemption, like Lomez. Others are desperate and confused, either battered by the streets or part of the streets. Working with them, it gets to the point that if you don't burn out or just scab over, you learn to recognize the nuances. Nick's been hurt, and his self-esteem is next to zero. He turned to a gang because he needed to be part of something, anything. Now he has you. No matter how much he might try to shake you loose, he wants you. He needs you."

"Maybe. If he ever starts to trust me, he might be able to turn a corner." He hadn't realized how much it was weighing on him. "He won't talk to me about my father, about what it was like when I was gone."

"He will, when he's ready."

"The old man wasn't so bad, Rachel. He'd never have made father of the year, but—hell." He let out a breath in disgust. "He was a hard-nosed, hard-drinking Irish son of a bitch who should never have given up the sea. He ran our lives like we were green crewmen on a sinking ship. All shouts and bluster and the back of his hand. We never agreed on a damn thing.''

''Families often don't.''

''He never got over my mother. He was in the South Pacific when she died.''

Which meant Zack would have been alone. A child, alone. Her fingers tightened on his.

''He came back, mad as hell. He was going to make a man out of me. Then Nadine and Nick came along, and I was old enough to go my own way. You could say I abandoned ship. So he tried to make a man—his kind of man—out of Nick.''

''You're beating yourself up again over something you can't change. And couldn't have changed.''

''I guess I keep remembering how it was that first year I came back. The old man was so fragile. He couldn't remember things, kept wandering out and getting lost. Damn it, I knew Nick was running wild, but I didn't have my legs under me. Having to put the old man in a home, watching him die there, trying to keep the bar going. Nick got lost in the shuffle.''

''You found him again.''

He started to speak again, then sat back with a sigh. ''Hell of a time to be dumping this on you.''

''It's all right. I want to help.''

''You've already helped. Do you want more soup?''

Subject closed, Rachel realized. She could press, or she could give him room. One favor deserved another, she decided, and smiled. ''No, thanks. It really did the job.''

He wanted to say more, a whole lot more. He wanted to hold her again, and feel her head resting on his shoulder. He wanted to sit and watch her sleep on the couch again. And if he did any one of those things, he wouldn't make it to the door.

"I'll clear it up and get out of your hair. I imagine you'd like some time alone."

She frowned after him as he walked into the kitchen. She had wanted time alone, hadn't she? So why was she trying to think of ways to stall him, keep him from walking out the door.

"Hey, look." She pushed away from the table to wander in after him. He was already pouring the remaining soup in a container. "It's still early. We might be able to salvage some of the day."

"You need rest."

"I had rest." Feeling awkward, she ran water over the bowls he'd stacked in the sink. "We could probably make at least one museum, or catch a matinee. I don't want to think you spent your whole day off mopping up after me."

"Will you quit worrying about my day off?" Zack slapped the container on a shelf in the refrigerator. "I'm the boss, remember? I can take another."

"Fine." She slammed the water off. "See you around."

"Man, you've got a short fuse." Amused, he put his hands on her shoulders and rubbed. "Don't get yourself worked up, sugar. All in all, I had a very eventful day."

She closed her eyes, feeling those rough fingers through the silk of her blouse. "Any time, Muldoon."

He could smell her hair, and he had to fight the urge to bury his face in it. It wouldn't be possible to stop there. "You going to be all right alone? I could call the cop to come stay with you."

"No. I'm fine." Gripping the edge of the counter, she stared hard at the wall. "Thanks for the first aid."

"My pleasure." Damn it, he was stalling when he should be out the door. Away from her. "Maybe we can have an early dinner one night this week."

She pressed her lips together. The way his hands were rubbing up and down her arms made her want to whimper. "Sure. I'll check my schedule."

He turned her around. He couldn't be sure if she moved into his arms or if he'd pulled her there, but he was holding her. Her lips were parting for his. "I'll call you."

"Okay." Her eyes fluttered closed as the kiss deepened.

"Soon." He felt the breath backing up in his lungs as she molded against him.

"Um-hmm…" As his tongue danced over hers, she gave a quick sigh that caught in the middle.

He tore his mouth away to nibble along her jaw. "One more thing."

"Yes?"

"I'm not leaving."

"I know." Her arms curled around his neck as he lifted her. "It's just chemistry."

"Right." Struggling to remember her bruises, he rained soft kisses over her face.

"Nothing serious." She shuddered, nipping at his neck. "I can't afford to get involved. I have plans."

"Nothing serious," he agreed, blood pounding in his head, in his loins. He jerked open a door and found himself facing a closet. "Where's the damn bedroom?"

"What?" She focused, realized he'd carried her out

of the kitchen. "This is it. The couch..." She nipped his ear. "It pulls out. I can..."

"Never mind," he managed, and settled for the rug.

Chapter Seven

He ripped her blouse. It wasn't only passion that made him grab and tear. He couldn't bear to see her wear it another moment, to see that vivid blue stained with spots of blood.

Yet the sound of it, of the silk rending beneath his fingers, and her gasp of shocked excitement, spread fire through his gut.

"The first time I saw you..." His breath was already short and fast when he tossed the mangled blouse aside. "From the first minute, I wanted this. Wanted you."

"I know." She reached for him, amazed at how deep and ripe a need could be. "Me, too. It's crazy," she said against his mouth. "Insane." Her skin trembled as he tugged the straps of her chemise from her shoulders to replace them with impatient lips. "Incredible."

Glorying in it, she arched against him when he took her breasts in those greedy, rough-palmed hands. Then his mouth—oh, his mouth, hot and seeking—closed over her to tug and suckle. *Hurry,* was all she could think, *hurry, hurry,* and her nails scraped heedlessly up his sides as she dragged his sweater over his head.

Flesh to flesh was what she wanted. Skin already hot, already damp. The feel of his lips against her thundering heart had her locking her fists in his hair, pressing him closer. She fretted for more. Even as the storm built to a crisis point inside her, she met, she ached, and she demanded.

Her fingers dug into his broad shoulders when he slid down, setting off hundreds of tiny eruptions by streaking hungry, openmouthed kisses down her torso. Then back, quickly back, to drown her in desire with his lips on hers.

He couldn't stop himself from taking. No matter that he had once imagined making slow, tortuously slow, love to her on some huge, soft bed. The desperation of what was overpowered any fantasy of what might have been.

She possessed him. Obsessed him. No mystical siren could have stolen his mind and soul more completely.

A button popped from her skirt as he fought to drag it down her hips. He thought he might go mad if he didn't rip aside all obstacles, if he didn't see her. All of her.

Half-crazed, he peeled off her stockings, and the delicate lace that had secured them. Somewhere through the roaring in his brain he heard her throaty cry when his fingers brushed against her thigh. Fighting to hold back, he knelt between her legs, filling himself with the sight of her, slim and golden and naked, her hair tousled around her face, her eyes dark and heavy.

She reared up, too desperate to wait even another moment. Her mouth closed avidly over his, and her fingers tore at the snap of his jeans.

"Let me," she said in a husky whisper.

"No." He slipped a hand behind her back to support her, and brought the other down to cover the source of heat. "Let me."

The volcano he'd imagined erupted at the first touch. Her body shuddered, quaked. And he watched, impossibly aroused, as her head fell back. Not surrender. Even in his own delirium, he understood that she was not surrendering. It was abandonment, the pure, unleashed quest for pleasure. He gave her more, and gave to himself, stroking that velvet fire, letting his tongue slide over hers in a delicious, matching rhythm.

How could she have known that desire could be dark and deadly? Or that she, always so sure, always so cautious, would throw reason to the winds for more of the dangerous delights? No, not just more. All of them, she thought dizzily. All of him. She would have all. Locking her legs around his hips, she took him into her.

She heard his gasp—the first one ended with a groan. She saw his eyes, cobalt now, and fixed on hers as he shifted to fill her. A sword to the hilt. Then he moved, and she with him. Lost in the whirlwind, she heard nothing but the screaming of her own heart.

* * *

"The bigger they are," Rachel murmured some time later.

"Hmm?"

Smiling to herself, she lifted one of Zack's hands, let it go and watched it drop limply to the rug. "The harder they fall." She rolled over and propped her elbows on his chest so that she could study him. If she hadn't known better, she would have thought he was sleeping—or unconscious. His breathing had slowed—somewhat—but his eyes were still closed. It had been some time since he'd moved a single muscle.

"You know, Muldoon, you look like you went ten rounds with the champ."

His lips curved. It was about all he had the energy for. "You pack a hell of a punch, sugar."

As a matter of principle, she bit his shoulder. "Don't call me 'sugar.' But, since you mention it, you didn't do too badly yourself."

He opened one eye. "Too badly? I melted you down to a gooey puddle."

True enough, she admitted, but she wouldn't stroke his ego by agreeing. "I'll say that you have a certain unrefined style that is strangely appealing." She trailed a fingertip down his chest. "But the simple fact is, I had to carry you." That got his other eye open, she thought with satisfaction. "Not that I minded. I didn't have anything else pressing to do this afternoon."

"You carried me?"

"Metaphorically speaking."

His opinion of that was short and rude. "Want to take me on again? Champ?"

She fluttered her lashes. "Any time. Any place."

"Here and now." She was laughing as he rolled her over, but the laughter ended on a hiss of pain when he bumped her bruised cheek. "Klutz," she said as he jerked back and swore.

"I'm sorry."

"Come on, Zack." She smiled, wanting to lighten the concern in his eyes and bring back the laughter. "I was only kidding."

Ignoring that, he turned her head for a closer look at the mark on her cheek. "I should have put ice on that. He didn't break the skin, but it's..."

She could feel the tension hardening his shoulders. Instead of trying to stroke it away, she pinched him. "Listen, Buster, I come from tough stock. I got worse than that wrestling with my brothers."

"If he ever gets out—"

"Stop it." Very firmly she put her hands on either side of his face. "Don't say anything you might regret. Remember, I'm an officer of the court."

"I wouldn't regret it." He tugged her upward until she was sitting beside him. They were circled, he realized, by the tattered remains of her clothes. "And I don't regret this—except for the unrefined style."

She let out an impatient breath. "Look, if you can't take a joke, learn to."

"Wait until I'm finished before you swipe at me, okay? I swear, you come on faster than a typhoon." He tucked her hair back and kissed her once, hard. "I wasn't going to stay. Not today. I figured a bout of hot sex wasn't the best encore after you'd been strangled."

"I wasn't—"

He interrupted her. "Close enough. You know that I wanted you however I could get you, Rachel. I sure as hell didn't make a secret of it. But it occurs to me that you were upset and vulnerable and I took advantage of that."

She had to wait nearly a full minute before she could speak. "Don't make me mad at you, Muldoon. And don't insult me."

"All I'm trying to say is… I don't know what the hell I'm trying to say," he muttered, and tried again. "Except—well, maybe I could have pulled that stupid couch out instead of using the floor."

Eyes narrowed, she leaned her face close to his. Her eyes were the color of gold doubloons, and just as exotic. "I like the floor. Get it?"

He was starting to feel better. Zack knew that tending to fragility was out of his league. But this tough, hardheaded woman was just his style. Watching her, he picked up her ruined blouse. "I ripped your clothes off."

"Proud of yourself?"

He tossed it aside. "Yeah. I can wait, if you want to put some more on. Then I can rip them off you again."

She bit the inside of her lip, but didn't quite defeat the smile. "Those were ruined anyway. Next time I'll have to bill you for damages. I'm on a budget."

Chuckling, he flicked her earring with his finger. "I'm crazy about you."

Her heart did a fast skip and shudder. The statement was as romantic as a whispered endearment to her. "Hey, don't get sloppy on me."

"Crazy," he said again, amazed and delighted at

the faint blush that stole into her cheeks. "And did I mention that your body makes me wild?"

She was a great deal more comfortable with that. "No." She tilted her head. "Why don't you?"

"From stem to stern," he said, letting his hand speak more eloquently. "Forward and aft. Port and starboard."

"Oh, God." She gave an exaggerated sigh and shiver. "Salty talk. I just love a man out of uniform." More than willing to be aroused, she nuzzled her lips against his. "Tell me something, sailor."

"You bet."

"Which part is the stern?"

"I'll show you." Very gently, he touched his lips to her bruised throat. "Honey, we better pull that couch out before this gets out of hand again."

"Okay." There was something unspeakably erotic about a callused finger stroking the underside of her breast. "If you want."

Though the idea had merit, the couch seemed entirely too far away. "Or we could do it later. Tell you what, if you'd say something in Ukrainian, I'd forget we were on the floor. And I promise to make you forget it, too."

"Why should I say something in Ukrainian?"

"Because it drives me insane."

She tilted her head back. "Are you putting me on?"

"Uh-uh." His tongue traced a slow, teasing circle on her lips. "Go ahead. Say anything."

After a little sigh, she twined her arms around his neck. Against his ear, she murmured the words, then chuckled when he groaned.

"What did it mean?" he demanded, busying himself by nibbling his way along her shoulder.

"Loosely translated? I said you were a big, pigheaded fool."

"Mmm...are you sure you didn't say how much you wanted my body?"

"No. This is how you say that."

She told him, but by the time she was finished, he was already obliging her.

In the dark, he drew her close. They had managed, finally, to pull out the bed. Now they were tangled in her sheets. The afternoon had become evening, and evening night.

"I'd like to stay," he said quietly.

"I know." It was silly, she thought, to be unhappy that he would go. She'd always jealously prized her nights alone. "But you can't. It's too soon to trust Nick overnight."

"If things were different..." Damn, he hadn't expected it to be so frustrating. "I'd like to take you back home with me. I'd like to have you in my bed tonight, wake up with you tomorrow."

"He's not ready for that, either." She wasn't sure she was ready herself. "Until I have a chance to smooth things out with him, and make him understand, it's probably best if he doesn't know we're..."

What were they? The question ran through both their heads. Neither of them voiced it.

"You're right." The mattress creaked as he shifted. "Rachel, I want to be with you again. It doesn't just have to be in bed." He traced the curve of her cheek. "Or on the floor."

"I want to be with you." She touched her fingers to the back of his hand. "It's good. And that's enough."

"Yeah." He was nearly sure it was. "I can take some time Wednesday. How about an early dinner?"

"I'd like that." They fell into silence again, until she sighed. "You'd better go."

"I know."

"Maybe Sunday you and Nick could come to dinner at my parents'. We talked about it before, remember?"

"That would be good." He kissed her again, and the kiss went on and on. "Just once more."

"Yes." She enfolded him. "Just once more."

Rachel shifted the phone to her other ear, scribbled on a legal pad and stared dubiously at the stack of files on her desk.

"Yes, Mrs. Macetti, I understand. What we need are a couple of good character witnesses for your son. Your priest, perhaps, or a teacher." As she listened to the rapid-fire broken English, she wondered if she could catch the attention of any of her harried co-workers and hope that they'd feel sorry enough for her to bring her a cup of coffee. "I can't tell you that, Mrs. Macetti. Our chances are very good for a suspended sentence and probation, since Carlo wasn't driving. But the fact is, he was riding in a stolen car, and…"

She trailed off, carefully folding the page she'd written on. "Uh-huh. Well, as I explained before, it would be rather difficult to convince anyone he didn't know the car was stolen, since the locks had been sprung and the engine hot-wired." Satisfied with the

shape of her paper airplane, she shot it out her door.
It was as good as a note in a bottle.

"I'm sure he's a good boy, Mrs. Macetti." Rachel
rolled her eyes. "Bad companions, yes. Let's hope that
this experience will have him keeping his distance
from the Hombres. Mrs. Macetti. Mrs. Macetti," Rachel said, trying to be firm, "I'm doing everything I
can. Try to be optimistic, and I'll see you in court next
week. No—no, really. I'll call you. Yes, I promise.
Goodbye. Yes, absolutely. Goodbye."

Rachel hung up the phone, then dropped her head
on her desk. Ten minutes of trying to deal with the
frantic mother of six was as exhausting as a full day
in court.

"Tough day?"

Lifting her head, Rachel spotted Nick in her doorway. He had her paper airplane in one hand, and a
large paper cup in the other.

"Tough month." Her gaze locked on the steaming
cup. "Tell me that's coffee."

"Light, no sugar." He stepped in and offered it.
"Your note sounded desperate." As she took the first
sip, he grinned. "I was coming down the hall, and it
hit me in the chest. Nice form."

"I find they make excellent interoffice memos."
Another sip and she felt the caffeine begin to pump
through her system. "Since you saved my life, what
can I do for you?"

"I was just kicking around. Thought maybe we
could grab some lunch."

"I'm sorry, Nick." She gestured to the clutter on
her desk. "I'm swamped."

"They don't let you eat?" Because he found he

enjoyed seeing her here, entrenched in the business of justice, he eased a hip down on the corner of the desk.

"Oh, they throw us some raw meat now and again." Lord, he was flirting with her, she realized. Rachel gauged the files piled in front of her, calculated how much time she had before her meeting with the DA to bargain on a half a dozen cases. It was going to be close. "Actually, I would like to talk to you, if you have a few minutes."

"I'm on six to two tonight, so I've got plenty of minutes."

"Good." She stood, easing by him to close the door. The moment she turned back, she realized he'd taken that gesture the wrong way. His hands went to her waist. She had a moment to think that in a few years that combination of smooth moves and rough manners would devastate hordes of women. Then she managed to slip aside.

"Nick," she began, then hesitated. "Sit down." When he settled in her battered office chair, she sat behind the desk. "We're going on three weeks. I'd like to know how you're feeling."

"I'm cool."

"What I mean is, when we go back in front of Judge Beckett, it's very likely she'll give you probation—unless you make a big mistake in the meantime."

"I don't plan on mistakes." The chair creaked rustily as he leaned back. "Going to jail isn't high on my list these days."

"Glad to hear it. But she may also ask about your plans. This might be the time to start thinking about that, whether you'd like to make the situation with Zack more permanent.''

"Permanent?" He gave a quick laugh. "Hey, I don't know about that. I'll probably want my own place, you know. Zack and me...well, maybe we're getting on a little better, but he cramps my style. Kind of hard to have a lady over when big brother can walk in any time." He flicked his green eyes over her face. "Know what I mean?"

An opening, she thought, and dived in. "Do you have a girl?"

His smile was very male and very attractive. "I'm more interested in women. Women with big brown eyes."

"Nick—"

"You know, when I was walking over here, I started to think how getting busted turned out to be a pretty lucky break." He lifted her hand, brushing his thumb over her knuckles before toying with her fingers. His eyes never left hers. "Otherwise, I wouldn't have needed such a great-looking lawyer."

"Nick, I'm twenty-six." It wasn't what she'd meant to say, or how she'd meant to say it, but he only tilted his head.

"Yeah? So?"

"And I'm your court-appointed guardian."

"Kind of an interesting situation." His smile spread. "It'll be over in about five weeks."

"I'll still be seven years older than you."

"More like six," he said easily. "But who's counting?"

"I am." Frustrated, she started to rise, then realized it would be best if she stayed in the position of authority behind the desk. "Nick, I like you, very much. And I meant what I said when I told you I wanted to be your friend."

"You can't let the age thing bother you, babe." When he rose, she realized she'd miscalculated by staying behind the desk. When he came around to sit on the edge of it, she was trapped between him and the wall.

"Of course I can. I was in college when you were starting puberty."

"Well, I've finished now." He grinned and traced his finger down her cheek. And his eyes narrowed. "Is that a bruise?"

"I ran into something," she said, and tried again. "The bottom line is, I'm too old for you."

He frowned at the bruise another minute, then lifted his eyes to hers. "I don't think so. Let me put it this way. Do you figure a woman shouldn't get tangled up with a guy six years older than she is?"

"That's entirely different."

"Sexist," he said clucking his tongue. "Here I figured you'd be all for equal rights."

"Of course I am, but—" She broke off with a hiss of breath.

"Gotcha."

"Regardless of age—" since that wasn't working, she thought "—I'm your guardian, and it would be wrong, certainly unethical, for me to encourage or agree to anything beyond that. I care about what happens to you, and if I've given you the impression that I'm interested in anything more than friendship, I'm sorry."

He considered. "I guess you take your work pretty seriously."

"Yes, I do."

"I can dig it. No pressure, right?"

Relief made her sigh. "Right." She rose, giving his hand a quick squeeze. "You're all right, Nick."

"You too." They both looked around when her phone began to shrill. "I'll let you get back to serving justice," he told her, then had her mouth dropping open as he brought her hand to his lips. "Five weeks isn't so long to wait."

"But—"

"Catch you later." He strolled out, leaving Rachel wondering if it would help to beat her head against the wall.

Nick was feeling great. He had the whole day ahead of him, money in his pocket, and a gorgeous woman planted in his heart. He had to grin when he thought about the way he'd flustered her. He hadn't realized it could be so satisfying to make a woman nervous.

And imagine a knockout like Rachel worrying about her age. Shaking his head, he jogged down to the subway. Maybe he'd thought she was a couple of years younger, but it didn't matter one way or the other. Everything about her was dead-on perfect.

He wondered how Zack would react when he saw Nick LeBeck strut into the bar one night with Rachel on his arm. He didn't imagine Zack would think of him as a kid when everybody saw he'd bagged a babe like Rachel Stanislaski.

Wrong, he told himself as he hopped on a car that would take him to Times Square. That was no way to talk about a classy lady. What they'd have was a relationship. As the subway car rattled and squeaked, he occupied himself by daydreaming about what they'd do together.

There would be dinners and long walks, quiet talks. They'd go listen to music, and dance. Now and again they'd have a lazy evening snuggled up in front of the television.

Nick considered it a sign of his commitment that he hadn't put sex at the top of the list.

On top of the world, he came out into the bustle and blare of Times Square and decided to use some of his loose change for a little pinball.

The arcade was noisy, and there was a loud rock backbeat blasting over the metallic sounds of beeps and buzzes. Though he'd missed the freedom of being able to breeze into an arcade any time he chose, he had to admit it felt good to be able to spend money he'd earned.

No sneaking around, no vague sense of guilt. Maybe he didn't have the gang to hang around with, but he didn't feel nearly as lonely as he'd thought he would.

It wasn't something he'd admit out loud, but he was getting a kick out of working in the kitchen with Rio. The big cook had plenty of stories, many of them about Zack. When he listened to them, Nick almost felt as though he'd been part of it.

Of course, he hadn't, Nick reminded himself, using expert body English to play out the ball. There was no possible way he could explain how miserable he'd been when Zack shipped out. Then he'd had no one again. His mother had tried, he supposed, but she'd always been more shadow than substance in his life.

It had taken all her energy to put food on the table and clothes on his back. She'd had little of herself left over once that was done.

Then there had been Zack.

Nick could still remember the first time he'd seen his stepbrother. In the kitchen of the bar. Zack had been sitting at the counter, gobbling potato chips. He'd been tall and dark, with an easy grin and a casually generous manner. Once Nick had gotten up the courage to follow him around, Zack hadn't tried to shake him off.

It was Zack who'd brought him into an arcade the first time, propped him up and shown him how to make the silver balls dance.

It was Zack who'd taken him to the Macy's parade. Zack who had patiently taught him to tie his shoes. Zack who'd clobbered him when he chased a ball into traffic.

And it was Zack who, barely a year later, had left him with a sick mother and an overbearing stepfather. Postcards and souvenirs hadn't filled the hole.

Maybe Zack wanted to make up for it, Nick thought with a shrug, then swore when the ball slipped by the flipper. And maybe, deep down, Nick wanted to let him.

"Hey, LeBeck." The slap on his shoulder nearly made Nick lose the next ball. "Where you been hiding?"

"I've been around." Nick sliced a quick glance at Cash before concentrating on his game. He wondered if Cash would make any comment about him not wearing his Cobra jacket.

"Yeah? Thought you'd dropped down the sewer."

Cash leaned against the machine, as always, appreciating Nick's skill. "Haven't lost your touch."

"I've got great hands. Ask the babes."

Cash snorted and lighted a crushed cigarette. His last. Since Reece had copped less than ten cents on the dollar for the stolen merchandise, Cash's share was long gone. "Man, the chicks see that ugly face and you never get a chance to use your hands."

"You've got your butt mixed up with my face." Nick eased back on his heels, satisfied with his score and the free game he'd finessed. "Want to take this one?"

"Sure." After stepping behind the machine, Cash began to bull his way through the game. "You still hanging with your stepbrother?"

"Yeah, got a few more weeks before we go back to court."

Cash lost the first ball and pumped up another. "You got a tough break, Nick. I mean that, man. I feel real bad about the way it went down."

"Right."

"No, man. Really." In his sincerity, Cash lost track of the ball and let it slip away. "We screwed up, and you took the heat."

Slightly mollified, Nick shrugged. "I can handle it."

"Still sucks. But hey, it can't be so bad working a bar. Plenty of juice, right?"

Nick smiled. He wasn't about to admit he'd downed no more than two beers in the past three weeks. And if Zack got wind of that much, there'd be hell to pay. "You got it, bro."

"I guess the place does okay, right? I mean, it's popular and all."

"Does okay."

"Must be plenty of sexy ladies dropping in, looking for action."

The neighborhood bar ran more to blue-collar workers and families, but Nick played along. "The place is lousy with them. It's pick and choose."

Cash laughed appreciatively even as he blew his last ball. "Want to go doubles?"

"Why not?" Nick dug in his pocket for more tokens. "So what's going on with the gang?"

"The usual. T.J.'s old man kicked him out, so he's bunking with me. Jerk snores like a jackhammer."

"Man, don't I know it. I put up with him a couple of nights last summer."

"Couple of the Hombres crossed over to our turf. We handled them."

Nick knew that meant fists, maybe chains and bottles. Occasionally blades. It was odd, he thought, but all that seemed so distant to him, distant and useless. "Yeah, well..." was all he could think of to say.

"Some people never learn, you know. Got a cigarette? I'm tapped."

"Yeah, top pocket." Nick racked up another ten thousand points while Cash lit up.

"Hey, I got a connection at this strip joint downtown. Could get you in."

"Yeah?" Nick answered absently as he sent the ball bouncing.

"Sure. I'd like to make that other business up to you. Maybe I'll drop by one night and we'll hang out."

"Forget it."

"No, man, really. I'll spring for the brew, too. Don't tell me slippery LeBeck can't slip out."

"I can get out when I want. Just walk out the kitchen."

"Around the back?"

"Yeah. Zack's usually tied up at the bar until three. Two on Sundays. I can get around Rio when I want to, or take the fire escape."

"You got a place upstairs?"

"Mmm... Your ball."

When they switched positions, Cash continued to question him, making it casual. The cash went in a safe in the office. Business usually peaked by one on Wednesdays. There were three ways in. The front door, the back, and through the upstairs apartment.

By the time Nick had trounced him three games in a row, Cash had all he needed. He made his excuses and wandered out to meet with Reece.

He didn't feel good about conning Nick. But he *was* a Cobra.

Chapter Eight

Zack stepped out of the shower, grateful the endless afternoon was over. He didn't mind paperwork. Or at least he didn't hate it. Well, the truth was, he hated it, but accepted that it was a necessary evil.

He'd made his orders, paid his invoices and tallied his end-of-the-month figures. Well, maybe he was a week or so behind the end of the month, but still, he figured he was doing pretty well.

And so was the business.

It looked as though he'd finally pulled it out of the hole his father's illness and the resulting expenses had dug. Paying off the loan he'd taken to square things for Nick would pinch a little, but in another year he'd be able to do more than look at boats in catalogs.

He wondered how Rachel would feel about taking a month off and sailing down to the Caribbean. He liked to imagine her lying out on the polished deck, wearing some excuse for a bikini. He liked the idea of watching her hair blow around her face when it caught the wind.

Of course, he'd have to take some time to check the boat out, test the rigging. He thought he'd be able to talk Nick into a day sail, or maybe a weekend. He wanted the two of them to be able to get away—away from the bar, the city, and the memories that tied them to both.

With a towel slung around his hips, he walked to the bedroom to dress. He hoped, sincerely, that the Sunday dinner at the Stanislaskis' would crack the kid's defenses a little more. Whenever Rachel spoke about her family, it made him think of what they—of what Nick—had missed.

All the kid needed was a little time to see how things could be. They were nearly halfway through the trial run, and apart from a few skirmishes, it had gone smoothly enough.

He had Rachel to thank for that, Zack thought as he tugged on a pair of jeans. He had Rachel to thank for a lot of things. Not only had she given him a second chance with Nick, but she'd added something incredible to his life. Something he'd never expected to have. Something he'd—

On a long breath, he stared hard into the mirror. When a man was going down for the third time, he recognized the signs.

Don't be an idiot, Muldoon, he told his reflection. Keep it steady as she goes. The lady wants to keep it simple, and so do you.

It wouldn't do to forget it.

"Hot date?" Feigning disinterest, Nick slouched against the doorjamb. He'd been passing and had caught the way Zack was staring blindly into the mirror.

"Huh? Yeah, I guess you could say that." Nick dragged a hand through his wet hair and scattered drops of water. "I didn't know you were back."

"I'm on at six." For reasons Nick couldn't understand, he was swamped by the memory of the times he'd stood in the bathroom watching Zack shave. How it had made him feel when Zack slapped shaving cream on his face. "Rio's got beef stew on special tonight. Too bad you'll miss it."

Zack grabbed a shirt. "You take my share or Rio'll make me eat it for breakfast."

Nick grinned, then remembered himself and smirked. "You take a lot of crap from him."

"He's bigger than I am."

"Yeah, right."

Watching Nick in the mirror, Zack buttoned his shirt. "He likes to think he's looking out for me. It doesn't cost me anything to let him. He ever tell you about how he got that scar down the side of his face?"

"He said something about a broken bottle and a drunk marine."

"The drunk marine was going for my throat with that broken bottle. Rio got in his way. The way I see it, I owe Rio a lot more than putting up with his nagging." Tucking in his shirt, Zack turned, grinned. "And you're getting paid to put up with it."

"He's okay." Nick would have liked to ask more, like why a drunk marine had wanted to slice Zack's throat, but he was afraid Zack would just shrug it off.

"Listen, if you get lucky tonight, don't worry about coming back."

Zack's fingers paused on the snap of his jeans. Tucking his tongue in his cheek, he wondered how Rachel would take his brother's turn of phrase. "Thanks for the thought, but I'll be home."

"For bed check," Nick muttered.

"Call it what you want," Zack shot back, then bit off an oath. Come hell or high water, they were going to get through one conversation without raised voices. "Listen, I don't figure you're going to climb out the window. Hell, you could do that while I'm here. It could be the lady won't want company overnight."

Mollified, Nick hooked his thumbs in his pockets. "They didn't teach you a hell of a lot in the navy, did they, bro?"

In an old gesture they'd both nearly forgotten, Zack rubbed his knuckles over Nick's head. "Kiss my butt." With his jacket slung over his shoulder, he headed out. "And don't wait up. I'm feeling lucky."

Long after the door shut behind Zack, Nick was still grinning.

Rachel was just unlocking the outside door when Zack strode up behind her. "Good timing," he said, and pressed a kiss to the back of her neck.

"For you, maybe. Everything ran over today. I was hoping to get back and soak in the tub before you got here."

"You want to soak?" The minute they were in the elevator, he had her against the wall. "Go ahead. I'll scrub your back."

"What a guy." When his mouth closed over hers,

it hurt, somewhere deep, reminding her just how much she'd wanted to be with him again. "You smell good."

"Must be these." He pulled a paper cone filled with roses from behind his back.

Her heart wanted to sigh, but she resisted. "Another bribe?" She couldn't resist the urge to bury her face in the blooms.

"There was a guy selling them a couple of blocks down. He looked like he could use a couple bucks."

"Softy." She handed him her keys so that he could unlock her door and she could continue to sniff the roses.

"Keep it to yourself."

"It'll cost you." After kicking the door closed with her foot, she dumped her briefcase and laid the spray of roses on a table. "Pay up, Muldoon," she demanded, tossing her arms around him.

There was such joy in it. Heat, yes. And the sweet, sharp ache of need. But the joy was so unexpected, so fast and full, that she laughed against his mouth as he twirled her around.

"I missed you." He continued to hold her, inches off the floor.

"Oh, yeah?" With her hands linked comfortably around his neck, she smiled. "Maybe I missed you, too. Some. How long are you going to hold me up here?"

"This way I can look right at you. You're beautiful, Rachel."

It wasn't the words so much as the way he said them that brought a lump to her throat. "You don't have to soften me up."

"I don't know how to tell you how beautiful—except that sometimes when I look at you, I remember how the sea looks, right at sunrise, when all that color spills out of the sky, kind of seeps over the horizon and falls into the water. Just for a few minutes, everything's so vivid, so...I don't know, special. When I look at you, it's like that."

Her eyes had darkened with an emotion she couldn't begin to analyze. All she could do was rest her cheek against his. "Zack." His name was a sigh, and she knew she would cry any minute if she didn't lighten the mood. "Roses and poetry, all in one day. I don't know what to say to you."

Enchanted, he buried his face in her hair. "That's a first."

"We're not going to get—"

"Sloppy," he finished for her, laughing. "Us? Are you kidding?" But when he sat on the couch, he kept her cuddled in his lap. "Let me see that bruise."

"It's nothing," she said, even as he tilted her head for a closer inspection. "The worst of it was that the word got out and I had to deal with all this sympathy and advice. If those cops had kept their mouths shut, I could have said I'd walked into a door."

"Take off the jacket and sweater."

She arched a brow. "You're such a romantic, Muldoon."

"Can it. I want to see your neck."

"It's fine."

"Which is why you're wearing a sweater that comes up to your chin."

"It's very fashionable."

"Peel it off, babe, or I'll have to do it for you."

Her eyes lit. "Ah, threatening a public official." After kicking off her shoes, she tossed up her chin. "Try it, Buster. Let's see how tough you are."

She didn't put up much of a fight, but the initial wrestling was enough to arouse them both. By the time he had her pinned to the couch, her arms over her head and her wrists cuffed in his hand, they were both breathing hard.

"I took it easy on you," she told him.

"I could see that." Her jacket was crumpled on the floor beside them. Smiling, Zack began to inch her sweater upward, letting his fingers skim over the silky material beneath.

Her breath caught, and released unsteadily. "That's not my neck," she managed as his hand cupped and molded her breast.

"Just checking." Watching her, always watching her, he teased the nipple until it was hot and hard. "You're quick to the touch, Rachel."

His touch, she thought, trembling. Only his.

Slowly, determined to savor every moment, he slipped the sweater up. He released her wrists to tug it off, then clasped them again.

"Zack."

He ignored her flexing hands. "My turn at the helm," he said quietly. "I told you once I wanted to drive you crazy. Do you remember?"

He was. He already was. "I want to touch you."

"You will." He skimmed a fingertip over her neck first, carefully studying the bruises. They were fading to yellow. "I don't want to see you hurt again." Gently he lowered his head to trail a necklace of kisses over the marks. "Not ever again."

"It doesn't hurt." Her pulse jackhammered under his nuzzling lips. "I don't need to be seduced."

"Yes, you do. But you're afraid to be, which makes the whole idea damn near irresistible. You're just going to have to trust me." He shifted so that he could unzip her skirt and slip it off. "I have places to take you." His mouth lowered to hers, rubbing, then nibbling. "Strange, wonderful places." Then diving deep.

The journey wasn't calm, but she had no choice but to go where he took her. This eagerness for pleasure, this immediacy of need, was still so new that she had no defense against it. His hand slid over her, lingering here, exploiting there, while his mouth devoured hers with a relentless hunger.

No escape, she thought desperately as he brought her close, painfully close, to that first tumultuous release. She was trapped in him, utterly lost in a tangled maze of sensations. She writhed beneath his hand, too steeped in her own needs to know how deliciously wanton her movements were.

"I didn't have time to appreciate these last time." Zack trailed his fingers up the sheer stocking to the pristine white garter. She would think them practical, he knew. He thought them erotic.

With an expert flick of his fingers that had her moaning, he released one stocking, then the other, before tormenting them both by peeling them, inch by lazy inch, down her legs.

He had to kneel on the floor to taste her calves, the backs of her knees, the glorious satin skin of her thighs. She cried out when he slid his tongue beneath her panties to sample the hot, sensitive flesh underneath. Fighting impatience, he tugged them off to give himself the freedom to taste more of her.

As the first wave swamped her, she arched like a bow, leaping into Ukrainian when the aftershocks shuddered through her. Freed, her hands groped for him until they were struggling together to strip off his clothes. Heat to heat, she pressed against him, overbalancing him, until she straddled him and her mouth could merge hotly with his.

"Now" was all he said, all he *could* say, as he gripped her hips.

"I really did mean to take you out," Zack said when they lay on the couch in a tangle of limbs.

"I bet."

He smiled, recognized the sleepy satisfaction in her voice. "Really. We can get dressed and try again."

With a half laugh, she pressed her lips to his chest. His heart was still thundering. "You're not going anywhere, Muldoon. Not till I'm finished with you."

"If you insist."

"That's what free delivery's for. How about Chinese?"

"You're on. Who's going to get up and call?"

She shifted for the pleasure of rubbing her cheek against his skin. "We'll flip for it."

He lost, and Rachel took advantage of the moment to grab a quick, bracing shower. When she came back, her hair damp and curly, a plain white terry-cloth robe skimming her knees, he was pouring them both a glass of wine.

"I think I'm repeating myself," he said, offering her a glass. "But you sure look good wet."

He'd tugged on his jeans, but hadn't bothered with his shirt. Rachel trailed a finger down his chest. "You could have joined me."

"We'd have missed the delivery boy."

"Since he's bringing egg rolls, you have a point." She moved to the kitchen to get some plates, then set them on the table by the window. "And I do have to refuel. I only had time for a candy bar at lunch." Because the mood seemed right, she lit candles. "Nick dropped by the office."

"Oh."

"I wish I had had more time...." She touched match to wick and watched the candle flare. "He caught me between phone calls and before a plea-bargaining meeting."

He watched her move around the room in her practical terry-cloth robe, turning the light into romance with her candles. He wondered if she realized how compelling that contrast was. "You don't have to explain to me, Rachel."

She shook out a match, struck another. It wasn't that she was superstitious, but there was no use taking chances with three on a match. "I have to explain to myself. He wanted to go to lunch, and I just couldn't swing it. I did talk to him about...the situation."

"About the fact that he's fallen in lust with you."

"I wouldn't put it like that." She sighed heavily when the intercom buzzed. After flipping it on, she released the security lock for the delivery boy. "He's simply misinterpreted gratitude and friendship."

Zack took one long look at her in the candleglow. "Whatever you say."

Disgusted, she went back to the table and sat. "You're buying, Muldoon."

He took out his wallet agreeably. He had the tab and the tip ready when the delivery arrived. After carrying three bulging bags to the table, he unpacked the little white cartons. In moments the air was filled with exotic aromas.

"Do you want to tell me the rest?"

"Well…" Rachel wound some noodles around her chopsticks. "I started off explaining the difference in our ages. Umm…" She chewed appreciatively. "He didn't buy it," she said over a mouthful. "He had a very convincing argument, and since I couldn't override it, I changed tactics."

"I've seen you in court," he reminded her.

"I explained the ethics of my being his guardian, and how it wasn't possible for us to go beyond those terms." Thoughtful, she scooped up some sweet and sour pork. "He seemed to understand that."

"Good."

"I thought it was. I mean, he agreed with me. He was very mature about it. Then, when he was leaving, he said how it wasn't so hard to wait five more weeks."

Zack said nothing for a moment. Then, with a half laugh, he picked up his wine. "You've got to give the kid credit."

"Zack, this is serious."

"I know. I know. It's sticky for both of us, but you have to admire the way he turned it around on you."

"I told you he was smooth." After peeking in another carton, she nibbled on some chilled chicken and bean sprouts. "Don't you know any nice teenage girls you could nudge in his direction?"

"Lola's got one," Zack said, considering. "I think she's sixteen."

"Lola has a teenager?"

"Three of them. She likes to say she started young so that she could lose her mind before she turned forty. I can feel her out about it."

"It couldn't hurt. I'm going to try again, though I'm hoping the feeling will pass in another week or two."

"I wouldn't count on it." Reaching across the table, he linked his fingers with hers. "You stick in a man's mind."

"Does that mean you're thinking of me when you're mixing drinks and flirting with the customers?"

"I never flirt with Pete."

She laughed. "I was thinking more of those two 'babes' who drop in. The blonde and the redhead. They always order stingers."

"You are observant, Counselor."

"The redhead's got her big green eyes on you."

"They're blue."

"A-ha!"

He shook his head, amazed he'd fallen so snugly into the trap. "It pays to know your regulars. Besides, I like brown eyes—especially when they lean toward gold."

She let his lips brush hers. "Too late." With her head close to his, she laughed again. "It's all right, Muldoon. I can always borrow Rio's meat cleaver if you notice more than her eyes."

"Then I'm safe. I've never paid any attention to

those cute little freckles over her nose. Or that sexy dimple in her chin.''

Eyes narrowed, Rachel bit his lip. "Get any lower, and you'll be in deep water."

"That's okay. I'm a strong swimmer."

Hours later, when Zack crawled into a cold, empty bed, he warmed himself by thinking of it. It had been nice, just nice, to laugh together over the cardboard boxes and chopsticks. They'd sampled each other's choices, talking while the candles had burned low. Not about Nick, not about work, but about dozens of other things.

Then they'd made love again, slowly, sweetly, while the night grew late around them.

He'd had to leave her. He had responsibilities. But as he settled his body toward sleep, he let his mind wander, imagining what it could be like.

Waking up with her. Feeling her stretch against him as the alarm rang. Watching her. Smiling to himself as she hurried around the apartment, getting dressed for work.

She'd be wearing one of those trim suits while they stood in the kitchen sharing coffee, talking over their plans for the day.

Sometimes they'd steal a quick lunch together, because they both hated to have a whole day pass without touching. When he could, he'd slip away from work so that he could walk home with her in the evening. When he couldn't, he'd look forward to seeing her come through the door, slide onto a stool at the bar, where she'd eat Rio's chili and flirt with him.

Then they would go home together.

One balmy weekend they would set sail together. He'd teach her how to man the tiller. They'd glide out over blue water, with the sails billowing....

The waves were high as mountains, rearing up to slap viciously at the ship. The bellow of the wind was like a thousand women screaming. Burying a fear that he knew could be as destructive as the gale, he scrambled over the pitching deck, clinging to the slippery rail as he shouted orders.

The rain was lashing his face like a whip, blinding him. His red-rimmed eyes stung from the salt water. He knew the boat was out there—radar had it—but all he could see was wall after wall of deadly water.

The next wave swamped the deck, sucking at him. Lightning cracked the sky like a bullet through glass. The ship heeled. He saw the seaman tumble, heard the shout as his hands scrambled on the deck for purchase. Zack leaped, snagging a sleeve, then a wrist.

A line. For God's sake, get me a line.

And he was dragging the dead weight back from the rail.

Wind and water. Wind and water.

There, in a flash of lightning, was the disabled boat. Lower the tow line. Make it fast. As the lightning stuttered against the dark, he could see three figures. They'd lashed themselves on—a man to the wheel, a woman behind him, a young girl to the mast.

They were fighting, valiantly, but a forty-foot boat was no match for the fury of a hurricane at sea. It was impossible to send out a launch. He had to hope one of them could hold the boat steady while another secured the tow.

Signal lights flashed instructions through the storm.

It happened fast. Another spear of lightning, and the mast cracked, falling like a tree under an ax. Horrified, he watched the young girl being dragged with it into the swirling water.

No time to think. Pure instinct had Zack grabbing a flotation device and diving into the face of the storm.

Falling, falling, endlessly, while the gale tumbled his body like dice in a gambler's hand. Black, pitch-black, then the white flare of lightning. Hitting a wall of water that felt like stone. Having it close relentlessly over your head. Like death.

Zack awoke gasping for air and choking against the nightmare water. Sweat had soaked through to the sheets, making him shiver in the chill. With a groan, he let his head fall back and waited for the first grinding ache of nausea to pass.

The room tilted once as he staggered to his feet. From past experience, Zack knew to close his eyes until it righted again. Moving through the dark, he went into the bathroom to splash the cold sweat from his face.

"Hey, you okay?" Nick was hovering in the doorway. "You sick or something?"

"No." Zack cupped a hand near the faucet, catching enough water to ease his dry throat. "Go back to bed."

Nick hesitated, studying Zack's pale face. "You look sick."

"Damn it, I said I'm fine. Beat it."

Nick's eyes darkened with angry hurt before he swung away.

"Hey, wait. Sorry." Zack let out a long breath. "Nightmare. Puts me in a lousy mood."

"You had a nightmare?"

"That's what I said." Embarrassed, Zack snatched up a towel to dry off.

It was hard for Nick to imagine big, bad Zack having a nightmare, or anything else that would make him sweat and go pale. "Uh, you want a drink?"

"Yeah." Steadier now, Zack lowered the towel. "There's some of the old man's whiskey in the kitchen."

After a moment, Zack followed Nick out. He sat on the arm of a chair while Nick splashed three fingers of whiskey into a tumbler. He took it, swallowed, then hissed. "I can't figure out how he had a liver left at the end."

Nick wished he'd pulled pants over his briefs. At least he'd have had pockets to dip his hands into. "I think when he started to forget stuff, it helped him to blame it on the whiskey instead of—you know."

"Alzheimer's. Yeah." Zack took another swallow, let it lie on his tongue a moment so that his throat could get used to the idea.

"I heard you thrashing around in there. Sounded pretty bad."

"It was pretty bad." Zack tilted the glass, watched the whiskey lap this way and that. "Hurricane. One mean bitch. I never understood why they started naming them after guys, too. Take it from me, a hurricane's all woman." He let his head fall back again, let his eyes close. "It's been nearly three years, and I haven't been able to shake this lady."

"You want to—" Nick cut himself off. "That should help you sleep."

Zack knew what Nick had wanted to ask. And he did want to. It might be best for both of them if they talked it through. "We were off of Bermuda when we got the distress call. We were the closest ship, and the captain had to make a choice. We turned back into the hurricane. Three civilians in a pleasure boat. They'd been thrown off course and hadn't been able to make it to shore before the storm hit."

Saying nothing, Nick sat on the arm of the couch so that he was facing his brother.

"Seventy-five knot winds, and the seas—they must have been forty feet. I've been through a hurricane after it's made landfall. It can be bad, real bad, but it's nothing like it is when it's at sea. You don't know scared until you see something like that. Hear something like that. The lieutenant took a rap on the head, it put him out. We came close to losing some of the crew over the side. Sometimes it was black, so black you couldn't see your own hands—but you could see that water rising up. Then the lightning would hit, and blind you."

"How were you supposed to find them in all that?"

"We had them on radar. The quartermaster could've slipped that ship through the crack of dawn. He was good. We spotted them, thirty degrees off to starboard. They'd tied the kid—little girl—to the main mast. The man and woman were fighting to keep it afloat, but they were taking on water fast. We had time. I remember thinking we could pull it off. Then the mast cracked. I thought I heard the girl scream, but it was probably the wind, because she went under pretty quick. So I went in.''

''You went in?'' Nick repeated, wide-eyed. ''You jumped in the water?''

''I was over the side before I thought about it. I wasn't being a hero, I just didn't think. Believe me, if I had...'' He let the words trail off, then swallowed the rest of the whiskey. ''It was like jumping off a skyscraper. You don't think you're ever going to stop falling. It was end over end, forever, giving you plenty of time to realize you've just killed yourself. It was stupid—if the wind had been wrong it would have just smashed me against the side of the ship. But I was lucky, and it tossed me toward the boat. Then I hit. God, it was like ramming full-length into concrete.''

He hadn't known until later that he'd snapped his collarbone and dislocated his left shoulder.

''I couldn't get my bearings. The water kept heaving me around, sucking me down. It was so black, the searchlight barely cut through. There I was, drowning, and I couldn't even remember what I was doing. It was blind luck that I found the mast. She was all tangled up in the line. I don't know how many times we went under while I was trying to get her loose. My hands were numb, and I was working blind. Then I had her, and I managed to get the flotation on her. They said I got the tow line secured, but I don't remember. I just remember hanging on to her and waiting for the next wave to finish us off. Next thing, I was waking up in the infirmary. The kid was sitting there, wrapped in a blanket and holding my hand.'' He smiled. It helped to think about that part. Just that part. "She was one tough little monkey. A damn admiral's granddaughter."

"You saved her life."

"Maybe. For the first couple of months, I jumped off that deck every time I closed my eyes. Now it's only once or twice a year. It still scares the breath out of me."

"I didn't think you were scared of anything."

"I'm scared of plenty," Zack said quietly as he met his brother's eyes. "For a while I was scared I wouldn't be able to stand on deck and look out at the water again. I was scared to come back here, knowing that once I did, my whole life was going to change. And I'm scared of ending up like the old man, sick and feeble and used up. I guess I'm scared you're going to walk out that door in a few weeks, feeling the same about me you did when you walked in."

Nick broke the gaze first, staring over Zack's shoulder at the shadowy wall. "I don't know how I feel. You came back because you had to. I stayed because there was no place else to go."

There was no arguing with the truth. As far as Zack could see, Nick had summed it up perfectly. "We never had much of a shot before."

"You didn't hang around very long."

"I couldn't get along with the old man—"

"You were the only one he cared about," Nick blurted out. "Every day I'd have to hear about how great you were, how you were making something out of yourself. What a hero you were. And how I was nothing." He caught himself, swallowed the need. "But that's cool. You were his blood, and I was just something that got dumped on him when my mother died.''

"He didn't feel that way. He didn't," Zack insisted. "For God's sake, Nick, when I lived with him, he was never satisfied with me, either. I was here, and my mother wasn't. That was enough to make him miserable every time he looked at me. Hell, he didn't mean it." Zack closed his eyes and missed the flicker of surprise that passed over Nick's face. "It was just the way he was. It took me years to realize he was always on my back because it was the only way he knew to be a father. It was the same with you."

"He wasn't my..." But this time Nick trailed off without finishing the sentence, or the thought.

"Toward the end, he asked for you. He really wanted to see you, Nick. Most of the times he came around like that, he thought you were still a little kid. And sometimes—most times, really—he just got the two of us mixed up together. Then he'd yell at me for both of us." He said it with a smile—a smile that Nick didn't return. "I'm not blaming you for staying away, or for holding all those years of criticism and complaints against him. I understand that it was too late for him, Nick. It doesn't have to be too late for you."

"What does it matter to you?"

"You're all the family I've got." He rose and laid a hand on Nick's shoulder, relaxing when it wasn't shoved off. "Maybe, when it comes right down to the bottom line, you're all the family I've ever had. I don't want to lose that."

"I don't know how to be family," Nick murmured.

"Me either. Maybe we can figure it out together."

Nick glanced up, then away. ''Maybe. We're stuck with each other a few more weeks, anyway.''

It would do, Zack thought as he gave Nick's shoulder a quick squeeze. It would do for now. ''Thanks for the drink, kid. Do me a favor and don't mention the nightmare business to anyone.''

''I can dig it.'' Nick watched Zack start back toward the bedroom. ''Zack?''

''Yeah.''

He didn't know what he wanted to say—just that it felt good, that he felt good. ''Nothing. Night.''

''Good night.'' Zack eased back into bed with a sigh, certain he'd sleep like a baby.

Chapter Nine

Something had changed. Rachel couldn't put her finger on it, but as she sat between Zack and Nick on the subway to Brooklyn she knew there was something going on between them. Something different.

It made her nerves hum. It made her wonder if she'd made a mistake in bringing the problems of the men who flanked her into her parents' home.

And her problem, as well, she admitted. After all, she wouldn't deny she cared about both of them more than what could be considered professional. She felt a kinship with Nick—the younger-sibling syndrome, she supposed. Added to that, she'd been telling the simple truth when she confessed to Zack that she had a weakness for bad boys.

She wanted to do more for Nick LeBeck than help him stay out of jail.

As for Nick's big brother, she'd long since crossed all professional boundaries with him, into what could only be termed a full-blown affair. Even sitting beside him in the rumbling car, she thought about the last time they'd been together, alone. And it took no effort at all to imagine what it would be like the next time they could steal a few hours.

Her mother was bound to sense it, Rachel mused. Nothing got past Nadia Stanislaski when it came to her children. She wondered what her mother would think of him. What she would think of the fact that her baby girl had taken a lover.

For two people who had vowed not to complicate matters, she and Zack had done a poor job of it, Rachel decided. She'd been so certain she could keep her priorities well in line, accept the physical aspects of a relationship with a man she liked and respected without dwelling on the thorny issue of what-happens-next.

But she was thinking about Zack too much, already slotting herself as part of a couple when she'd always been perfectly content to go along single.

Now, when she imagined moving along without him, the picture turned dull and listless.

Her problem, Rachel reminded herself. After all, they had made a pact, and she never went back on her word. It was something she would have to deal with when the time came. Much more immediate was the nagging sensation that the relationship of the men beside her had taken a fast turn without her being aware of it.

To offset the feeling, she kept up a steady stream of conversation until they reached their stop.

"It's only a few blocks," Rachel said, dragging her

hair back as a brisk autumn wind swirled around them. "I hope you don't mind the walk."

Zack lifted a brow. "I think we can handle it. You seem nervous, Rachel. She seem nervous to you, Nick?"

"Pretty jumpy."

"That's ridiculous." She headed into the wind, and the men fell in beside her.

"It's probably the thought of having a criminal type sit down to Sunday dinner," Zack commented. "Now she's going to have to count all the silverware."

Shocked at the statement, Rachel started to respond, but Nick merely snorted and answered for himself. "If you ask me, she's worried about inviting some Irish sailor. She has to worry if he'll drink all the booze and pick a fight."

"I can handle my liquor, pal. And I don't plan on picking a fight. Unless it's with the cop."

Nick crunched a dry leaf as it skittered across the sidewalk. "I'll take the cop."

Why, they're *joking* with each other, Rachel realized. Like brothers. Very much like brothers. Delighted, she linked arms with both of them. "If either of you takes on Alex, you'll be in for a surprise. He's meaner than he looks. And the only thing I'm nervous about is that I won't get my share of dinner. I've seen both of you eat."

"This from a woman who packs it away like a linebacker."

Rachel narrowed her eyes at Zack. "I merely have a healthy appetite."

He grinned down at her. "Me too, sugar."

She was wondering how to control the sudden leap

of her heart rate when a car skidded to a halt in the street beside them. "Hey!" the driver called out.

"Hey back." Rachel broke away to walk over to greet her brother and sister-in-law. Bending into the tiny window of the MG, she kissed Mikhail and smiled at his wife. "Still keeping him in line, Sydney?"

Cool and elegant beside her untamed-looking husband, Sydney smiled. "Absolutely. Difficult jobs are my forte."

Mikhail pinched his wife's thigh and nodded toward the sidewalk. "So what's the story there?"

"They're my guests." She gave Mikhail a long, warning look that she knew was wasted on him before calling to Nick and Zack. "Come meet my brother and his long-suffering wife. Sydney, Mikhail, this is Zackary Muldoon and Nicholas LeBeck."

His eyes shielded by dark glasses, Mikhail took a careful survey. He had a brother's natural lack of faith in his sister's judgment. "Which is the client?"

"Today," Rachel said, "they're both guests."

Sydney leaned over and jammed her elbow sharply in Mikhail's ribs. "It's very nice to meet you, both of you. You're in for quite a treat with Nadia's cooking."

"So I hear." Zack kept his eyes on Mikhail as he answered, and lifted a proprietary hand to Rachel's shoulder.

Mikhail's fingers drummed on the steering wheel. "You own what? A bar?"

"No, actually, I'm into white slavery."

That got a chuckle from Nick before Rachel shook her head. "Go park your car."

As they retreated to the sidewalk, Nick smiled over

at Rachel. "I see what you mean now about older brothers. Being a pain must go with the position."

"Responsibility," Zack told him. "We just pass on the benefit of our experience."

"No," Rachel said, "what you are is nosy." Amused, she gestured toward the sound of voices and laughter. Mikhail and Sydney were already at the door of the row house, hugging and being hugged. "This is it." When Rachel spotted Natasha, she gave a cry of pleasure and dashed up the steps.

Hanging back a little, Zack watched Rachel embrace her sister. Natasha was slighter, more delicately built, with rich brown eyes misted with tears, and tumbled raven curls raining down her back. Zack's first thought was that this could not be the mother of three Rachel had described to him. Then a young boy of six or seven squeezed between the women and demanded attention.

"You let in the cold!" This was bellowed from inside the house in a rumbling male voice that carried to the sidewalk and beyond. "You are not born in barn."

"Yes, Papa." Her voice sounded meek enough, but Rachel winked at her nephew as she lifted him up for a kiss. "My sister, Natasha," she continued, as they stood in the open doorway. "And my boyfriend, Brandon. And," she said when a toddler wandered up to hang on Natasha's legs, "Katie."

"You pick me up," Katie demanded, homing in on Nick. "Okay?" She was already holding up her arms, smiling flirtatiously. Nick cleared his throat and glanced at Rachel for help. When he only got a smile and a shrug, he bent down awkwardly.

"Sure. I guess."

An expert at such matters, Katie settled herself on his hip and wound an arm around his neck.

"She enjoys men," Natasha explained. When her father bellowed again, she rolled her eyes. "Come inside, please."

Zack was struck by the sounds and the scents. Home, he realized. This was a home. And stepping inside made him realize he'd never really had one himself.

The scents of ham and cloves and furniture polish, the clash of mixed voices. The carpet on the stairway leading to the second floor was worn at the edges, testimony to the dozens of feet that had climbed up or down. The furniture in the cramped living room was faded with sun and time, crowded now with people. A gleaming piano stood against one wall. Atop it was a bronze sculpture. He recognized the faces of Rachel's family, melded together, cheek to cheek, flanked by two older, proud faces that could only be her parents'.

He didn't know much about art, but he understood that this represented a unity that could not be broken.

"So you bring your friends, then leave them in the cold." Yuri sat in an armchair, cuddling a sprite of a girl. His big workingman's arms nearly enveloped the pretty child, who had a fairy's blond hair and curious eyes.

"It's only a little cold." Rachel bent to kiss her father, then the girl. "Freddie, you get prettier every time I see you."

Freddie smiled and tried to pretend she wasn't staring at the young blond man who was holding her little sister. But she had just turned thirteen, and whole worlds were opening up to her.

Rachel went through another round of introductions. Freddie turned the name Nick LeBeck over in her head while Yuri shouted out orders.

"Alexi, bring hot cider. Rachel, take coats upstairs. Mikhail, kiss your wife later. Go tell Mama we have company."

Within moments, Zack found himself seated on the couch, scratching the ears of a big, floppy dog named Ivan and discussing the pros and cons of running a business with Yuri.

Nick felt desperately self-conscious with a baby on his knee. She didn't seem to be in any hurry to get down. And the little blond girl named Freddie kept studying him with solemn gray eyes. He glanced away, wishing their mother would come along and do something. Anything. Katie snuggled up and began to toy with his earring.

"Pretty," she said, with a smile so sweet he couldn't help but respond. "I have earrings, too. See?" To show off her tiny gold hoops, she turned her head this way and that. "'Cause I'm Daddy's little gypsy."

"I bet." Unconsciously he lifted a hand to stroke her hair. "You kind of look like your Aunt Rachel."

"I can take her." Freddie had worked up her courage and now she stood beside the couch smiling down at Nick. "If she's bothering you."

Nick merely moved his shoulders. "She's cool." He struggled to find something to say. The girl was china-doll pretty, he thought, and as foreign to him as

Rachel's Ukraine. "Uh...you don't look a whole lot like sisters."

Freddie's smile bloomed warm and her fledgling woman's heart tapped a little faster. *He'd noticed her.* "Mama's my stepmother, technically. I was about six when she and my father got married."

"Oh." A *step,* he thought. That was something he knew about, and sympathized with. "I guess it was a little rough on you."

Though she was baffled, Freddie continued to smile. After all, he was talking to her, and she thought he looked like a rock star. "Why?"

"Well, you know..." Nick found himself flustered under that steady gray stare. "Having a stepmother—a stepfamily."

"That's just a word." Gathering her nerve, she sat on the arm of the couch beside him. "We have a house in West Virginia—that's where Dad met Mama. He teaches at the university and she owns a toy store. Have you ever been to West Virginia?"

Nick was still stuck on her answer. *It's just a word.* He could hear in the easy tone of her voice that she meant just that. "What? Oh, no, never been there."

Inside the warm, fragrant kitchen, Rachel was laughing with her sister. "Katie certainly knows how to snag her man."

"It was sweet the way he blushed."

"Here." Nadia thrust a bowl into her eldest daughter's hands. "You make biscuits. The boy had good eyes," she said to Rachel. "Why is he in trouble?"

Sniffing a pot of simmering cabbage, Rachel smiled. "Because he didn't have a mama and papa to yell at him."

"And the older one," Nadia continued, opening the oven to check her ham. "He has good eyes, too. And they're on you."

"Maybe."

After smacking her daughter's hand away, Nadia replaced the lid on the pot. "Alex grumbles about them."

"He grumbles about everything."

Natasha cut shortening in the bowl and grinned. "I think it's more to the point that Rachel has her eye on Zack every bit as much as he has his on her."

"Thanks a lot," Rachel said under her breath.

"A woman who doesn't look at such a man needs glasses," Nadia said, and made her daughters laugh.

When her curiosity got to be too much for her, Rachel opened the swinging door a crack and peeked out. There was Sydney, sitting on the floor and keeping Brandon entertained with a pile of race cars. The men were huddled together, arguing football. Freddie was perched on the arm of the sofa, obviously in the first stages of infatuation with Nick. As for Nick, he seemed to have forgotten his embarrassment and was bouncing Katie on his knee. And Zack, she noted with a smile, was leaning forward, entrenched in the hot debate over the upcoming game.

By the time the table was set and groaning under the weight of platters of food, Zack was thoroughly fascinated with the Stanislaskis. They argued, loudly, but without any of the bitterness he remembered from his own confrontations with his father. He discovered that Mikhail was the artist who had crafted the sculpture on the piano, as well as all the passionate pieces in Rachel's apartment. Yet he talked construction and building codes with his father, not art.

Natasha handled her children with a deft hand. No one seemed to mind if Brandon created a racket imitating race cars or if Katie climbed all over the furniture. But when it was time to stop, they did so at little more than a word from their mother or father.

Alex didn't seem like such a tough cop when he was being barraged by his family's teasing over his latest lady friend—a woman, Mikhail claimed, who had the I.Q. of the cabbage he was heaping on his plate.

"Hey, I don't mind. That way I can do the thinking for her."

That earned an unladylike snort from Rachel. "He wouldn't know how to handle a woman with a brain."

"One day one will find him," Nadia predicted. "Like Sydney found my Mikhail."

"She didn't find me." Mikhail passed a bowl of boiled potatoes to his wife. "I found her. She needed some spice in her life."

"As I recall, you needed someone to knock the chip off your shoulder."

"It was always so," Yuri agreed, shaking his fork. "He was a good boy, but— What is the word?"

"Arrogant?" Sydney suggested.

"Ah." Satisfied, Yuri dived into his meal. "But it's not so bad for a man to be arrogant."

"This is true." Nadia kept an eagle eye on Katie, who was concentrating on cutting her meat. "So long as he has a woman who is smarter. Is not hard to do."

Female laughter and male catcalls had Katie clapping her hands in delight.

"Nicholas," Nadia said, pleased that he was going back for seconds, "you will go to school, yes?"

"Ah...no, ma'am."

She urged the basket of biscuits on him. "So you know what work you want."

"I... Not exactly."

"He is young, Nadia," Yuri said from across the table. "Time to decide. You're skinny." He pursed his lips as he studied Nick. "But have good arms. You need work, I give you job. Teach you to build."

Speechless, Nick stared. No one had ever offered to give him anything so casually. The big, broad-faced man who was plowing through the glazed ham didn't even know him. "Thanks. But I'm sort of working for Zack."

"It must be interesting to work in a bar. Brandon, eat your vegetables, or no more biscuits. All the people you meet," Natasha continued, saving Katie's glass from tipping on the floor without breaking rhythm.

"You don't meet a whole lot of them in the kitchen," Nick muttered.

"You have to be twenty-one to tend bar or serve drinks," Zack reminded him.

Noting Nick's mutinous expression, Rachel broke in. "Mama, you should see Zack's cook. He's a giant from Jamaica, and he makes the most incredible food. I've been trying to charm some recipes out of him."

"I will give you one to trade."

"Make it the glaze for this ham, and I guarantee he'll give you anything." Zack sampled another bite. "It's great."

"You will take some home," Nadia ordered. "Make sandwiches."

"Yes, ma'am." Nick grinned.

* * *

Rachel bided her time, waiting until dinner was over and three of the four apple pies her mother had baked had been devoured. With just a little urging, Nadia was persuaded to play the piano. After a time, she and Spence played a duet, the music flowing out over the sound of clattering dishes and conversation.

She saw the way Nick glanced over, watching, listening. As cleverly as a general aligning his troops, she dropped down on the bench when Spence and Nadia took a break. She held out a hand, inviting Nick to join her.

"I shouldn't have had that second piece of pie," she said with a sigh.

"Me either." It was difficult to decide how to tell her the way the afternoon had made him feel. He wouldn't have believed people lived this way. "Your mom's great."

"Yeah, I think so." Very casually, she turned and began to noodle with the keys. "She and Papa love these Sundays when we can all get together."

"Your dad, he was saying how the house would get bigger when the kids left home. But now he thinks they'll have to add on a couple of rooms to hold everyone. I guess you get together like this a lot."

"Whenever we can."

"They didn't seem to mind you brought me and Zack along."

"They like company." She tried a chord, wincing at the clash of notes. "This always looks so easy when Spence or Mama does it."

"Try this." He put his hand over hers, guiding her fingers.

"Ah, better. But I don't see how anyone can play different things with each hand. At the same time, you know."

"You don't think about it that way. You just have to let it happen."

"Well..."

She trailed off and, unable to resist, he began to improvise blues. When the music moved through him, he forgot he was in a room crowded with people and let it take over. Even when the room fell silent, he continued, wrapped up in the pleasure of creating sound and feeling from the keys. When he played, he wasn't Nick LeBeck, outcast. He was someone he didn't really understand yet, someone he couldn't quite see and yearned desperately to be always.

He eased into half-remembered tunes, filling them out with his own interpretation, letting the music swing with his mood from blues to boogie-woogie to jazz and back again.

When he paused, grinning to himself from the sheer pleasure it had given him to play, Zack laid a hand on his shoulder and snapped him back to reality.

"Where'd you learn to do that?" The amazement in Zack's voice was reflected in his eyes. "I didn't know you could do that."

With a shrug, Nick wiped his suddenly nervous hands on his thighs. "I was just fooling around."

"That was some fooling around."

Cautious, trying to put a label on the tone of Zack's voice, Nick glanced back. "It's no big deal."

Grinning from ear to ear, Zack shook his head. "Man, to somebody who can't play 'Chopsticks,' that was one whale of a big deal.'' Pride was bubbling through the amazement. ''It was great. Really great.''

The pleasure working its way into him made Nick almost as uneasy as the criticism he'd expected. It was then he realized that everyone had stopped talking and was looking at him. Color crept into his cheeks. ''Look, I said it was no big deal. I was just banging on the keys.''

''That was some very talented banging.'' With Katie on his hip, Spencer moved to the piano. ''Ever think about studying seriously?''

Flabbergasted, Nick stared down at his hands. It had been one thing to sit across the table from Spencer Kimball, and another entirely to have the renowned composer discussing music with him. ''No... I mean, not really. I just fool around sometimes, that's all.''

''You've got the touch, and the ear.'' Catching Rachel's eye, he passed her Katie and changed positions with her so that he sat with Nick on the edge of the piano bench. ''Know any Muddy Waters?''

''Some. You dig Muddy Waters?''

''Sure.'' He began to play the bass. ''Can you pick it up?''

''Yeah.'' Nick laid his hands on the keys and grinned. ''Yeah.''

''Not too shabby,'' Rachel murmured to Zack.

He was still staring at his brother, dumbfounded. ''He never told me. Never a word.'' When Rachel reached for his hand, he gripped hard. ''I guess he did to you.''

''A little, enough to make me want to try this. I didn't know he was that good.''

''He really is, isn't he?'' Overwhelmed, he pressed

his lips to Rachel's hair. Nick was too involved to notice, though several pair of eyes observed the gesture. "Looks like I'm going to have to get my hands on a piano."

Rachel leaned her head against his shoulder. "You're all right, Muldoon."

It took him nearly a week to arrange it, but taking another deep dip into his savings, Zack bought an upright piano. With Rachel's help, he dragged furniture around the apartment to make room for it.

Puffing a bit, her hands on her hips, she surveyed the space they had cleared under the window. "I wonder if it wouldn't be better against that wall there."

"You've already changed your mind three times. This is it." He took a long pull from a cold beer. "For better or worse."

"You're not marrying the stupid piano. You're arranging it. And I really think—"

"Keep thinking, and I'll pour this over your head." He caught her chin to tilt her head up for a kiss. "And it's not a stupid piano. The guy assured me it was the best for the money."

"Don't get started on that again." She eased closer to link her arms around his neck. "Nick doesn't need a baby grand."

"I'd just like to have done a little better for him."

"Muldoon." She pressed her mouth to his. "You did good. When's it supposed to get here?"

"Twenty minutes ago." Wound up, he began to pace. "If they blow this after I went through all that business to get Nick out for a few hours—"

Rachel interrupted him, amused and touched. "It's

going to be fine. And I think it was inspired of you to use beer nuts to get him out of the way.''

''He was steaming.'' With a grin, Zack dropped down on the couch. ''Argued with me for ten minutes about why the hell he had to go check on a missing delivery of beer nuts when he was getting paid to wash dishes.''

''I think he'll forgive you when he gets back.''

''Hey up there.'' Rio's musical voice echoed up the stairway. ''We got us one fine piano coming in. Best you come down and take a look.''

Rachel tried to stay out of the way—though several times, as they muscled and maneuvered the piano up those steep stairs, she wanted to offer advice. The best part was watching Zack, which she did the entire time the instrument was hauled, set into place and tuned. He worried over the piano like a mother hen, wiping smudges from the surface, opening and closing the lid on the bench.

''That looks real fine.'' Rio folded his massive arms over his chest. ''Be good to have music when I cook. You do right by that boy, Zack. He's going to make himself somebody. You'll see. Now I'm going to fix us something special.'' He grinned at Rachel. ''When you going to bring that mama of yours by here so we can talk food?''

''Soon,'' Rachel promised. ''She's going to bring you an old Ukrainian recipe.''

''Good. Then I give her my secret barbecue sauce. I think she must be a fine woman.'' He started out just as Nick came clattering up the steps. ''What's your hurry, boy? Got a fire in your pocket?''

''Damn beer nuts'' was all Nick said as he pushed

by. He swung into the apartment, ready for a fight. "Listen, bro, the next time you want somebody to—" Everything went out of his mind when he spotted the piano standing new and shiny under the window.

"Sorry about the wild-goose chase." Nervous, Zack jammed his hands in his pockets. "I wanted to get you out so we could get this in." He shifted back on his heels when Nick remained silent. "So, what do you think?"

Nick swallowed hard. "What did you do, rent it or something?"

"I bought it."

Because his fingers itched to feel the keys, he, too, stuck them in his pockets. Rachel nearly sighed. They looked like two stray dogs that didn't know whether to fight or make friends.

"You shouldn't have done that." The strain in Nick's voice made it come out curt and sharp.

"Why the hell not?" Zack shot back. His hands were now balled into fists and straining against denim. "It's my money. I thought it would be nice to have some music around here. So, do you want to try it out or not?"

There was an ache spreading, twisting in his gut and burning the back of his throat. He had to get out. "I forgot something," he muttered, and strode stiffly out the door.

"What the hell was that?" Zack exploded. He snatched up his beer, then set it down again before he gave in to the temptation to hurl the bottle against the wall. "If that little son of a—"

"Hold it." Rachel's order snapped out as she thumped a fist against Zack's chest. "Oh, the pair of you are a real prize. He doesn't know how to say thank you, and you're too stupid to see he was so overwhelmed he was practically on the verge of tears.''

"That's bull. He all but tossed it back in my face."

"Idiot. You gave him a dream. It's very possibly the first time anyone ever understood what he wanted, deep down, and gave him a shot at it. He didn't know how to handle it, Zack, any more than you would.''

"Listen, I—" He broke off and swore, because it made sense. "What am I supposed to do now?''

"Nothing." Cupping his face in her hands, she pulled it toward hers to kiss him. "Nothing at all. I'm going to go talk to him, okay?" She pulled back and started for the door.

"Rachel." He took a deep breath before crossing to her. "I need you." He watched surprise come into her eyes as he took her hands and brought them to his lips. "Maybe I don't know how to handle that, either.''

Something fluttered around her heart. "You're doing all right, Muldoon.''

"I don't think you understand." He didn't, either. "I really need you.''

"I'm right here.''

"But are you going to stay here, once your obligation to Nick is over?''

The fluttering increased. "We've got a couple of weeks before we have to think about that. It's..." Steady, Rachel, she warned herself. Think it through. "It's not just Nick I care about." She tightened her fingers on his briefly before drawing away. "Let me go find him. We'll talk about the rest of this later.''

"Okay." He stepped back from her, and from what

he was feeling. "But I think we are going to have to talk about it. Soon."

With a quick nod, she hurried down the steps. Rio merely gestured toward the front of the bar, and, grateful she didn't have to talk for a moment, she went out to look.

She found him standing on the sidewalk with his hands balled in his pockets, staring at the late-afternoon traffic. Oh, she knew a portion of what he was feeling. How Zackary Muldoon could get inside you and pull your emotions apart before you had a chance to defend yourself.

Later, she promised herself, she would think about what he'd done to *her* emotions. For now, she would concentrate on Nick.

She stepped up beside him and brushed at the hair on his shoulders. "You doing okay?"

He didn't look at her, just continued to watch the fits and starts of traffic. "Why did he do that?"

"Why do you think?"

"I didn't ask him for anything."

"The best gifts are the ones we don't ask for."

He shifted, meeting her eyes for the barest of moments. "Did you talk him into it?"

"No." Trying to be patient, she took him by the arms so that he had to face her. "Open your eyes, Nick. You saw the way he reacted when he heard you play. He was so proud of you he could barely talk. He wanted to give you something that would matter to you. He didn't do it so you'd be obligated to him, but because he loves you. That's what families do."

"Your family."

She gave him a quick shake. "And yours. Don't try

to con me with that bull about not being real brothers. You care just as much about him as he does about you. I know how much it meant to you to walk in there and see that piano. Mama had the same look on her face on Mother's Day, but it was easier for her to show what she was feeling. You just need a little practice.''

Closing his eyes, he laid his brow against hers. "I don't know what to say to him. How to act. Nobody's ever... I've never had anybody. When I was a kid, I just wanted to hang around him. Then he took off."

"I know. Try to remember he wasn't much more than a kid himself when he did. He's not going anywhere now." Rachel kissed both his cheeks, as her mother might have done. "Why don't you go back inside, Nick, and do what you do best?"

"What's that?"

She smiled at him. "Play it by ear. Go on. He's dying for you to try it out."

"Yeah. Okay." He took a step back. "You coming?"

"No, I've got some things to do." Some things to think about, she thought, correcting herself. "Tell Zack I'll see him later."

But she waited after he'd gone in. Standing on the sidewalk, she watched the window. And after a while, very faintly, she heard the sound of music.

Chapter Ten

"Yo, Rachel." Pete straightened on his stool and sucked in some of his comfortable stomach when he spotted Rachel swinging through the front door of the bar. "How 'bout I buy you a drink?"

"I might just let you do that." But her smile was for Zack as she hung her coat on one of the hooks by the door. As she crossed the room, she shot a meaningful glance at the blonde who was seductively wrapped around a bar stool, purring an order for another drink while she walked her fingers up Zack's arm. "Busy night?"

Lola juggled a tray as she passed. "That one's on her third stinger," she said to Rachel under her breath. "And those big blue eyes of hers have been crawling all over the boss for two hours."

"That's all she'll do—unless she wants those eyes black-and-blue."

Lola gave a snap of appreciative laughter. "Atta girl. Hey, hold on a minute." With a skill Rachel admired, Lola served a full tray of drinks, emptied ashtrays and replaced an empty basket of chips. "See the brunette by the juke?"

With her lips pursed, Rachel studied the slim jean-clad hips and the waterfall of honey-brown hair. "Don't tell me I have to worry about her, too?"

"No, *I* do. That's my oldest."

"Your daughter? She's gorgeous."

"Yeah. That's why I have to worry. Anyway, Zack's been hinting around about how he'd like Nick to meet some people closer to his own age, so I talked her into coming in, having one of Rio's burgers."

"And?"

"Nick looked. Actually, he was pretty enthusiastic about busing tables tonight. But he didn't make a move in her direction."

"Looking's good," Rachel mused. "It wouldn't bother you if he was interested enough to ask her out?"

"Nick's okay. Besides, my Terri can take care of herself." Lola winked. "Takes after her mom. Keep your pants on," she shouted to the table of four that was signaling to her. "Catch you later."

"Well, now..." Rachel eased onto the stool between Harry and Pete. A glass of white wine was already waiting for her. "What's the latest?"

"Seven-letter word for rapture," Harry told her. "Ending in 'y'."

Rachel smiled into her wine. *"Ecstasy,"* she said, watching Zack.

"Okay!" Pleased with that, he skimmed over the

blank spaces in his puzzle. "Here's another seven. Characterized by a lack of substance."

"Perfect," she murmured, shifting her gaze to the blonde, who was leaning her cleavage over the bar. "Try *vacuous*."

"Damn, you're good."

"Harry," she gave him a smile that had him going beet red, "I'm terrific. Keep an eye on things for me. I want to talk to Nick."

Pete watched her go, sighed. "If I was twenty years younger, thirty pounds lighter, didn't have a wife who'd slit my wrists and still had all my hair..."

"Yeah. Keep dreaming." Harry signaled for another round.

The minute she passed into the kitchen, Rachel took a deep breath. It always smelled like heaven. "Okay, Rio, what's good tonight?"

"Everything's always good." He grinned, wiping his big hands on his apron. "But tonight my fried chicken's number one."

"There must be a drumstick with my name on it. Hey, Nick." Now as at home here as she was in her mama's kitchen, she eased against the counter where he was stacking the dishes. "How's it going?"

"By last count, I've washed six thousand and eighty-two plates." But he smiled when he said it. "Zack mentioned you might be coming by tonight. I've been looking for you."

Rio handed her a plate heaped with fried chicken, creamed potatoes and coleslaw. "If I came by any more often, they'd have to roll me in and out the door."

"You eat." Rio gestured with his spatula before he flipped burgers. "I like to see a woman with hips."

"You're about to." Her willpower was nonexistent when she was faced with Rio's extra-spicy chicken. Rachel began to eat where she stood. "Definitely number one," she said with her mouth full. Rio grinned. "So, did you want to see me about anything in particular?" she asked Nick.

"No." He brushed a hand down her hair. "I just wanted to see you."

Whoops. "Nick, I really think—"

"We've only got a couple of weeks to go."

"I know." She shifted slightly, putting the plate between them. "In fact, I was able to speak to the DA, tell him about your progress. He doesn't plan on making an objection to the suspended sentence and probation we expect from Judge Beckett."

"I knew I could count on you, but I wasn't just thinking about that."

She knew very well what he was thinking of, and she'd put off dealing with it long enough. "Rio—" she set the plate aside "—I need to talk to Nick for a minute. Can you handle things without him if we go upstairs?"

"No problem. He just wash twice as fast when he come back."

She would be calm, Rachel promised herself as they started upstairs. She would be logical, and she would be in control. "Okay, Nick," she said the minute they stepped into the apartment. And that was all she said, because she found herself being thoroughly kissed. "Stop." Her voice was muffled, but it was firm, and the hands she shoved against his shoulders did the rest.

"I've missed you, that's all." He gentled his grip, then released her completely when she stepped back. "It's been a long time since we had a chance to be alone."

Pressing her hands to her temples, she sighed. "Oh, Nick. I've made a mess of this." The confused churning of emotion was clear in her eyes as she stared at him. "I kept telling myself it would resolve itself, even though I knew it wouldn't." In a gesture that mirrored the helplessness she was feeling, she let her hands drop to her sides. "I don't want to hurt you."

There was a quick warning twist in his gut. People only said that stuff about not hurting you in that particular tone of voice when they were about to. "What are you talking about?"

"About you and me—about you thinking there's a you and me." She turned away, hoping she could find the right words. "I tried to explain it to you before, but I did a poor job of it. You see, initially I was so surprised that you would think of me that way. I didn't—" With a sound of disgust, she turned to face him again. "I'm not handling it any better now."

"Why don't you just say what you mean?"

"I care about you, not only as my client, but as a person."

That all-too-familiar light came into his eyes. "I care about you, too."

When he took a step toward her, she lifted her hands, palms out. "But not that way, Nick. Not... romantically."

His eyes narrowed, and she watched, hurting, as he absorbed the rejection. "You're not interested in me."

"I am interested in you, but not the way you think you'd like me to be."

"I get the picture." Trying to tough it out, he hooked his thumbs in his front pockets. "You think I'm too young."

She thought about the way she'd just been kissed, and let out a long breath. "That argument doesn't seem altogether valid. It should, but you're not a typical teenager."

"So what is it? I'm just not your type?"

When she thought of how much he and Zack had in common, she had to block a quick laugh. "That doesn't work either." Sorry that she was going to hurt him, knowing she had to, Rachel did her best with the truth. "What I feel for you is the same sort of thing I feel for my brothers. I'm sorry it's not what you want, Nick, but it's all I can give." She wanted to reach out, touch his arm, but she was afraid he'd shrug her off. "I'm sorry, too, that I didn't put it just that way weeks ago. I didn't seem to know how."

"I feel like an idiot."

"Don't." She couldn't keep herself from reaching out now, taking his hand in hers. "There's nothing for you to feel like an idiot about. You were attracted, and you were honest about it. And underneath all my confusion and dismay," she added, trying out a smile, "I was very flattered."

"I'd rather you said you were tempted."

"Maybe." Her smile warmed, squeezing his battered heart. "For a moment. I hope it doesn't hurt you to have me say it, but I do want to be your friend."

"Well, you gave it to me straight." And he supposed he would have to accept it. A babe was just a babe, he tried to tell himself. But he knew there was no one else like Rachel. "No hard feelings."

"Good." She wanted to kiss him, but figured it was best not to push her luck. Or his. She did take his other hand. "I always wanted a younger brother."

He wasn't quite ready to take that position. "Why?"

"For the purest of reasons," she told him. "To have somebody I could push around." When he smiled, she felt the first genuine tug of relief. "Come on, get back to work."

She walked down with him, certain they had progressed to the next stage. To reassure herself, she stayed in the kitchen for a few minutes, pleased when she felt no lingering tension from Nick's direction.

When she slipped out, she looked immediately for Zack.

"In the office," Pete told her, grinning. "You should go right on in."

"Thanks." She was puzzled by the chuckles that rumbled around the bar, but when she glanced back, everyone looked busy and innocent. Too innocent, Rachel thought as she pushed open Zack's office door.

He was there all right, big as life, standing in front of his shipshape desk. There was a curvy blonde wrapped around him, clinging like cellophane.

With one brow arched, Rachel took in the scene. The blonde was doing her best to crawl up Zack's body. She nearly had him pinned to the desk, and Zack was tugging at the arms that roped his neck. The expression on his face, Rachel mused—a kind of baffled embarrassment—was worth the price of admission all by itself.

"Listen, honey, I appreciate the offer. Really. But I'm not—" He broke off when he spotted Rachel.

That expression, she decided, was even better. This one had traces of shock, chagrin and apology, all seasoned with a nice dollop of fear.

"Oh, God." He managed to pry one arm from around his neck, and he tried to shake her off, but she transferred her grip to his waist.

"Excuse me," Rachel said, her tongue firmly in her cheek. "I can see you're busy."

"Damn it, don't shut the door." His eyes widened when the blonde shifted to give his bottom a nice, intimate squeeze. "Give me a break, Rachel."

"You want a break?" She glanced back to where the regulars had moved closer, craning their necks to catch the show. "He wants a break," she told them. Very casually, she strolled across the threshold. "Which leg would you like me to break, Muldoon? Or would you prefer an arm? Maybe your neck."

"Have a heart." The blonde was giggling now as she tugged at his sweater. "Help me get her off. She's plowed."

"I'd think a big strong man like you could handle that all by yourself."

"She moves like a damn eel," he muttered. "Come on, Babs, let go. I'll call you a cab."

She was slithering over him, Rachel noted, and with a sigh she took charge. Gripping the blonde's artfully tangled mane in one hand, she tugged. Hard. The quick squeal of pain was very satisfying. Following up on it, Rachel shoved her face close. "You're trespassing, dear."

Babs weaved, gave a glazed-eyed grin. "I didn't see any signs."

"Consider yourself lucky I don't make you see stars." Using the hair as a leash, Rachel pulled the squeaking blonde to the door. "This way out."

"I'll take it from here." Lola slipped an arm around the blonde's waist. "Come on, sweetie, you're looking a little green."

"He's just so damn cute," Babs sighed as she stumbled toward the ladies' room with Lola.

"Call her a cab," Zack shouted. After one heated glare at the grinning faces of his customers, he slammed the door shut. "Listen, Rachel..." Besides being mortified, he was out of breath, and he took a moment to steady himself. "It wasn't the way it looked."

"Oh?" The situation was too entertaining to resist. She sauntered over to his desk, scooted onto the edge and crossed her legs. "How did it look, Muldoon?"

"You know damn well." He blew out a breath, tucked his useless hands in his pockets. "She got herself wasted on a couple of stingers. I came in to call her a cab, and she followed me." His brows drew together when Rachel lifted a hand to examine her nails. "She attacked me."

"Want to press charges?"

"Don't get cute with me." As embarrassing moments went, Zack considered this in the top ten. "I was trying to...defend myself."

"I could see it was a pitched battle. You're lucky you came out of it alive."

"What was I supposed to do, knock her cold?" He

paced from one wall to the other. "I told her I wasn't interested, but she wouldn't back off."

"You're just so damn cute," Rachel said, fluttering her lashes.

"Funny," he tossed over his shoulder. "Really funny. You're going to play this one out all the way, aren't you?"

"Bingo." She picked up a letter opener from his desk, tested the point, thoughtfully. "As counsel for the defense, I have to ask if you feel that strutting behind the bar in those snug black jeans—"

"I don't strut."

"I'll rephrase the question." She flicked the tip of the letter opener with her thumb. "Can you say—and I remind you, Mr. Muldoon, you're under oath—can you tell this court you haven't done anything to entice the defendant, to make her believe you were available? Even willing?"

"I never... Well, I might have before you..." As a man of the sea, Zack knew when to cut line. He crossed his arms over his chest. "I take the Fifth."

"Coward."

"You bet." He eyed the letter opener warily. "You don't plan to use that on any particularly sensitive part of my anatomy?"

Letting her gaze skim down, Rachel touched her tongue to her upper lip. "Probably not."

His smile came slowly and was full of relief. "You're really not mad, are you, sugar?"

"That I walked in and found you in a compromising position with a blond bombshell?" After a quick laugh, she shifted her grip on the letter opener. "Why should I be mad, sugar?"

"You may have saved my life." He thought he'd gauged her mood correctly, but his approach was still cautious. "You don't know what she said she was going to do to me." He gave a mock shudder, and slipped his arms around her, as if for support. "She's a yoga instructor."

"Oh, my." Biting back a grin, Rachel patted his back. "What did she threaten you with?"

"Well, I think it went something like…" He leaned close to her ear, whispering. He heard Rachel's surprised chuckle. "And then…"

"Oh, *my*" was all she could say. She swallowed once. "Do you think that's anatomically possible?"

"I think you'd have to be double-jointed, but we could give it a try."

Wicked laughter gleaming in her eyes, she tilted her head back. "I don't care what you say, Muldoon. I think you liked being pawed."

"Uh-uh." He nuzzled her neck. "It was degrading. I feel so…cheap."

"There, there. I saved you."

"You were a regular Viking."

"And you know what they say about Vikings…" she murmured as she turned her mouth to his.

"Go ahead," he said invitingly. "Use me."

"Oh, I plan to."

The kiss was long and satisfying, but as it began to heat he tore his mouth from hers to bury his face in her hair.

"Rachel, you don't know how good you feel. How right."

"I know this feels right." Eyes shut tightly, she held him close.

"Do you?"

"Yes. I think…" She let her words trail off into a sigh. She'd been doing a great deal of thinking over the past few days. "I think sometimes people just fit. The way you told me once before."

He drew back, cupping her face in his hands. His eyes were very dark, very intense, on hers. She wasn't entirely sure what she was reading in them, but it made her heart trip-hammer into her throat. "We fit. I know you said you didn't want to get involved. That you have priorities."

She linked her fingers around his wrists. "I said a lot of things."

"Rachel, I want you to move in with me." He saw the surprise in her eyes and hurried on before she could answer. "I know you wanted to keep it simple. So did I. This doesn't have to be a complication. You'd have time to think about it. We have to wait until everything's straightened out with Nick. But I need for you to know how much I want to be with you—not just snatching time."

She let out an unsteady breath. "It's a big step."

"And you don't do things on impulse." He lowered his lips to brush hers. "Think about it. Think about this," he whispered, and took the kiss deep, deep, fathoms deep, until thinking was impossible.

"Zack, I need to—" Nick burst into the office, and froze. He saw Rachel pressed against his brother, her hands fisted in his hair, her eyes soft and clouded.

They cleared quickly enough, and now there was alarm there, and apology. But as Nick stared at them, all he could see was the red mist of betrayal.

She shouted his name as Nick leaped. Zack saw the

blow coming, and he let it connect. It rocked him back
on his heels. He tasted blood. Instinct had him gripping Nick's wrists to prevent another punch, but Nick
twisted away, agile as a snake, and braced for the next
round.

"Stop it!" Heedless that the next fist could fly any
second, Rachel stepped furiously between them, shoving them apart. "This isn't the way."

Clamping down on his own temper, Zack merely
lifted her up and set her aside. "Stay clear. You want
to go a round in here?" he said to Nick. "Or take it
outside?"

"Of all the—"

"Anywhere you say," Nick snapped, cutting Rachel off. "You son of a bitch. It was always you."
He shoved, but the bright hurt in his eyes kept Zack
from striking back. "You always had to come out on
top, didn't you?" His breathing was labored as he
rammed Zack back against the wall. "All this crap
about family. Well, you know where you can stick it,
bro."

"Nick, please." Rachel lifted a hand, but let it drop
when he turned those furious eyes on her.

"Just shut up. That whole line of bull you handed
me upstairs. You've got real talent, lady, because I
was buying it. You knew how I felt, and all the time
you're making it with him behind my back."

"Nick, it wasn't like that."

"You lying bitch."

His head snapped back when Zack clipped him with
a backhand. There was blood on both sides now.
"You want to take a swing at me, go ahead. But you
don't talk to her like that."

Teeth gritted, Nick wiped the blood from his lip. He wanted to hate. Needed to. "The hell with you. The hell with both of you."

He swung on his heel and darted out.

"Oh, God." Rachel covered her face, but it did nothing to erase the image of the hurt she'd seen in Nick's eyes. The damage, she thought miserably, that she had done. "What a mess. I'm going after him."

"Leave him alone."

"It's my fault," she said, dropping her arms to her sides. "I have to try."

"I said leave him alone."

"Damn it, Zack—"

"Excuse me." There was a rap on the door, which Nick had left hanging open. Rachel turned and bit back a groan.

"Judge Beckett."

"Good evening, Ms. Stanislaski. Mr. Muldoon, I dropped in for one of your famous manhattans. Perhaps you could mix one for me while I have a conference with your brother's attorney."

"Your Honor," Rachel began, "my client..."

"I saw your client as he roared out of here. Your mouth's bleeding, Mr. Muldoon." She turned and shot a look at Rachel. "Counselor?"

"Perfect timing," Rachel said under her breath. "I'll handle this," she said to Zack. "Don't worry. And once Nick works off a little steam—"

"He'll come back smiling?" Zack finished. His temper was fading, but guilt was moving full steam ahead. "I don't think so. And it's not your fault." He wished he had more than his own empty sense of failure to give her. "He's my brother. I'm responsible."

He shook his head before she could speak. "Let me go fix the judge her drink."

He brushed by her. Rachel reached out to stop him, then let her hand fall away. There was nothing she could say to ease the hurt. But she had a chance to minimize the damage with Judge Beckett.

She found the judge looking attractive and relaxed at a table on the far side of the bar. Yet the aura of power the woman had when wearing black robes on the bench wasn't diminished in the least by the trim blue slacks and white sweater she wore tonight.

"Have a seat, Counselor."

"Thank you."

Beckett smiled, tapping rose-tipped nails on the edge of the table. "I can see the wheels turning. How much do I tell her, how much do I evade? I always enjoy having you in my courtroom, Ms. Stanislaski. You have style."

"Thank you," Rachel said again. Their drinks arrived, and she took the time while they were served to gather her thoughts. "I'm afraid you might, understandably, misinterpret what you saw tonight, Your Honor."

"Are you?" With a smile, Beckett sampled her drink. She shifted her gaze to meet Zack's and sent him an approving smile. "And what would you consider my interpretation?"

"Obviously, Nick and his brother were arguing."

"Fighting," Beckett corrected, stirring the cherry around in her drink before biting it from its stem. "Arguing involves words. And, while words may leave scars, they don't draw blood."

"You don't have brothers, do you, Your Honor?"

"No, I don't."

"I do."

With a lift of a brow, Beckett sipped again. "All right, I'll sustain that. What were they arguing about?"

Rachel eased around the boggy ground. "It was just a misunderstanding. I won't deny both of them are hotheaded, and that with their type of temperament a misunderstanding can sometimes evolve into..."

"An argument?" Beckett suggested.

"Yes." Needing to make her point, Rachel leaned forward. "Judge Beckett, Nick has been making such incredible progress. When I was first assigned to his case, I very nearly dismissed him as just another street punk. But there was something that made me reevaluate him."

"Haunted eyes do that to a woman."

Surprised, Rachel blinked. "Yes."

"Go on."

"He was so young, and yet he'd already started to give up on himself, and everyone else. After I met Zack, and found out about Nick's background, it was easy to understand. There's never been anyone permanent in his life, anyone he felt he could count on and trust. But with Zack...he wanted to. No matter how tough and disinterested he tried to act, the longer he was with Zack, the more you could see that they needed each other."

"Just how involved are you with your co-guardian?"

With her face carefully blank, Rachel sat back in her seat. "I believe that's irrelevant."

"Do you? Well." She gestured with her hand. "Continue."

"For nearly two months, Nick has stayed out of trouble. He's been handling the responsibilities Zack has given him. He's developing outside interests. He plays the piano."

"Does he?"

"Zack bought him one when he found out."

"That doesn't seem like something that would make fists fly." A faint smile played around her mouth as she gestured with her manhattan. "You're dodging the point, Counselor."

"I want you to understand that this probationary period has been successful. What happened tonight was simply a product of misunderstandings and hot tempers. It was the exception rather than the rule."

"You're not in court."

"No, Your Honor, but I don't want you to hold this against my client when I am."

"Agreed." Pleased with what she saw in Rachel, what she heard, and what she sensed, Beckett rattled the ice in her glass. "Explain tonight."

"It was my fault," Rachel said, pushing her wine aside. "It was poor judgment on my part that caused Nick to feel, to believe he felt…something."

Beckett pursed her lips. "I begin to see. He's a healthy young man, and you're an attractive woman who's shown an interest in him."

"And I blew it," Rachel said bitterly. "I thought I'd handled it. I was so damn sure I was on top of everything."

"I know the feeling." Beckett sampled a beer nut thoughtfully. "Off the record. Start at the beginning."

Hoping her own culpability would lighten Nick's load, even if it got her thrown off the case, Rachel explained. Beckett said nothing, only nodding or making interested noises now and again. "And when he walked into the office and saw Zack and me together," she concluded, "all he saw was betrayal. I know I had no right to become involved with Zack. Excuses don't cut it."

"Rachel, you're an excellent attorney. That doesn't preclude your having a private life."

"When it endangers my relationship with a client—"

"Don't interrupt. I'll grant that you may have exercised poor judgment in this instance. I'll also grant that one can't always choose the time, place or circumstances for falling in love."

"I didn't say I was in love."

Beckett smiled. "I noticed that. It's easier to beat yourself up about it if you tell yourself love had nothing to do with it." Her smile widened. "No rebuttal, Counselor? Just as well, because I haven't finished. I could tell you you've lost your objectivity, but you already know that. I, for one, am not entirely sure objectivity is always the answer. There are so many shades between right and wrong. Finding the one that fits is something we struggle with every day. Your client is trying to find his. You may not be able to help."

"I don't want to let him down."

"Better you should do what's possible to prevent him from letting himself down. Sometimes it works, sometimes it doesn't. You'll discover how often it doesn't when it's your turn to sit on the bench."

The understanding in Beckett's eyes had Rachel reaching for her wine again. "I didn't know I was that transparent."

"Oh, to one who's been there, certainly." Amused, Beckett tapped her glass against Rachel's. "A few more years of seasoning, Counselor, and you'll make quite a competent judge. That *is* what you want?"

"Yes." She met Beckett's eyes levelly. "That's exactly what I want."

"Good. Now, since I've had a drink and I'm feeling rather mellow, I'll tell you something—off the record. It was almost thirty years ago that I was you. So very close to who and what you are. Things were more difficult for women in our position than they are now. They're far from perfect now," she added, setting her glass aside, "but some of the battles are over. I had to make choices. Those professional-versus-personal choices that men rarely have to make. Do I have a family or do I have a career? I don't regret choosing my career."

She glanced back at the bar, at Zack, and sighed. "Or only rarely. But times change, and even a professionally ambitious woman doesn't have to make an either-or decision. She can have both, if she's clever. You strike me as a clever woman."

"I like to think so," Rachel murmured. "But it doesn't make it any less terrifying."

"That kind of terror makes life worthwhile. I don't think nerves will stop you, Counselor. I don't think anything will. In the meantime, see that you and your client are prepared for the hearing."

When Beckett rose, Rachel was instantly on her feet. "Judge Beckett, about tonight—"

"I came in for a drink. It's a nice bar. Clean, friendly. As for my decision, that will depend on what I see and hear in my courtroom. Understood?"

"Yes. Thank you."

"Tell Mr. Muldoon he makes an excellent manhattan."

With her emotions still in a state of upheaval, Rachel watched Beckett stroll out.

"How bad is it?" Zack asked from behind her.

Rachel merely shook her head, reaching back to take his hand. "She likes the way you mix a drink." Turning to him, she comforted him with a hug. "And I think I've just met another intelligent woman with a weakness for bad boys. It's going to be all right."

"If Nick doesn't come back..."

"He'll be back." She needed to believe it. Needed to make Zack believe it. "He's mad, and he's hurt, but he's not stupid." She gave his hand another quick squeeze and smiled up at him. "He's too much like you."

"I shouldn't have hit him."

"Intellectually, I agree. Emotionally..." Because passion was a part of her life, she shrugged it off. "I've seen my brothers pound on each other too often to believe it's the end of the world. I've got to go." She touched a gentle kiss to his swollen lip. "When he comes back, it's probably best if I'm not here. But I want you to call me when he shows up, no matter what time it is."

"I don't like you going home alone," he said as he walked with her to where her coat was hanging.

"I'll take a cab." The fact that he didn't argue made

her realize just how distracted he was. "We're going to work this out, Zack. Trust me."

"Yeah. I'll call you."

She stepped outside and headed down to the corner to hail a cab. Trust me, she'd told him. She could only hope she deserved that trust.

Chapter Eleven

She nearly called Alex when she got home, but she was afraid that if her brother put out feelers, even unofficially, Nick would only be more furious.

All she could do was wait. And wait alone.

An odd triangle they made, she thought as she wandered restlessly around her apartment with a rapidly cooling cup of tea. Nick, young and defiant, seeing rejection and betrayal everywhere, even as he looked so desperately for his place in the world. And Zack, so innately generous, so fueled by passion and so vulnerable to his brother. And herself, the objective, logical and ambitious attorney who'd fallen in love with them both.

Maybe she should be writing soap operas, she thought as she dropped down on the couch. She curled up her legs, cupping her mug in both hands. If she had the imagination for that, at least she might be able to write herself out of this situation.

Oh, how had it happened? she wondered, and closed her tired eyes. She was the one who had had things aligned so clearly. Hadn't she always known exactly where she was going and how she was going to get there? Every obstacle that could possibly block her path had been considered and weighed. All the options, all the ways of going around or through those obstacles, had been calculated.

All of them.

Except Zackary Muldoon.

By becoming involved with him, by letting her emotions rule her head, she'd made a mess of everything. It was entirely possible that Nick, pumped by hurt and frustration, would race headlong into trouble before the night was over. However understanding and compassionate Judge Beckett was, if Nick broke his probation, she would have no choice but to sentence him.

Even if the sentence was light, how could she forgive herself? How could Zack forgive her for failing? And, worst of all, how could Nick rebound from that final rejection when society put him behind bars?

She wanted to believe he'd go back to Zack. Angry, yes...defiant, certainly...maybe even spoiling for a fight. All those things could be dealt with, if only he went back.

But if he didn't...

The sound of her buzzer had her jolting. Well aware that it was after midnight, she unfolded herself, hoping it was Zack coming by to tell her Nick was safe and sound.

"Yes?"

"I want to come up." It was Nick's voice, edgy and demanding. Rachel had to bite back a cry of relief.

"Sure." She kept her tone light as she released the lock. "Come ahead."

She pressed her fingers against her eyes to push back the tears that filled them. It was stupid to get so emotional. Hadn't logic told her he'd have to come back? Hadn't she said as much to Zack?

But when the knock rapped sharply at her door, she was swinging it open, and the words were tumbling out. "I was so worried. I was going to go after you, but I didn't know where to start to look. Oh, Nick, I'm sorry. I'm so sorry."

"Sorry it blew up in your face?" He shoved the door closed behind him. He hadn't intended to come here, but he'd been walking, walking. Then it had seemed like the only place to go. "Sorry I came in and found you with Zack?"

It was far from over, Rachel realized. What she saw in his eyes was just as dangerous as what had been in them when he'd leaped across the office at Zack. "I'm sorry I hurt you."

"You're sorry I found out what you really are. You're nothing but a liar."

"I never lied to you."

"Every time you opened your mouth." He hadn't moved away from the door, and his hands were balled into fists, white-knuckled, at his side. "You and Zack. The whole time you were pretending to care about me, acting as if you liked being with me, you were making it with him."

"I do care—" she began, but he cut her off.

"I can see what a kick the two of you must've gotten out of it. Poor, pathetic Nick, mooning around, trying to make something of himself because he had a case on the sexy lawyer. I guess the two of you lay in bed and laughed yourself sick."

"No. It was never like that."

"Are you going to tell me you didn't go to bed with him?"

He saw the truth in her eyes before her own temper kicked in. "You're out of line. I'm not going to discuss—"

His hands shot out, snatching the lapels of her robe and swinging her around. Her back rammed hard into the door. The first bubble of fear evaporated in her throat as Nick pushed his face close to hers. All she could see was his eyes, sharp green and glinting with fury.

"Why did you do it? Why did you have to make a fool out of me? Why did it have to be my brother?"

"Nick." She had his wrists now, and she tried to drag them away. But rage had added weight to his sinewy strength.

"Do you know how it makes me feel to know that while I was imagining us you were with him? And he knew. He knew."

Her breath was hitching, but she fought to control it. "You're hurting me."

She thought the statement would come out calm, even authoritative. Instead, it was shaky, and the fear underneath it clear even in his reckless state. His eyes went blank for a moment, then focused on his hands. They were digging into her shoulders. Appalled, he pulled them away and stared at her.

"I'm going."

Sometimes all you had was impulse. Rachel went with it and pressed her back against the door. "Don't. Please. Don't go like this."

There was a churning in his stomach that was pure self-loathing. "I never pushed a woman around before. It's as low as it gets."

"You didn't hurt me. I'm okay."

What she was, he noted, was deathly pale. "You're shaking."

"Okay, I'm shaking. Can we sit down?"

"I shouldn't have come here, Rachel. I shouldn't have jumped on you that way."

"I'm glad you came. Let's leave it at that for a minute. Please, let's sit down."

Because he was afraid she'd stay pressed against the door trembling until he agreed, he nodded. "You've got some things to toss back at me. I figure I owe you that." As he sat, his shoulders slumped. "I guess you'll ask to be taken off the case."

"That has nothing to do with this. But no." She thought about picking up her cold tea, but she was afraid her hands weren't steady enough. "This is personal, Nick. I'm the one who screwed up by blurring the lines. I knew better. There's no excuse." Inhaling deeply, she linked her fingers in her lap. "What happened between Zack and me wasn't planned, and it certainly wasn't professional."

He gave a quick snort. "Now you're going to tell me you couldn't help yourself."

"No," she said quietly. "I could have. There's always a choice. I didn't want to help myself."

Her answer, and the tone of it, had him frowning.

He'd been certain she would try to find an easy way out. "So, you chose him."

"What happened was immediate, and maybe a little overwhelming..." She wasn't certain there were words to describe what had happened between her and Zack. "In any case, I could have stopped it. Or at least postponed it. I didn't, and that fault lies with me. The fact that we were both your guardians made it a poor call, but—" She shook her head. "No buts. It was a poor call." Her eyes met his, pleaded for trust. "We never thought of you as poor or pathetic. We never laughed at you. Whatever you think of me, don't let it ruin what you've started to get back with Zack."

"He moved in on me."

"Nick." Her voice held both patience and compassion. "He didn't. You know he didn't."

He did know, wondered if he had always known, that his relationship with Rachel had never been anything more than a fantasy. But knowing it didn't ease the raw wounds of rejection.

"I cared about you."

"I know." Her eyes filled again, and spilled over before she could prevent it. "I'm sorry."

"God, Rachel. Don't." He didn't think he could stand it. First he'd terrified her, and now he was making her cry. "Don't do that."

"I won't." But as quickly as she swiped at the tears, more fell. "I just feel so lousy about it all. When I look back, I can see a dozen ways I should've handled things. I'm usually in control." Her breath hitched as she fought for composure. "I hate, I really hate, that I've come between the two of you."

"Hey, come on." He was totally at a loss. When

he rose to cross to her, he was surprised he didn't leave a trail of slime on her rug. "Listen, take it easy, okay?" He patted her shoulder awkwardly. "I've been dumped before."

All that did was force her to fumble in the pocket of her robe for a tissue. "Don't hate him because of this."

"Don't ask for miracles."

"Oh, Nick, if you could only see through all the mistakes to what you mean to him."

"No lectures." Since her tears seemed to be drying up, he felt he could take a stand on that. "You carry on like you're in love with him." He was stunned when he saw the look in her eyes, the miserable, heart-sick look, before they filled again. "Oh, man." While she crumpled into sobs, he readjusted his thinking. "You mean it's not just sex?"

"It was supposed to be." His arm went around her tentatively, and she leaned into it. "Oh, God, how did I get into all this? I don't want to be in love with anybody."

"That's rough." It occurred to Nick that he was holding her close but there weren't any tingles or tugs. The hell of it was, he was feeling almost brotherly. No one had ever cried on his shoulder before, or looked to him for support. "How about him? Is he stuck in the same groove?"

"I don't know." She sniffled, blew her nose. "We haven't talked about it. We aren't going to talk about it. The whole thing's ridiculous. I'm ridiculous." Thoroughly ashamed, she eased back. "Let's just say it's been an emotional night all around. Please, don't say anything to him about this."

"I figure that's up to you."

"Good. I appreciate it." Still shaky, she wiped at a stray tear with the back of her hand. "Don't hate me too much."

"I don't hate you." He leaned back, suddenly exhausted. "I don't know what I feel. Maybe I thought I could come up here tonight and prove to you I was the better man. Pretty stupid."

"You're both pretty special," she told him. "Why else would a nice, sensible woman like me fall for both of you?"

He turned his head to give her a weak smile. "You sure can pick 'em."

"Yeah." She touched his cheek. "I sure can. Tell me you're going back."

His lips flattened. "Where else would I go?"

That didn't satisfy her. "Tell me you're going back to talk things through with him, to work things out."

"I can't tell you that."

When he started to stand, she took his hand. "Let me go back with you. I want to help. I need to feel as though I've made some of this up to the two of you."

"You didn't do anything but fall for the wrong guy."

She took a great deal of comfort from the familiar smirk. "You may be right. Let me come anyway."

"Suit yourself. You might want to wash your face. Your eyes are red."

"Great. Give me five minutes."

Rachel could feel Nick start to tense up half a block from Lower the Boom. His shoulders were hunched, his brows were lowered, his hands were jammed in his pockets.

Typical, she thought. The male animal ruffles his fur and bares his teeth to show the opposing male how tough he is.

She kept the observation to herself, knowing neither of these males would appreciate it.

"Here's the idea," she said, pausing by the door. "It was a pretty slow night, and it's already after one. We'll wait until the bar closes, and you two can say your piece. I'll be mediator."

Nick wondered if she had any idea how hard it was for him to face what was on the other side of that door. "Whatever."

"And if there are any punches thrown," she added as she pulled the door open, "I'll throw them."

That brought the ghost of a smile to his face. It faded as soon as they stepped in.

Rachel had been right. It was a slow night, as it often was in the middle of the week. Most of the regulars had already headed off to home and hearth. A few diehards lingered at the bar, which Zack was manning alone. Lola was busy wiping down the tables. She glanced up, shot Rachel a satisfied look, then went back to work.

Zack took a pull from a bottle of mineral water. Rachel saw his eyes change, recognized the relief in them before the shutters came down.

"Hey, barkeep—" Rachel slid onto a stool "—got any coffee?"

"Sure."

"Make it two," she said, sending a meaningful glance in Nick's direction.

He said nothing, but he did sit beside her.

"There's an old Ukrainian tradition," she began when Zack set the cups on the bar. "It's called a family meeting. Are you up for it?"

"Yeah." Zack inclined his head toward his brother. "I guess I can handle it. What about you?"

"I'm here," Nick muttered.

"Hey." A man, obviously well on his way to being drunk, leaned heavily on the bar a few stools away. "Am I going to get another bourbon over here?"

"Nope." Carrying the pot, Zack crossed over. "But you can have coffee on the house."

The man scowled through red-rimmed eyes. "What the hell are you, a social worker?"

"That's me."

"I said I want a damn drink."

"You're not going to get another one here."

The drunk reached out and grabbed a handful of Zack's sweater. Considering Zack's size, Rachel took this to be a testament to the bourbon already in his system.

"This a bar or a church?"

Something flickered in Zack's eyes. Rachel recognized it, and was slipping out of her seat when Nick clamped a warning hand on hers.

"He'll handle it," he said simply.

Zack lowered his gaze to the hands on his sweater, then shifted it back to the irate customer's face. When he spoke, his voice was surprisingly mild. "Funny you should ask. I knew this guy once, down in New Orleans. He favored bourbon, too. One night he went from bar to bar, knocking them back, then staggering back out on the street. Story goes that he got so blind drunk he wandered into a church, thinking it was another bar. Weaved his way up to the front—you know, where the altar is? Slammed his fist down and ordered himself a double. Then he dropped dead. Stone dead.'' Zack pried the fingers from his sweater. ''The way I figure it, if you drink enough bourbon so you don't know where you are, you could wake up dead in church.''

The man swore and snatched up the coffee. ''I know where the hell I am.''

''That's good news. We hate hauling out corpses.''

Rachel heard Nick's muffled chuckle and grinned. ''Truth or lie?'' she whispered.

''Probably some of both. He always knows how to handle the drunks.''

''He wasn't doing very well with the blonde earlier.''

''What blonde?''

''Another story,'' Rachel said, and smiled into her coffee. ''Another time. Listen, would you be more comfortable doing this upstairs, or—'' She broke off when she heard a crash from the kitchen. ''Lord, it sounds like Rio knocked over the refrigerator.'' She started to rise and go check. Then froze. The kitchen door swung open. Rio staggered out, blood running down his face from a wound on his forehead. Behind him was a man in a stocking mask. He was holding a very large gun to Rio's throat.

''Party time,'' he snarled, then shoved the big man forward with the butt of the gun.

''Jumped me,'' Rio said in disgust as he staggered against the bar. ''Come in front upstairs.''

There was a quick giggle as two more armed men,

their features distorted by their nylon masks, stepped in. "Don't anybody move." One of them accentuated the order by blasting away at the ship's bell over the bar. It clanged wildly.

"Lock the front door, you jerk." The first man gestured furiously. "And no shooting unless I say so. Everybody empty their pockets on the bar. Make it fast." He gestured the third man into position so that the whole bar was covered. "Wallets, jewelry, too. Hey, you." He lifted the barrel of the gun toward Lola. "Dump out those tips, sweetheart. You look like you'd earn plenty."

Nick didn't move. Couldn't. He knew the voice. Despite the distorted features, all three gunmen were easy for him to recognize. T.J.'s giggle and shambling walk. Cash's battered denim jacket. The scar on Reece's wrist where an Hombre blade had caught him.

These were his friends. His family.

"What the hell are you doing?" he demanded as T.J. pranced around the bar, scooping the take into a laundry bag.

"Empty them," Reece demanded.

"You've got to be crazy."

"Do it!" He swung the barrel toward Rachel. "And shut the hell up."

Nick kept his eyes on Reece as he complied. "This is the end, man. You crossed the line."

Behind the mask, Reece only grinned. "On the floor!" he shouted. "Facedown, hands behind your heads. Not you," he said to Zack. "You empty out the cash register. And you—" he grabbed Rachel's arm "—you look like mighty fine insurance. Anybody gets any ideas, I cash her in."

"Leave her the hell—"

"Nick!" Zack's quick and quiet order cut him off. "Back off." As he emptied the till, he watched Reece. "You don't need her."

"But I like her."

Rachel swallowed as the hand tightened on her arm, squeezing experimentally.

"Fresh meat," he called out, smacking his lips. T.J. erupted into giggles. "Maybe we'll take you along with us, sweet thing. Show you a real good time."

The furious retort burned the tip of her tongue. Rachel gritted her teeth against it. The heel of her foot on his instep, she thought. An elbow to his windpipe. She could do it, and the idea of taking him out had her blood pumping fast. But if she did, she knew the other two would open fire.

When Nick strained forward, Reece locked his arm around Rachel's throat. "Try it, dishwasher." His teeth flashed in a brutal challenge. "Do it, man. Take me on."

"Cool it." Reece's attitude toward the woman was making Cash nervous. "Come on, we came for the money. Just the money."

"I take what I want." He watched as T.J. scooped the contents of the till into his sack. "Where's the rest?"

"Slow night," Zack told him.

"Don't push me, man. There's a safe in the office. Open it."

"Fine." Zack moved slowly, passing through the opening of the bar. He had to control the urge to fight, to grab the little sneering-voiced punk and pound his face to pulp. "I'll open it as soon as you let her go."

"I got the gun," Reece reminded him. "I give the orders."

"You've got the gun," Zack agreed. "I've got the combination. You want what's in the safe, you let her go."

"Go on," Cash urged. His hands were sweating on the gun he held. "We don't need the babe. Shake her loose."

Reece felt his power slipping as Zack continued to watch him with cold blue eyes. He wanted to make them tremble. All of them. He wanted them to cry and beg. He was the head of the Cobras. He was in charge. Nobody was going to tell him any different.

"Open it," he said between his teeth. "Or I'll blow a hole in you."

"You won't get what's inside that way." Out of the corner of his eye, Zack saw Rio shift from his prone position. The big man was braced for whatever came. "This is my place," Zack continued. "I don't want anyone hurt in my place. You let the lady go, and you can take what you want."

"Let's trash the dump," T.J. shouted, and swung his gun at the glasses hanging over the bar. Shards went flying, amusing him enough to have him breaking more. "Let's kick butt and trash it." He grabbed up a vodka on the rocks and slurped it down. Then, howling, he hurled the glass to the floor.

The sound of the wreckage, and the muffled cries of the hostages on the floor, pumped Reece full of adrenaline. "Yeah, we'll trash this dump good." Over Cash's halfhearted objections, he fired at the overhead television, blasting out the screen. "That's what I'm going to do to the safe. I don't need a damn woman."

He shoved Rachel aside, and she overbalanced, landing on her hands and knees. "And I don't need you."

He swung the gun toward Zack, savoring the moment. He was about to take a life, and that was new. And darkly exciting.

"This is how I give orders."

Even as Zack braced to jump, Nick was springing to his feet. Like a sprinter off the mark, he lunged, hurling full force into Zack as Reece's gun exploded.

There were screams, dozens of them. Rachel swung out with a chair, unaware that one of them was her own. She felt the chair connect, heard a grunt of pain. She caught a glimpse of the mountain that was Rio whiz past. But she was already scrambling over to where Zack and Nick lay limp on the floor.

She saw the blood. Smelled it. Her hands were smeared with it.

The room was like a madhouse around her. Shouts, crashes, running feet. She heard someone weeping. Someone else being sick.

"Oh, God. Oh, please." She was pressing her hands against Nick's chest as Zack sat up, shaking his head clear.

"Rachel. You're—" Then he saw his brother, sprawled on the floor, his face ghostly pale. And the blood seeping rapidly through his shirt. "*No!* Nick, no!" Panicked, Zack grabbed for him, fighting Rachel off as she tried to press her hands to the wound.

"Stop! You have to stop! Listen to me—keep your hands there. Keep the pressure on. I'll get a towel." With prayers whirling in her head, she scrambled up to her feet and dashed behind the bar. "Call an ambulance," she shouted. "Tell them to hurry." Because terror left no room for fumbling, she clamped down on it. Kneeling by Zack, she pushed his hands aside and pressed the folded towel on Nick's wound. "He's young. He's strong." The tears were falling even as she felt frantically for Nick's pulse. "We're not going to let him go."

"Zack." Rio crouched down. "They got away from me. I'm sorry. I'll go after them."

"No." Revenge glittered in his eyes. "I'll go after them. Later. Get me a blanket for him, Rio. And more towels."

"I've got some." Lola passed them to Rachel, then dropped a hand on Zack's head. "He's a hero, Zack. We don't let our heroes die."

"He got in the way," Zack said as grief welled into his throat. "Damn kid was always getting in the way." He looked at Rachel, then covered her hands with his over his brother's chest. "I can't lose him."

"You won't." She heard the first wail of sirens and shuddered with relief. "We won't."

Endless hours in the waiting room, pacing, smoking, drinking bitter coffee. Zack could still see how pale Nick had been when they rushed him through Emergency and into an elevator that snapped shut in Zack's face.

Helpless. Hospitals always made him feel so helpless. Only a year had passed since he'd watched his father die in one. Slowly, inevitably, pitifully.

But not Nick. He could cling to that. Nick was young, and death wasn't inevitable when you were young.

But the blood. There had been so much blood.

He looked down at the hands that he'd scrubbed clean, and could still see his brother's life splattered across them. In his hands. That was all he could think. Nick's life had been in his hands.

"Zack." He stiffened when Rachel came up behind him and rubbed his shoulders. "How about a walk? Some fresh air?"

He just shook his head. She didn't press. It was useless to suggest he try to rest. She couldn't. Her eyes were burning, but she knew that if she closed them she would see that last horrible instant. The gun swinging toward Zack. Nick leaping. The explosion. The blood.

"I'm going to find food." Rio pushed himself off the sagging sofa. The white bandage gleamed against his dark brow. "And you're going to eat what I bring you. That boy's going to need tending soon. You can't tend when you're sick." With his lips pressed tightly together, he marched out into the hallway.

"He's crazy about Nick," Zack said, half to himself. "It's eating at him that he didn't round up three armed men all by himself."

"We'll find them, Zack."

"I thought he would hurt you. I saw it in his eyes. That kind of sickness can't be disguised by a mask. He was going to hurt somebody, wanted to hurt somebody, and he had you. I never even thought about Nick."

"It's not your fault. No," she said sharply when he tried to pull away. "I won't let you do that to yourself. There were a lot of people in that bar, and you were doing your best to protect all of them. What happened to Nick happened because he was trying to protect you. You're not going to turn an act of love into blame."

This time, when she put her arms around him, he went into them. "I need to talk to him. I don't think I could handle it if I don't get to talk to him."

"You're going to have plenty of time to talk."

"I'm sorry." Alex hesitated at the doorway. His heart was thumping, as it had been ever since he'd gotten the news. "Rachel, are you all right?"

"I'm fine." She kept one arm firm around Zack's waist as she turned. "It's Nick…"

"I know. When the call came in, I asked to handle it. I thought it would be easier on everybody." His eyes shifted to Zack's, held. "Is that okay with you?"

"Yeah. I appreciate it. I've already talked to a couple of cops."

"Why don't we sit down?" He waited while Zack sat on the edge of a chair and lit another cigarette. "Any news on your brother's condition?"

"They took him into surgery. They haven't told us anything."

"I might be able to find something out. Why don't you tell me about these three creeps?"

"They wore stocking masks," Zack began wearily. "Black clothes. One of them wore a denim jacket."

Rachel reached for Zack's hand. "The one who shot Nick was about five-eight or nine," she added. "Black hair, brown eyes. There was a scar on his left wrist. On the side, about two inches long. He wore engineer's boots, worn down at the heel."

"Good girl." Not for the first time, Alex thought that his sister would have made a damn good cop. "How about the other two?"

"The one who wanted to trash the place had a high-pitched giggle," Zack remembered. "Edgy. Skinny guy."

"About five-ten," Rachel put in. "Maybe a hundred and thirty. I didn't get a good look at him, but he had light hair. Sandy blond, I think. The third one was about the same height, but stockier. At a guess, I'd say the guns made him nervous. He was sweating a lot."

"How about age?"

"Hard to say." She looked at Zack. "Young. Early twenties?"

"About. What are the chances of catching them?"

"Better with this." Alex closed his notebook. "Look, I won't con you. It won't be easy. Now if they left prints, and the prints are on file, that's one thing. But we're going to work on it. *I'm* going to work on it," he added. "You could say I've got a vested interest."

"Yeah." Zack looked at Rachel. "I guess you do."

"Not just for her," Alex said. "I've got a stake in the kid, too. I like to see the system work, Muldoon."

"Mr. Muldoon?" A woman of about fifty dressed in green scrubs came into the room. When Zack started to rise, she gestured to him to stay where he was. "I'm Dr. Markowitz, your brother's surgeon."

"How—" He had to pause and try again. "How is he?"

"Tough." As a concession to aching feet and lower back pain, she sat on the arm of a chair. "You want all the technical jargon so I can show off, or you want the bottom line?"

The next lick of fear had his palms damp. "Bottom line."

"He's critical. And he's damn lucky, not only to have had me, but to have taken a bullet at close range that missed the heart. I put his chances now at about seventy-five percent. With luck, and the constitution of youth, we'll be able to bump that up within twenty-four hours."

The coffee churned violently in his stomach. "Are you telling me he's going to make it?"

"I'm telling you I don't like to work that hard and long on anyone and lose them. We're going to keep him in ICU for now."

"Can I see him?"

"I'll have someone come down and let you know when he's out of Recovery." She stifled a yawn and noted that she'd spent yet another sunrise in an operating room. "You want all the crap about how he'll be out for several more hours, won't know you're there, and how you should go home and get some rest?"

"No thanks."

She rubbed her eyes and smiled. "I didn't think so. He's a good-looking boy, Mr. Muldoon. I'm looking forward to chatting with him."

"Thanks. Thanks a lot."

"I'll be checking in on him." She rose, stretched, and narrowed her eyes at Alex. "Cop."

"Yes, ma'am."

"I can spot them a mile away," she said, and walked out.

Chapter Twelve

The pain was a thin sheet of agony layered under dizziness. Every time Nick surfaced, he felt it, wondered at it, then slipped away again into a cocoon of comforting unconsciousness. Sometimes he tried to speak, but the words were disjointed and senseless even to him.

He heard a disconcerting beeping, annoying and consistent, that he didn't recognize as his heartbeat on the monitor. The squeak of crepe-soled shoes against tile was muffled by the nice, steady humming in his ears. The occasional prodding and poking as his vital signs were checked and rechecked was only a minor disturbance in the huge, dark lack of awareness that covered him.

Sometimes there was a pressure on his hand, as if someone were holding it. And a murmuring—someone speaking to him. But he couldn't quite drum up the energy to listen.

Once he dreamed of the sea in a hurricane, and watched himself leap off the deck of a pitching ship into blackness. But he never hit bottom. He just floated away.

There were other dreams. Zack standing behind him at a pinball machine, guiding his hands, laughing at the whirl of bells and whistles.

Then Cash was there, leaning on the machine, the smoke from his crooked cigarette curling up in front of his face.

He saw Rachel, smiling at him in a brightly lit room, the smell of pizza and garlic everywhere. And her eyes were bright, interested. Beautiful.

Then they were drenched with tears. Overflowing with apologies.

The old man, shouting at him. He looked so sick as he stumbled to the top of the stairs. *You'll never amount to anything. Knew it the first time I laid eyes on you.* Then that blank, slack look would come over his face, and he could only whine, *Where have you been? Where's Zack? Is he coming back soon?*

But Zack was gone, hundreds of miles away. There was no one to help.

Rio, frying potatoes and cackling over one of his own jokes. And Zack, always back to Zack, coming through the kitchen. *You going to eat all the profits, kid?* An easy grin, a friendly swipe as he went out again.

The gleaming piano—that polished dream—and Zack standing beside it, grinning foolishly. Then the glitter of the overhead light on the barrel of a gun. And Zack—

With a grunt, he threw off sleep, tried to struggle up.

"Hey, hey...take it easy, kid." Zack sprang up from the chair beside the bed to press a gentle hand on Nick's shoulder. "It's okay. You got no place to go."

He tried to focus, but the images around him kept slipping in and out like phantoms in shadows. "What?" His throat was sand-dry and aching. "Am I sick?"

"You've been better." And so have I, Zack thought, fighting to keep his hand from shaking as he lifted the plastic drinking cup. "They said you could suck on this if you came around again."

Nick took a pull of water through the straw, then another, but didn't have the energy for a third. At least his vision had cleared. He took a long, hard look at Zack. Dark circles under tired eyes in a pale face prickled by a night's growth of beard.

"You look like hell."

Grinning, Zack rubbed a hand over the stubble. "You don't look so hot yourself. Let me call a nurse."

"Nurse." Nick shook his head, almost imperceptibly, then frowned at the IV. "Is this a hospital?"

"It ain't the Ritz. You hurting?"

Nick thought about it and shook his head. "Can't tell. Feel...dopey."

"Well, you are." Swamped with relief, Zack laid a hand on Nick's cheek, left it there until embarrassment had it dropping away. "You're such a jerk, Nick."

Nick was too bleary to hear the catch in Zack's

voice. "Was there an accident? I..." And then it came flooding back, a tidal wave of memory. "At the bar." His hand fisted on the sheets. "Rachel? Is Rachel all right?"

"She's fine. Been in and out of here. I had Rio browbeat her into getting something to eat."

"You." Nick took another long look to reassure himself. "He didn't shoot you."

"No, you idiot." His voice broke, then roughened. "He shot you."

When his legs went watery, Zack sat again, buried his face in his hands. The hands were trembling. Nick stared, utterly amazed, as this man he'd always thought was the next best thing to superhuman struggled for composure.

"I could kill you for scaring me like this. If you weren't flat on your back already, I'd damn well put you there."

But insults and threats delivered in a shaky voice held little power. "Hey." Nick lifted a hand, but wasn't sure what to do with it. "You okay?"

"No, I'm not okay," Zack tossed back, and rose to pace to the window. He stared out, seeing nothing, until he felt some portion of control again. "Yeah, yeah, I'm fine. Looks like you're going to be that way, too. They said they'd move you down to a regular room sometime soon, if you rated it."

"Where am I now?" Curious, Nick turned his head to study the room. Glass walls and blinking, beeping machines. "Wow, high tech. How long have I been out?"

"You came around a couple times before. They said you wouldn't remember. You babbled a lot."

"Oh, yeah. About what?"

"Pinball machines." Steadier now, Zack walked back to the bed. "Some girl named Marcie or Marlie. Remind me to pump you on that little number later." It pleased him to see a faint smile curve Nick's lips. "You asked for french fries."

"What can I say? It's a weakness. Did I get any?"

"No. Maybe we'll sneak some in later. Are you hungry?"

"I don't know. You didn't tell me how long."

Zack reached for a cigarette, remembered, and sighed. "About twelve hours since they finished cutting you up and sewing you back together. I figure if he'd shot you in the head instead of the chest, you'd have walked away whistling." He tapped his knuckles on Nick's temple. "Hard as a rock. I owe you one, a big one."

"No, you don't."

"You saved my life."

Nick let his heavy lids close. "It's kind of like jumping off a ship in a hurricane. You don't think about it. Know what I mean?"

"Yeah."

"Zack?"

"Right here."

"I want to talk to a cop."

"You've got to rest."

"I need to talk to a cop," Nick said again as he drifted off. "I know who they were."

Zack watched him sleep and, since there was no one to see, brushed gently at the hair on his brother's forehead.

* * *

"I told you his condition is good," Dr. Markowitz repeated. "Go home, Mr. Muldoon."

"Not a chance." Zack leaned against the wall beside the door to Nick's room. He was feeling a great deal better since they'd brought his brother out of ICU, but he wasn't ready to jump ship.

"God save me from stubborn Irishmen." She aimed a hard look at Rachel. "Mrs. Muldoon, do you have any influence with him?"

"I'm not Mrs. Muldoon, and no. I think we might pry him away once he checks in on Nick. My brother shouldn't be with him much longer."

"Your brother's the cop?" She sighed and shook her head. "All right. I'll give you five minutes with my patient, then you're out of here. Believe me, I'll call Security and have them toss you out if necessary."

"Yes, ma'am."

"That goes for that giant who's been lurking around the corridors, too."

"I'll take them both home," Rachel promised. She looked around quickly as the door opened. "Alexi?"

"We're finished." He couldn't keep the satisfied gleam out of his eyes. "I've got some rounding up to do."

"He identified them?" Zack demanded.

"Cold. And he's raring to testify."

"I want—"

"No chance," Alex said quickly, noting Zack's clenched fists. "The kid figured out how to do it the right way, Muldoon. Take a lesson. Keep him in line, Rach."

"I'll try," she murmured as her brother hurried off. "Zack, if you're going in there to talk to him, pull it together."

"That son of a bitch shot my brother."

"And he'll pay for it."

With a curt nod, Zack walked by her and into Nick's room. He stood at the foot of the bed, waiting. "How are you feeling?"

"Okay." He was exhausted after his interview with Alex, but he wasn't finished. "I need to talk to you, to tell you. Explain."

"It can wait."

"No. It was my fault. The whole thing. They were Cobras, Zack. They knew when to come in and how, because I told them. I didn't know...I swear to God I didn't know what they were going to do. I don't expect you to believe me."

Zack waited a moment until he got his bearings. "Why shouldn't I believe you?"

Nick squeezed his eyes tight. "I messed up. Like always." He poured out the entire story of how he'd run into Cash at the arcade. "I thought we were just talking. And all the time he was setting me up. Setting you up."

"You trusted him." Zack came around the side of the bed to put a hand on Nick's wrist. "You thought he was your friend. That's not messing up, Nick, it's just trusting people who don't deserve it. You're not like them." When Nick's eyes opened again, Zack took a firm hold of his hand. "If you messed up anything, it was yourself by trying to be like them. And that's done."

"I won't let them get away with it."

"*We* won't," Zack told him. "We're in this to-gether."

"Yeah," Nick said on a long breath. "Okay."

"They're going to kick me out of here so you can get some rest. I'll be back tomorrow."

"Zack," Nick called out as his brother hit the door. "Don't forget the fries."

"You got it."

"Okay?" Rachel asked when Zack came out.

"Okay." Then he gathered her up, held her hard and close. She was slim and small, and as steady as an anchor in a storm-tossed sea. "Come home with me, please," he murmured against her hair. "Stay with me tonight."

"Let's go." She pressed a kiss to his cheek. "I can buy a toothbrush on the way."

Later, when he fell into an exhausted sleep, she lay beside him and kept watch. She knew it was the first time he'd done more than nod off in a chair in nearly forty-eight hours. Odd, she thought as she watched his face in the faint, shadowy light that sneaked through the windows. She'd never considered herself the nur-turing type. But it had been very satisfying to simply lie beside him and hold him until the strain and fatigue of the past few days had toppled him into sleep.

The bigger they are, she thought again, pressing a light kiss to his forehead.

Still, as tired as she was, and as relieved, she couldn't find escape in sleep herself. How daunting it was to realize she'd come to a point in her life where she wasn't sure of her moves.

Love didn't run on logic. It didn't follow neat lines

or a list of priorities. Yet, in a matter of days, the bond that had brought them together would be broken. They would go into court, and it would be resolved one way or the other.

Now was the time to face the what-happens-next.

He'd asked her to move in with him. Rachel shifted to watch the pattern of shadows on the ceiling. It could be enough. Or much too much. Her problem now was to decide what she could live with, and what she could live without.

She was very much afraid that the one thing she couldn't live without was sleeping beside her.

He shuddered once, made a strangled sound in his throat before ripping himself awake. Instantly she moved to soothe.

"Shh..." She touched a hand to his cheek, to his shoulder, stroking. "It's all right. Everything's all right."

"Hurricanes," he murmured, groggy. "I'll tell you about it sometime."

"Okay." She rested a hand on his heart, as if to slow its rapid pace. "Go back to sleep, Muldoon. You're worn out."

"It's nice that you're here. Real nice."

"I like it, too." One brow arched as she felt his hand slide up her thigh. "Don't start something you won't be able to finish."

"I just want my T-shirt back." He moved his hand up her makeshift nightie until her warm, soft breast filled his palm. Comfort. Arousal. Perfection. "Just as I thought. This is a completely nonregulation body."

The stirring started low and deep, working its way through her. "You're pushing your luck."

"I was having this dream about the navy." His fatigue had everything moving in slow motion, making it all the more erotic when he slipped the shirt up and off. Her arms seemed to flow over her head and down again like water. "It makes me remember what it was like being at sea for months without seeing a woman." He lowered his mouth to flick his tongue over her. "Or tasting one."

She sighed luxuriously, and even that slight movement heightened his need. "Tell me more." His mouth met hers, so soft, so sweet.

"When I woke up just now, I could smell your hair, your skin. I've been waking up wanting you for weeks. Now I can wake up and have you."

"Just that easy, huh?"

"Yeah." He lifted his head and smiled down at her. "Just that easy."

She trailed a finger down his back as she considered. "I've got only one thing to say to you, Muldoon."

"What?"

"All hands on deck." With a laugh, she rolled on top of him.

And it was very, very easy.

"You're not being sensible," she said to Nick as she walked up the courthouse steps beside him, supporting his arm. "It's the simplest thing in the world to get a postponement under the circumstances."

"I want it over," he repeated, and glanced over at Zack.

"I'm with you."

"Far be it from me to fight the pair of you," she said in disgust. "If you keel over—"

"I'm not an invalid."

"You're two days out of the hospital," she pointed out.

"Dr. Markowitz gave him the green light," Zack put in.

"I don't care what Dr. Markowitz gave him."

"Rachel." A little winded from the climb, but still game, Nick shook off her hand. "Stop playing mother."

"Fine." She tossed up her hands, then lowered them again to fuss with Nick's tie, brush the shoulders of his jacket. She caught Zack's grin over Nick's shoulder and scowled. "Shut up, Muldoon."

"Aye, aye, sir."

"He thinks he's so cute with the nautical talk." She stood back to study her client. He was still a little pale, but he would do. "Now, are you sure you remember everything I explained to you?"

"Rachel, you went over the drill a dozen times." Letting out a huff of breath, he turned to his brother. "Can I have a minute with her?"

"Sure." Zack tossed a look over his shoulder. "Hands off."

"Yeah, yeah." The smirk was back, but it was good-natured rather than nasty. "Listen, Rachel, first I want to tell you how... Well, it was really nice of your family to come by the hospital the way they did. Your mom—" he pushed restless hands in his pockets, then pulled them out again "—bringing me cookies, and all the other stuff. Your father, coming by to hang out and play checkers."

It should have sounded corny, he reflected. But it didn't.

"They came to see you because they wanted to."

"Yeah, but...well, it was nice. I even got a card from Freddie. And the cop—he was okay."

"Alex has his moments."

"What I'm trying to say is, whatever happens today, you've done a lot for me. Maybe I don't know where I'm going, but I know where I'm not. I owe that to you."

"No, you don't." Worried she might cry, she made her tone brisk. "A little, sure, but most of it was right here." She tapped a finger on his heart. "You're okay, LeBeck."

"Thanks. One more thing." He glanced over to be sure Zack was out of earshot. "I know I made things a little sticky before. Zack's been making noises that you might be moving in. I just wanted you to know that I wouldn't be in the way."

"I haven't decided what I'm going to do. Regardless, you wouldn't be in the way. You're family. Got it?"

His lips curved. "I'm getting it. If you decide to throw him over, I'm available."

"I'll keep it in mind." She gave his jacket one last tug. "Let's go."

There was no reason to be nervous, she told herself as she led Nick to the defense table. Her statement was well prepared, and she had a sympathetic judge on the bench.

She was terrified.

She rose with the rest of the court when Judge

Beckett came in. Ignoring the twisting in her gut, she gave Nick a quick, confident smile.

"Well, well, Mr. LeBeck," Beckett began, folding her hands. "How time flies. I hear through the grapevine that you ran into a bit of trouble recently. Are you quite recovered?"

"Your Honor..." Puzzled by the break in courtroom routine, Rachel rose.

"Sit, sit, sit." Beckett gestured with the back of her hand. "Mr. LeBeck, I asked how you're feeling."

"I'm okay."

"Good. I'm also informed that you identified the three desperadoes who broke into Mr. Muldoon's bar. Three members of the Cobras—an organization with which you were associated, I believe—who are now in custody awaiting trial."

Rachel tried again. "Your Honor, in my final report—"

"I read it, thank you, Counselor. You did an excellent job. I'd prefer to hear from Mr. LeBeck directly. My question is, why did you identify these men, who a relatively short time ago you chose to protect?"

"Stand up," Rachel hissed under her breath.

Frowning, Nick complied. "Ma'am?"

"Was the question unclear? Shall I repeat it?"

"No, I got it."

"Excellent. And your answer?"

"They messed with my brother."

"Ah." As if she were a teacher congratulating a much-improved student, Beckett smiled. "And that changes the complexion of things."

Forgetting all Rachel's prompting, he took the natural stance. The aggressive one. "Listen, they broke in, busted Rio's head open, shoved Rachel around and waved guns all over the place. It wasn't right. Maybe you think turning them in makes me a creep, but Reece was going to shoot my brother. No way he was going to walk from that."

"What I think it makes you, LeBeck, is a clear-thinking, potentially responsible adult who has grasped not only the basic tenets of right and wrong, but also of loyalty, which is often more valuable. You will likely make more mistakes in your life, but I doubt you will make the kind that will bring you back into my courtroom. Now, I believe the district attorney has something to say."

"Yes, Your Honor. The state drops all charges against Nicholas LeBeck."

"All *right!*" Rachel said, springing to her feet.

"Is that it?" Nick managed.

"Not quite." Beckett pulled the attention back to the bench. "I get to do this." She slapped the gavel down. "Now that's it."

With a laugh, Rachel threw her arms around Nick's neck. "You did it," she murmured to him. "I want you to remember that. You did it."

"I'm not going to jail." He hadn't been able to allow anyone, even himself, to see how much that had terrified him. He gave Rachel one last squeeze before turning to Zack. "I'm going home."

"That's right." Zack held out a hand. Then, with an oath, he dragged Nick into a hug. "Play your cards right, kid, I'll even give you a raise."

"Raise, my butt. I'm working my way up to partner."

"If you gentlemen will excuse me, I have other clients." She gave each of them a highly unprofessional kiss.

"We have to celebrate." Zack caught her hands. There was nothing he could say. Too much that needed to be said. "Seven o'clock, at the bar. Be there."

"I wouldn't miss it."

"Rachel," Nick called out, "you're the best."

"No." She tossed a laugh over her shoulder. "But I will be."

She was a little late. It couldn't be helped. How could she have known she'd get a case of criminal assault tossed at her at six o'clock?

Two years with the PD's office, she reminded herself, grinning a little, as she pushed open the door of the bar.

When the cheer went up, she stopped cold. There were streamers, balloons, and several people in incredibly stupid party hats. A huge banner hung across the back wall.

Next to Rachel, Perry Mason is a Wimp.

It made her laugh, even as Rio hauled her onto his shoulders and carried her to the bar. He set her down, and someone thrust a glass of champagne in her hand.

"Some party."

Zack tugged at her hair until she turned her face for a kiss. "I tried to make them wait for you, but they got caught up."

"*I'll* catch up..." she began. Then her mouth dropped open. "Mama?"

"We've already eating Rio's short ribs," Nadia informed her. "Now your papa is going to dance with me."

"Maybe I dance with you later," Yuri informed his daughter as he swept Nadia off for what was surely to be a polka.

"You invited my parents. And—" She shook her head in wonder. "That's Alex stuffing meatballs in his face."

"It's a private party." Zack clinked his glass against hers. "Nick made up the list. Take a look."

She craned her neck and spotted him at a table. "Isn't that Lola's daughter?"

"She's really impressed that he's been shot."

"It's one of the top ten ways to impress a woman."

"I'll keep it in mind. Want to dance?"

She took another sip of champagne. "I'd bet a week's pay you don't know how to polka."

"You lose," he said, and grabbed her hand.

It went on for hours. Rachel lost track of the time as she sampled the enormous spread Rio had prepared and washed it down with champagne. She danced until her feet went numb and ultimately collapsed to sing Ukrainian folk songs with her slightly snookered father.

"Good party," Yuri said, swaying a bit, while his wife helped him into his coat.

"Yes, Papa."

He grinned as he leaned toward Rachel. "Now I go home and make your mama feel like a girl."

"Big talk. You'll snore in truck on the way home."

He leered at his wife. "Then you wake me up."

"Maybe." She kissed her daughter. "You make me very proud."

"Thank you, Mama."

"You're a smart girl, Rachel. I'll tell you what you should already know. When you find a good man, you lose nothing by taking hold, and everything by letting go. You understand me?"

"Yes, Mama." Rachel looked over at Zack. "I think I do."

"This is good."

Rachel watched them walk out, arm in arm.

"They're pretty great," Nick said from behind her.

"Yes, they are."

"And your brother's not so bad—for a cop."

"I'm pretty fond of him, all in all." With a sigh, she brushed a streamer from her hair. "Looks like the party's over."

"This one is." Smiling to himself, he turned away to help Rio gather up some of the mess. If Nick knew his brother—and he was beginning to believe he did—Rachel was in for another surprise before the evening was over.

Zack tolerated the cleanup crew for nearly twenty minutes before ordering Rio home and Nick to bed. If he didn't get Rachel to himself, he was going to explode. "We'll get the rest tomorrow."

"You're the boss." Rio gave Rachel a wink as he shrugged into his coat. "For the time being."

Zack shook a nearly empty bottle. "There's a little champagne left. How about it?"

"I think I could choke it down." She settled at the bar and, aiming her best provocative look at him, held out her glass. "Buy me a drink, sailor?"

"Be my pleasure." After filling her glass, he slid

the bottle aside. "There's nothing I can say or do to repay you."

"Don't start."

"I want you to know how much I appreciate everything. You made all the difference."

"I was doing my job, and following my conscience. No one needs to thank me for that."

"Damn it, Rachel, let me explain how I feel."

Nick swung in from the kitchen. "If that's the best you can do, bro, you need all the help you can get."

The single glance Zack shot in his direction was explosive. "Go to bed."

"On my way." But he walked to the juke and popped in a few quarters. After punching some buttons, he turned back to them. "You two are a real case. Take it from someone who knows you both have weaknesses, and cut to the chase." With a shake of his head, he dimmed the lights and walked out.

"What the hell was that?" Zack demanded.

"Don't ask me. Weaknesses? I don't have any weaknesses."

Zack grinned at her. "Me either." He came around the bar. "But it's nice music."

"Real nice," she agreed, going willingly into his arms to sway there.

"Things have been a little hectic."

"Hmm... Just a little."

"I'd like to talk to you about what I asked you a while back. About moving in."

She shut her eyes. She'd already decided the answer was no. As hard as it was to resist a half a loaf, she would hold out for the whole one. "This may not be the time to go into it."

"I can't think of a better one. The thing is, Rachel, I don't want you to move in."

"You—" She stiffened, then shoved away, nearly toppling him over. "Well, that's just fine."

"What I want—"

"Stuff what you want," she tossed back at him. "Isn't that just typical? After I clean up the mess for you, you brush me off."

"I'm not—"

"Shut up, Muldoon. I'll have my say."

"Who could stop you?" he muttered.

Her heels slapped the floor as she tried to walk off her anger. "You're out of order, Buster. You're the one who kept pushing your way in, pushing your way in." She demonstrated by making shoving motions with her hands. "Just wouldn't take no for an answer."

"You didn't say no," he reminded her.

"That's irrelevant." Facing him, she fisted her hands on her hips. "So, you don't want me to move in. Fine. My answer was an unqualified no anyway."

"Great." He stepped closer so that he had to lean over to shout in her face. "Because I'm not settling for you packing up a few things and coming by to play house. I want you to marry me."

"And if you think— Oh, God." She swayed back, forward, then pressed a hand to his chest for balance. "I have to sit down."

"So sit." He nipped her around the waist and plopped her down on the bar. "And just listen. I know we said no long-term commitments. You didn't want them, and neither did I. But we're turning the page here, Rachel, and there's a whole new set of rules."

"Zack, I—"

"No. You're not going to get me tangled up in an argument." She was too good at winning those, and he'd be damned if he was going to lose this time. "I've thought this through. You've got your priorities, and that's fine." He grabbed her hands, hard. Rachel decided she'd check for broken fingers later. Right now, she couldn't feel anything but amazement. "All you have to do is add one to the list. Me. I didn't plan on falling in love with you, but that's the way it is, so deal with it."

"Me either," she murmured, but he plowed on.

"Maybe you think you don't have room..." His grip tightened, and he ignored her quick yelp. "What did you say?"

"I said, 'Me either.'"

"'Me either' what?"

"You said, 'I didn't plan on falling in love with you,' and I said, 'Me either.'" She let out a long, shaky sigh when his hands slid limply from hers. "But that's the way it is, so deal with it."

"Oh, yeah?"

"Yeah." Perched on the bar, she linked her arms around his neck, lowered her brow to his. Amazing, she thought. He was as scared as she was. "You beat me to it, Muldoon. I was going to turn you down because I love you too much, and I wasn't going to settle for anything less with you than everything. It's had me going in circles for days."

"Weeks." He brought his mouth to hers. "I was going to try to ease you into it, but I couldn't wait. I even talked to your father about my intentions to-night."

Unsure whether to laugh or groan, she drew back. "You did not."

"I plied him with vodka first, just in case. He told me he wanted more grandchildren."

She felt her heart swell. "I'd like to accommodate him."

Something caught in his chest, then broke beautifully free. "No kidding?"

And here it was, she thought, looking down into his eyes. A whole new set of rules. A whole new life for the taking. "No kidding. I want a family with you. I want it all with you. That's my choice."

He cupped her face in his hands. "You're everything I've wanted and never thought I'd have."

"You're everything I wanted," she repeated. "And pretended not to." When she lowered her lips to his, she felt the sting of tears in her throat. "We're not going to get sloppy, are we, Muldoon?"

"Who, us?" He grinned as she slid off the bar and into his arms. "Not a chance."

* * * * *

A Note from the Author

I happen to feel I'm an expert on womanhood as I've been surrounded by men all my life. I was the youngest of five and the only daughter. Outnumbered. This meant learning to use basic female traits to my advantage. Now, I'm not talking about wimpy tears and whining. Though they have their uses. I'm talking about the female mind, with all its interesting twists and angles. And the female heart, with its deep wells and often incomprehensible logic. As a girl, I learned to appreciate and to enjoy femininity, the kind that has nothing to do with lace and flounces and everything to do with emotion.

It was fortunate I learned—I now have a husband and two sons and am once more outnumbered.

When I first met Rachel Stanislaski, she was a law student, the youngest child and second daughter of

Ukrainian immigrants. Though I found each and every member of the Stanislaski family fascinating, Rachel was special because of her personal ambitions, the strength of her convictions and the way they merged and melded with her strong love of family.

When I met Zack Muldoon, I knew it would take a very special woman to match him. Rachel, with her wit, her temper, her sense of justice and her deep well of compassion, fit the bill.

I'm delighted to participate in Silhouette's celebration of womanhood, and hope that Rachel will hold a special place in your heart. She does in mine.

Take 4 bestselling love stories FREE

Plus get a FREE surprise gift!

Special Limited-time Offer

Mail to Silhouette Reader Service™

3010 Walden Avenue
P.O. Box 1867
Buffalo, N.Y. 14240-1867

YES! Please send me 4 free Silhouette Special Edition® novels and my free surprise gift. Then send me 6 brand-new novels every month, which I will receive months before they appear in bookstores. Bill me at the low price of $3.34 each plus 25¢ delivery and applicable sales tax, if any.* That's the complete price and a savings of over 10% off the cover prices—quite a bargain! I understand that accepting the books and gift places me under no obligation ever to buy any books. I can always return a shipment and cancel at any time. Even if I never buy another book from Silhouette, the 4 free books and the surprise gift are mine to keep forever.

235 BPA A3UV

Name	(PLEASE PRINT)	
Address		Apt. No.
City	State	Zip

This offer is limited to one order per household and not valid to present Silhouette Special Edition® subscribers. *Terms and prices are subject to change without notice. Sales tax applicable in N.Y.

USPED-696   ©1990 Harlequin Enterprises Limited

LOVE *or* MONEY?
Why not Love *and* Money!
After all, millionaires
need love, too!

How to Marry a
MILLIONAIRE

Suzanne Forster,
Muriel Jensen
and
Judith Arnold

bring you three original stories
about finding that one-in-a million man!

Harlequin also brings you
a million-dollar sweepstakes—enter
for your chance to win a fortune!

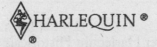

HARLEQUIN ®

Look us up on-line at: http://www.romance.net

HTMM

**Harlequin®
Historical**

A clandestine night of passion
An undisclosed identity
A hidden child

RITA Award nominee

Miranda
Jarrett

presents...

THE SECRETS OF
Catie Hazard

Available in April,
wherever Harlequin Historicals are sold.

Bestselling Author

MARGOT DALTON

explores every parent's worst fear...the
disappearance of a child.

First Impression

Three-year-old Michael Panesivic has vanished.

A witness steps forward—and his story is chilling.
But is he a credible witness or a suspect?

Detective Jackie Kaminsky has three choices:
1) dismiss the man as a nutcase,
2) arrest him as the only suspect,
   or
3) believe him.

But with a little boy's life at stake, she can't afford to
make the wrong choice.

Available in April 1997 at your favorite retail outlet.

HARLEQUIN SUPERROMANCE®

SISTERS

A trilogy by three of your favorite authors.

Peg Sutherland
Ellen James
Marisa Carroll

A golden wedding *usually* means a family celebration.

But the Hardaway sisters drifted apart years ago. And each has her own reason for wanting no part of a family reunion. As plans for the party proceed, tensions mount, and it begins to look as if their parents' marriage might fall apart before the big event. Can the daughters put aside old hurts and betrayals...for the sake of the family?

Follow the fortunes of AMY, LISA and MEGAN in these three dramatic love stories.

April 1997—AMY by Peg Sutherland
May 1997—LISA by Ellen James
June 1997—MEGAN by Marisa Carroll

Available wherever Harlequin books are sold.

SIS

You are cordially invited to a

HOMETOWN REUNION

September 1996—August 1997

Bad boys, cowboys, babies. Feuding families,
arson, mistaken identity, a mom on the run...
Where can you find romance and adventure?
Tyler, Wisconsin, that's where!

So join us in this not-so-sleepy little town and
experience the love, the laughter and the
tears of those who call it home.

WELCOME TO A
HOMETOWN REUNION

Daphne Sullivan and her little girl were hiding
from something or someone—that much was
becoming obvious to those who knew her. But
from whom? Was it the stranger with the dark
eyes who'd just come to town? Don't miss
Muriel Jensen's *Undercover Mom,* ninth in a
series you won't want to end....

Available in May 1997
at your favorite retail store.

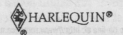

HARLEQUIN®

Look us up on-line at: http://www.romance.net

HTR9